A Modern Buccaneer

Rolf Boldrewood

ESPRIOS DIGITAL PUBLISHING

A MODERN BUCCANEER

I desire to acknowledge my indebtedness to Mr. Louis Becke, author of *By Reef and Palm*, as to the South Sea Island portion of *A Modern Buccaneer*, with the exception of the chapter headed "Poisoned Arrows," which is founded upon the diary of a Whaling Cruise by my late father.

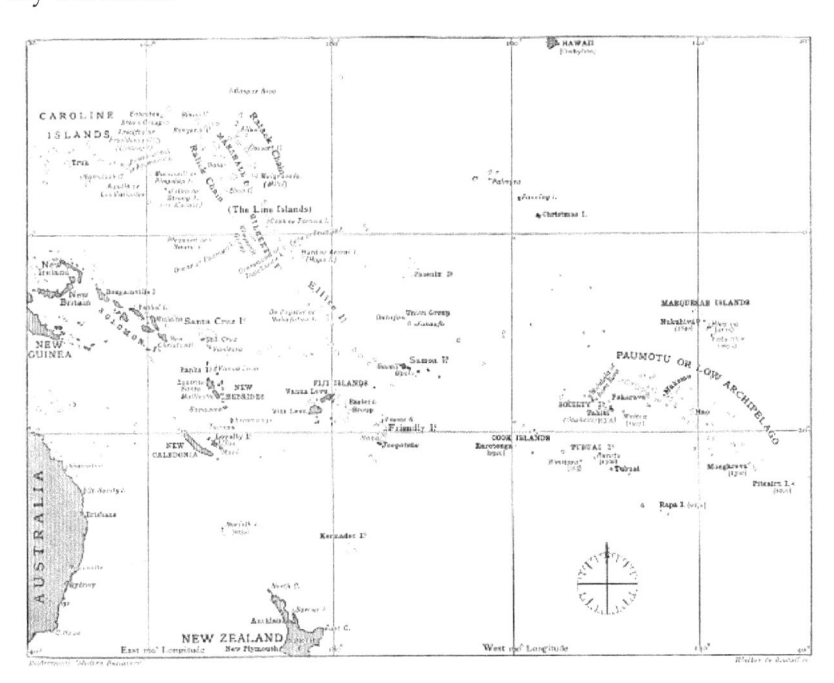

Boldrewood's "Modern Buccaneer"
Walker & Boutall sc.

A MODERN BUCCANEER

BY

ROLF BOLDREWOOD

AUTHOR OF 'ROBBERY UNDER ARMS'

London

MACMILLAN AND CO.
AND NEW YORK
1894

All rights reserved

COPYRIGHT
1894
BY
MACMILLAN AND CO.

First Edition (3 Vols.) April 1894
Second Edition (1 Vol.) October 1894

CONTENTS.

CHAPTER I.
My First Voyage

CHAPTER II.
William Henry Hayston

CHAPTER III.
In Samoa

CHAPTER IV.
Samoa to Millé

CHAPTER V.
The Brig Leonora

CHAPTER VI.
Captain Ben Peese

CHAPTER VII.
Cruising among the Carolines

CHAPTER VIII.
Poisoned Arrows

CHAPTER IX.
Halcyon Days

CHAPTER X.
Murder and Shipwreck

CHAPTER XI.
A King and Queen

CHAPTER XII.
"My Lords of the Admiralty"

CHAPTER XIII.

H.M.S. Rosario

CHAPTER XIV.

Norfolk Island — Arcadia

CHAPTER XV.

Epithalamium

CHAPTER XVI.

A Swim for Life

CHAPTER XVII.

"Our Jack's come Home to-day"

CHAPTER I

MY FIRST VOYAGE

Born near Sydney harbour, nursery of the seamen of the South, I could swim almost as soon as I could walk, and sail a boat at an age when most children are forbidden to go near the water. We came of a salt-water stock. My father had been a sea-captain for the greater part of his life, after a youth spent in every kind of craft, from a cutter to a man-of-war. No part of the habitable globe was unfamiliar to him: from India to the Pole, from Russia to the Brazils, from the China Sea to the Bight of Benin—every harbour was a home.

He had nursed one crew frost-bitten in Archangel, when the blankets had to be cut up for mittens; had watched by the beds of another, decimated by yellow fever in Jamaica; had marked up the "death's-head and cross-bones" in the margin of the log-book, to denote the loss by tetanus of the wounded by poisoned arrows on Bougainville Island; and had fought hand to hand with the stubborn Maories of Taranaki. Wounds and death, privation and pestilence, wrecks and tempests were with him household words, close comrades. What were they but symbols, nature-pictures, the cards dealt by fate? You lost the stake or rose a winner. Men who had played the game of life all round knew this. He accepted fortune, fair or foul, as he did the weather—a favour or a force of nature to be enjoyed or defied. But to be commented upon, much less complained of? Hardly. And as fate had willed it, the worn though unwearied sea-king had seen fit to heave anchor, so to speak, and moor his vessels—for he owned more than one—in this the fairest haven of the southern main. Once before in youth had he seen and never forgotten the frowning headlands, beyond which lay so peerless a harbour, such wealth of anchorage, so mild a clime, so boundless an extent of virgin soil; from which he, "a picked man of countries," even then prophesied wealth, population, and empire in the future.

Here, then, a generation later, he brought his newly-wedded wife. Here was I, Hilary Telfer, destined to see the light.

From the mid-city street of Sydney is but a stone's throw to the wharves and quays, magnificent water-ways in which those ocean palaces of the present day, the liners of the P. and O. and the Orient, lie moored, and but a plank divides the impatient passenger from the busy mart. Not that such stately ships were visitors in my school-boy days. Sydney was then a grass-grown, quiet seaport, boasting some fifty thousand inhabitants, with a fleet of vessels small in size and of humble tonnage.

But, though unpretending of aspect, to the eager-hearted, imaginative school-boy they were rich as Spanish galleons. For were they not laden with uncounted treasure, weighed down with wealth beyond the fabled hoards of the pirates of the Spanish Main, upon whose dark deeds and desperate adventures I had so greedily feasted?

Each vessel that swept through the Heads at midnight, or marked the white-walled mansions and pine-crowned promontories rise faintly out of the pearl-hued dawn, was for me a volume filled with romance and mystery. Sat there not on the forecastle of that South Sea whaler, silent, scornful, imperturbable, the young Maori chief, nursing in his breast the deep revenge for a hasty blow, which on the return voyage to New Zealand and the home of his tribe was to take the form of a massacre of the whole ship's company?

Yes, captain and officers, passengers and crew, every man on that ship paid the death penalty for the mate's hard word and blow. The insult to a Rangatira must be wiped out in blood.

The trader of the South Sea Islands was a marine marvel which I was never weary of studying.

I generally managed to make friends with one or other of the crew, who permitted me to explore the lower deck and feed my fancy upon the treasures from that paradise with which the voyager from an enchanted ocean had surely freighted his vessel. Strange bows and arrows—the latter poison-tipped, as I was always assured, perhaps as a precautionary measure—piles of shaddocks, tons of bananas, idols, skulls, spears, clubs, woven cloth of curious fabric, an endless store of unfamiliar foreign commodities.

Among the crew were always a few half-castes mingled with the grizzled, weather-beaten British sea-dogs. Perhaps a boat's crew of the islanders themselves, born sailors, and as much at home in water as on land.

Seldom did I leave, however unwillingly, the deck of one of these fairy barques, without registering a vow that the year in which I left school should see me a gay sailor-boy, bound on my first voyage in search of dangerous adventures and that splendidly untrammelled career which was so surely to result in fortune and distinction.

Then the whaleships! In that old time, Sydney harbour was rarely without a score or more of them. In their way they were portents and wonders of the deep. Fortune failed them at times. The second year might find them far from full of the high-priced whale-oil. The capricious cetacean was not to be depended upon in migration from one "whaling ground" to another. Sometimes a "favourite" ship—lucky in spite of everything—would come flaunting in after an absence of merely eleven or twelve months—such were the *Florentia* and the *Proteus*—full to the hatches, while three long years would have elapsed before her consort, sailing on the same day and fitted up much in the same way, would crawl sadly into Snail's or Neutral Bay, battered and tempest-tossed, but three-quarter full even then, a mark for the rough wit of the port, to pay off an impoverished crew and confront unsmiling or incredulous owners.

Every kind of disaster would have befallen her. When she got fast to a ninety-barrel whale, her boats would be stoven in. When all was well, no cheery shout of "There she spouts!" would be heard for days. Savage islanders would attack her doggedly, and hardly be beaten off. Every kind of evil omen would be justified, until the crew came to believe that they were sailing with an Australian Vanderdecken, and would never see a port again.

The grudging childish years had rolled by, and now I was seventeen years of age—fitted, as I fully believed, to begin the battle of life in earnest, and ardent for the fray. As to my personal qualifications for a life on the ocean wave, and well I knew no other would have contented me, let the reader judge. At the age when tall lads are often found to have out-grown their strength, I had attained the fullest stature of manhood; wide-chested and muscular, constant exercise with oar and sail had developed my frame and toughened my sinews, until I held myself, with some reason, to be a match in strength and activity for most men I was likely to meet.

In the rowing contests to which Australians of the shore have always been devoted, more particularly the privileged citizens of Sydney, I had always taken a leading part. More than once, in a hard-fought finish, had I been lifted out fainting or insensible.

My curling fair hair and blue eyes bore token of our Norse blood and Anglo-Norman descent. The family held a tradition that our surname came from Taillefer, the warrior minstrel who rode in the forefront of Duke William's army at Hastings. Strangely, too, a passionate love of song had always clung to the race. "Sir Hilary charged at Agincourt," as saith the ballad. Roving and adventure ran in the blood for generations uncounted.

For all that trouble arose when I announced my resolve. My schoolmates had settled down in the offices of merchants, bankers, and lawyers, why could not I do the same? My mother's tears fell fast as she tried in vain to dissuade me from my resolution. My father was neutral. He knew well the intensity of the feeling. "If born in a boy," he said, "as it was in me, it is his fate—nothing on earth can turn him from it; if you stop him you will make a bad landsman and spoil a good sailor. Let him go! he must take his chance like another man. God is above the wave as over the earth. If it be his fate, the perils of the deep will be no more than the breezes of the bay."

It was decided at length that I should be allowed to go on my way. To the islands of the South Pacific my heart pointed as truly as ever did compass needle to the North.

I had read every book that had ever been written about them, from Captain Cook's *Voyages* to *The Mutiny of the Bounty*. In my dreams how many times had I seen the purple mountains, the green glow of the fairy woodlands, had bathed in the crystal streams, and heard the endless surf music on the encircling reef, cheered the canoes loaded with fruit racing for their market in the crimson flush of the paradisal morn, or lingered amidst the Aidenns of the charmed main, where the flower-crowned children of nature—maidens beauteous as angels—roamed in careless happiness and joyous freedom! It was an entrancing picture.

Why should I stay in this prosaic land, where men wore the hideous costume of their forefathers, and women, false to all canons of art, still clung to their outworn garb?

What did I care for the sheep and cattle, the tending of which enriched my compatriots?

A world of romance, mystery, and adventure lay open and inviting. The die was cast. The spell of the sea was upon me.

My father's accumulations had amounted to a reasonable capital, as things went in those Arcadian non-speculative days. He was not altogether without a commercial faculty, which had enabled him to make prudent investments in city and suburban lands. These the steadily improving markets were destined to turn into value as yet undreamed of.

It was not thought befitting that I should ship as an apprentice or foremost hand, though I was perfectly willing, even eager, for a start in any way. A more suitable style of equipment was arranged. An agreement was entered into with the owner of a vessel bound for San Francisco viâ Honolulu, by which a proportion of the cargo was purchased in my name, and I was, after some discussion, duly installed as supercargo. It may be thought that I was too young for such a responsible post. But I was old for my age. I had a man's courage and ambition. I had studied navigation to some purpose; could "hand reef and steer," and in the management of a boat, or acquaintance with every rope, sail, and spar on board of a vessel, I held myself, if not an A. B., fully qualified for that rank and position.

Words would fail to describe my joy and exultation when I found myself at length on blue water, in a vessel which I might fairly describe as "our little craft," bound for foreign parts and strange cities. I speedily made the acquaintance of the crew—a strangely assembled lot, mostly shady as to character and reckless as to speech, but without exception true "sailor men." At that time of day, employment on the high seas was neither so easy to obtain nor so well paid as at present. The jolly tars of the period were therefore less independent and inclined to cavil at minor discomforts. Once shipped, they worked with a will, and but little fault could be found with their courage or seamanship.

Among other joys and delights which I promised myself, had been a closer acquaintance with the life and times of a picturesque and romantic personage, known and feared, if all tales were true, throughout the South Seas. This was the famous, the celebrated Captain Hayston, whose name was indeed a spell to conjure with from New Zealand to the Line Islands.

Much that could excite a boyish imagination had been related to me concerning him. One man professing an intimate knowledge had described him as "a real pirate." Could higher praise be awarded? I put together all the tales I had heard about him—his great stature and vast strength, his reckless courage, his hair-breadth escapes, his wonderful brig,—cousin german, no doubt, to the "long low wicked-looking craft" in the pages of *Tom Cringle's Log*, and other veracious historiettes, "nourishing a youth sublime," in the long bright summer days of old; those days when we fished and bathed, ate oysters, and read alternately from early morn till the lighthouse on the South Head flashed out! My heroes had been difficult to find hitherto; they had mostly eluded my grasp. But this one was real and tangible. He would be fully up to description. His splendid scorn of law and order, mercy or moderation, his unquestioned control over mutinous crews and fierce islanders, illumined by occasional homicides and abductions, all these splendours and glories so stirred my blood, that I felt, if I could only once behold my boyhood's idol, I should not have lived in vain. Among the crew, fortunately for me as I then thought, was a sailor who had actually known in the flesh the idol of my daydreams.

"And it's the great Captain Hayston you'd like to hear about," said Dan Daly, as we sat together in the foc'sle head of the old barque *Clarkstone*, before we made Honolulu. Dan had been a South Sea beach-comber and whaler; moreover, had been marooned, according to his own account, escaping only by a miracle; a trader's head-man—once, indeed, more than half-killed by a rush of natives on the station. With every kind of dangerous experience short of death and burial he was familiar. On which account I regarded him with a fine boyish admiration. What a night was it, superbly beautiful, when I hung upon his words, as we sat together gazing over the moonlit water! We had changed our course owing to some dispute about food between captain and crew, and were now heading for the island of Rurutu, where fresh provisions were attainable. As I listened spellbound and entranced, the barque's bows slowly rose and fell, the wavering moonlight streamed down upon the deck, the sails, the black masses of cordage, while ghostly shadows moved rhythmically, in answering measure to every motion of the vessel.

"You must know," said Dan, in grave commencement, "it's nigh upon five years ago, when I woke up one morning in the 'Calaboose' as they call the 'lock-up' in Papiete, with a broken head. It's the port of the island of Tahiti. I was one of the hands of the American brig *Cherokee*, and we'd put in there on our way to San Francisco from Sydney. The skipper had given us liberty, so we went ashore and began drinking and having some fun. There was some wahines in it, in coorse—that's whats they call the women in thim parts. Somehow or other I got a knock on the head, and remembered nothing more until I woke up in the 'Calaboose,' where I was charged with batin' a native till he was nigh dead. To make a long story short, I got six months 'hard,' and the ship sailed away without me.

"When I'd served my time, I walks into the American Consulate and asks for a passage to California.

"'Clear out,' says the Consul, 'you red-headed varmint, I have nothing to say to you, after beating an inoffensive native in the manner you did.'

"'By the powers,' says I to myself, 'you're a big blackguard, Dan Daly, when you've had a taste of liquor, but if I remember batin' any man black, white, or whitey-brown, may I be keel-hauled. Howsomdever, that says nothing, the next thing's a new ship.'

"So I steps down to the wharf and aboord a smart-looking schooner that belonged to Carl Brander, a big merchant in Tahiti, as rich as the Emperor of China, they used to say. The mate was aboord. 'Do you want any hands?' says I.

"'We do,' says he. 'You've a taking colour of hair for this trade, my lad.'

"'How's that?'

"'Why, the girls down at Rimitara and Rurutu will just make love to you in a body. Red hair's the making of a man in thim parts.'

"Upon this I signed articles for six months in the schooner, and next day we sailed for a place called Bora-bora in the north-west. We didn't stay there long, but got under weigh for Rurutu next day. We weren't hardly clear of Bora-bora when we sights a brigantine away to windward and bearing down on us before the wind. As soon as she got close enough, she signalled that she wanted to send a boat aboard, so we hove to and waited.

"Our skipper had a look at the man who was steering the boat, whin he turns as pale as a sheet, and says he to the mate, 'It's that devil Hayston! and that's the brigantine he and Captain Ben Peese ran away with from Panama.'

"However, up alongside came the boat, and as fine a looking man as ever I set eyes on steps aboard amongst us.

"'How do ye do, Captain?' says he. 'Where from and whither bound?'

"The skipper was in a blue funk, I could see, for this Bully Hayston had a terrible bad name, so he answers him quite polite and civil.

"'Can you spare me half a coil of two-inch Manilla?' asks the stranger, 'and I'll pay you your own price?'

"The skipper got him the rope, the strange captain pays for it, and they goes below for a glass of grog. In half an hour, up on deck they comes again, our skipper half-seas over and laughing fit to kill himself.

"'By George!' says he, 'you're the drollest card I ever came across. D—n me! if I wouldn't like to take a trip with you myself!' and with that he struggles to the skylight and falls in a heap across it.

"'Who's the mate of this schooner?' sings out Hayston, in such a changed voice that it made me jump.

"'I am!' said the mate, who was standing in the waist.

"'Then where's that Mangareva girl of yours? Come, look lively! I know all about her from that fellow there,' pointing to the skipper.

"The mate had a young slip of a girl on board. She belonged to an island called Mangareva, and was as pretty a creature, with her big soft eyes and long curling hair, as ever I'd seen in my life. The mate just trated her the same as he would the finest lady, and was going to marry her at the next island where there was a missionary. When he heard who the strange captain was, he'd planted her down in the hold and covered her up with mats. He was a fine manly young chap, and as soon as he saw Hayston meant to take 'Taloo,' that was her name, he pulls out a pistol and says, 'Down in the hold, Captain Hayston! and as long as God gives me breath you'll never lay a finger on her. I'll put a bullet through her head rather than see her fall into the hands of a man like you.' The strange captain just gives a laugh and pulls his long moustache. Then he walks up to the mate and slaps him on the shoulder.

"'You've got the right grit in you,' says he. 'I'd like to have a man like you on board my ship;' and the next second he gripped the pistol out of the mate's hand and sent it spinning along the deck. The mate fought like a tiger, but he was a child in the other man's grasp. All the time Hayston kept up that devilish laugh of his. Then, as he saw me and Tom Lynch coming to help the mate, he says something in a foreign lingo, and the boat's crew jumps on board amongst us, every one of them with a pistol. But for all that they seems a decent lot of chaps.

"Hayston still held the mate by his wrists, laughing in his face as if he was having the finest fun in the world, when up comes Taloo out of the hold by way of the foc'sle bulk-head, with her long hair hanging over her shoulders, and the tears streaming down her cheeks.

"She flings herself down at the Captain's feet, and clasps her arms round his knees.

"'No, no! no kill Ted!' she kept on crying, just about all the English she knew.

"'You pretty little thing,' says he, 'I wouldn't hurt your Ted for the world.' Then he lets go the mate and takes her hand and shakes it.

"'What's your name, my man?'

"'Ted Bannington!' says the mate.

"'Well, Ted Bannington, look here; if you'd showed any funk I'd have taken the girl in spite of you and your whole ship's company. If a man don't think a woman good enough to fight for, he deserves to lose her if a better man comes along.'

"Taloo put out one little hand, the other hand and arm was round the mate's neck, shaking like a leaf too.

"'I'm so sorry if I've hurt your wrists,' says he to the mate, most polite. Then he gave some orders to the boat's crew, who pulled away to the brigantine. After they had gone he walked aft with the mate, the two chatting like the best friends in the world, and I'll be hanged if that same mate wasn't laughing fit to split at some of the yarns the other chap was spinning, sitting on the skylight, with the Captain lying at their feet as drunk as Davy's sow.

"Presently the boat comes alongside agin, and a chap walks aft and gives the strange captain a parcel.

"'You'll please accept this as a friendly gift from Bully Hayston,' says he to the mate; and then he takes a ten-dollar piece out of his pocket and gives it to Taloo. 'Drill a hole in it, and hang it round the neck of your first child for luck.'

"He shakes hands with her and the mate, jumps into the boat, and steers for the brigantine. In another ten minutes she squared away and stood to the south-east.

"'Come here, Dan,' says the mate to me; 'see what he's given me!' 'Twas a beautiful chronometer bran new, in a splendid case. The mate said he'd never seen one like it before.

"Well, that was the first time I ever seen Bully Hayston, though I did a few times afterwards, and the brigantine too.

"They do say he's a thundering scoundrel, but a pleasanter-spoken gentleman I never met in my life."

CHAPTER II

WILLIAM HENRY HAYSTON

These were the first particulars I ever heard of the man who had afterwards so great an influence upon my destiny that no incident of my sojourn with him will ever be forgotten. A man with whom I went into the jaws of death and returned unhurt. A man who, no matter what his faults may have been, possessed qualities which, had they been devoted to higher aims in life, might have rendered him the hero of a nation.

Our Captain's altercation with the crew nearly blossomed into a mutiny. This was compromised, however, one of the conditions of peace being that we should touch at Rurutu, one of the five islands forming the Tubuai group. This we accordingly did, and, steering for San Francisco, experienced no further adventures until we sighted the Golden Gate. When our cargo was sold I left the ship.

My occupation being from this time gone, I used to stroll down to the wharf from my lodgings in Harvard Street to look at the foreign vessels. Wandering aimlessly, I one day made the acquaintance of a "hard-shell down-easter," with the truly American name of Slocum, master of a venerable-looking rate called the *Constitution*. He himself was a dried-up specimen of the old style of Yankee captain, with a face that resembled in colour a brown painted oilskin, and hands like an albatross's feet. He had been running for a number of years to Tahiti, taking out timber and returning with island produce.

Not being a proud man, he permitted me to stand drinks for him in a well-known liquor saloon in Third Street, where we had long yarns over his trading adventures in the Pacific.

One Sunday morning, I remember it as if yesterday, we were sitting in a private room off the bar. Slocum was advising me to come with him on his next trip and share the luxuries of the *Constitution's* table, for which he asked the modest sum of a hundred dollars to Tahiti and back, when we heard some one enter and address the bar-keeper. "Great Scott!" came the reply, "it's Captain Hayston! How air you, Captain, and whar d'ye come from?"

"I've come to try and find Ben Peese. We're going to form a new station at Arrecifu. He left me at Yap in the Carolines to come here and buy a schooner with a light draught; but he never turned up; I'm afraid that after he left Yap he met with some accident."

The moment Slocum heard the stranger's voice his face underwent a marvellous change. All his assurance seemed to have left him. He whispered to me, "That's Bully Hayston! I guess I'll lie low till he clears out. I don't want to be seen with him, as it'll sorter damage my character. Besides, he's such a vi'lent critter."

The next moment we heard the new-comer say to the barman, —

"Say, Fred, I've been down to that old schooner the *Constitution*, but couldn't find Slocum aboard. They told me he often came here to get a cheap drink. I want him to take a letter to Tahiti. Do you know where he is?"

Slocum saw it was of no use attempting to "lie low," so with a nervous hand he opened the door.

I've knocked about the world a good deal since I sat in the little back parlour in Third Street, Frisco, but neither before nor since I left Strong's Island have I seen such a splendid specimen of humanity as the man who then entered.

Much that I am about to relate I learned during my later experience.

William Henry Hayston was born in one of the Western States of America, and received his education at Norfolk, Virginia. As his first appointment he obtained a cadetship in the United States Revenue Service, subsequently retiring to become captain of one of the large lake steamers.

In '55 he joined the navy, serving with great gallantry under Admiral Farragut. The reported reason of his leaving the service was a disagreement with Captain Carroll, afterwards commander of the rebel cruiser *Shenandoah*. So bitter was their feud, that years afterwards, when that vessel was in the South Pacific, her commander made no secret of his ardent wish to meet Hayston and settle accounts with him, even to the death.

Hayston was a giant in stature: six feet four in height, with a chest that measured, from shoulder to shoulder, forty-nine inches; and there was nothing clumsy about him, as his many antagonists could testify. His strength was enormous, and he was proud of it. But, apart from his magnificent physique, Hayston was one of the most remarkably handsome men about this time that I have ever seen. His hair fell in clusters across his forehead, above laughing eyes of the brightest blue; his nose was a bold aquiline; a well-cut, full-lipped mouth that could set like fate was covered by a huge moustache. A Vandyke beard completed the *tout ensemble* of a visage which, once seen, was rarely forgotten by friend or foe. Taking him altogether, what with face, figure, and manner, he had a personal magnetism only too fatally attractive, as many a man—ay, and woman too—knew to their cost. He was my beau ideal of a naval officer—bold and masterful, yet soft and pleasant-voiced withal when he chose to conciliate. His sole disfigurement—not wholly so, perhaps, in the eye of his admirers—was a sabre cut which extended from the right temple to his ear.

For his character, the one controlling influence in his life was an ungovernable temper. It was utterly beyond his mastery. Let any one offend him, and though he might have been smiling the instant before, the blue eyes would suddenly turn almost black, his face become a deep purple. Then it was time for friend or foe to beware. For I never saw the man that could stand up to him. Strangely enough, I have sometimes seen him go laughing through a fight until he had finished his man. At other times his cyclone of a mood would discharge itself without warning or restraint. It was probably this appalling temper that gained him a character for being bloodthirsty; for, once roused, nothing could stop him. Yet I do him the justice to say that I never once witnessed an act of deliberate cruelty at his hands. In the islands he was surrounded by a strange collection of the greatest scoundrels unhung. There, of necessity, his rule was one of "blood and iron."

And now for his pleasing traits. He was one of the most fascinating companions possible. He possessed a splendid baritone voice and affected the songs of Schumann and the German composers. He was an accomplished musician, playing on the pianoforte, violin, and, in default of a better instrument, even on the accordion. He spoke German, French, and Spanish, as well as the island languages, fluently. Generous to a fault, in spite of repeated lessons, he would insist on trusting again and again those in whom he believed. But once convinced that he had been falsely dealt with, the culprit would have fared nearly as well in the jaws of a tiger. He was utterly without fear, under any and all circumstances, even the most desperate, and was naturally a hater of every phase of meanness or cowardice. But one more trait, and my sketch is complete. He had a fatal weakness where the fairer sex was concerned. To one of them he owed his first war with society. To the consequences of that false step might have been traced the reckless career which dishonoured his manhood and led to the final catastrophe.

"Come, gentlemen!" he said on entering—in so pleasant and kindly a tone, that I felt drawn towards him at once, "let us sit down and have a drink together."

We went back to the room, Slocum, I could see, feeling intensely uncomfortable, fidgeting and twisting. As we sat down I took a good look at the man of whom I had heard so much. Heard of his daring deeds in the China seas; of a wild career in the Pacific Islands; of his bold defiance of law and order; besides strange tales of mysterious cruises in the north-west among the Caroline and Pellew Islands.

"And how air yer, Captain?" said Slocum with forced hilarity.

"I'm devilish glad to see *you*," replied Hayston; "what about that barque of mine you stripped down at the Marshalls, you porpoise-hided skunk?"

"True as gospel, Captain, I didn't know she was yours. There was a trader at Arnu, you know the man, an Italian critter, but they call him George Brown, and he says to me, 'Captain Slocum,' says he, 'there's a big lump of a timber-ship cast away on one of them reefs near Alluk, and if you can get up to her you'll make a powerful haul. She's new coppered, and hasn't broke up yet.' So I gave him fifty dollars, and promised him four hundred and fifty more if his news was reliable; if that ain't the solid facts of the case I hope I may be paralysed."

"Oh! so it was George who put you on to take my property, was it? and he my trader too; well, Slocum, I can't blame you. But now I'll tell you my '*facts*': that barque was wrecked; the skipper and crew were picked up by Ben Peese and taken to China. He bought the barque for me for four hundred dollars, and I beat up to Arnu, and asked George if he would get me fifty Arnu natives to go with me to the wreck and either try and float it or strip her. The d—d Marcaroni-eating sweep promised to get me the men in a week or two, so I squared away for Madura, where I had two traders. Bad weather came on, and when I got back to Arnu, the fellow told me that a big canoe had come down from the Radacks and reported that the barque had gone to pieces. The infernal scoundrel! Had I known that he had put you on to her I'd have taken it out of his hide. Who is this young gentleman?"

"A friend of mine, Captain, thinking of takin' a voyage with me for recruitin' of his health," and the lantern-jawed Slocum introduced us.

Drawing his seat up to me, Hayston placed his hand on my shoulder, and said with a laugh, looking intensely at Slocum, who was nervously twisting his fingers, "Oh! a recruitin' of his health, is he? or rather recruitin' of your pocket? I'm glad I dropped in on you and made his acquaintance. I could tell him a few droll stories about the pious Slocum."

Slocum said nothing, but laughed in a sickly way.

Leaning forward with a smiling face, he said, "What did you clear out of my barque, you good Slocum?"

"Nigh on a thousand dollars."

"You know you lie, Slocum! you must have done better than that."

"I kin show my receipts if you come aboard," he answered in shaky tones.

"Well, I'll take your word, you sanctimonious old shark, and five hundred dollars for my share."

"Why, sartin, Captain! that's fair and square," said the other, as his sallow face lighted up, "I'll give you the dollars to-morrow morning."

"Right you are. Come to the Lick house at ten o'clock. Say, my pious friend, what would our good Father Damien think if I told him that pretty story about the six Solomon Island people you picked up at sea, and sold to a sugar planter?"

The trader's visage turned green, as with a deprecating gesture towards me he seemed to implore Hayston's silence.

"Ha! ha! don't get scared. Business matters, my lad," he said, turning to me his merry blue eyes, and patting me on the back. "Where are you staying here?"

I told him. Then as we were rising to go, speaking to me, and looking Slocum in the face, he said, "Don't have any truck with Master Slocum, he'll skin you of every dollar you've got, and like as not turn you adrift at some place you can't get away from. Isn't that so, my saintly friend?"

Slocum flinched like a whipped hound, but said nothing. Then, shaking hands with me, and saying if ever I came to the Pacific and dropped across him or Captain Ben Peese I should meet a hearty welcome, he strode out, with the shambling figure of the down-easter under his lee.

That was the last I saw of the two captains for many a long day, for a few days later the *Constitution* cleared out for Tahiti, and I couldn't learn anything more about Hayston. Whether he was then in command of a vessel, or had merely come up as passenger in some other ship, I could not ascertain. All the bar-keeper knew about him was that he was a gentleman with plenty of money and a h—l of a temper, if anybody bothered him with questions.

Little I thought at the time that we were fated to meet again, or that where we once more forgathered would be under the tropic sun of Polynesia.

CHAPTER III

IN SAMOA

From what I have said about Hayston, it will readily be understood that every tale relating to him was strangely exciting to my boyish mind. For me he was the incarnation of all that was utterly reckless, possibly wicked, and of course, as such, possessed a fascination that a better man would have failed to inspire.

My hero, however, had disappeared, and with him all zest seemed to have gone out of life at Frisco. So after mooning about for a few weeks I resolved on returning to Sydney.

My friends on the Pacific slope did their best to dissuade me, trying to instil the idea into my head that I was cut out for a merchant prince by disposition and intellect. But I heeded not the voice of the charmer. The only walk in life for which I felt myself thoroughly fitted was that of an armed cruiser through the South Sea Islands. All other vocations were tame and colourless in comparison. I could fancy myself parading the deck of my vessel, pistol at belt, dagger in sheath, a band of cut-throats trembling at my glance, and a bevy of dark-skinned princesses ready to die for me at a moment's notice, or to keep the flies from bothering, whichever I preferred.

I may state "right here," as the Yankees have it, that I did not become a "free trader," though at one time I had a close shave of being run up to the yardarm of a British man-of-war in that identical capacity. But this came later on.

I returned, therefore, to my native Sydney in due course of time, and as a wholesome corrective after my somewhat erratic experiences, was placed by my father in a merchant's office. But the colourless monotony became absolutely killing. It was awful to be stuck there, adding up columns of pounds, shillings, and pence, and writing business letters, while there was stabbing, shooting, and all sorts of wild excitement going on "away down in the islands."

It was about this time that I made the acquaintance of certain South Sea Islanders belonging to whalers or trading vessels. With one of them, named George, a native of Raratonga, I became intimate. He impressed me with his intelligence, and amused me with his descriptions of island life. He had just returned from a whaling voyage in the barque *Adventurer* belonging to the well-known firm of Robert Towns & Company.

So when George, having been paid off in Sydney with a handsome cheque, confided to me that he intended going back to the Navigators' Islands, where he had previously spent some years, in order to open a small trading station, my unrest returned. He had a hundred pounds which he wished to invest in trade-goods, so I took him round the Sydney firms and saw him fairly dealt with. A week afterwards he sailed to Samoa via Tonga, in the *Taoji Vuna*, a schooner belonging to King George of that ilk.

Before he left he told me that two of his countrymen were trading for Captain Hayston—one at Marhiki, and one at Fakaofo, in the Union group. Both had made money, and he believed that Captain Hayston had fixed upon Apia, the chief port of Samoa, as his head-quarters.

Need I say that this information interested me greatly, and I asked George no end of questions. But the schooner was just leaving the wharf in tow of a tug, and my dark-skinned friend having shipped as an A. B., was no longer of the "leisure classes." So, grasping my hand, and tell ing me where to hear of him if I ever came to Samoa, we parted.

Before going further let me explain the nature of a Polynesian trader's mission.

On the greater number of the islands white men are resident, who act as agents for a firm of merchants, for masters of vessels, or on their own account. In some cases a piece of ground is rented from the king or chief whereon to make the trading station. In others the rulers are paid a protection fee. Then, if a trader is murdered, his principal can claim blood for blood. This, however, is rarely resorted to. A trader once settled on his station proceeds to obtain cocoa-nuts from the natives, for which he pays in dollars or "trade." He further employs them to scrape the fruit into troughs exposed to the sun, by which process the cocoa-nut oil is extracted. Of late years "copra" has taken the place of the oil. This material—the dried kernel of the nut—has become far more valuable; for when crushed by powerful machinery the refuse is pressed into oil-cake, and proved to be excellent food for cattle.

To be a good trader requires pluck, tact, and business capacity. Many traders meet their death for want of one or other of these attributes. All through the South Seas, more especially in the Line Islands, are to be found the most reckless desperadoes living. Their uncontrolled passions lead them to commit acts which the natives naturally resent; the usual result being that if the trader fails to kill or terrorise them, they do society a kindness by ridding it of him. Then comes the not infrequent shelling of a native village by an avenging man-of-war. And thus civilisation keeps ever moving onwards.

The traders were making fortunes in the South Seas at that time, according to George. I returned to business with a mind full of projects. The glamour of the sea, the magic attraction of blue water, was again upon me; I was powerless to resist. My father smiled. My mother and sisters wept afresh. I bowed myself, nevertheless, to my fate. In a fortnight I bade my relations farewell—all unworthy as I felt myself of their affection. Inwardly exultant, though decently uncheerful, I took passage a fortnight later in a barque trading to the Friendly and Navigators' Islands. She was called the *Rotumah*, belonging to Messrs. M'Donald, Smith, & Company, of Hunter Street, Sydney. Her captain was a Canadian named Robertson, of great experience in the island trade.

There were two other passengers—a lady going to join her brother who was in business at Nukulofa, in Tonga, and a fine old French priest whom we were taking to Samoa. The latter was very kind to me, and during our passage through the Friendly Islands I was frequently the guest of his brother missionaries at their various stations in the groups.

How shall I describe my feelings, landed at last among the charmed isles of the South, where I had come to stay, I told myself? Generally speaking, how often is there a savour of disappointment, of anticipation unrealised, when the wish is achieved! But the reality here was beyond the most brilliant mental pictures ever painted. All things were fresh and novel; the coral reefs skirting the island shore upon which the surf broke ceaselessly with sullen roar; cocoa-palms bowed with their feathery crests above a vegetation richly verdurous. The browns and yellows of the native villages, so rich in tone, so foreign of aspect, excited my unaccustomed vision. Graceful figures, warm and dusky of colouring, passed to and fro. The groves of broad leafed bananas; the group of white mission houses; the balmy, sensuous air; the transparent water, in which the very fish were strange in form and hue,—all things soever, land and water, sea and sky, seemed to cry aloud to my eager, wondering soul, "Hither, oh fortunate youth, hast thou come to a world new, perfect, and complete in itself—to a land of Nature's fondness and profuse luxuriance, to that Aïdenn, long lost, mysteriously concealed for ages from all mankind."

At the Marist Mission at Tongatabu I was received most kindly by the venerable Father Chevron, the head of the Church in Tonga. His had been a life truly remarkable. For fifty years he had laboured unceasingly among the savage races of Polynesia, had had hairbreadth escapes, and passed through deadliest perils. Like many of his colleagues he was unknown to fame, dying a few years later, beloved and respected by all, yet comparatively "unhonoured and unsung." During the whole course of my experiences in the Pacific I have never heard the roughest trader speak an ill word of the Marist Brothers. Their lives of ceaseless toil and honourable poverty tell their own tale. The Roman Catholic Church may well feel proud of these her most devoted servants.

One morning Captain Robertson joined me; the Father seemed pleased to see him. On my mentioning how kindly they had treated me, a stranger and a Protestant, he replied,—

"Ay, ay, my lad; they are different from most of the missionaries in Tonga, anyway, as many a shipwrecked sailor has found. If a ship were cast away, and the crew hadn't a biscuit apiece to keep them from starving, they wouldn't get so much as a piece of yam from some of the reverend gentlemen."

I asked Father Chevron if he knew Captain Peese and Captain Hayston.

"Yes! I am acquainted with both; of the latter I can only say that when I met him here I forgot all the bad reports I had heard about him. He cannot be the man he is reputed to be."

I was sorry to part with the good Father when the time came to leave. But a native messenger arrived next day with a note from the captain, who intended sailing at daylight.

So I said farewell and went on board.

We called at Hapai and Vavau, the two other ports of the Friendly Islands, sighting the peak of Upolu, in the Navigators', three days after leaving the latter place.

We rounded the south-east point of Upolu next day, running in so close to the shore that we could see the natives walking on the beaches. Saw a whaleboat, manned by islanders and steered by a white man, shoot through an opening in the reef opposite Flupata. For him we tarried not, in spite of a signal, running in as we were with the wind dead aft, and at four o'clock in the afternoon anchored in Apia harbour, opposite the American consulate.

The scenery around Apia harbour is beauteous beyond description. Spacious bays unfold themselves as you approach, each revealing the silvery white-sanded beach fringed with cocoa-palms; stretching afar towards the hills lies undulating forest land chequered with the white houses of the planters. The harbour itself consists of a horseshoe bay, extending from Matautu to Mullinu Point. Fronting the passage a mountain rears its summit cloud-enwrapped and half-hidden, narrow paths wind through deep gorges, amid which you catch here and there the sheen of a mountain-torrent. On the south the land heads in a graceful sweep to leeward, until lost in the all-enveloping sea-mists of the tropics, while the straggling town, white-walled, reed-roofed, peeps through a dark-green grove of the bananas and cocoa-palms which fringe the beach.

At this precise period I paid but little attention to the beauties of Apia, for in a canoe paddled by a Samoan boy sat my friend George. I hailed him; what a look of joy and surprise rippled over his dark countenance as he recognised me! With a few strokes of the paddle the canoe shot alongside and he sprang on deck.

"I knew you would come," he said; "I boarded every ship that put in here since I landed. Going to live here?"

"I think so, George! I have some money and trade with me; if I get a chance I'll start somewhere in Samoa."

He was delighted, and said I would make plenty of money by and by. He wouldn't hear of my going to an hotel. I must come with him. He had a Samoan wife at Lellepa, a village about a mile from Apia on the Matautu side.

It was dark when we landed. As we walked towards his home George pointed out a house standing back from the beach, which, he said, belonged to Captain Hayston.

That personage had just left Samoa, and was now cruising in the Line Islands, where he had a number of traders. He was expected back in two months. A short time before I arrived, the American gunboat *Narraganset* had suddenly put in an appearance in Apia where Hayston's brig was lying. Her anchor had barely sounded bottom, before an armed boat's crew left her side, boarded, took Hayston prisoner, and kept possession of the *Leonora*.

There was wild excitement that day in Apia. Many of the residents had a strong liking for Hayston and expressed sympathy for him. Others, particularly the German element, were jubilant, and expressed a hope that he would be taken to America in irons.

The captain of the *Narraganset* then notified his seizure to the foreign consuls, and solicited evidence regarding alleged acts of piracy and kidnapping. During this time Hayston was, so the Americans stated, in close confinement on board the man-of-war, but it was the general opinion that he was treated more as a guest than a prisoner. The trial came on at the stated time, but resulted in his acquittal. Either the witnesses were unreliable or afraid of vengeance, for nothing of a criminal nature could be elicited from them. Hayston was then conducted back to his brig, and in half-an-hour he had "dressed ship" in honour of the event. The next act was to give his crew liberty—when those bright particular stars sallied forth on shore, all more or less drunk, in company with the blue jackets from the man-of-war, and immediately set about "painting the town red," and looking for the witnesses who had testified against their commander. On the next night Hayston gave a ball to the officers, and, doubtless, from that time felt his position secure, as far as danger from warships of his own country was concerned.

All this was told to me by George as we walked along the track to his house, where we arrived just in time for a good supper. The place was better built than the ordinary native houses. The floor was covered with handsome clean mats on which, on the far end of the room, his wife and two daughters by a former marriage were sitting. They seemed so delighted at the idea of having me to live with them, that in a few minutes I felt quite at home. The evening meal was ready on the mats; the smell of roast pork and bread-fruit whetted my appetite amazingly; nor was it appeased until George and his wife had helped me to food enough to satisfy a boarding-school.

After supper the family gathered round the lamp which was placed in the middle of the room. There they went through the evening prayers; a hymn was sung, after which a chapter was read from a Samoan Testament, followed by a prayer from the master of the house.

I found that the custom of morning and evening prayers was never neglected in any Samoan household; for, whether the Samoans are really religious or no, they keep up a better semblance of it than many who have whiter skins.

That night George, who by the way was called Tuluia by his wife and daughters, made plans for our future. As we sat talking the others retired to a far corner, where they sat watching us, their big dark eyes dilated with interest. We agreed to buy a boat between us and make trading trips to the windward port as far as Aleipata. Then after smoking a number of "salui" or native cigarettes, we turned in.

All next day we were incommoded by crowds of inquisitive visitors, who came to have a look at me and learn why I had come to Samoa—George having told them merely that I was his "uo," or friend, treated most of them with scant courtesy, explaining that the natives about Apia are thorough loafers and beggars, and warning me not to sell any of them my "trade" unless I received cash in return. In the afternoon I landed my effects, but could scarcely get into the house for the crowds.

George's wife, it appeared, had been so indiscreet as to tell some of her relations that I had rifles for sale; as a consequence there were fully a hundred men eager to see them. Some had money, others wanted credit, others desired loose powder, and kept pointing to a shed close by, saying, "Panla pana fanua" (powder for the cannon). I discovered that under the shed lay a big gun which Patiole and Asi, two chiefs, had bought from Captain Hayston for six hundred dollars, but had run out of ammunition.

I had no powder to sell, but George found me a cash buyer for one of my Winchesters at seventy-five dollars. I could have sold the other three for sixty dollars each, but he advised me to keep them in order to get a better price up the coast. It was just on the eve of the second native war, so the Samoans were buying arms in large quantities. From some Californians' trading vessels they had brought about three hundred breech-loaders, and Hayston had sold them the cannon aforesaid, which he had brought from China in the *Leonora*.

The chief, Malietoa, had an idea of carrying the war into the enemy's country. His plan was to charter a vessel, and take five hundred men to Tuvali, the largest island in the group. Hayston had met a deputation of chiefs, and told them that for a thousand dollars he would land that number of Malietoa's warriors in any part of the group. Moreover, if they gave him ten dollars for every shot fired, he would land them under cover of four guns. But they were not to bring their arms, and were to arrange to have taumualuas, or native boats, to meet the brig off the coast and put them on board. This, he explained, was necessary to prevent the vessel being seized if they met a man-of-war, and so getting him into serious trouble.

The chiefs took this proposition in eagerly at first, but, on thinking it over, suspicions arose as to their reaching their destination safely; and, finally, after the usual amount of fawning and flattering, in which every Samoan is an adept, they told Hayston that they could not raise sufficient money, and so the matter ended.

The following months of my sojourn in Samoa passed quickly. George and I bought a cutter in which we made several trips to the windward villages, whence we ran down to the little island of Manono, situated between Upolu and Savaii. There we did a good business, selling our trade for cash to the people of Manono, and buying a cargo of yams to take to Apia, to sell to the natives there, who were short of food owing to the outbreak of hostilities.

On our way up we took advantage of a westerly wind, and made the passage inside the reef, calling at the villages of Multifanna and Saleimoa—visiting even places with only a few houses nestling amongst the cocoa-palms.

We left Saleimoa at dusk, and although we were deeply laden, we made good way. Whilst at the village I heard that a large Norwegian ship laden with guano had put into Apia, having sprung a leak and run short of provisions; also that there was not a yam to be had in the place. Our informant was a deserter from a man-of-war, living at Saleimoa. He had been tattooed, and was a thorough Samoan in appearance, but was anxious to get a passage to New Britain, being afraid to remain longer in his present quarters. He was known as "Flash Jack," and was held to be a desperate character. After a few drinks he became communicative, telling me certain things which he had better have kept to himself. He informed me that he intended to ship with Hayston, whose brig was expected daily with a hundred recruits for Goddeffroy and Sons' plantations. He advised me to keep my yams until the *Leonora's* cargo of "boys" arrived, as the Germans would pay me my own price for them, being short of food for their plantation labourers. In another few minutes Jack was drunk, and wanted to fight us, when two of his wives came on board, and after beating him with pieces of wood, carried him on shore and laid him in his bunk.

I determined, however, to take his advice about the yams, and was cogitating as to the price I should ask for them, when George, who was steering, called my attention to two "taumualuas" full of men, paddling quickly in from sea through an opening in the reef.

Not apprehending danger we kept on. Our boat was well known along the coast by the Tua Massaga or Malietoa faction, and we merely supposed that these boats were coming down from Apia to the leeward ports. It was a clear night; George called out the usual Samoan greeting, used when canoes meet at night. The next moment we saw them stop paddling, when, without a word of warning, we received a volley, the bullets striking the cutter in at least twenty places. How we escaped is a mystery. George got a cut on the shoulder from a piece of our saucepan, which was lying against the mast. It flew to pieces when struck, and I thought a shell had exploded.

Flinging ourselves flat on the deck, George called out to the canoes, which were now paddling quickly after us, and told them who we were, at the same time lowering our jib and foresail. The taumualuas dashed up, one on each side. Luckily some of the warriors instantly recognised us. They expressed great sorrow, and explained that they had mistaken us for a boat bringing up a war party from Savaii.

Every man was armed with a rifle, mostly modelled on the German needle-gun, and as they were all in full fighting costume they had a striking and picturesque effect. After mutual expressions of regard and a general consumption of cigarettes, we gave them a bottle of grog to keep out the cold night air, sold them some cartridges from my own private stock, and with many a vociferous "To Fa," we sailed away, and left them in the passage waiting for the expected invaders.

CHAPTER IV

SAMOA TO MILLÉ

Just as we parted from our warlike friends who had so nearly put an end to our cruises, one of the chiefs sang out that a large brig, painted white, was out at sea beating up to Apia. Turning his information over in my mind, the conviction grew upon me that she must be Hayston's vessel, the *Leonora*. It proved to be correct, for as we ran past Mulinu Point we saw her entering the passage leading to the harbour. She was about a mile distant from us, but I could see that she was a beautifully-built vessel, and could well believe the tales of her extraordinary speed. The Norwegian guano-man, an immense ship, the *Otto and Antoine*, was lying in the roadstead, and as the *Leonora* came to her moorings, we ran up between the two vessels and dropped anchor.

During the next few minutes I received no less than three different offers for our sixteen tons of yams. These I declined, and after waiting till I perceived that most of the shore visitors had left the brig, I took our dingey and pulled aboard.

Captain Hayston was below, and the Chinese steward conducted me into his presence. He looked at me steadily for a moment, as if trying to recall where he had seen me before, and then after my few words of explanation, gave me a hearty welcome to the South Seas.

Having told him how I came to visit Samoa, I offered him my yams, which he gladly purchased, paying me a good price for them in United States gold coin. This transaction being concluded, he asked me to meet him next day, when we could have a good long chat, at the same time desiring me to keep secret the fact of our previous meeting. What his reasons were I never knew; but as he seemed anxious on this matter, I told him that I had seldom mentioned the circumstance, and to no one in Samoa, with the exception of my mate Tuluia. I had indeed made few other acquaintances.

Although I should much have liked to have had a look round the brig, I could see the Captain wished to get on shore, so after shaking hands with him I returned to our cutter, where, in a few minutes, the brig's longboat came alongside, and we set to work getting out the yams. Hayston paid me without demanding to have them weighed, and George's dark face was wreathed in smiles when I showed him the money. He explained that two tons were very bad, and had they been seen by a purchaser would have been rejected.

Although only a Kanaka, George possessed true commercial instincts, and I felt sure he would grow rich.

The native war was now at its height, and the lines of the hostile party were so close to Matautu, the eastern part of Apia, that bullets were whistling over our heads all day long. The yam season being over, and the copra trade at a standstill, we gave up the cutter and settled for a while on shore. It was during this period that I was a constant visitor at the house of Mr. Lewis, the American Consul, where I generally found Hayston in company with Captain Edward Hamilton, the pilot, and another American, a whisky-loving, kava-drinking old salt, brimful of fun and good humour. He had been twenty years in Samoa, and was one of the best linguists I ever met with; was known to every native in the group, and had been several trips with Hayston to the north-west islands. He followed no known occupation, but devoted his time to idling and attending native dances.

Many a merry evening we spent together while the *Leonora* was recruiting, and I began to think Hayston was the most entertaining man I had ever met. He made no secret of some of his exploits, and in particular referred to the way in which he had beaten a certain German firm in the way of business, even breaking up their stations in the Line Islands. At that time these merchants had acquired a bad name for the underhand manner in which they had treated English and American traders; and for any man to gain an advantage over them was looked upon as a meritorious action.

By many people who cherished animosity against Hayston I had been led at first to look upon him as a thorough-going pirate and a bloodthirsty ruffian. Yet here I found him, if not respected, at least deemed a fit associate for respectable men. Moreover, his word was considered as good security in business as another man's bond. I well remember the days when he used to visit me at Leliepa, and we amused ourselves with pistol practice. He was a wonderful shot, and his skill excited the loud applause of the native chiefs. One fat old fellow, known as Pulumakau (the bullock), begged him to spend a day now and then in the lines with the native forces, and exercise his skill upon the enemy.

One day he took me on board with him in order to show me over the brig. He intended to leave in a few days, and I remarked, as we were pulled on board, that I should dearly like to have a trip with him some day.

He was silent for a minute, and then replied, "No! I shall be glad enough of your company as my guest, as I have taken a fancy to you; but it will be better for you to keep clear of me."

When we got on board I was struck with the beautiful order in which the vessel was kept, aloft and below; there was not a rope yarn out of place. Descending to the cabin I found it splendidly furnished for a vessel of her size.

The *Leonora* was 250 tons register, and had been built for the opium trade. During her career in Chinese seas she acquired the reputation of being the fastest vessel on the coast. She then carried eight guns. She had been several times attacked by pirates, who were invariably beaten off with loss. At the time of my visit she carried but one gun, which stood on the main deck, Hayston having sold two others of the same calibre to the natives. But for this, as far as I could see, she had a most peaceful appearance.

On the main deck, just abaft the foc'sle, was a deckhouse divided into compartments, forming the cook's galley and boats' crews' quarters, together with those belonging to the first and second mates. On the top of the house a whale-boat was carried, leaving room for two sentries to keep guard, a precaution which I afterwards found was, on certain occasions, highly necessary for the vessel's safety. The foc'sle was large, for she carried between twenty-five and thirty men. The thing that struck me most, however, was the bulkhead, which was loop-holed for rifles, so that if any disturbance took place in the forehold, which was sometimes filled with Kanaka labourers, the rebels could be shot down with ease and accuracy.

The most noticeable things about the gear were the topsails she carried, Cunningham's patent, in which there were no reef points.

The topsail yards revolved, so that you could reef as much as you liked, and all the work could be done from the main deck by the down haul. Many captains dislike this patent, but it behaved splendidly on the *Leonora* for all that.

The crew, or most of them, were ashore, and only the second mate, the Chinese carpenter, the steward, and ship's boys were on board. The mate was a muscular Fijian half-caste named Bill Hicks, known as a fighting man all over Polynesia. A native girl, called Liva, was sitting on the main hatch making a bowl of kava.

"Halloa! Liva," said the Captain, as we passed along the deck, "I thought you were married to one of the Dutch clerks at Goddeffroy's?"

"Avoe, lava, alii." "Quite true, Captain, but I've come to stay with Bill for a week."

The Captain and second mate laughed, and next day I learned that Bill had gone to the clerk's house at Matafele, the German quarter of the town, and though there were other Germans present, told Liva to pack up her clothes and come with him. She, nothing loth, did as he told her, and the Germans, seeing mischief in the half-caste's eye, offered no opposition.

The departure of the *Leonora* took place a few days afterwards, and I accepted the position of supercargo in a ketch which the junior partner of one of the principal firms in Samoa wished to send to the Marshalls to be sold. I expressed my doubts of her sea-worthiness for so long a voyage. However, he said there was no danger, as it would be a fine weather passage all the way through, adding that the king of Arnu, or Arrowsmith's Island, had commissioned Captain Hayston to buy a vessel for him in Samoa.

I thought his proposition over, and next day stated my willingness to undertake the venture, the owners promising to put the vessel in repair as soon as possible. She was hauled up to the beach in front of the British consulate, where for the next few weeks carpenters were at work, patching up and covering her rotten bottom with a thick coating of chunam. Notwithstanding these precautions no one except old Tapoleni, the Dutch skipper, could be induced to take charge of her.

During the time she was on the beach I made a trip to the beautiful village of Tiavea, doing a week's trading and pigeon shooting. On my return I found the town in a high state of excitement owing to a succession of daring robberies of the various stores. Strong suspicions were entertained with respect to a herculean American negro, known as Black Tom, who kept an extremely disorderly hotel where seamen were known to be enticed and robbed.

The old vessel was launched at last, and, to the manifest surprise of everybody, refrained from springing a leak. Things might easily have been worse; for what with the great age of her timber and the thickness of her hull the carpenters were barely able to make the copper hold.

Next day we took in our stores. I was surprised at the casks of beef, tins of biscuits, and quantities of other provisions put on board, and thought the owners extremely liberal. This favourable state of feeling lasted till we were well at sea, when I discovered all the beef to be bad, and the remainder of the stores unfit for any well-brought-up pig. When everything was aboard the owners gave me the following document:—

APIA, *3rd December, 187_.*

Dear Sir,—You will proceed to Millé, Mulgrave Island, for the purpose of selling the ketch *E. A. Wilson*. You will find Captain Hayston there waiting for you; so you will please consult with him, as he is acquainted with the parties who wish to purchase her. Try to obtain oil and copra to the amount of £500 for the vessel. Ship whatever produce you may get on board the *Leonora*, and get Captain Hayston to sign bills of lading. Do not sell the chronometer unless you get a good price for it. Sell the few things you take to the best advantage; none of the Samoans are to remain, but must come back to Apia. Have the ketch painted on your arrival at Millé. Wishing you a prosperous and speedy voyage.—We are, etc.,

BASCOM & CO.

I quote this letter *in extenso,* for later on it plays an important part in my narrative. Having carefully read it Mr. Bascom shook hands with me, wished me a pleasant voyage, and departed. I went aboard, the vessel being already hove short, and, as I thought, only waiting my arrival to sail.

Things looked much otherwise as I stepped on deck. The skipper was drunk and helpless. The decks were thronged with shore natives—men and women nearly all crying and half drunk, bidding farewell to one or other of the crew.

The mate, Jim Knowles, was a Tongan half-caste, who was afterwards hanged in Fiji for shooting Larsen, one of the Messrs. Goddeffroy's captains, dead on his own ship. He was the only sober man on board. He told me that one of Tapoleni's friends had come on board, and that she had been stowed away by that worthy, who swore that he would not leave her behind. To this Maa Maa I had a particular aversion, and always hated to see her come on board. She was ugly enough in all conscience, and had always been said to be the cause of quarrels and fights whenever the skipper took her on a trip. Taking Knowles with me, we lugged her on deck screaming and biting. As she refused to get into a canoe, Knowles threw her overboard, where some sympathising friends picked her up.

Just as this incident terminated I received a note from the owners, telling me to delay the vessel's departure for half-an-hour. Wondering what was in the wind, I set about restoring order. I found a lot of liquor in the foc'sle, which I took aft and locked up. Then with Knowles' aid I succeeded in clearing the decks of the women and shore loafers, who were lying about in all stages of intoxication.

At eleven o'clock we saw two boats pulling off from the shore, and noticed armed Samoans among the crews. As they came alongside I saw seated in one of them the figures of Black Tom and his son Johnny, both heavily ironed. In the stern sat his Samoan wife, a woman named Musia. A number of white residents were in charge of the lot, and I was informed that at an impromptu mass meeting, held that morning, it had been decided to expatriate Tom and his family for the good of the country; they had seized this favourable opportunity of carrying their resolution into effect.

This was a pretty state of affairs. I need scarcely explain my indignation at having two such characters as Black Tom and his son foisted on me as passengers. I was about to get into a boat and let them carry their own prisoners away, when I was told that I could land him and his family at the first land we made. This would be Quiros Island, bearing N.N.W. from Apia.

"All right, gentlemen," I replied, "and as everybody here happens to be drunk, I'll feel obliged if you will be good enough to lift the anchor and let us get away."

Tom and his family were accordingly put in the hold, and the newcomers having got the anchor up bade me farewell, chuckling at having rid themselves of Black Tom so cleverly. Whereupon they got into the boats and pulled ashore.

It was blowing stiffly as we ran through the passage, and certainly we presented a pretty spectacle, with our running gear all in disorder, and the crew drunk in the lee scuppers. I had the keys of the prisoners' irons, so giving the tiller to Knowles, I went below and liberated them.

"Tom," I said, "my instructions are to keep you in irons till we made the first land. Now, I've got nothing against you, but I don't want your company, and I consider I was served a shabby trick when they put you on board. I mean to be even with them. They said the first land. Now, I'll stand on this tack till midnight; then I'll put about and land you on the coast."

The negro's bloodshot eyes showed blind fury when I first approached him, but his look softened as I spoke. He laughed, evidently enjoying my suggestion.

"Thank you, sir, for taking the bracelets off us, but I don't care about landing in Samoa again, and I'll face the voyage with you. You're the first man that's spoke a kind word to me since I was rushed and tied in my own house—treated like a wild beast, and, by ——! I'll do any mortal thing in this world for you."

He then begged me not to land him at Quiros, but to let him remain on board until we met Captain Hayston who, he was sure, would give him a trading station. I promised him this, and in return, being a splendid cook, he provided me during the remainder of the voyage with all sorts of sea delicacies.

I will not speak of the dangers of that wearisome voyage; the drunkenness that I tried in vain to suppress; the erratic course we made to our destination. The skipper sobered up every two or three days, took the sun, worked out the ship's position, and let me steer any course I liked. Then he would fly to his bottle of "square-face," until I thought it necessary to rouse him again in order to ascertain our whereabouts. At last, after a forty-two days' passage, we sighted the low-lying coral islands enclosing the spacious lagoon of Millé.

CHAPTER V

THE BRIG LEONORA

The island of Millé is situated in the Radac or eastern portion of the Marshall group, discovered by a captain of that name in 1788. On the charts it bears the name of the Mulgrave Lagoon, and the reason is not far to seek. For the most part the islands of Polynesia are of volcanic origin, whilst the lagoons, which sometimes pass for islands, are exclusively of coral formation. The minute insects which form them build their submarine wall in a circle, which growing for ages, until it rises at low water above sea-level, gradually collects sand and debris, when it decomposes and becomes a solid. Then comes a day when wandering cocoa-nuts float to it and take up their abode on its shores. Gradually a ring of land is formed, varying in width, covered with a wreath of palms, sheltering within its circumference a peaceful sea, into which access is attainable by scattered channels only.

The spot we had reached was of this description.

Day was breaking when we first sighted the tops of the cocoa-palms, and putting the ketch dead before the wind we ran down to the passage. On going aloft I was glad to see the spars of a vessel showing about three miles distant. As none of the crew had ever visited the place before, we lay to and fired a gun. In about half-an-hour we saw a boat pulling towards us, with a tall man standing up steering. It was Hayston. Jumping aboard he shook me warmly by the hand, and said, "So you see we've met again! What sort of passage did you have?"

I recounted our misfortunes, adding the information that the ketch leaked terribly.

"Oh! that's just like Bascom," he remarked. "He told me that he'd send her down as sound as a bell. I never had a chance of looking at her when she was on the beach at Apia, and I certainly thought he would act squarely with me. But we'll talk business by and by."

He now took command of the ketch, and brought us into the lagoon, where we dropped anchor in ten fathoms alongside the brig. I then formally handed over my vessel to him, and wished the king of Arnu joy of his bargain. After receiving full particulars of the voyage, he called the skipper aft.

"Well, Captain Westendorf," he said, "you have most fortunately reached here safely, but more through good luck than good management. I know you to be an experienced and capable navigator, so that had you attended to your duty you would have made Millé ten or fifteen days, earlier. Now, you can go ashore and live with my trader till you get a passage back to Samoa, for I'll be hanged if I take you back. As for your crew, I don't want them either; you can take them with you or turn them adrift. The ketch I intend to leave here until I return from Ascension; but mark this—*and you know me*—don't attempt to board her during my absence; good day!"

I felt sorry at seeing the good-natured "Tapoleni" so humiliated; for with the exception of that one failing which has obscured brighter intellects, and which was the cause of all his troubles, he was a thoroughly honest old fellow.

Black Tom and his wife elected to remain at Millé until they found a suitable island on which to open a trading station. They parted from me with many professions of gratitude which I think were sincere. He afterwards became a wealthy man—such are fortune's vagaries in the islands; his son Johnny earnestly begged me to intercede with Captain Hayston on his account, and not to leave him on shore at Millé. I made the request, and the Captain told him to come aboard the *Leonora*.

During the afternoon Hayston and I went over the ketch in order to inspect the stores, gear, etc., when he asked me, now that my responsibility had ended, what were my intentions as to future movements? I told him I proposed to charter a native canoe for Arnu, there to await a passing vessel and a passage to Samoa. From this course, however, he dissuaded me, pointing out that I might have to stay there six months. He then offered me the position of supercargo on his brig at a fair salary, pressing for an immediate answer.

Thinking it better to be earning money than leading a life of idleness among the natives, I consented. "I accept your offer, Captain," I said;

"but there is one thing I wish you to understand, I am coming with you, not for the sake of the pay, but because I don't want to loaf about the Marshall group like a beach-comber, and, moreover, I should like to visit the Carolines. I don't particularly want to return to Samoa, and if I see a place I like I'll start trading. Now, I am willing to do duty as supercargo, even without pay, but I won't lend a hand in any transaction that I don't like the look of. So at our first difference you can set me ashore."

Hayston looked me straight in the face and held out his hand— "Well, now, that's a fair deal. I give you my word that I won't ask you to join in anything doubtful. The traders round here are the greatest scoundrels unhung, and I have to treat them as they treat me. My books are in a bad state, and you'll find work enough putting them straight; but I'll be glad of your company aboard, even if you never do a hand's turn." So the bargain was closed. I got my chest from the hold and sent it aboard the brig; the steward receiving instructions that I was to occupy the port side of the cabin. At dusk Hayston gave some of the crew liberty, and sent the rest with the mates to haul the ketch in and beach her as the tide was full. While he stood watching her from the brig's deck, he suddenly remarked that they were making a mess of it, and calling two boys to bring the dingey alongside, he was pulled into the shore.

There was a number of young women on board, natives of the Kingsmill group, good-looking, but wild in appearance. I was on deck and they were below, where I heard them laughing and talking, and saw they were seated on the lounge that ran round the cabin. They all seemed very merry over a game, much like "knucklebones," which they were playing with shells. A large canoe was bearing down on us from one of the islands in the lagoon, and just as she ran up in the wind ahead of us, allowing the topsail to drift down alongside, I heard a man's voice mingling with the girls'.

I was going forward to have a close look at the canoe, when I saw the Captain close alongside in the dingey. He had sailed out to the brig, having let the two boys remain on shore to assist at the ketch. Just as he stepped over the sail, the owner of the voice I had heard ran out of the cabin. Hayston gripped him by the arm, and I heard him sing out, "What, would you knife me?" The next minute the man was seized in the powerful arms, lifted high above his head, and then dashed upon the deck, where he lay perfectly still.

The Captain disappeared in the cabin, and running up I lifted the man's head. His back and neck seemed broken, and though I called loudly no one came from below. There were a lot of Arunai natives in the hold sleeping and smoking, but they took no notice of my calls, which, as I didn't know a word of their language, did not surprise me. The canoe had now come alongside, and the Captain reappeared upon deck. The chief seemed pleased to see him, and then a lot of natives clambered on board and carried the wounded man aboard their barque.

Having given them eight or ten pounds of tobacco, Hayston told them, partly in English and partly in the Millé dialect, that the man was shamming dead, and if he woke up on board they could chuck him overboard and let him swim. Then they hoisted sail again and stood away.

I felt horrified, for, although the Captain was certainly justified in defending himself from a man armed with a knife, I was shocked at witnessing the result. He, however, insisted that the fellow was only "foxing," and so the matter ended. When the boats returned from the ketch, I heard the women remark to the sailors that Siāké (Jack) had run away in a canoe, because "Kaptin" had beat him.

At daylight next morning we got under weigh, and I was astonished at the manner in which Hayston handled the brig through the narrow passage. After accomplishing this feat, we bore away for Ujillong, and the steward called us to breakfast.

Our destination was the almost unknown chain of coral islets forming Ujillong or Providence Island. Some fifteen months previously, Hayston had discovered a passage through the reef there, and sailed his brig in. He was delighted with the security afforded by the magnificent lagoon inside. The islets were covered with cocoa-nuts, and he at once decided upon forming a principal trading station there, making it a centre from whence he could work the islands in the North Pacific. There were only thirty natives on the whole lagoon, and with these he succeeded in establishing friendly relations, setting them to work in erecting dwelling-houses and oil-sheds.

We left in charge two white men named Jerry Jackson and Whistling Bill, together with a number of Line Island natives who were to assist in making oil. Hayston told me he intended to settle there himself and cruise among the Carolines and Marshalls, whilst Captain Peese, his colleague, would run a small vessel to China, making Ujillong his headquarters. On this occasion he expected to find that a large quantity of oil had been made in his absence, and was anxious to get there as quickly as possible.

During the day I had leisure to observe the crew, and considering that none of them were white men, the way in which the brig was worked was simply admirable. They treated the officers with great freedom of manner, but before the Captain they seemed absolutely to cower. There being some thirty of them they were by no means over-worked. They were allowed as much liquor as they chose to buy at a dollar a bottle for gin, beer at fifty cents, and rum at a dollar. With such license one would naturally think that insubordination would be rife. It was not so. But though they never broke out at sea, when once the brig anchored they became fiends incarnate. Gambling and drinking then commenced. The sounds of oaths, yells, and blows floated up from the foc'sle, mingling with the screams of the women, and the night was made horrible with their din.

Individual members of the crew of this strange vessel I shall describe later on—for the present *place aux dames*! Every officer had a native wife, and the Chinese carpenter two. Most of these women were natives of Arurai or Hope Island, one of the Kingsmill group. They were darker in complexion than the other Polynesians, and prone to violent jealousy of their protectors. It was by no means uncommon to see two of these girls fighting like demons on the main deck with their national weapons, wooden daggers set round with shark's teeth, while blood poured in streams from their lacerated limbs and bodies. There were several girls from Ocean and Pleasant Island, near the equator. Very good-looking were these last, and fair as to complexion. The principal belle, whose name was Nellie, was a very handsome half-caste—a native of Hope Island. Her father, a deserter from a whaler, had acquired such influence with the natives that they made him a war chief. He led them when they cut off an American whaler and killed the whole crew. Discarding civilised clothing, he became a native in all but colour, and finally met his death in a skirmish with a hostile tribe. This girl was his daughter, and had been given as a present to Hayston by the king of Arurai. Along with her beauty she had a violent and dangerous temper, and was never backward in using her knife on any woman that provoked her.

We had merely dropped Millé astern of us, when Hayston changed his mind about going to Arurai, and bore away to Pleasant Island. He told me that he had forgotten a promise made to the traders there to bring them supplies, but that he would call at Providence on our way back from the Carolines.

Pleasant Island (or Naura) is generally considered one of the Gilbert group, although it is far to the leeward, and the natives, together with those of Ocean Island (or Paanup), consider themselves a distinct people. The former island is in latitude 0.25 S., longitude 167.5 E., and the latter in latitude 0.505, longitude 169.30 E.

"We've got a bully breeze," said the Captain; "and there is a straight run of five hundred miles before we sight the cocoa-nuts on Pleasant Island. I'll show you what the *Leonora* can do."

Our course was something about S.W. by W., the wind increasing in strength as we put the helm up for Pleasant Island, and during the afternoon, so quickly was the brig slipping through the water, that Hayston said we should do the distance—four hundred and ninety-five miles—in forty-eight hours. I was astonished at the rate we travelled, and the Captain himself seemed pleased. Calling the hands aft, he gave them a glass of grog all round, and told the women to go on the main deck and dance. This created considerable amusement, for as the brig was running dead before the wind, and occasionally giving rolls, the dancers losing their balance got some heavy falls into the scuppers, while the others laughed and enjoyed their misfortunes.

We ran up under the leeside of the island just forty-four hours after leaving Millé, a trifle over eleven knots an hour. In a few minutes we were boarded by the traders, of whom there were six. They were certainly a rough lot. As each man lived under the protection of a particular chief, the island being divided into six districts, there was the keenest business rivalry among them.

Hayston called them down below, when they were soon pretty well drunk.

They had plenty of dollars, and bought largely of arms and ammunition. I was employed, with the second mate, in getting up the guns, principally Snider rifles, from the lazarette. I called to them, one by one, to come and pick what they wanted; however they seemed quite satisfied to let me give them what I liked.

The brig was standing off and on, close into the land, in charge of the boatswain, the mate being ill; Hayston was singing "The Zouave," and the traders were applauding uproariously, whilst two were dancing with Nellie and Sara, shouting and yelling like lunatics. The only one that was sober was a fine young fellow who seemed ill, and was supported by a native. This young fellow paid me for the arms bought by his comrades, saying, "They're all drunk now, and as I don't go in for that kind of thing myself, they've got me to do this business for them." The man who was dancing with Sara had a bag of dollars in his hand, and as he waltzed round the cabin he kept swinging it about and striking the woodwork of the cabin.

Carl, the sick man, called out to him, "I say, Ned, let me have that money now, I'm settling up for you." Swinging the bag of dollars round, Ned sent it full at liberty, and struck Carl in the chest, knocking him down. I picked him up, and thought by the pallor of his face that he was either killed or seriously injured.

The native who was with him called to some of his comrades, and a young woman came down and took his head in her lap, while I got a decanter of water. After a while he came round, and told me he was not much hurt, but that the bag of money was heavy and had bruised his chest greatly.

"You dog," he said, getting up and walking over to the other man, who was now sitting at the table talking to the Captain, "as sure as my name's Carl I'll make you suffer for this."

"Come, come," said Hayston, "it was only Ned's rough play. I don't think he meant to hurt you. Besides, I don't want to see white men fighting on board my ship."

"Look here, Captain," said he, pulling off his shirt, "look at my body, and tell me if Ned thought me a fit subject for a joke."

It makes me shudder now. There was an awful gash on his back, extending from his right shoulder to below the ribs on the right side. It was roughly sewn up here and there, and seemed to be healing, but the blow on the chest had made it bleed anew; a dark stream was soaking down his leg to the ground.

"By heaven! that is a terrible cut," said the Captain; "how in thunder did you get mauled like that?"

Carl, who was still very faint, told us that some time ago he had a fight with a native, and licked him. One night, as he was lying face downward on his mat, this man crept into his hut and struck him with a shark tooth sword. His native wife, who was coming into the house at the time, carrying two shells of toddy, dropped them, and flinging her arms round the man's legs, tripped him up, and held him, while Carl, all smothered in blood, shot him dead with his revolver.

"Ned!" said the Captain gravely, when Carl's tale was told, "did you know this young fellow had this gash in his back when you hove the bag at him?"

"Of course I did! why, d—n him, can't he take a joke? Naura's a rough shop for a man that can't stand a bit of fun."

"Put up your hands, you cowardly dog!" said the Captain, and in an instant the drunken traders cleared a space. "I'll teach you to hurt a wounded man."

Ned was as big a man as the Captain, and seemed to be the leading spirit of the gang. But the other traders, though armed with navy revolvers and derringers, did not seem inclined to interfere.

At the first round the big trader went down like a bullock, and lay on the cabin floor apparently lifeless. Hayston was like a mad animal when he tried to get him up, and the man fell helpless. Picking him up in his arms like a child, he carried him on deck, the rest of us following.

"Here! Naura men, where's Ned's boat?" he called out.

It was towing astern, and some one having hauled it up, Hayston dropped the man into it like a log of wood.

Then his good temper returned instantly, and he paid Carl every attention, insisting on dressing his wound. We remained out by Pleasant Island all day, and shipped a lot of oil, for which Hayston paid the traders in arms and ammunition; we then stood away for Ocean Island.

I learned that Carl had been a petty officer on board the U.S. cruiser *Wish-ton-wish*, but had deserted and made his way to Pleasant Island. He seemed superior to his companions in every way, and I was glad to be able to give him some books.

He told me that he belonged to the New England States, but that he could never return, and would put a bullet through his head rather than be taken back a disgraced man. I bade him farewell with regret, and learned two years afterwards that, a month after I saw him, he had blown his brains out, as the U.S. corvette *Rowena* touched at the island. Poor Carl! How many a tale of wasted life, of reckless deeds, and early death, could every island of the South Sea tell.

Although Hayston was an utterly reckless man in most matters, he was by no means foolhardy where the lives of others were concerned. During the time we spent at Pleasant Island every precaution was taken against a surprise.

All the crew carried revolvers, and two men were posted in the fore and main-tops armed with Winchesters. The natives of this island had cut off many ships in past years, and were now so well armed and determined that the utmost caution was needed.

It was here that I met an American named Maule—about as hard a specimen of an old style South Sea trader as one could fall across. He was extremely anxious that I should purchase two native girls from him. They were under his charge. It seems their father had been killed, and his own wife objected to their presence in his house.

I told him that I was supercargo, and therefore could not speculate on my own account. Besides, that sort of traffic was entirely out of my line. If he had curios, weapons, or Naura gods, I would deal, but there I drew the line.

"Well, blame my cats! if you ain't too disgustin' partickler! Want to stuff yer cabin with kyurosities and graven images, instead of dellikit young women. Now, lookee hyar—jest you take them two gals o' mine for thirty dollars, and you'll jest double your money from king Abinoka. He's jest mad after Naura girls, and buys 'em up by the dozen."

Finding that I wouldn't invest, he tried the Captain, telling him that the girls were anxious to get away from Pleasant Island, as their father was dead, and having no brothers, they could not get food enough from the people. His wife was jealous too, and had beaten them.

"Well, well!" said the Captain, "bring them aboard, and I'll give them a passage somewhere. I suppose by and by you'll tell some man-of-war captain that I stole them." So the trader sent them on board, and received in exchange some boats' gear and a keg of molasses.

The girls went aft, and remained with the others in the cabin for a few days. When we sighted Ocean Island, Hayston called me on deck, and said, "Come and see a bit of fun."

Old Mary was told to bring up her flock. The two Pleasant Island girls came up with the rest. They were about fourteen and fifteen years of age, and, from their close similarity, probably the children of the same mother—a somewhat unusual thing in the Gilbert group. They seemed frightened at being called up, and clung closely to Sara and Nellie. Their hair, Pleasant Island fashion, hung down straight upon their backs, and was carefully oiled and combed. A girdle of Pandanus leaf was their only garment. Speaking kindly to them, the Captain asked them if they would like to go ashore there and live. I give the conversation.

Captain.—"Well, will you go ashore here?"

Girls.—"Are there plenty of cocoa-nuts and fish?"

Captain.—"Pretty fair; but there are not always plenty."

Girls.—"What chiefs will take us and give us food?"

Captain.—"I don't know—there are more women there than men. All the young men have gone away in whaleships."

Girls.—"That's bad; the Ocean Island women will soon kill us strangers."

Captain.—"Most likely. Would you like to stay on the ship if I get you husbands?"

Girls.—"Yes! where are they?"

Captain.—"Boatswain, send Sunday and boy George here."

These were two boys who had been sailing with Hayston for some years. Both were about sixteen. Of George I will speak later on. Having come aft, the Captain, addressing them, said he was pleased at their steadiness, and as a reward for their good conduct, he had at great expense procured them wives, whom he hoped they would treat well. His speech was a humorous one, and the crew standing round grinned approvingly—Sunday and boy George being, apparently, looked upon as lucky youths, for the girls were undeniably good-looking. In fact, I never saw an ill-looking Pleasant islander.

"Now, Terau and N'jilong, you must draw lots for first pick. Carpenter, bring me two splinters of wood."

They were instructed by the other native girls how to draw lots, the result being that Terau picked boy George, and her sister took Sunday.

"Steward!" commanded Hayston, "bring up a couple of bottles of grog. And you, Sunday and boy George! before you begin your married life just listen to me! Call all hands aft!"

The crew came aft, and the Captain, who now seemed quite serious, said, "Now, boys, I have given these girls to Sunday and boy George. Don't let me hear of any one attempting to interfere with them, and if one of you puts his head into the boys' house while the girls are there alone, I'll make it warm for him. There's a couple of bottles of grog for the watch to drink their healths, and the steward has two more for the watch below. For'ard now, and you, boys, go and ask the supercargo for some cloth to rig your girls out with."

The *Leonora* was certainly a very sociable and domesticated ship.

We lay off and on at Ocean Island for a day or two, and engaged twenty-seven natives to proceed to Ponapé (Ascension Island) to work for Cappelle and Milne, a German firm. Then we made an easterly course to Taputanea (or Drummond Island), one of the Gilbert group, where Hayston had a trader.

The Drummond islanders are notorious throughout the Pacific for treachery and ferocity. They frequently cut off vessels, and murder all hands, being led on these occasions by renegade white men. When Commodore White's ships visited this spot in 1842 they murdered one of his seamen. A fight ensued, in which many were killed, and the town of Utiroa was laid in ashes. But the lesson had no great effect, and Hayston told me that they would not hesitate to attempt the capture of any vessel that could not make a good resistance.

We sighted the island at night-time, and lay off Utiroa till daylight. Then after putting the brig in a state of defence, and giving the command to the Fiji half-caste, Bill, telling him also to shoot a certain native if he saw him come alongside, Hayston had the longboat and whaleboat lowered.

Into the former he put a great quantity of trade, principally gin, rum, and firearms, giving me charge of the latter to cover him. I had six men with me, each armed with a Vetterlich rifle, and I carried my own Winchester—eighteen shot. Hayston gave me full instructions how to act if he was attacked; then we made for the town of Utiroa, the boats keeping alongside of each other. As we were pulling Hayston told me that he wished to get ashore before the canoes left, in order to interview his trader Jim in the presence of the people. This fellow, it appeared, was a fighting man who had great influence over the Drummond Island natives, with whom bloodshed and murder were acts of everyday occurrence. He always aided them in their tribal fights, and evinced a partiality for taking life that had won their warmest admiration. Hayston had brought him from Ponapé, where he was the terror of the white men, swaggering about

A Modern Buccaneer

the ports of the island, and using his pistol on any one that resented his conduct. But he was a good trader for all that, and had been placed in this trust because no other man could be found willing to risk his life among such a treacherous race.

Jim had not been installed a week at Utiroa, when a chief named Tabirau gave him one of his daughters for a wife, and was paid for her in trade according to custom. Shortly afterwards the girl ran home again, saying that the white man had beaten her for spoiling a razor.

Jim took his rifle, went to his father-in-law's house, and demanded the girl back. A number of natives followed up, anticipating that he would be killed, for Tabirau was a chief of note, not averse to the extermination of white men. As they expected, he refused to give up the girl unless Jim paid more trade, alleging that one of the muskets paid for her was no good. Without a moment's hesitation the trader shot him through the body, killing him instantly, and then clubbed the girl to death with the butt end of his rifle.

Instead of being murdered by the natives for this atrocious deed, he was looked upon as a hero, and all Tabirau's land, canoes, and property were made over to him. The people of Utiroa elected him to be their commercial ruler, refusing to sell oil or produce to any ship without his advice or consent. For a while his conduct had quite satisfied Hayston, until he learned that Jim had sold a lot of his oil to a Californian trader, boasting, besides, that Hayston dared not bring him to task for it.

It was now the Captain's intention to assert his authority, and break the trader's power over the natives. For this purpose he determined to meet him on shore, and let the natives see which was the better man.

As we approached the beach we saw fully five hundred natives assembled; all were armed, and many dressed in their thick armour of fibre, and wearing helmets of the skin of the porcupine fish. There was great excitement among them, though many of them seemed glad to see Hayston, calling out "Tiaka po, Kaptin" (How do you do). The main body, however, seemed ready to dispute our landing.

"Keep close up!" the Captain called out to me, "and don't let any of them see your arms, but be ready to drop it into them the first shot that is fired. But, for God's sake, don't miss. That villain Jim, you see, isn't here, though; those fellows mean mischief. However, land I must, and will." He then told the crew to run the boat on the beach, and standing up in the stern, called out to natives that he knew, pretending to see nothing unusual in their manner. At the moment that he stepped on the beach the whole body of natives formed in solid line in front of him, while hundreds of rifle muzzles were almost thrust in his face. He looked steadily at them, and commenced to talk with his hands in his trousers' pocket.

I forgot my instructions, and my crew seemed equally excited at the Captain's danger, for, without being told, they ran the whaleboat ashore and we all jumped out. The men in the other boat were standing up rifle in hand, and they followed us.

The Captain was speaking calmly to the natives, when he turned and saw me. "For God's sake, go back to the boats," he said, in a quiet tone; then raising his hand threateningly and roaring like a lion, he repeated the order in the Drummond Island dialect. I understood this hint, so we ran back, but kept our arms ready. Hayston's order to me seemed to have a good effect, for the fierce looks of the natives relaxed, and soon afterwards he called out that it was all right, and told me to give him two muskets and a box of tobacco out of the longboat. This was a present for two of the principal chiefs, who now shook hands with him, saying that Jim was in his house, and had told them that if Captain Hayston put his foot inside he would shoot him. Our former opponents seemed pretty equally divided in their opinions. Half of them were eager to see the fight between Jim and the Captain, and the others were ready to massacre the whole of us if but a single act of hostility was committed on either side.

Hayston ordered me then to come with him, and asked the natives' permission to allow me to bring my Winchester, as I was frightened of them. The boats were shoved out, the crew being told to jump ashore if they heard any firing, and fight their way to Jim's house. As I joined the Captain on the beach he told me that the natives thought he meant to kill Jim, and that they had felt him all over to see if he had concealed any arms, but that they seemed satisfied when they found none. I was astonished at his recklessness in not bringing weapons, and as we were escorted along the road by the natives, I told him that I had a derringer hidden among some tobacco in a canvas bag slung round my waist.

"No, no!" he said. "It will never do to see you give it to me now. Besides, I don't want any shooting if I can help it. There are many of these natives who will be glad to see Jim's power broken, and I want to get my hands on him before he puts a bullet into me. The rest is easy enough. If you see him taking a shot at me before I come up to him, you can use that rifle; but don't kill him if you can help it, and don't be alarmed about yourself. Take hold of this old nigger's hand who is walking beside you and you'll be all right. Just keep laughing and talking."

After a long walk we got up to the trader's house, and here the natives made a halt. I was beginning to feel horribly scared, and wished we were on board the brig again. Presently we were told that Jim was inside, and would not come out because he was sick. Walking steadily forward the Captain advanced to within a few feet of the house, and called out, "Well, this is a nice sort of welcome, Jim! Come out and show yourself."

The door opened, and I could see that the place was filled with natives, all of whom carried guns and seemed much excited.

Then Jim made his appearance and walked slowly up to the Captain. He was a tall man, dressed in pyjamas, with two navy revolvers in his belt. With his heavy red moustache and bloodshot eyes, he looked his character well—that of an unscrupulous and remorseless ruffian. Hayston had seated himself on a fallen cocoa-nut tree with his hands full of papers.

"How d'ye do, Jim?" he said, extending his hand to the trader and rising as he spoke. The moment the trader's hand touched his, he seized him by the throat and shook him like a dog shaking a rat; then spun him round violently and threw him against the stern of a canoe, where he lay half stunned. The natives gave a roar, but the Captain held up his hands—the tide seemed to turn at once in our favour, and one man went up to the trader, took away his pistols, and gave them to Hayston. The Captain addressed the principal chiefs, whom he told that Jim had robbed him, and that after he had made presents to the people, he intended to take the rest of the trade away.

We were moving into the house to take possession, when the trader, who had now recovered himself, got up and addressed the natives. I did not understand what he said, but Hayston evidently did. The effect of Jim's harangue was to render the natives undecided as to what course to adopt. One man, who spoke good English and had a rifle with a sword bayonet attached, said it did not matter if any one was killed, but they thought their white man did not have fair play.

"Jim," said the Captain, in his smoothest tones, "you say you can whip any man in the Pacific in four rounds. Well! now you have an opportunity to prove your words. If you are a better man than I am, I will let you keep what trade you have got, and shake hands afterwards."

Jim stripped to the waist, and called for one of his women to bring him a pair of "taka" or "cinnet" sandals, as he was barefooted.

He was shaking with rage and excitement, while Hayston showed no concern whatever. From the jump the trader forced the fighting, but in less time than I describe it, both of his eyes were nearly closed, and he had a terrific cut on his cheekbone. Some women then ran in and begged the Captain to desist. I believe he could have killed his man in another five minutes. He asked Jim if he was satisfied and would shake hands. But the trader would not answer, and then the Captain's face grew dark. Seizing him again by the throat he nearly strangled him, his eyes protruding horribly as he worked his arms in the air. When he let him go he fell like a log. "Carry him down to the boats and make him fast," he said to the interpreter.

We entered his house unmolested, and I took an inventory of his goods. There was very little trade left, but the natives said he had a lot of money given him by the skipper of the Californian vessel. This we found in a large soup and bouilli tin in his chest. It amounted to nearly seven hundred dollars, mostly in U.S. half-dollar coins.

The natives begged the Captain not to close the station up; if Jim was going away, they wished some one in his place. He said he would consider their wish after he got on board; but they must first help him to raft off twenty casks of oil that were lying in Jim's oil-shed.

We got off to the boats at last. The old man still kept hold of my left hand. This, the Captain had told me, he had done to protect me if any fighting took place; that if fighting had resulted I would not have been killed, but would have been regarded as the old man's prize. The natives launched their canoes and followed the boats in swarms when we set sail for the brig. As soon as we got alongside, Hayston asked the second mate if the native he had spoken of had shown up.

"No," said Bill; "he's gone away to Samoa, so they say here."

Hayston seemed pleased at this news, telling me that this man was a special enemy of his, into whom he meant to put a bullet if he could drop across him. As he was gone away he was saved an unpleasant task. Jim was taken for'ard, and the carpenter was ordered to put him in irons; thereupon he sulkily explained that he didn't intend to turn rusty.

"All right, then, Jim," replied the Captain. "I'm glad we're going to be friends again. But you can go ashore at Makin and stay there."

He then called for a man among his crew to take Jim's place on shore. After some hesitation a sturdy Rotumah native said he didn't mind, if the Captain gave him a wife. He couldn't speak the language, and if he took a Taputana woman she might plot to kill him and he be none the wiser.

"Boys!" called out the Captain, "is any one of you willing to give Willie his wife? I'll make it up to him. Besides, there'll be plenty more going through the Marshall group."

No one appeared struck with the idea. So the Captain called Sunday aft, and held brief conversation with him, after which the boy went into the deckhouse and brought out his wife and N'jilong. The poor girl shed a few tears at first and clung to Sunday's neck, but he finally induced her to go with Willie. She had come aboard almost naked, but went away with a well-filled chest and any amount of finery.

She parted from her sister in an apathetic manner, but her tears began to flow afresh when Sunday turned coolly from her and pursued his duties on the deck. Savage though she might be, she felt the parting from the hardened young wretch whom she had come to look on as her partner. However she lost nothing by the change. Her new husband was a steady, good fellow who treated her kindly. Years afterwards I met them both on one of the Ellice Islands and received a warm welcome. Willie had legally married her in Fiji, and they seemed a most affectionate couple, with children in whom their chief pride in life was centred.

CHAPTER VI

CAPTAIN BEN PEESE

For the next few weeks we cruised about among the islands of the Kingsmill and Gilbert groups, collectively known as the Line Islands. The most southerly of them is Arurai or Hope Island, in the latitude 2.41 S., longitude 177 E.—the most northerly, Makin or Butaritu, in latitude 3.20, 45 N.

We did good business generally going through this group, and steady going trade it was, varied only by the mad drunken bouts and wild dances which took place when we were at anchor—these last beyond description.

Just then I was badly hurt fishing on shore one day. It was peculiarly a South Sea accident. I was standing on a jutting ledge of coral, holding my rod, when it suddenly broke off, allowing me to fall downwards on sharp edges, where I was terribly cut about the legs and body. The green or live coral has the property of making a festering wound whenever it pierces the true skin, and for weeks, with my unhealed wounds, I was nearly mad with pain. The Captain did all he could for me, having a netted hammock slung on deck, where I could see all that was going on. One day in a fit of pain I fell out and nearly cracked my skull. All the native girls on board were most kind and patient in nursing me. So the Captain said the least I could do was to marry one, if only out of gratitude and to brush away the flies.

Whatever some people might call these poor girls they had at least one virtue, which, like charity, covereth a multitude of sins. Pity for any one in bodily pain they possessed in the highest degree. Many an hour did they sit beside me, bathing my aching head with a sponge and salt water—this last the universal and infallible cure.

We called at Peru or Francis Island, where we obtained nine natives—five men and four young women. The islanders here are rude and insulting to all strangers not carrying arms, and almost as threatening as those of Taputana. I was, however, too ill to go on shore here.

After a two months' cruise through this group we bore away for Strong's Island, distant some five hundred miles. We had favourable winds, and the brig's speed was something wonderful. In thirty-eight hours we had covered a distance of four hundred and ninety miles, when the lofty hills of this gem of the North Pacific, covered with brightest verdure, gladdened our eyes after the long, low-lying chains of islets and atolls of the Marshall and Kingsmill groups.

The brave "north-east trade" that had borne us so gallantly along died away to a zephyr as we drew near the land, and saw once more the huge rollers thundering on the weather point of the island.

Calling first at Chabral harbour we did a little trading, and then sailed down the coast close to the shore—so deep runs the water—till we reached Utwé.

Here we found three American whalers put in for food and water. Hayston seemed anxious to get away, so, after exchanging courtesies with the skippers, we ran round to Coquille harbour, where we lay several days trading and painting ship. We cleared the harbour at daylight, with the sea as smooth as glass and wind so light that the *Leonora* could scarcely stem the strong easterly current. Still keeping a north-west course, we sailed away over the summer sea while scarce a ripple broke its glassy surface, until we sighted Pingelap or M'Askill's, a hundred and fifty miles from Strong's Island.

These were discovered by Captain Musgrave, of the American whaler *Sugar Cane*, in 1793. They are densely covered with cocoa-palms, and though wholly of coral formation, are a good height above sea-level.

The Captain had a trader here named Sam Biggs—a weak-kneed, gin-drinking cockney. How ever such a character could have found his way to these almost unknown islands passed my comprehension! We ran in close to the village—so near that, the wind being light, we nearly drifted onto the beach, and lowered the starboard quarter boat to tow out again.

Whilst waiting for the trader I had a good look at the village, which I was surprised to hear contained 500 inhabitants. As, however, these islands—there are three of them, Takai, Tugula, and Pingelap—are wondrous fertile, they support their populations easily.

Presently the trader came off in a canoe, and, shambling along the deck, went down below to give in his report. He said that things were very bad. A few months back the American missionary brig *Morning Star* had called and prevailed on the king to allow two teachers to be landed. After making presents to the chiefs and principal men, they had got their promise to accept Christianity and to send the white man Biggs about his business. They had also told the natives that Captain Hayston was coming with the intention of carrying them off in bondage to work on the plantations in Samoa. Also that Mr. Morland, the chief missionary, was now in Honolulu, begging for a man-of-war to come to Pingelap and fight Captain Hayston's ship with his big guns and sink her.

All South Sea islanders are easily influenced. In a few hours after the teachers landed the whole village declared for Christianity, burned their idols, and renounced the devil and all his works, *i.e.* Captain Hayston and the brig *Leonora*.

The Captain's face darkened as he listened; then he asked the trader what he had done in the matter. The man, blinking his watery eyes, said he had done nothing; that he was afraid the natives would kill him, and asked to be taken away.

Jumping up from the table, Hayston grasped him by the collar, and asked me to look at him and say what he should do with such a white-livered hound, who would let one of the finest islands in the Pacific be handed over to the sanctimonious pack on board the *Morning Star*, and let the best trading station he, Hayston, owned be ruined?

I suggested that he should be detained on board till we met the *Morning Star*, and then be given to Mr. Morland to keep.

"By ——! just the thing! but just let me tell you, you drunken hound, that when I picked you up a starving beach-comber in Ponapé, I thought you had at least enough sense to know that I am not a man to be trifled with. I was the first man to place a trader on Pingelap. I overcame the natives' hostility, and made this one of the safest islands in the group for whaleships to call at. Now I have lost a thousand dollars by your cowardice. So take this to remember it by."

Then, holding him by one hand, he shook him like a rag, finally slinging him up the companion way, and telling the men to tie him up.

"Lower away the longboat," he roared, "I'll teach the Pingelap gentry how to dance." I went with him, as I wanted to get some bananas and young cocoa-nuts. In five minutes we drew up on the beach.

The head-men of the island now came forward to meet the Captain, and to express their pleasure at seeing him. But he was not to be mollified, and sternly bade them follow him to the largest house in the town where he would talk to them.

The boy Sunday, who was a native of Pingelap, came with us to act as interpreter. Behind the crowd of natives were the two Hawaiian teachers, dressed in white linen shirts and drill trousers. They had their wives with them, dressed in mixed European and native costume.

None of us had arms, nor did we think them necessary. Hitherto these people had been slavish admirers of Hayston, and he assured me that he would reassert his former influence over them in ten minutes. The crowd swarmed into the council-house and sat down on their mats. The Captain remained standing.

His grand, imposing form, as he stood in the centre of the house and held up his hands for silence, seemed to awe them as would a demigod, and murmurs of applause broke from them involuntarily.

"Tell them, Sunday," he said, fixing his piercing blue eyes on the cowering forms of the two missionary teachers, "that I have come to talk peace, not to fight. Ask them who it was years ago, when the hurricane came and destroyed their houses and plantations—when their little ones were crying with hunger—that brought them to his ship and fed them? Have they forgotten who it was that carried them to Ponapé, and there let them live on his land and fed them on his food till they grew tired of the strange land, and then brought them back to their homes again?"

Sunday translated, and the silence was unbroken till the Captain resumed, "Did not the men of Pingelap say then that no man should be more to them than me—that no one else should place a white man here? And now a strange ship comes, and the men of Pingelap have turned their faces from me?"

A scene of wild excitement followed, the greater number crowding round the Captain, while with outstretched hands and bent heads they signified respect.

The two teachers were walking quickly away with their wives, when the Captain called them back, and in a pleasant voice invited them to come on board and see if there was anything there that they would like their wives to have for a present.

Before returning on board Sunday told the Captain that the chiefs and people desired to express their sorrow at receiving the missionaries, and that they would be glad if he took them away. Since the visit of the *Morning Star* an epidemic had broken out resembling measles, which had already carried off fifty or sixty of them. Already their superstitious fears led them to regard the sickness as a punishment for having broken their treaty with Hayston. So they offered us six young women as a present; also ten large turtles, and humbly begged him to allow his trader to remain.

The Captain made answer that he did not want six young women— there were plenty on board already; but he would take two, with the ten turtles, and ten thousand cocoa-nuts. The said presents were then cheerfully handed over; the two girls and the turtles going off in the Captain's boat, while the cocoa-nuts were formed into a raft and floated alongside the ship.

While these weighty matters were being arranged I walked round to the weather side of the island with Sunday, who wanted to show me a pool in which the natives kept some captive turtle. On our way we came across some young boys and girls catching fish with a seine. They brought us some and lit a fire. We stayed about an hour with them, having great fun bathing in the surf.

Happening to look out to sea, I saw a big ship coming round the point under easy sail; from her rig and the number of boats she carried I knew her at once to be a whaler. We ran ashore and dressed, and as two of the children offered to show us a short cut through the forest to the village, we ran all the way and got opposite the brig just in time to see the Captain leaving her side to board the whaler. I hailed the brig, and they sent me the dingey, in which I followed Hayston. She proved to be the *Josephine*, just out from Honolulu—a clean ship, not having taken a fish. The captain was a queer-looking old fellow dressed like a fisherman. He received us with civility, yet looked at the Captain curiously. His crew were all under arms. Each man had a musket, a lance, or a whaling spade— these two last very formidable weapons—in his hand.

Captain Long was candid, and admitted that as soon as he sighted our brig he had armed his men, for the wind was so light that he would have no chance of getting away. Hayston laughingly asked him if he thought the brig was a pirate.

The whaler replied, "Why, certainly. Old Morland and Captain Melton told me two years ago that you sailed a brig with a crew of darned cut-throat niggers, and would take a ship if you wanted her, so I made up my mind to have a bit of shootin' if you boarded us."

"Well, Captain Long," said Hayston, in his easy, pleasant way, "come over to my little vessel and see the pirate at home."

The invitation was accepted, and as we pulled over amicably, the skipper cast an admiring glance at the graceful *Leonora* as she floated o'er the still, untroubled deep. As we stepped over the ship's side we were met by Bill Hicks, the second mate, whose savage countenance was illumined by a broad smile as he silently pointed to the queer entertainment before us.

"Great ancestral ghosts! d'ye carry a troupe of ackeribats aboard this hyar brig?" quoth the skipper, pointing to four undraped figures capering about in the mad abandonment of a Hawaiian national dance.

The mate explained briefly that he had given the native teachers grog, after which nothing would satisfy them but to show the crew how they used to dance in Lakaina in the good old days. Their wives were also exhilarated, and having thrown off their European clothes, were dancing with more vigour than decorum to the music of an accordion and a violin. The Hope Island girl, Nellie, was seated in a boat we carried on deck playing the accordion, and with her were the rest of the girls laughing and clapping their hands at the antics of the dancers. The stalwart Portuguese, Antonio, was perched on the water-tank with his fiddle, and the rest of the crew who were not at work getting the cocoa-nuts on board were standing around encouraging the quartette by shouts and admiring remarks.

As the whaling skipper gazed with astonishment at the sight, Hayston said, "Ay, there you see the Honolulu native teacher in his true colours. His Christianity is like ours—no better, no worse—to be put on and off like a garment. Once give a Sandwich Island missionary a taste of grog and his true instincts appear in spite of himself. There is *nothing* either of those men would not do now for a dollar; and yet in a day or two they will put on their white shirts, and begin to preach again to these natives who are better men than themselves."

We went below, and after a glass of wine or two the skipper was about to leave, after promising to sell us some bolts of canvas, when the Chinese steward announced that they were fighting on deck. We ran up and saw Antonio and boy George struggling with knives in their hands. The Captain caught Antonio a crack on the head, which sent him down very decisively, and then pitched George roughly into the boat with the girls, telling them to stop their infernal din. The two teachers' wives were then placed in old Mary's care below, and told to lie down and sleep.

The two Pingelap girls who came on board were very young, and seemed frightened at their surroundings, wailing and moaning with fear, so Hayston gave them trinkets and sent them back to the chiefs, getting two immense turtles in exchange.

The wind now died away. All night the brig lay drifting on the glassy sea. At breakfast-time we were almost alongside of the whaler, and the two crews were exchanging sailors' courtesies when five or six whales hove in sight.

All was changed in a moment. Four boats were lowered as if by magic from the whaler, and the crews were pulling like demons for the huge prizes.

The whales were travelling as quickly as the boats, but towards the ships, and in another quarter of an hour three of the boats got fast, the fourth boat also, but had to cut away again.

Our crew cheered the boats, and as there was no wind for the vessel to work up to the dead whales which were being towed up, I took the brig's longboat and six men to help the boats to get the whales alongside.

A breeze sprung up at noon, so after bidding good-bye to the whaler, we stood away for Ponapé, making W.N.W. We were ten days out from Pingelap before we sighted Ponapé's cloud-capped peaks. The wind was very light for the whole way, the brig having barely steerage way on her. Hayston was anxious to reach the island, for there he expected to meet his partner, the notorious Captain Ben Peese.

Here he told me that if things went well with them they would make a fortune in a few years; that he had bought Peese's schooner and sent him to Hong Kong with a load of oil to sell, arranging to meet him in Jakoits harbour in Ponapé on a day named. They were then to proceed to Providence Island, which was a dense grove of cocoa-nut trees. He was sanguine of filling two hundred and fifty casks now in the brig's hold with oil when we reached there.

Twenty miles from shore we spoke an American whaleship from New London. She was "trying out," and signalled to send a boat. The Captain, taking me with him, went on board, when we were met by a pleasant, white-haired old man, Captain Allan.

His first words were, "Well, Captain Hayston, I have bad news. Peese has turned against you. He returned to Ponapé from China a week ago, and cleared out your two stations of everything of value. He had a big schooner called the *Vittoria*, and after gutting the stations, he told the chiefs at Kiti harbour that you had sent him for the cattle running there. He took them all away—thirty-six head."

The Captain said nothing. Turning away he looked at the brig, as if in thought, then asked Allan if he knew where Peese had gone.

"To Manila; Peese has made friends there, and engaged with the Governor-General of the Philippines to supply the garrison with forty head of cattle. I knew the cattle were yours, and warned the chiefs not to let Peese take them away. But he threatened them with a visit from a Spanish man-of-war, and Miller backed him up. He had a strong party with him to enforce his demands."

"Thank you, Allan!" Hayston said very deliberately and calmly; "I was half afraid something like this would happen, but I thought the man I took out of the slums of Shanghai and helped like a brother was the last person to have robbed me. It has shown me the folly of trusting any one. You are busy, Allan! so will leave you."

Bidding adieu to the good skipper we stepped into our boat. Hayston was silent for ten minutes. Then he put his hand on my knee, and looking into my face with the expression I had never seen him wear since he fought the trader at Drummond Island, said, "Hilary! did you ever know me to say I would do a thing and not do it?"

"No! but I have often wished you would *not* keep your word so strictly. Some day you will regret it."

"Perhaps so. But listen to me. This man—this Peese—I found in Shanghai years ago, ill and starving. There was something in his face which roused my interest; I took him on board my vessel and treated him as a brother. I was then high in favour with the Chinese authorities. Not as I am now—hunted from port to port—forced to take up this island life and associate with ruffians who would shoot and rob me if they did not fear me. I went to a mandarin—a man who knew the stuff I was made of, and what I had done in the Chinese service—and asked for preferment for Peese. It was done. In a week he was put in command of a transport, and with his commission in his hand he came aboard my ship and swore he would never forget who it was that had saved him. He spoke but the bare truth, for I tell you this man was dying—dying of starvation. Well! it was he who led me afterwards, by his insidious advice and by collusion with Portuguese collie merchants, into risky dealings.

At first all went well. We so used our positions in the Imperial service that we made over fifteen thousand dollars in three months, exclusive of the money used in bribing Chinese officials. The end came by and by, when I nearly lost my head in rescuing Peese from a gunboat in which he lay a prisoner. Anyhow I lost my rank, and the Viceroy issued a proclamation in the usual flowing language, depriving me of all honours previously conferred. We escaped, it is true, but China was closed to me for ever. Since then I have stood to Peese faithfully. Now, you see the result. He is a d—d clever fellow, and a good sailor, no doubt of that. But mind me when I say that I'll find him, if I beggar myself to do it. And when I find him, he dies!"

I said nothing. He could not well let such treachery and ingratitude pass, and Peese would deserve his fate. However, they never met. Peese, like Hayston, appeared to have his hand against every man, as every man had his hand against Peese.

He met his fate after this fashion:—

A daring act of piracy—seizing a Spanish revenue vessel under the very guns of a fort—and working her out to sea with sweeps, outlawed him. Caught at one of his old haunts in the Pelew Islands, he was heavily ironed and put on board the cruiser *Hernandez Pizarro*, for conveyance to Manila, to await trial.

One day he begged the officers of the corvette to allow him on deck as the heat was stifling. He was brought up and his leg-irons widened so that he could walk. Peese was always an exceedingly polite man. He thanked the officers for their courtesy, and begged for a cigar.

This was given him, and he slowly walked the decks, dragging his clanking chains, but apparently enjoying the flavour of his cigar. Standing against a gun, he took a last look at the blue cloudless sky above him, and then quietly dropped overboard. The weight of his irons, of course, sank him "deeper than plummet lies".... So, and in such manner, was the appropriate and befitting ending of Benjamin Peese, master mariner—"*Requiescat in pace!*"

CHAPTER VII

CRUISING AMONG THE CAROLINES

Our first port of call at Ponapé was Jakoits harbour. It was here we were to land some Line Islanders we had brought from various places in the Gilbert group. Hayston had brought them to the order of the firm of Johann Guldenstern and Sons of Hamburg, whose agents and managers at Ponapé were Messrs. Capelle and Milne. Their trading stations were at Jakoits Islands, where resided the manager of the business. The senior partner of the firm—a burly, bullying Scot—had for some time been carrying on a rather heated correspondence with Hayston, whom he had accused of kidnapping the firm's traders. He had not as yet encountered the Captain, but had told various whaling skippers and others that if half a dozen good men would back him up, he would seize Hayston, and keep him prisoner till H.M. warships *Tuscarora* or *Jamestown* turned up.

Occasionally Hayston had by letter warned him to beware, as he was not a man to be trifled with. Talk and threats are easy when the enemy is distant; so Miller, during his cruisings in the schooner *Matauta*, would exhibit to various traders the particular pistol he intended to use on Hayston. Representing a powerful firm, he had almost unlimited influence in Ponapé. Hayston told me that he believed Peese would never have dared to have looted his trading stations and taken his cattle if Miller had not sided with him.

"Now," said the Captain, as we were slowly sailing into Jakoits, "I'm in a bit of a fix. I must let Miller come aboard and treat him civilly for a bit, or he will pretend he knows nothing of this consignment of natives I have for him. He lies easily, and may declare that he has received no instructions from Kleber, the manager at Samoa, to receive these niggers from me, much less pay for them. But once I have the cash in hand, or his firm's draft, I mean to bring him up with a round turn."

We dropped anchor in the lovely harbour, almost underneath the precipitous Jakoits Islands, on which were the trading stations. There were five whalers lying at anchor, having run in according to custom to get wood, water, and other necessaries. One of these was a brig, the *Rameses* of Honolulu. Dismantled and deserted-looking—in a little secluded cove—she had not a soul on board but the captain, and he was mad. Of him and his vessel later on.

A Yankee beach-comber of a pilot, named Joe Kelman, met us as we came in; not that his services were required, but evidently for his own gratification, as he was bursting with news. As he pulled alongside the Captain told me that he was a creature of Miller's, and a thundering scoundrel on his own account as well. But he would settle it with him and his principal also in a few days.

With a countenance expressive of the deepest sorrow the beach-comber, as he sent glass after glass of grog down his throat, told his doleful tale—how Peese had come with a crew of murdering Spaniards, and played h—l with the "Capting's" property; stole every hoof of his cattle, but four which were now running at Kiti harbour; how Capting Miller had been real cut up at seeing Peese acting so piratical, and said that though he and Captain Hayston was sorter enemies, he thought Peese was "blamed downright ongrateful," etc.

"That's all right, Joe," answered the Captain with the pleasantest laugh, "that's only a stroke of bad luck for me. I bear Captain Miller no ill will from the letters he has written me, and for this part—we are both hot-tempered men, and may have felt ourselves injured by each other's acts—as he tried to save my property, I shall be glad to meet him and thank him personally."

"Well, that's suthinlike," said the beach-comber, "I'd be real sorry to see two such fine lookin' men shootin' bullets into each other. Besides, pore Miller's sick. Guess I'll cut ashore now, Captain. Kin I take any message?"

Hayston said he would give him a few lines, and, sitting down, wrote a short but polite note to Miller, stating that he had a number of labourers for him, which he would be glad to have inspected and landed. He regretted his illness, but would come ashore as soon as he (Miller) was well enough to receive him.

The beach-comber took the letter and went ashore. Hayston turned to me with a laugh: "Do you see that? The gin-drinking scoundrel is playing pilot-fish. He has come to learn if I suspect anything of the game his master is playing. Here's a canoe; you'll see I'll get the truth out of these natives."

The canoe was paddled by a very old man and a boy. There were also a lot of young girls. The Captain declined to entertain visitors at present, there being too much work to do, and cross-examined the old man as to Miller and his men. He said there were no white men now at Jakoits; furthermore, that when the *Leonora* was sighted, Miller had gone off to the four whaleships and had a long talk with the captains. He had taken two guns from the *Seabreeze*, and loaded them as soon as he got ashore. The natives were told there were going to be a big fight; that Captain Miller had got sixty natives in his house, and the two guns placed in front of the landing-place. Hayston gave the old man a present, and suggested that he should dispose of his cargo to one of the whaleships. The old fellow shook his head sadly, saying he had come too late.

Turning to me, the Captain said, "There's news for you; Miller must have thought I meant to go for him as soon as we met, and has his people ready to give me a warm reception. If I had not these Kanakas on board I'd give him as much fighting as he cares for, and put a firestick in his station to finish up with." A few minutes later we saw a boat put off from Jakoits with a big burly man sitting in the stern. At the same time one of the whalers' boats came aboard, in which were the four captains. He greeted them warmly, and we all trooped below.

One of them, a wizened little man with a wonderful vocabulary of curses, said, looking at the others: "Well, gentlemen, before we accept Captain Hayston's hospitality we ought to tell him that we lent Captain Miller two guns to sink this brig with."

"Gentlemen," said Hayston, standing at the head of his table, with his hands resting upon it, "I know all about that, but you are none the less welcome. Miller will be here in a few minutes, and I must beg of you not to let him know that I have been informed of the warm reception he had prepared for me. Besides, they tell me he is ill."

"Oh, h—l! Ill! That's curious; he was in powerful good health an hour or two ago," and the skippers looked at each other and winked.

Presently we returned to the deck, just as the bluff personage of whom we were talking clambered up the ship's side and came aft.

The whaling captains and I watched the meeting with intense interest. Miller was evidently ill at ease, but seeing Hayston walking towards him with outstretched hand and a smile on his face, he made a great effort at self-command, and shook hands vigorously.

"Well, we've met at last, Captain Hayston, and ye see I'm no feared to come aboard and speak up till ye like a man."

"My dear sir," replied Hayston, grasping his hand with a prolonged shake, "I was just telling these gentlemen how I regretted to hear of your illness, for, although we have carried on such a paper warfare, I'm convinced that we only need to meet to become good friends."

Here one of the American captains came up, and, looking the newcomer straight in the face, said, "Well, I *am* surprised at meeting you here. Reckon you can sick and well quicker'n any man I ever come across."

No notice was taken by Miller of this and other sarcastic remarks while he hurried on his business with Hayston. Much grog was drunk, and then the Captain passed the word for all hands to muster on deck—the crew to starboard, the Kanaka passengers on the port side.

The "labour" was then inspected, and passed by their new proprietor, who, now very jovial and unsteady on his pins, took them on shore without delay. He returned shortly and paid for them in cash. Next morning several traders came on board, and any amount of beach-combers, for Ponapé is their paradise. Mr. Miller came with an invitation to visit him on shore. Having business to attend to I stayed on board, promising to follow later on. As Hayston was leaving the brig, Miller said, in presence of the traders,—

"Eh, Captain Hayston, but ye're no siccan a terrible crater as they mak' ye oot. Man, I hae my doots if ye could pommel me so sevairly as ye've inseenuated."

"Mr. Miller," said the Captain, stopping dead, and taking him by the shoulder, "you are now on board my ship, and I will say nothing further than that if you have any doubt on the subject I am perfectly willing, as soon as we reach your station, to convince you that you are mistaken."

The traders, who had hitherto backed up their colleague, applauded loudly, evidently expecting Miller to take up the challenge. He, however, preferred to treat it as a joke. I knew that the Captain was labouring under suppressed wrath because he was so cool and polite. I knew, by the ring in his voice, that he meant mischief, and at any moment looked to see the hot blood surging to his brow, and his fierce nature assert itself.

About an hour later the mate of one of the whaleships came on board to have dinner with me, and told me that Hayston had given Miller a terrible thrashing in his own house, in the presence of his backers and the American captains. It seems that Hayston led the conversation up to Captain Peese's recent visit, and then suddenly asked Miller if he had not told the natives that Captain Peese must take the cattle, and that he (Hayston) dared not show up in Ponapé again, or else he would long since have appeared on the scene.

Possibly Miller thought his only chance was to brazen it out, for, though he had a following of the lowest roughs and beach-combers, who were at that moment loafing about his house and grounds, and Hayston was unarmed, he could see by the coolness of the American captains that he could not count on their support. At last he said, with a forced laugh,—

"Come, let us have nae mair fule's talk. We can be good friends pairsonally, if we would fain cut each other's throats in business. I'll make no secret of it, I did say so, and thocht I was playing a good joke on ye."

"So that's your idea of a joke, is it," said Hayston, grimly, "but now I must have mine, and as it takes a surgical operation to get one into a Scotchman's brain, I'll begin at once."

He gave Miller a fearful knocking about there and then. The captains picked him up senseless, with a head considerably altered for the worse. After which Hayston washed his hands, and went on board one of the whaleships to dinner.

He then sent for the chiefs of the various districts, telling them to meet him at Miller and Lapelle's station on a certain day and hour. When they were all assembled, he induced Miller to say that he sincerely regretted having told them such lies, as he knew the cattle did belong to Captain Hayston. Finally they shook hands, and swore to be friends in future; Hayston, in a tone of solicitude, informing him that he would send him some arnica, as his head appeared very bad still. The parting scene must have been truly ludicrous. Shaking him warmly by the hand, Hayston said, "Good-bye, old fellow; we've settled our little difficulty, and will be better friends in future. If I've lost cattle, I've gained a friend." Begging the favour of a kiss from the women present he then departed, full of honours and dignities; and in another hour we were sailing round the coast to Metalauia harbour.

Here we bought a quantity of hawkbill turtle shell. While it was being got on board, the Captain and I spent two days on shore exploring the mysterious ruins and ancient fortifications which render the island so deeply interesting; wonderful in size, Cyclopean in structure. It is a long-buried secret by whom and for what purpose they were erected. None remain to tell. "Their memorial is perished with them."

In one of the smaller islands on which those ruins are situated, Hayston told me that a Captain Williams, in 1836, had found over £10,000 worth of treasure. He himself believed that there were rich deposits in other localities not far distant.

To this end we explored a series of deathly cold dungeons, but found nothing except a heavy disc of a metal resembling copper several feet under ground.

This was lying with its face to the stone wall of the subterranean chamber—had lain there probably for centuries.

Its weight was nearly that of fifty pounds. It had three holes in the centre. We could form no idea as to its probable use or meaning. I was unwilling to part with it, however, and taking it on board, put it in my cabin.

While we were at Metalauia, Joe Keogh came on board, bringing with him three native girls from the Andema group, a cluster of large coral islands near the mainland, belonging to the three chiefs of the Kité district. He had gone forward, when the Captain saw him and called him aft.

He at once accused Joe of being treacherous, telling him that the whaling captains had given him a written statement to the effect that he had taken a letter from Miller to the Mortlock group, where an American cruiser was surveying, asking the captain if he would take Hayston to California, as he (Miller) and Keogh would engage to entice him ashore and capture him if the cruiser was close at hand.

Not being able to deny the charge, Keogh was badly beaten, and sent away without the girls, who were taken aft. Like the Ponapé natives, they were very light-coloured, wearing a quantity of feather head-dress and other native finery. They agreed to remain on board during the cruise through the Caroline group, and were then to be landed at their own islands.

They were then sent to keep the steward company in the cabin, and put to making hats and mats, in which they excelled. At Kité harbour we took on board the bull and three cows which Peese had not succeeded in catching. On returning to Jakoits harbour in a fortnight's time, I was told that I might take up my quarters on shore, while the cabin was redecorated. I therefore got a canoe and two natives, with which I amused myself with visiting the native village and pigeon-shooting.

One day I fell across a deserted whaling brig. Her crew had run away, and the ship having contracted debts, was seized by Miller and Lapelle. The captain alone was left. He was now ship-keeper, and his troubles had so preyed on his mind that he had become insane.

I watched him. It was a strange and weird spectacle; there lay the vessel, silent, solitary—"a painted ship upon a painted ocean."

Her brooding inmate would sometimes pace the deck for hours with his arms folded; then would throw himself into a cane lounge, and fixing his eyes upon the sky, mutter and talk to himself.

At other times he would imagine that the ship was surrounded by whales, and rush wildly about the decks, calling on the officers to lower the boats. Not succeeding, he would in despair peer down the dark, deserted foc'sle, begging the crew to be men, and get out the boats.

We cruised now for some weeks to and fro among the lovely islands of the Caroline group, trading in turtle shell, of which we bought great quantities. What a halcyon time it was! There was a luxurious sense of dreamy repose, which seemed unreal from its very completeness.

The gliding barque, the summer sea, the lulling breeze, the careless, joyous children of nature among whom we lived, — all were fairy-like in combination.

When one thought of the hard and anxious toilers of civilisation, from whom we had come out, I could fancy that we had reached the lotus-land of the ancients, and could well imagine a fixed unwillingness to return to a less idyllic life. Hayston was apparently in no hurry.

At any particular island that pleased him he would lie at anchor for days. Then we would explore the wondrous woods, and have glorious shooting trips on shore.

We met some truly strange and original characters in these waters — white men as well as natives. The former, often men of birth and culture, were completely lost to the world, to their former friends and kinsfolk.

Return? not they! Why should they go back? Here they had all things which are wont to satisfy man here below. A paradise of Eden-like beauty, amid which they wandered day by day all unheeding of the morrow; food, houses, honours, wives, friends, kinsfolk, all provided for them in unstinted abundance, and certain continuity, by the guileless denizens of these fairy isles amid this charmed main. Why — why, indeed, should they leave the land of magical delights for the cold climate and still more glacial moral atmosphere of their native land, miscalled home?

Then, perhaps, in the former life beyond these crystal seas — where the boom of the surf upon the reef is not heard, and the whispering palm leaves never talk at midnight — some imprudence, some mistake at cards may have occurred, who knows! These things happen so easily.

The temptation of a moment—a lack of resolve at the fateful crisis—and they are so deadly difficult of reparation. Difficult—nay impossible.

Where, then, can mortal find such an asylum for weary body and restless soul as this land of Lethe? Where life is one long dream of bliss, and where death comes as a lingering friend rather than a swift executioner.

It added materially to my enjoyment of the whole adventure, that wherever we went we were always honoured personages, favoured guests. Everywhere the people had the greatest admiration for Hayston's personal qualities—his strength, his fearlessness, his prompt determination in the face of danger and difficulty. That his word was invariably law to them was fully evident.

One day, however, as a kind of drawback to all these satisfactions, I suddenly noticed that the girl Terau, who had been given to boy George, appeared to be very ill, if not dying. That young savage had obtained permission from the Captain to keep her on board, although she was most anxious to get ashore at Ponapé.

She would often get into one of the boats and sit there all day—sad and silent—knitting a head-dress from the fibres of the banana plant. Not being able to talk to her myself, I got a native of Ocean Island, whose dialect resembled her own, to ask her if she was ill.

The girl made no answer. She covered her face with her hands. I then saw that every movement of her body gave her pain. At length she murmured something to the Ocean islander, slowly took from her shoulders the mat which covered them, and looking at me, said, "Teorti fra mati Terau" (George has nearly killed Terau). I was horrified to see that the poor girl's back was cut and swelled dreadfully. Her side, also, she said, was very bad, and it hurt her to breathe.

We lifted her carefully out of the boat, and carried her between us to the skylight, where we placed her in a comfortable position.

I found the Captain lying down, and asked him to come on deck, where, lifting the mat from the girl's bruised shoulders, I showed him the terrible state she was in.

"Do you mean to allow such brutality to be practised on a poor girl? Why, I believe she is dying!"

He said nothing, except "Come below." Sitting down at the table, he said, "I will not punish that boy. But I would be glad if you will see him, and induce him to treat the girl kindly."

I called George, who was in the deck-house playing cards, and asked him what he would take for Terau.

The lad thought for a moment, and asked me if the Captain had told me to come to him about her?

I said, "Yes! he had." But that I wanted him either to give or sell me the girl, adding that he had better be quick about it, as Terau seemed sinking fast.

"Oh! if that is so, you give me what you like for her. Don't want no dead girls 'bout me."

I called up three of the crew as witnesses, whereupon George sold me the victim of his brutality for ten dollars and a German concertina.

"Now, George," I said, "I am going to put Terau ashore, and if you touch her again, or even speak to her, I'll knock your infernal soul out of your black body."

He grinned, and replied that he was only too glad to get rid of her; and returning into the deck-house, began at once to play on the concertina.

A few days after this transaction we touched at Ngatik or Los Valientes Island, and I was pleased to find here a trader whose wife was a native of Pleasant Island.

I asked them if they would like to have Terau to live with them, and the wife at once expressed her willingness as well as joy at seeing one of her own countrywomen.

Returning on board, I inquired of Terau if she would not like to go ashore and live with these people, who would treat her kindly. During my ownership she had regained her strength in great degree, Nellie having agreed to attend on her, and the Chinese steward saw that she had nourishing food.

She preferred to go ashore, being still afraid of George's ill-treatment; I did not tell her of the trader's wife being a countrywoman, trusting it would prove a joyful surprise. I was not mistaken. The two women rushed into each other's arms, and wept in their impulsive fashion. I felt certain that here poor Terau would receive kind treatment.

Before returning on board the trader told me that Terau had related her story to them, and that the Ngatik women, who were in the house, told her to make the white man who had been so kind to her "the present of poverty." This ceremonial consisted in her cutting off her hair close to the head, and, together with an empty cocoa-nut shell and a small fish, offering it to me. The trader said this was to express her gratitude—the empty shell and small fish signifying poverty, while the gift of hair denoted that she was a bondswoman to me for life.

I felt sorry that the poor child should have cut off her beautiful hair, which was tied round the centre with a band of pandanus leaf, and put in my hand; but I felt a glow of pleasure at being able to place her with people who would be good to her; and thanking her for the gift, to which she added a thick plate of turtle shell, I said farewell, and returned to the brig.

The Captain called me below, and shook my hand.

"I'm glad," he said, "that poor girl has left the ship; but I must repay you the money you gave George for her."

This I refused to take. I felt well repaid by the unmistakable gratitude Terau had evinced towards me from the moment the Ocean islander and I had carried her pain-racked form below.

CHAPTER VIII

POISONED ARROWS

The weather had changed, and been cloudy and dull for several days. We were all rather in the doldrums too. We had been bearing eastward on the line. Suddenly Hayston said, "Suppose we put in at Santa Cruz. We want the water casks filled. I'm not very fond of the island, for all its name. Sacred names and bloodshed often go together with Spaniards. However, I know the harbour well, and the yams are first-rate." So at daylight we bore up, at eight bells we entered the heads with both anchors bent to the chains, and at noon were beating up the harbour. By two o'clock we cast anchor in thirty fathoms. Out came the canoes, and we soon began trading with the natives.

We kept pretty strict watch, however. The men, to my fancy, had a sullen expression, and the women, though not bad-looking, seemed as if it cost them an effort to look pleasant.

Our girls wouldn't have anything to say to them. Hope Island Nellie, in particular, said she'd like to shoot half of them; that they'd killed a cousin of hers, who was only scratched with a poisoned arrow, and that it was one of the Captain's mad tricks to go there at all.

However, Hayston, as usual, was spurred on by opposition to have his own way, and to do even more than he originally intended. He told me afterwards that he only wanted to get some yams in the harbour, and that the water would have held out longer—until we got to a known safe island.

So on Sunday we sent two boats on shore, and got the casks filled with water immediately. Our provisions were taken out and examined. Trading with the natives went on merrily.

On Monday the weather was fine. We got a couple of rafts out with water, and laid in yams enough to last for the rest of our cruise. Hayston laughed, and said there was nothing like showing natives that you were not afraid of them. "Eh, Nellie? What you think now?"

"Think Captain big fool," said Nellie, who was in a bad temper that morning. "Ha! you see boat crew; by God! man wounded—I see them carry him along."

Sure enough, we could see the two boats' crews coming down to the beach. They were carrying one man, while two supported another, who seemed hardly able to walk. "Get out the boats!" roared Hayston. "I'll teach the scoundrels to touch a crew of mine."

All was now bustle and commotion. Every man on the ship that could be spared, and Hope Island Nellie to boot, who had begged to be allowed to go with the attacking party, and whose ruffled temper was restored to equanimity by the chance of having a shot at her foes, and avenging her cousin's death. We left a boat's crew watch, and made for the shore, Nellie sitting in the bow of the Captain's boat with a Winchester rifle across her knees, and her eyes sparkling with a light I had never seen in a woman's face before. It was the light of battle come down through the veins of chiefs and warriors of her people for centuries uncounted.

We left a couple of men in each boat, telling them to keep on and off until we returned; the wounded men were carefully laid on mats in one of their own boats; and forth we went—a light-hearted storming party, and attacked the town of the treacherous devils. Hayston was in a frightful rage, cursing himself one moment for relaxing his usual caution, and devoting the Santa Cruz natives in the next to all the fiends of hell for their infernal causeless treachery. He raged up again and again to the cluster of huts, thickly built together with palisades here and there, which made excellent cover for shooting from, backed up by the green wall of the primeval forest. I could not but admire him as he stood there—grand, colossal, fearless, as though he bore a charmed life, while the deadly quivering arrows flew thick, and more than one man was hit severely. Only that our fire was quick and deadly with the terrible Winchester repeaters, and that the savages—bold at first—were mowed down so quickly that they had to retreat to a distance which rendered their arrows powerless, we should have had a muster roll with gaps in it of some seriousness. Hayston was a splendid rifle shot, and for quick loading and firing had few equals. Every native that showed himself within range went down ere he could fit an arrow to his bowstring. And there was Hope Island Nellie by his side, firing nearly as fast, and laughing like a child at play whenever one of her shots told.

Then the arrows grew fewer. Just before they ceased I had fired at a tall native who had been conspicuous through the fight. He fell on his face. Nellie gave a shout, and loaded her own rifle on the chance of another shot, straining her bright and eager eyes to see if another lurking form was near enough for danger. Well for me was it that she did so! Staggering to his feet, a wounded native fitted an arrow to his bow, and sent it straight for my breast before I could raise my gun to my shoulder. Nellie made a snap shot at him, and, either from exhaustion or the effect of her bullet, he fell prone and motionless.

I felt a scratch on my arm—bare to the shoulder—as if a forest twig had raised the skin. "Look!" said Nellie, and her face changed. As she spoke, she passed her finger over the place, and showed it bloodstained. "The crawling brute's arrow hit you there. Let me suck the poison. If you don't"—as I made a gesture of dissent—"you die, twel' days."

"Don't be a fool!" said Hayston. "You're a dead man if you don't. As it is, you must run your chance. Some of these fellows will lose the number of their mess, I'm sorry to say."

So the girl, who had been but the moment before thirsting for blood, and firing into the mob of half-frightened, yet ferocious savages, pressed her soft lips on my arm, like a young mother soothing a babe, and with all womanly tenderness bound up the injured place, which had now begun to smart, and, to my excited imagination, commenced to throb from wrist to shoulder.

"Strange child, isn't she?" laughed Hayston. "If she'd only been born white, and been to boarding-school down east, what a sensation she'd have created in a ball-room!"

"Better as she is, perhaps," said I. "She has lived her life with few limitations, and enjoyed most of it."

The excited crew rushed in and finished every wounded man in a position to show fight. Nellie did not join in this, but stood leaning on her rifle—*la belle sauvage*, if ever there was one—brave, beautiful, with a new expression like that of a roused lioness on her parted lips and blazing eyes.

As for Hayston, he was a fatalist by constitution and theory. "A man must die when his time comes," he had often said to me. "Until the hour of fate he cannot die. Why, then, should he waste his emotions by giving way to the meanest of all attributes—personal fear?"

He had none, at any rate. He would have walked up to the block without haste or reluctance, had beheading been the fashionable mode of execution in his day, chaffed his executioner, and with a bow and a smile for the handsomest woman among the spectators, quitted with easy grace a world which had afforded him a fair share of its rarest possessions.

By his order the town was fired and quickly reduced to ashes, thus destroying a number of articles—mats, utensils, wearing apparel, weapons, etc.—which, requiring, as they do, considerable skill and expenditure of time, are regarded as valuable effects by all savages.

The attack had been early in the day. We cut down as many cocoa-nut trees as we could, and finally departed for the ship, towing out with us a small fleet of canoes, to be broken up when we got to the brig. The sick men were sent below, and such remedies as we knew of were applied. They were—all but one—silent and downhearted. They knew by experience the sure and deadly effect of the poison manufactured among the Line Islands. Subtle and penetrating! But little hope of recovery remains.

About four o'clock next morning we began to heave at the windlass, and got under weigh at eight. The wind was light and variable, and our progress slow. As we got abreast of the hostile village we gave them a broadside. But the sullen devils of Santa Cruz were not cowed yet. A second fleet of canoes swarmed around the ship. They made signals of submission and a desire to trade, but when they got near enough sent a cloud of arrows at the ship, many of which stuck quivering in the masts, though luckily no one was hit. Their yells and screams of wrath were like the tumult of a hive of demons. We were luckily well prepared, and we let them have the carronades over and over again, sinking a dozen of their canoes, and doing good execution among the crews when their black heads popped up like corks as they swam for the nearest canoes. While this took place we unbent the starboard chain, stowed it and the anchor, and clearing the heads, bade adieu to the inhospitable isle.

On the next day all hands were engaged in cleaning our armoury, which it certainly appeared necessary to keep in good order. Hope Island Nellie polished her Winchester rifle till it shone again, besides showing an acquaintance with the machinery of the lock and repeating gear was nothing new to her.

"You ought to make a notch in the stock for every man you kill, Nellie," said Hayston, as we were lying on the deck in the afternoon, while the *Leonora* was gliding on her course like the fair ocean bird that she was.

Nellie frowned. "No like that talk," she answered. "Might have to put 'nother notch yet for Nellie—who knows?"

"Who knows, indeed, Nellie?" answered the Captain. "None of us can foresee our fate," he added with a tinge of sadness, which so often mingled with his apparently most careless moments. "We don't even know who's going to die from those arrow scratches yet."

Here the girl looked over at me. "How you feel, Hil'ree?" she said, as her voice softened and lost its jesting tone.

"Feel good," I said, "think getting better."

"You no know," she answered gravely. "You wait." And she began to count. She went over the fingers of her small, delicately-formed left hand,—wonderful in shape are the hands and feet of some of these Island girls,—and after counting from little finger to thumb *twice*, touched the two first fingers, and looked up. "How many?" she asked.

"Twelve," I said; I had followed the counts with care, you may be sure.

"Twel' day, you see," she said; "perhaps you all right—perhaps"—and here she gave a faint but accurate limitation of the dreadful shudder which precedes the unspeakable agonies of tetanus.

"Nellie's right," said Hayston; "keep up your spirits, for you won't know till then whether you're to go to sleep in your hammock in blue water or not."

This was a cheerful prospect, but I had come through many perils, and missed the grim veteran by so many close shaves, that I had grown to be something of a fatalist like Hayston.

"Well! if I go under it won't be your fault, Nellie! So, Captain, remember I make over to her all the stuff in my trade chest. Send any letters and papers to the address you know in Sydney, and a bank draft for what you will find in the dollar bag. Nellie will have some good dresses anyhow."

"Dress be hanged!" quoth Nellie, who was emphatic in her language sometimes. "You go home to mother yet;" and she arose and left hurriedly. Poor Nellie!

In that day when we and others who have sinned, after fullest knowledge of good and evil "know the right and yet the wrong pursue," shall be arraigned for deeds done in the flesh, will the same doom be meted out to this frank, untaught child of Nature and her sisters? I trow not. I must say that for a day or two before the fated twelfth which Nellie so stoutly insisted upon, I felt slightly anxious. What an end to all one's hopes, longings, and glorious imaginings, to be racked with tortures indescribable before dying like a poisoned hound, all because of the instinctive, senseless act of a stupid savage!

To die young, too, with the world but opening before me! Life with its thousand possibilities just unrolled! One's friends, too,—the weeping mother and sisters, whose grief would never wholly abate this side of time; the old man's fixed expression of sorrow. These thoughts passed through my brain, with others arising from and mingled with them, as I left my hammock early on the twelfth day. I dressed quickly, and going on deck, that daily miracle occurred— "the glorious sun uprist."

The dawnlight now began to infuse the pearly rim, which, imperceptibly separating from the azure grey horizon, deepened as it touched the edge of the vast ocean plain. Faintly glimmering, how magically it transformed from a dim, neutral-tinted waste to an opaline clarity of hue—a fuller crimson. Then the wondrous golden globe heaved itself over the edge of our water-world all silently, and the day, the 19th of October, began its course.

Should I live to see its close?

How strange if all this time the subtle poison should have lurked in one's veins until the exact moment, when, like a modern engine of devilry—an infernal machine with a clock and apparatus—set to strike and detonate at a given and calculated hour, the death-stroke should sound!

We had breakfasted, and were lying on the deck chatting and reading, as the *Leonora* glided over the heaving bosom of the main—the sun shining—the seabirds sailing athwart our course with outstretched, moveless wings—the sparkling waters reflecting a thousand prismatic colours, as the brig swiftly sped along her course—all nature gaily bright, joyous, and unheeding. Suddenly one of the wounded men, Henry Stephens by name, raised himself from his mat with a cry so wild and unearthly that half the crew and people started to their feet.

"My God!" he exclaimed, as he sank down again upon his mat, "I'm a dead man—those infernal arrows."

"Poor Harry!" said Nellie, who by this time was bending over him, "don't give in—by and by better—you get down to bunk. Carry him down, you boys!"

Two of the crew lifted the poor fellow, who even as they raised him had another fearful paroxysm, drawing his frame together almost double, so that the men could scarcely retain their hold.

"Carry him gently, boys!" said Hayston; "go to the steward for some brandy and laudanum, that will ease the pain."

"And is there no cure—no means of stopping this awful agony?"

"Not when tetanus once sets in," said Hayston; "it's not the first case I've seen."

The other man was quite a young fellow, and famed among us for his entire want of fear upon each and every occasion. He laughed and joked the whole time of the fight with the Santa Cruz islanders, said that every bullet had its billet, and that his time had not come.

"He believed," he said, "also that half the talk about death by poisoned arrows was fancy. Men got nervous, and frightened themselves to death." He was not one of that sort anyhow. He had laughed and joked with both of us, and even now, when poor Harry Stephens was carried below, and we could hear his cries as the increasing torture of the paroxysms overcame his courage and self-control, he joked still.

The day was a sad one. Still the brig glided on through the azure waveless deep—still the tropic birds hung motionless above us—still the breeze whispered through our swelling sails, until the soft, brief twilight of the tropic eve stole upon us, and the stars trembled one by one in the dusky azure, so soon to be "thick inlaid with patines of bright gold."

"Reckon I've euchred the bloodthirsty niggers this time," said Dick, with a careless laugh, lighting his pipe as he spoke. "This is 'Twelfth night.' That's the end of the time the cussed poison takes to ripen, isn't it, Nellie?" he laughed. "It regular puts me in mind of old Christmas days in England, and us schoolboys counting the days after the New Year! What a jolly time it was! Won't I be glad to see the snow, and the bare hedges, and the holly berries, and the village church again? Dashed if I don't stay there next time I get a chance, and cut this darned slaving, privateering life. I'll—oh! my God—ah—a—h!"

His voice, in spite of all his efforts, rose from a startled cry to a long piercing shriek, such as it curdled our blood to hear.

Hayston came up from the cabin, followed by Nellie and the other girls. All crowded round him in silence. They knew well at the first cry he was a doomed man.

"Carry him down, lads!" he said, as he laid his hand on his forehead and passed it quietly over his clustering hair—"poor Dick! poor fellow!" At this moment another frightful spasm shook the seaman's frame, and scarcely could the men who had lifted him from the deck on which he had been lying control his tortured limbs. As they reached the lower deck another terrible cry reached our ears, while the continuous groaning of the poor fellow first attacked made a ghastly and awful accompaniment to the screams of the latest victim.

As for me, I walked forward and sat as near as I could get to the *Leonora's* bows, where I lit my pipe and awaited the moment in which only too probably my own summons would come in a like pang of excruciating agony. The gleaming phosphorescent wavelets of that calm sea fell in broken fire from the vessel's side, while the hissing, splashing sound deadened the recurring shrieks of the doomed sufferers, and soothed my excited nerves.

Now that death was so near, in such a truly awful shape, I began seriously to reflect upon the imprudence, nay, more, the inexcusable folly of continuing a life exposed to such terrible hazards.

If my life was spared I would resolve, like poor Dick, to stay at home in future. The resolution might avail me as little as it had done in his case.

As I sat hour after hour gazing into the endless shadow and gleam of the great deep, a strange feeling of peace and resignation seemed to pass suddenly over my troubled spirit. I felt almost tempted to plunge beneath the calm bosom of the main, and so end for aye the doubt, the fear, the rapture, and despair of this mysterious human life. All suddenly the moon rose, sending before her a brilliant pathway, adown which, in my excited imagination, angels might glide, bearing messages of pardon or reprieve. A distinct sensation of hope arose in my mind. A dark form glided to my side, and seated itself on the rail.

"You hear eight bell?" she said. "Listen now, you all right—no more poison—he go away." She held my hand—the pulse was steady and regular. In spite of my efforts at calmness and self-control, I was sensible of a strange exaltation of spirit. The heaven above, the sea below, seemed animate with messengers of pardon and peace. Even poor Nellie, the untaught child of a lonely isle, "placed far amid the melancholy main," seemed transformed into a celestial visitant, and her large, dark eyes glowed in the light of the mystic moon rays.

"You well, man Hil'ree!" she said in the foc'sle vernacular. "No more go maté. Nellie so much glad," and here her soft low tones were so instinct with deepest human feeling that I took her in my arms and folded her in a warm embrace.

"How's poor Dick?" I asked, as we walked aft to where Hayston and the rest of the cabin party were seated.

"Poor Dick dead!" she said; "just die before me come up."

The people we had brought for the big firm, mostly Line Island natives, were quiet and easily controlled. Hayston now and then executed orders of this sort, though he would have scorned the idea of turning the *Leonora* into a labour vessel. He was naturally too humane to permit any ill-treatment of the recruits, and having his crew under full control, always made matters as pleasant for these dark-skinned "passengers" as possible.

But there were voyages of very different kind,—voyages when the recruiting agents were thoroughly unscrupulous, caring only for the numbers—by fair means or foul—to be made up. Sometimes dark deeds were done. Blood was shed like water; partly from the fierce, intractable nature of the islanders—sometimes in pure self-defence. But "strange things happen at sea." One labour cruise of which Hayston told me—he heard it from an English trader who saw the affair—was much of that complexion. We had plenty of time for telling stories in the long calm days which sometimes ran into weeks. And this was one of them.

One day a white painted schooner, with gaff-headed mainsail, and flying the German flag, anchored off Kabakada, a populous village on the north coast of New Britain. She was on a labour cruise for the German plantations in Samoa.

Not being able to secure her full complement of "boys" in the New Hebrides and Solomon groups, she had come northward to fill up with recruits from the naked savages of the northern coast of New Britain.

In those days the German flag had not been formally hoisted over New Britain and New Ireland, and apart from the German trading station at Matupi in Blanche Bay, which faces the scarred and blackened sides of a smouldering volcano springing abruptly from the deep waters of the bay, the trading stations were few and far between.

At Kabakada, where the vessel had anchored, there were two traders. One was a noisy, vociferous German, who had once kept a liquor saloon in Honolulu, but, moved by tales of easily accumulated wealth in New Britain, he had sold his business, and settled at his present location among a horde of the most treacherous natives in the South Seas. His rude good nature had been his safety; for although, through ignorance of the native character, he was continually placing his life in danger, he was quick to make amends, and being of a generous disposition and a man of means, enjoyed a prestige among the natives possessed by no other white man.

His colleague—or rather his opponent, for they traded for opposition firms—was a small, dark Frenchman, an ex-bugler of the Chasseurs d'Afrique, who had spent some years of enforced retirement at New Caledonia. His advent to New Britain had been made in the most private manner, and his reminiscences of the voyage from the convict colony with his four companions were not of a cheerful nature.

Ten miles away, at the head of a narrow bay that split the forest-clad mountains like a Norwegian fiord, lived another trader, an English seaman. He had been on the island about two years, and was well-nigh sickened of it. Frequently recurring attacks of the deadly malarial fever had weakened and depressed him, and he longed to return to the open, breezy islands of eastern Polynesia, where he had no need to start from his sleep at night, and, rifle in hand, peer out into the darkness at the slightest noise.

The labour schooner anchored about a mile from the German trader's house, and about two hours afterwards the boat of the Englishman was seen pulling round Cape Luen, and making for Charlie's station. This was because all three traders, being on friendly terms, it would have been considered "playing it low down" for any one of them to have boarded the schooner alone.

The day was swelteringly hot, and the sea between the gloomy outlines of Mau Island and the long, curving, palm-shaded beaches of New Britain shore was throwing off great clouds of hot, steamy mist. As the Englishman's boat was about half-way between the steep-wooded point of Cape Luen and Kabakada, she altered her course and ran into the beach, where, surrounded by a cluster of native huts, was the station of Pierre. This was to save the little Frenchman the trouble of launching his clumsy boat. Pierre, dressed in white pyjamas, with a heavy Lefaucheux revolver in his belt and a Snider rifle in his hand, came out of his house. Addressing his two wives in emphatic language, and warning them to fire off guns if anything happened during his absence on board the schooner, he swaggered down the beach and into the boat.

"How are you, Pierre?" said the Englishman, languidly. "I knew you and Hans Muller would expect me to board the schooner with you, or else I wouldn't have come. Curse the place, the people, the climate, and everything!"

The little Frenchman grinned, "Yes, it ees ver' hot; but nevare mind. Ven ve get to de 'ouse of de German we shall drink some gin and feel bettare. Last veek he buy four case of gin from a valeship, and now le bon Dieu send this schooner, from vich we shall get more."

"What a drunken little beast you are!" said the Englishman, sourly. "But after all, I suppose you enjoy life more than I do. I'd drink gin like water if I thought it would kill me quick enough."

"My friend, it is but the fevare that now talks in you. See me! I am happy. I drink, I smoke, I laugh. I have two wife to make my café and look aftare my house. Some day I walk in the bush, then, whouff, a spear go through me, and my two wife will weep ven they see me cut up for *rosbif*, and perhaps eat a piece themselves."

The Englishman laughed. The picture Pierre drew was likely to be a true one in one respect. Not a mile from the spot where the boat was at that moment were the graves of a trading captain, his mate, and two seamen, who had been slaughtered by the natives under circumstances of the most abominable treachery. And right before them, on the white beach of Mau Island, a whaler's boat's crew had been speared while filling their water casks, the natives who surrounded them appearing to be animated by the greatest friendliness.

Such incidents were common enough in those days among the islands to the westward of New Guinea, and the people of New

Britain were no worse than those of other islands. They were simply treacherous, cowardly savages, and though occasionally indulging in cannibalistic feasts upon the bodies of people of their own race, they never killed white men for that purpose. Many a white man has been speared or shot there, but their bodies were spared that atrocity—so in that respect Pierre did his young wives an injustice. They would, if occasion needed it, readily poison him, or steal his cartridges and leave him to be slaughtered without the chance of making resistance, but they wouldn't eat him.

"It's the *Samoa*," said the German, as he shook hands with us. "And the skipper is a d—d Dutchman, but a good sort" (having once sailed in a Yankee timber ship, trading between Sydney and the Pacific slope, Hans was now an American), "and as soon as it gets a bit cool, we'll go off. I know the recruiter, he's a chap with one arm."

"What?" said the Englishman, "you don't mean Captain Kyte, do you?"

"That's the man. He's a terror. Guldensterns pay him $200 a month regular to recruit for them, and he gets a bonus of $10 each for every nigger as well. We must try and get him a few here to fill up."

"*You* can," said the Englishman, "but I won't. I'm not going to tout for an infernal Dutch black-birder."

As soon as a breeze set in the three traders sailed off. The schooner was a fine lump of a vessel of about 190 tons register, and her decks were crowded with male and female recruits from the Solomon group. There were about fifty in all—thirty-five or forty men and about a dozen women.

The captain of the schooner and his "recruiter," Captain Kyte, received the traders with great cordiality. In a few minutes the table was covered with bottles of beer, kummel, and other liquor, and Hans was asserting with great vehemence his ability to procure another thirty "boys."

Kyte, a thin man, with deep-set grey eyes, and a skin tanned by twenty years' wanderings in the South Seas, listened quietly to the trader's vapourings, and then said, "All right, Hans! I think, though, we can leave it till to-morrow, and if you can manage to get me twenty 'boys,' I'll give you five dollars a head for them, cash."

The traders remained on board for an hour or two, and in the meanwhile the captain of the schooner sent a boat ashore to fill water casks from the creek near the trader's house. Six natives got in—four of whom were seamen from the schooner and two Solomon Island recruits; these two recruits led to all the subsequent trouble.

Kyte was a wonderfully entertaining man, and although his one arm was against him (he had lost the other one by the bursting of a shell), he contrived to shoot very straight, and could hold his own anywhere.

He was full of cynical humour, and the Englishman, though suffering from latent fever, could not but be amused at the disrespectful manner in which the American spoke of his employers. The German firm which in a small way was the H.E.I.C. of the Pacific; indeed, their actions in many respects, when conducting trading arrangements with the island chiefs, were very similar to those of the Great East India Company—they always had an armed force to back them up.

"I should think you have natives enough on board as it is, Captain Kyte," the Englishman was saying, "without taking any more."

"Well, so I have in one way. But these d—d greedy Dutchmen (looking the captain and mate of the schooner full in the face) like to see me come into Apia harbour with about 180 or 200 on board. The schooner is only fit to carry about ninety. Of course the more I have the more dollars I get. But it's mighty risky work, I can tell you. I've got nearly sixty Solomon boys on board now, and I could have filled down there, but came up along here instead. You see, when we've got two or three different mobs on board from islands widely apart they can't concoct any general scheme of treachery, and I can always play one crowd off against the other. Now, these Solomon Island niggers know me well, and they wouldn't try any cutting off business away up here—it's too far from home. But I wouldn't trust them when we are beating back through the Solomons on our way to

A Modern Buccaneer

Samoa—that's the time I've got a pull on them, by having New Britain niggers on board."

"You don't let your crew carry arms on board, I see," said the Englishman.

"No, I don't. There's no necessity for it, I reckon. If we were anywhere about the Solomon Islands, and had a lot of recruits on board, I take d—d good care that every man is armed then. But here, in New Britain, we could safely give every rifle in the ship to the 'recruits' themselves, and seeing armed men about them always irritates them. As a matter of fact, these 'boys' now on board would fight like h—l for us if the New Britain niggers tried to take the ship. Some men, however," and his eyes rested on Pierre, Hans, and the captain, "like to carry a small-arms factory slung around 'em. Have another drink, gentlemen? Hallo, what the h—l is that?" and he was off up on deck, the other four white men after him.

The watering party had come back, but the two Solomon islanders (the recruits) lay in the bottom of the boat, both dead, and with broken spears sticking all over their bodies. The rest of the crew were wounded—one badly.

In two minutes Captain Kyte had the story. They were just filling the last cask when they were rushed, and the two Solomon islanders speared and clubbed to death. The rage of the attackers seemed specially directed against the two recruits, and the crew—who were natives of Likaiana (Stewart's Island)—said that after the first volley of spears no attempt was made to prevent their escape.

The face of Captain Kyte had undergone a curious change. It had turned to a dull leaden white, and his dark grey eyes had a spark of fire in them as he turned to the captain of the schooner.

"What business had you, you blundering, dunder-headed, Dutch swab, to let two of my recruits go ashore in that boat? Haven't you got enough sense to know that it was certain death for them. Two of my best men, too. Bougainville boys. By ——! you'd better jump overboard. You're no more fit for a labour schooner than I am to teach dancing in a ladies' school."

The captain made no answer. He was clearly in fault. As it was, no one of the boat's crew were killed, but that was merely because their European clothing showed them to be seamen. The matter was more serious for Kyte than any one else on board. The countrymen of the murdered boys looked upon him as the man chiefly responsible. He knew only one way of placating them—by paying some of the dead boys' relations a heavy indemnity, and immediately began a consultation with five Solomon islanders who came from the same island.

In the mean time the three traders returned to the shore, and Hans, with his usual thick-headedness, immediately "put his foot in it," by demanding a heavy compensation from the chief of the village for the killing of the two men.

The chief argued, very reasonably from his point of view, that the matter didn't concern him.

"I don't care what you think," wrathfully answered the little trader, "I want fifty coils, of fifty fathoms each, of *dewarra*. If I don't get it"— here he touched his revolver.

Now, dewarra is the native money of New Britain; it is formed of very small white shells of the cowrie species, perforated with two small holes at each end, and threaded upon thin strips of cane or the stalk of the cocoa-nut leaf. A coil of dewarras would be worth in European money, or its trade equivalent, about fifty dollars.

The chief wasn't long in giving his answer. His lips, stained a hideous red by the betel nut juice, opened in a derisive smile and revealed his blackened teeth.

"He will fight," he answered.

"You've done it now, Hans," said the Englishman, "you might as well pack up and clear out in the schooner. You have no more sense than a hog. By the time I get back to my station I'll find it burnt and all my trade gone. However, I don't care much; but I hope to see you get wiped out first. You deserve it."

All that night the native village was in a state of turmoil, and when daylight came it was deserted by the inhabitants, who had retreated to their bush-houses; the French trader, who had walked along the beach to his station, returned at daylight and reported that not a native was in his town, even his two wives had gone. Nothing, however, of his trade had been touched.

"That's a good sign for you," said the Englishman. "If I were you, Pierre, I would go quietly back, and start mending your fence or painting your boat as if nothing had happened. They won't meddle with you."

But this was strongly objected to by his fellow-trader, and just then a strange sound reached them, — the wild cries and howls of chorus, in a tongue unknown to the three men. It came from the sea, and going to the door they saw the schooner's two whaleboats, packed as full of natives as they could carry, close in to the shore. Instead of oars they were propelled by canoe paddles, and at each stroke the native rowers fairly made the boats leap and surge like steam launches in a sea-way. But the most noticeable thing to the eyes of the traders was the glitter of rifle barrels that appeared between the double row of paddlers. In another five minutes the leading boat was close enough for the traders to see that the paddlers who lined the gunwales from stem to stern had their faces daubed with red and blue, and their fighting ornaments on. In the body of the boats, crouching on their hams, with elbows on knees, and upright rifles, were the others, packed as tightly as sardines.

"Mein Gott!" gasped Muller, "they have killed all hands on the schooner and are coming for us. Look at the rifles." He dashed into his trade-room and brought out about half a dozen Sniders, and an Epsom salts box full of cartridges. "Come on, boys, load up as quick as you can."

"You thundering ass," said the Englishman, "look again; can't you see Kyte's in one boat steering?"

In another minute, with a roar from the excited savages, the first boat surged up on the beach, and a huge, light-skinned savage seized Kyte in his arms as if he were a child and placed him on the land. Then every man leaped out and stood, rifle in hand, waiting for the other boat. Again the same fierce cry as the second boat touched the shore; then silence, as they watched with dilated eyes and gleaming teeth the movements of the white man.

For one moment he stood facing them with outstretched hand uplifted in warning to check their eager rush. Then he turned to the traders—

"The devils have broken loose. Have you fellows any of your own natives that you don't want to get hurt? If so, get them inside the house, and look mighty smart about it."

"There's not a native on the beach," said the German, "every mother's son of them has cleared into the bush, except this man's boat's crew," pointing to the English trader; "they're in the house all right. But look out, Captain Kyte, those fellows in the bush mean fight. There's two thousand people in this village, and many of them have rifles—Sniders—and plenty cartridges. I know, because it was I who sold them."

Kyte smiled grimly. There was a steely glitter of suppressed excitement in his keen grey eyes. Then he again held up his hand to his followers—

"Blood for blood, my children. But heed well my words—kill not the women and children; now, go!"

Like bloodhounds slipped from the leash, the brown bodies and gleaming rifle barrels went by the white men in one wild rush, and passed away out of sight into the comparatively open forest that touched the edge of the trader's clearing.

"There they go," said Kyte quietly, as he sat down on the edge of the trader's verandah and lit a cigar, "and they'll give those smart niggers of yours a dressing down that will keep them quiet for the next five years (he was right, they did). Well, I had to let them have their own way. They told me that if I didn't let them have revenge for the two men that I would be unlucky before I got to Samoa,—a polite way of saying that they would seize the schooner and cut our throats on the way up. So to save unpleasantness, I gave each man a Snider and twenty-five cartridges, and told them to shoot as many *pigs and fowls* as they liked. You should have heard the beggars laugh. By the way, I hope they do shoot some, we want pork badly."

"Hallo, they've got to Tubarigan's, the chief's bush-house, and fired it!" said Muller.

A column of black smoke arose from the side of the mountain, and in another second or two loud yells and cries of defiance mingled with the thundering reports of the Sniders and the crackling of the flames.

The little Frenchman and Muller played nervously with their rifles for a moment or two; then meeting the answering look in each other's eyes, they dashed into the trees and up the jungle-clad mountain side in the direction of the smoke and fighting.

The native houses in New Britain are built of cane, neatly lashed together with coir cinnet, and the roofs thatched with broad-leaved grass or sugar-cane leaves. They burn well, and as the cane swells to the heat each joint bursts with a crack like a pistol shot.

"Look now," said Kyte to his companion, pointing along the tops of the hills. Clouds of black smoke and sheets of flame were everywhere visible, and amidst the continuous roar of the flames, the crackling of the burning cane-work of the native houses, and the incessant reports of the Sniders, came savage shouts and yells from the raiders, and answering cries of defiance from the New Britain men, who retreated slowly to the grassy hills of the interior, whence they watched the total destruction of some four or five of their villages. These bush-houses are constructed with great care and skill by the natives, and are generally only a short distance from the main village on the beach; every bush-house stands surrounded by a growth of carefully-tended crotons of extraordinary beauty and great variety of colour, and in the immediate vicinity is the owner's plantation of yams, taro, sugar-cane, bananas, and betel nuts.

In the course of an hour or two the Solomon islanders ceased firing, and then the two white men, looking out on the beach, saw a number of the beaten villagers fleeing down to the shore, about half a mile away, and endeavouring to launch canoes.

"By — —!" exclaimed Kyte, "my fellows have outflanked them, and are driving them down to the beach. I might get some after all for the schooner. Will you lend me your boat's crew to head them off? They are going to try and get to Mau Island."

"No," said the Englishman, "I won't. If Pierre and the German are such idiots as to go shooting niggers in another man's quarrel, that's no reason why I should take a hand in it."

Kyte nodded good-humouredly, and seemed to abandon the idea; but he went into the house after a while, and came out again with a long Snider in his hand.

In a few minutes the Solomon islanders began to return in parties of two or three, then came the two white men, excited and panting with the lust of killing.

Kyte held a whispered consultation with one of his "boys,"—a huge fellow, whose body was reeking with perspiration and blood from the scratches received in the thorny depths of the jungle,—and then pointed to the beach where four or five white-painted canoes had been launched, and were making for an opening in the reef. To reach this opening they would have to pass in front of the trader's house, for which they now headed.

Kyte waited a moment or two till the leading canoe was within four or five hundred yards, then he raised his rifle, and placing it across the stump of his left arm, fired. The ball plumped directly amidships, and two of the paddlers fell. The rest threw away their paddles and spears, and swam to the other canoes.

"Now we've got them," said Kyte, and taking about twenty of his boys, he manned his two boats and pulled out, intercepting the canoes before they could get through the reef into the open.

Then commenced an exciting chase. The refugees swam and dived about in the shallow water like frightened fish, but their pursuers were better men at that game than they, and of superior physique. In twenty minutes they were all captured, except one, who sprang over the edge of the reef into deep water and was shot swimming.

There were about five-and-twenty prisoners, and when they were brought back in the boats and taken on board the schooner it was found that the chief was among them. It may have occurred to him in the plantation life of the after time that he had better have stayed quiet. The Englishman, disgusted with the whole affair, went off with the other white men, leaving his boat's crew for safety in the trader's house, for had the Solomon islanders seen them they would have made quick work of them, or else Kyte, to save their lives, would have offered to take them as recruits.

The two other traders decided to leave in the schooner. They had made the locality too warm for themselves, and urged the Englishman to follow their example.

"No," he said, "I've been a good while here now, and I've never shot a nigger yet for the fun of the thing. I'll take my chance with them for a bit longer. The chances are you fellows will get your throats cut before I do."

However, the schooner arrived safely at Samoa with her live cargo, but Kyte reported to his owners that it would not be advisable to recruit in New Britain for a year or two.

CHAPTER IX

HALCYON DAYS

We were now bound for Arrecifos Island, Hayston's central station, but had first to call at Pingelap and Strong's Island, where we were to land our cattle and ship a few tuns of oil.

Nine days after leaving Ponapé, as the sun broke through the tropic haze, the lookout reported smoke in sight. The Captain and I at once went aloft, and with our glasses made out a steamer a long distance off.

Hayston said he thought it was the *Resacca*, an American cruiser. Possibly she might overhaul us and take us into Ponapé. Unless the breeze freshened we could not get away from her.

We were heading N.N.E. close hauled, and the steamer appeared to be making for Ponapé. She was sure to see us within an hour unless she changed her course.

The *Leonora* was kept away a couple of points, but the wind was light, and we were only travelling about four knots.

At breakfast time we could see the man-of-war's spars from the deck, and the breeze was dying away. The Captain and I went on the foreyard and watched her.

She had not as yet changed her course, but apparently did not seem anxious to overtake us.

At length Hayston said with a laugh, as he took a long look at her, "All right, keep full, and by (to the man at the wheel) − −, brace up the yards again, she doesn't want to stop us. It's that old Spanish gunboat from Manila, a 'side wheeler.' I was told she was coming down to Ponapé from Guam to look after some escaped Tagalau prisoners. She'd never catch us if she wanted to with anything like a breeze."

That night the Captain seemed greatly relieved. He told me that it would prove a bad business for him if an American cruiser took him; and although he did not anticipate meeting with one in these parts, he gave me full instructions how to act in the event of his seizure. He placed in my charge two bags of gold coin of two thousand dollars each, and a draft for a thousand dollars on Goddefroys' in Samoa.

After which he declared that the ship was getting dull lately, and ordered the steward's boy to beat the gong and call out the girls for a dance.

For the next hour or two wild merriment prevailed. Antonio, the Portuguese, with his violin, and the Captain with his flute, furnished the music, while half a dozen of the girls were soon dancing with some of the picturesque ruffians of the foc'sle.

For days and days we had scarcely shifted tack or sheet, so gentle and steady was the wind that filled our sails; but the easterly equatorial counter current that prevails in these calm seas was sweeping us steadily on towards Strong's Island at the rate of two or three knots an hour.

On some days we would lower a floating target and practise with the long gun carried amidships, on others the Captain and I would pass away an hour or two shooting at bottles with our rifles or revolvers.

Hayston was a splendid shot, and loud were the exclamations from the crew when he made an especially clever shot; at other times he would sit on the skylight, and with the girls around him, sewing or card-playing, tell me anecdotes of his career when in the service of the Chinese Government.

There were on board two children, a boy and girl—Toby and Kitty—natives of Arurai or Hope Island. They were the Captain's particular pets, in right of which he allowed them full liberty to tease any one on the ship.

He was strongly attached to these children, and often told me that he intended to provide for them.

Their father, who was one of his boat's crew, had fallen at his side when the natives of the island had boarded the vessel. On his next cruise he called at Arurai and took them on board, the head chief freely giving his permission to adopt them. I mention this boy and girl more particularly, because the American missionaries had often stated in the Honolulu journals "that Hayston had kidnapped them after having killed their father."

His story was that on his first visit to the Pelew Islands with Captain Peese, the vessel they owned, a small brigantine, was attacked by the natives in the most daring manner, although the boarding nettings were up and every preparation made to repel them.

He had with him ten seamen—mostly Japanese. Captain Peese was acting as first mate. An intelligent writer has described these Pelew islanders, the countrymen of the young Prince Lee Boo, whose death in England caused genuine sorrow, as "delicate in their sentiments, friendly in their disposition, and, in short, a people that do honour to the human race."

The Captain's description of the undaunted manner in which fifty of these noble islanders climbed up the side of the brigantine, and slashed away at the nettings with their heavy swords, was truly graphic. Stripped to the waist they fought gallantly and unflinchingly, though twelve of their number had been killed by the fire of musketry from the brigantine. One of them had seized Captain Peese by his beard, and, dragging him to the side, stabbed him in the neck, and threw him into the prahu alongside, where his head would have soon left his body, when Hayston and a Japanese sailor dashed over after him, and killed the two natives that were holding him down, while another was about to decapitate him. At this stage three of the brigantine's crew lay dead and nearly all were wounded, Hayston having a fearful slash on the thigh.

There were seventeen islanders killed and many badly wounded before they gave up the attempt to cut off the vessel.

The father of Kitty and Toby was the steward. He had been fighting all through like a demon, having for his weapon a carpenter's squaring axe. He had cut one islander down with a fearful blow on the shoulder, which severed the arm, the limb falling on the deck, when he was attacked by three others. One of these was shot by a Japanese sailor, and another knocked down by the Captain, when the poor steward was thrust through from behind and died in a few minutes.

The Captain spoke highly of the courage and intelligence of the Pelew islanders, and said that the cause of the attack upon the vessel was that, being under the Portuguese flag—the brigantine was owned by merchants in Macao—the natives had sought to avenge the bombardment of one of their principal towns by two Portuguese gunboats a year previously.

Hayston afterwards established friendly relations with these very people who had attacked him, and six months afterwards slept ashore at their village alone and unarmed.

From that day his perfect safety was assured. He succeeded in gaining the friendship of the principal chiefs by selling them a hundred breech-loading rifles and ten thousand cartridges, giving them two years' time to pay for them. He also gave nearly a thousand dollars' worth of powder and cartridges to the relatives of the men killed in attempting to cut off the brigantine.

Such was one of the many romantic incidents in Hayston's career in the wild islands still further to the north-west. That he was a man of lion-like courage and marvellous resolution under the most desperate circumstances was known to all who ever sailed with him. Had not his recklessness and uncontrollable passions hurried him on to the commission of deeds that darkened for ever his good name, his splendid qualities would have earned him fame and fortune in any of those national enterprises which have in all ages transformed the adventurer into the hero.

One day, while we sat talking together, gazing upon the unruffled deep,—he had been explaining the theory of the ocean currents, as well as the electrical phenomena of the Caroline group, where thunder may be heard perhaps six times a year, and lightning seen not once,—I unthinkingly asked him why he did not commit his observations to paper, as I felt sure that the large amount of facts relating to the meteorology of the Pacific, of which he was possessed, would be most valuable, and as such secure fitting recognition by the scientific world.

He smiled bitterly, then answered, "Hilary, my boy, it is too late. I am an outlaw in fact, if not in name. The world's doors are closed, and society has turned its back on me. Out of ten professed friends nine are false, and would betray me to-morrow. When I think of what I once was, what I might have been, and to what I have now fallen, I am weary of existence. So I take the world as it comes, with neither hope nor fear for the morrow, knowing that if I do not make blue shark's meat, I am doomed to leave my bones on some coral islet."

And thus the days wore on. We still drifted under cloudless skies, over the unfretted surface of the blue Pacific, the brig's sails ever and anon swelling out in answer to the faint, mysterious breeze-whispers, to fall languidly back against her spars and cordage.

Passing the Nuknor or Monteverde Islands, discovered by Don Juan Monteverde in 1806, in the Spanish frigate *La Pala*, we sailed onward with the gentle N.E. trades to Overluk, and then to Losap. Like the people of Nuknor, the Losap islanders were a splendid race and most hospitable. Then we made the Mortlock group, once so dreaded by whaleships. These fierce and warlike islanders made most determined efforts to cut off the whaleships *Dolly Primrose* and *Heavenly City*. To us, however, they were most amiable in demeanour, and loud cries of welcome greeted the Captain from the crowd of canoes which swarmed around the brig.

Then commenced one of the reckless orgies with which the brig's crew were familiar. Glad to escape the scene, I left the brig and wandered about in the silent depths of the island forest.

The Captain here, as elsewhere, was evidently regarded as a visitor of immense importance, for as I passed through the thickly populated villages the people were cooking vast quantities of pigs, poultry, and pigeons.

The women and girls were decorating their persons with wreaths of flowers, and the warriors making preparations for a big dance to take place at night. I had brought my gun with me, and shot some of the magnificent pigeons which throng the island woods, which I presented to the native girls, a merry group of whom followed me with offerings of cocoa-nuts, and a native dish made of baked bananas, flavoured with the juice of the sugar-cane.

I could not have eaten a fiftieth part of what was offered, but as declining would have been regarded as a rudeness, I begged them to take it to the chief's house for me.

On my return a singular and characteristic scene presented itself. I could not help smiling as I thought what a shock it would have given many of my steady-going friends and relatives in Sydney, most of whom, if untravelled, resemble nothing so much as the inhabitants of English country towns, and are equally apt to be displeased at any departure from the British standard of manners and morals.

The Captain was seated on a mat in the great council-house of the tribe, talking business with a white-headed warrior, whom he introduced as the king of the Mortlock group. The women had decorated the Captain's neck and broad breast with wreaths—two girls were seated a little farther off, binding into his hat the tail-feathers of the tropic bird. He seemed in a merry mood, and whispering something to the old man, pointed to me.

In a moment a dozen young girls bounded up, and with laughing eyes and lips, commenced to circle around me in a measure, the native name of which means "a dance for a husband."

They formed a pretty enough picture, with their waving arms and flowing flower-crowned hair. I plead guilty to applauding vociferously, and rewarding them with a quantity of the small red beads which the Mortlock girls sew into their head-dresses.

Thus, with but slight variations, our life flowed, if monotonously, pleasantly, even luxuriously on—as we sailed to and fro amid these charmed isles, from Namoluk to Truk, thence to the wondrously beautiful Royalist Islands, inhabited by a wild vigorous race. They also made much of us and gave dances and games in honour of our visit.

And still we sailed and sailed. Days passed, and weeks. Still glided we over the summer sea—still gazed we at a cloudless sky—still felt we the languorous, sighing breath of the soft South Pacific winds.

Day by day the same flock of predatory frigate birds skimmed and swept o'er the glittering ocean plain, while high overhead the wandering tropic birds hung motionless, with their scarlet tail-feathers floating like lance pennons in relief against the bright blue heavens.

Now, the Captain had all a true seaman's dislike to seeing a sea-bird shot. One day, off Ocean Island, Jansen, the mate, came out of the cabin with a long, smooth bore, which he proceeded to load with buck shot, glancing the while at two graceful tropic birds, which, with snow-white wings outspread, were poised in air directly over the deck, apparently looking down with wondering eye at the scene below.

"What are you going to shoot, Jansen?" inquired the Captain, in a mild voice.

The mate pointed to the birds, and remarked that his girl wanted the feathers for a head-dress. He was bringing the gun to his shoulder, when a quick "Put down that musket," nearly caused him to drop it.

"Jansen!" said the Captain, "please to remember this,—never let me see you or any other man shoot a sea-bird from the deck of this ship. Your girl can live without the feathers, I presume, and what is more to the point, I *forbid* you to do it."

The mate growled something in an undertone, and was turning away to his cabin, when Hayston sprang upon him like a panther, and seizing him by the throat, held him before him.

"By ——! Jansen," he said, "don't tempt me too far. I told you as civilly as possible not to shoot the birds—yet you turn away and mutter mutinously before my men. Listen to me! though you are no seaman, and a thorough 'soldier,' I treat you well for peace' sake. But once give me a sidelook, and as sure as God made me, I'll trice you up to the mainmast, and let a nigger flog you."

He released his hold of the mate's throat after this warning. The cowed bully staggered off towards his cabin. After which the Captain's mood changed with customary suddenness; he came aft, and began a game with Kitty and her brother—apparently having forgotten the very existence of Jansen.

The calm, bright weather still prevailed—the light air hardly filling our sails—the current doing all the work. When one afternoon, taking a look from aloft, I descried the loom of Kusaie or Strong's Island, on the farthest horizon.

"Land ho!" The watch below, just turning out, take up the cry as it goes from mouth to mouth on deck. Some of them gaze longingly, making calculations as to the amount of liberty they are likely to get, as well as the work that lies before them.

Early next morning we had drifted twenty miles nearer, whereupon the Captain decided to run round to the weather side of the island first, and interview the king, before going to Utwé or South harbour, where we proposed to do the most of our trading.

Suddenly, after breakfast, a serious disturbance arose between the Chinese carpenter and Bill Hicks, the fierce Fijian half-caste, who was second mate. The carpenter's provisional spouse was a handsome young woman from the Gilbert group, who rejoiced in the name of Ni-a-bon (Shades of Night). Of her, the carpenter, a tall, powerfully-built Chinaman, who had sailed for years with Hayston in the China Seas, was intensely jealous. So cunning, however, was she in evading suspicion, that though every one on board was aware of the state of affairs, her lawful protector suspected nothing.

However, on this particular morning, Nellie, the Hope Island girl, being reproved by the second mate for throwing pine apple and banana peel into the ship's dingey, flew into a violent rage, and told the carpenter that the second mate was stealing Ni-a-bon—and, moreover, had persuaded her to put something into his, the carpenter's, food, to make him "go maté," *i.e.* sicken and die.

Seizing an axe, the Chinaman sallied on deck, and commenced to exact satisfaction by aiming a blow at Ni-a-bon, who was playing cards with the other girls. The girl Mila averted the blow, and the whole pack fled shrieking to the Captain, who at once called upon Bill for explanation.

He did not deny the impeachment, and offered to fight the carpenter for Ni-a-bon. The Captain decided this to be eminently right and proper; but thought the carpenter was hardly a match for the mate with fists. Bill promptly suggested knives. This seemed to choke off the carpenter, as, amid howls from the women, he stepped back into his cabin, only to reappear in the doorway with a rifle, and to send a bullet at the mate's head, which missed him.

"At him, Billy," cried the Captain, "give him a good licking—but *don't hurt his arms*; there's a lot of work to be done to the bulwarks when we get the anchor down again."

The second mate at once seized the carpenter, and dragging him out of his cabin, in a few minutes had so knocked his features about that he was hardly recognisable.

Ni-a-bon was then called up before the Captain and questioned as to her preference, when, with many smiles and twisting about of her hands, she confessed to an ardent attachment to the herculean Bill.

The Captain told Bill that he would have to pay the carpenter for damages, which he assessed at ten dollars, the amount being given, not for personal injury, but for the loss sustained by his annexation of the fascinating Ni-a-bon.

At sunset we once more were off Chabral harbour, where we ran in and anchored—*within fifty yards* of the king's house.

CHAPTER X

MURDER AND SHIPWRECK

We found the island in a state of excitement. Two whaleships had arrived, bringing half a dozen white men, and who had a retinue of nearly a hundred natives from Ocean and Pleasant Islands. The white men had to leave Pleasant Island on account of a general engagement which had taken place; had fled to the ships for safety, taking with them their native wives, families, and adherents.

The other men were from Ocean Island, a famine having set in from drought in that lovely isle. They had also taken passage with their native following, to seek a more temporarily favoured spot. The fertility of Kusaie (Strong's Island) had decided them to remain.

Strange characters, in truth, were these same traders, now all quartered at Chabral harbour! They were not without means, and so far had conducted themselves decently. But their retinue of savage warriors had struck terror into the hearts of the milder natives of Kusaie.

Let me draw from the life one of the patriarchs of the movement, on the occasion of his embarkation.

Ocean Island, lat. 0° 50' south, long. 168° east.

A fantastic, lonely, forbidding-looking spot. Circular in form, with rounded summit, and a cruel upheaved coral coast, split up into ravines running deep into the land. Here and there, on ledges overlooking the sea, are perched tiny villages, inhabited by as fierce and intractable a race of Malayo-Polynesians as ever lacerated each other's bodies with sharks'-tooth daggers, after the mad drunkenness produced by sour toddy.

Mister Robert Ridley, aged seventy, sitting on a case in his house, on the south-west point of Paanopa, as its people call Ocean Island, with a bottle of "square face" before him, from which he refreshes himself, without the intervention of a glass, is one of the few successful deserters from the convict army of New South Wales. At the present moment he is an ill-used man. For seven years he has been the boss white man of Paanopa, ever since he left the neighbouring Naura or Pleasant Island, after seeing his comrades fall in the ranks one by one, slain by bullet or the scarce less deadly drink demon. Now, solitary and saturnine, he has to bow to Fate and quit his equatorial cave of Adullam, because a mysterious Providence has afflicted his island with a drought.

From out the open door he sees the *Josephine*, of New Bedford, Captain Jos Long, awaiting the four whaleboats now on the little beach below his house, which are engaged in conveying on board his household goods and chattels, his wives and his children, with *their* children, and a dusky retinue of blood-relations and retainers; for the drought had made food scarce. Blood had been shed over the ownership of certain cocoa-nut trees; and old Bob Ridley has decided to bid farewell to his island, and to make for Ponapé in the Carolines. So the old man sits alone and awaits a call from the last boat. Perhaps he feels unusual emotion stirring him, as the faint murmur of voices ascends from the beach. He would be alone for awhile to conjure up strange memories of the past, or because the gin bottle is but half emptied.

"The *Josephine*, of New Bedford!" he mutters, as a grim smile passes over his bronzed, sin-wrinkled countenance; "why, *t'other one* was from New Bedford too. This one's larger—a six-boat ship—and carries a big afterguard. Still the job could be done agin. But—what's the good now! If Joe, the Portuguese, was here with me I'd say it *could* be done." Another gulp at the "square face." "Damn it! I'm an old fool. There's too many of these here cussed blubber-hunting Yankees about now. Say we took the ship, we'd never get away with her. Please God, I'll go to Ponapé and live like a d—d gentleman. There's some of the old crowd there now, and I a'n't so old yet."

And here, maybe, the old renegade falls a thinking afresh of "the other one" from New Bedford, that made this very island on the evening of the 3rd of December 1852.

Out nearly two years, and working up from the Line Islands towards Honolulu, the skipper had tried to make Pleasant Island, to get a boat-load of pigs for his crew, but light winds and strong currents had drifted him away, till, at dawn, he saw the rounded summits of Ocean Island pencilled faintly against the horizon, and stood away for it. "We can get a few boat-loads of pigs and 'punkins' there, anyhow," he said to the mate.

The mate had been there before, and didn't like going again. That was in 1850. Sixteen white men lived there then, ten of whom were runaway convicts from Sydney or Norfolk Island. He told his captain that they were part of a gang of twenty-seven who had at various times been landed from whalers at Pleasant Island in 1845. They had separated—some going away in the *Sallie* whaler, and others finding their way to Ocean Island. Now, the *Sallie was never heard of again*, the mate remarked. The captain of the *Inga* looked grave, but he had set his heart upon the pigs and "punkins." So at dusk the brig hove to, close to the south-west point, and as no boats came off the skipper went ashore.

There were nearly a thousand people on Ocean Island then, and he felt a trifle queer as the boat was rushed by the wild, long-haired crowd, and carried bodily on shore.

Through the gathering darkness he saw the forms of white men trying to push their way through the yellow crowd of excited natives. Presently a voice called out, "Don't be scared, mister! Let the niggers have their way and carry up the boat."

He let them have their way, and after being glared at by the red light of cocoa-nut torches borne by the women, he was conducted to one of three houses occupied by the six gentlemen who had arranged to leave the continent of Australia without beat of drum.

Bob Ridley's house was the scene of rude and reckless revelry that night. A jar of the *Inga's* rum had been sent for, and seated around on the boxes that lined the side of the room the six convicts drank the raw spirit like milk, and plied the captain for news of the outer world two years old. Surrounding the house was a throng of eager, curious natives, no longer noisy, but strangely silent as their rolling, gleaming eyes gloated over the stone jar on the table. Presently a native, called "Jack" by his white fellow residents, comes to the door and makes a quick sign to Bob and a man named Brady, who rose and followed him into a shed used as a cook-house. Jack's story is soon told. He had been to the brig. She had thirty-two hands, but three men were sick. A strict watch was kept by the mate, not more than ten natives were allowed on board at once. In the port bow boats and the starboard quarter boats hanging on the davits there were two sailors armed with muskets.

Another of the white men now slunk into the cook-house where the three talked earnestly. Then Brady went back and told the captain that the brig was getting into the set of the outer currents, and would be out of sight of land by daylight unless he made sail and worked in close again. Upon which the captain shook hands all around, and was escorted to his boat, promising to be back at daylight and get his load of "punkins."

Brady and two others went with the captain for company, and on the way out one of his new friends—a tall, ghastly creature, eternally twisting his long fingers and squirting tobacco juice from his evil-seeming mouth—told the captain that he "orter let his men take a run ashore to get some cocoa-nuts and have a skylark." When they got aboard the captain told the mate to take the sentries out of the boats, to make sail, and run in close out of the currents, as it was all right. The captain and the guests went below to open another jar, while the mate and cooper roused up the hands who were lying about yarning and smoking, and told them to make sail. In the house ashore Bob Ridley with his two companions and Jack were planning *how the job was to be done.*

Two boats came ashore at daylight, and in addition to the crews there were ten or a dozen liberty men who had leave till noon to have a run about the island. The captain still bent on his "punkins," took a boat-steerer and two other hands to put the coveted vegetables into bags and carry them down to the boats. The pumpkins, Ridley said, grew on his own land quite close; the men could pick them off the vines, and the natives carry them down. So they set off up the hill until the pumpkin patch was reached. Here old Bob suddenly felt ill, and thought he would go back to take a swig at the rum jar and return, but if the captain wanted a good view from the top of the island Jack would show him round. So leaving the men to bag the pumpkins, the skipper and Jack climbed the path winding through the cocoa-nuts to the top of the hill. The sun was hot already, and the captain thirsty. Jack, out of his hospitable heart, suggested a drink. There were plenty of cocoa-nuts around growing on short, stumpy trees, a couple of which he twisted off, and without husking one with his teeth, as is often done, cut a hole in the green husk and presented it to the skipper to drink from. The nut was a heavy one; taking it in both hands the doomed sailor raised it to his lips and threw back his head. That was his last sight of the summer sky that has smiled down on so many a deed of blood and rapine. For Jack at that moment lifted his right arm and drove the knife to the hilt through his heart.

As Jack hurried back to be in good time for the "grand coup"—the cutting off of the brig—he saw that the boat-steerer and his two hands *had finished gathering the pumpkins*. Two bags were filled and tied, while beside them were the three bodies of the gatherers, each decently covered with a spreading cocoa-nut branch. The ten "liberty men" had been induced by a bevy of laughing island nymphs to accompany them along the ledge of the steep coast cliff to a place where, as Jack had told them, they would find plenty of nuts—a species of almond peculiar to Ocean and Pleasant Islands. Half-an-hour's walk took them out of sight and hearing of the *Inga*, and then the "liberty men" saw that the girls had somehow dropped behind, and were running with trembling feet into the maze of the undergrowth. The startled men found themselves in an amphitheatre of jagged rough coral boulders, covered over with a dense verdure of creepers, when suddenly Brady and fifty other devils swept down upon them without a cry. It was soon over. Then the blood-stained mob hurried back to the little beach.

The mate of the *Inga* was a raw-boned Yankee from Martha's Vineyard. Fearless, and yet watchful, he had struck the tall renegade as "a chap as was agoin' to give them trouble if they didn't stiffen him fust in the cabin." It was then noon, and as eight bells struck the crew began to get dinner. The mate, before he went below, took a look at the shore and fancied he saw the boat shoving off with the captain.

"Yes," chimed in Wilkins, one of the guests, "that's him; he's got a boat-load, and all the canoes comin' off 's a lot of our own niggers bringin' off cocoa-nuts."

"Then let's get dinner right away," answered the mate, who knew the captain would make sail as soon as ever he found his "punkins" safe aboard.

Had he known that the captain was lying staring up at the sun on the hilltop among the dwarf palms, he might even then have made a fight of it, short of half the crew as he was.

It was not to be.

They went below—he and his guests, the third mate and the carpenter; the cooper was left in charge of the ship.

The boats and canoes came alongside at once, pulling hard. Suddenly the cooper heard a cry from a man in the waist of the ship that chilled his blood, while over the bulwarks swarmed the copper-skinned crowd, knife and club in hand. As he rushed to the companion, the tall renegade looked up and saw the time had come.

Then began the butchery. The ship's officers rushed on deck, leaving behind only the negro steward and a boy with the three convicts. Two shots were fired in the cabin, after which the three demons hurried up to join in the melée. In ten minutes there was not a man of the crew alive, except the cooper in the maintop, with a bloody whale-spade in his fast relaxing grasp. Brady and Bob were agreed "to give the old cove a chance to get eat up by the sharks," and ironically advised him to take a header and swim ashore. But the cooper, with his feet dangling over the futtocks and his head sunk on his chest, made no sign. He fell back as a streak of red ran slowly between the planking of the maintop and trickled down the mast to the deck.

It was a disappointment when the white murderers gathered in the cabin to find so small a quantity of rum in the *Inga's* lazarette. But they were consoled by two bags of Mexican dollars—"Money for the punkins," grinned Brady, which would buy them twice as much as they wanted when next ship came along. And then as the principal business was over, the harmony began, and amidst rum and unholy jesting, a division of the effects in the cabins was made, while unto Jack and his myrmidons were abandoned all and sundry that could be found for'ard.

When the heavy-laden boats had been sent again and again to the shore, a fire was lighted in the cabin by the tall renegade, and the white men pushed off. But it suddenly occurred to Messrs. Ridley and Brady that "such a hell of a blaze might be seen by some other blubber-hunters a long way on a dark night," so the boat was put back and the brig hurriedly scuttled. And you can drop a lead line close to the edge of the reef anywhere about Ocean Island, and get no soundings at forty fathoms.

Soon after we anchored an urgent message was sent to the Captain by King Tokusar and Queen Sê, imploring him to come ashore and advise them. The Captain had of late seemed averse to going anywhere without my company, and asked me to come with him. So, getting into the whaleboat, we were pulled on shore, landing at a massively-built stone wharf which formed part of the royal premises.

I may here mention that the headquarters of the American Mission had been at Kusaie for many years. The people were all Christians, and to a certain degree educated. Their island took rank, therefore, as the most successful result of missionary enterprise in the North Pacific.

A native college had been built, to which were brought from outlying islands those natives who were destined for the ministry. However, about a year previously the Board of Mission had changed their headquarters to Ebon, an island of the Marshall group, leaving but one native missionary on Kusaie in charge of the flock. His name was Likiak Sâ. There are coloured Chadbands as well as white ones;

and for pure, unmitigated hypocrisy the European professor would have had but little show in a prize contest.

The head of the American Mission, Mr. Morland, had built himself an exceedingly comfortable stone house in Lêlé. As he was away at present in the brig *Morning Star*, his residence was occupied by his fellow-worker, Likiak Sâ, h is wife, and an exceedingly pretty girl named Kitty of Ebon, who acted as housekeeper to Mr. and Mrs. Morland when at home.

The missionaries had tried hard to prevent the people of Kusaie from selling produce to the whaleships, alleging that their visits were fruitful of harm. The old king, however, whose power had declined sensibly since the arrival of the missionaries, withstood their orders; and finally insisted upon the privilege of permitting them to visit the island, and to purchase the pigs, poultry, and fruit from the islanders which would otherwise lie useless on their hands.

This King Tokusar was a curious compound of shrewdness, generosity, cant, and immorality, each alternately gaining the upper hand.

On entering the "palace," which was exceedingly well furnished, we found him seated in an armchair in his reception room. He was dressed in a black frock-coat and white duck trousers: the latter somewhat of a military cut, falling over patent leather shoes. On one side of the chair, lying on its broad arm, was a ponderous copy of the Scriptures in the Kusaie dialect. On the other arm was placed one of the long clay pipes known as churchwardens.

Behind him, with her much bejewelled fingers clasping the back of her consort's chair, was Queen Sê, a pretty little woman, with a pleasant, animated expression of countenance. Further inside the apartment were the queen's female attendants, sitting in the ungraceful manner peculiar to the Pingelap and Kusaie women.

The king looked worn and ill, as he croaked out, "How you do, Captain? I glad to see you again. I thank God he bin good to you — give you good voyage. How much oil you bin buy at Ponapé?"

Shaking hands warmly with the king, Hayston introduced me in form, and then to Her Majesty, who smiled graciously, tossing back her wavy black hair, so as to show her massive gold ear-rings. Chairs were brought, when a truly amusing conversation took place.

King.—"Well, Captain! you d—d clever man. I want you give me advice. You see—all these men come to Kusaie. Well—me afraid, take my island altogether. What you think?"

Captain.—"Oh no, king! I'll see they do you no harm. I think some of them go away in the *Leonora.*"

King.—(Much doubting) "Oh! thank you. I no want too many white men here—no Christians like Kusaie men. No believe God, no Jesus Christ." (Then with sudden change of tone) "I say, Capt'n Hayston, one of you men no pay my people when you here last—no pay anybody."

Captain.—"Very bad man, king, how much he cheat people out of?"

King.—(With inquiring look at queen) "Oh! about three dollars."

Captain.—"I'll attend to it, king—I'll see it paid."

King.—"Thank you, Capt'n. What you say this young gentleman's name?"

Captain.—"His name is Hilary Telfer."

King.—"You like Strong's Island, young gentleman? Pretty girl, eh? Same as Captain?" Here he gave a wheezing laugh, and clapped his hands on the Captain's knees.

I told him I thought the Strong Island girls very pretty. The queen communicated this to the attendants. After which I was the recipient of various nods and winks and wreathed smiles.

An enormous roasted hog was then carried in by two of the king's cooks, after which a number of servitors appeared carrying taro, yams, and other vegetables—again yet more, bearing quantities of fish. We seated ourselves at a small table—the Captain opposite the king, while the lively little queen and I were *vis-a-vis*.

"Make up to her," whispered the Captain, "flatter her to the masthead if you wish to be in clover for the rest of your stay. Never mind old Tokusar."

Acting on this hint I got on famously with her South Sea majesty, discovering in due course that she was a really clever little woman, as well as an outrageous flirt.

Presently the boats came ashore again, and the steward was ushered in, carrying a large box.

"King!" said the Captain, "I know you are sick, and need something to make you strong. Pray accept a small present from my table." The present consisted of two bottles of brandy, with the same quantity of gin, and a dozen of beer.

"Oh! thank you, Capt'n—you really very kind. By George! I like you too much."

The queen cast a reproachful glance at Hayston. I could see she did not appreciate the gift. Her lord soon had a bottle of brandy opened, out of which he poured himself an able seaman's dose. The Captain took a little, and I—for once in my life—shared a bottle of Tennant's bitter beer with a real queen.

The king rose up, with a broad smile illumining his wrinkled face, and said, with his glass to his lips, "Capt'n, and Capt'n's friend, I glad to see you." Presently, however, with a scared face, he said something to his consort at which she seemed disconcerted, and then told us they had forgotten to say grace.

This, in a solemn manner, Hayston requested me to do, and, as I was bending my head and muttering the half-forgotten formula, the king leaned over and whispered to him, "I say, Capt'n, how many labour boys you want take away in brig?"

This made me collapse entirely, and I indulged in a hearty laugh. The Captain and the queen followed suit, and, at some distance, the king's cackling merriment.

It certainly was a jolly dinner. The king was growing madder ever minute, alternately quoting Scripture and swearing atrociously. After which he told me that he liked to be good friends with Mr. Morland, and that he had given up all his bad habits. But, changing his mood again, he confided to me that he wished he was young again, and concluded by expressing a decided opinion as to the beauty of Kitty of Ebon, Mrs. Morland's housekeeper.

The queen now rose from the table and asked me to smoke a cigar. She produced a work-box in which were cigarettes and some Manila cheroots. Most graciously she lighted one for me.

The king was now more than half-seas over. He laughed hilariously at the Captain's stories, and, with some double-barrelled oaths, announced his determination to return to the worship of the heathen gods and to increase the number of his wives.

Queen Sê smiled, and blowing out the smoke from between her pouting red lips, said, "Hear the old fool talk!"

That night there was high revel on board the *Leonora* after we had taken our farewell of the king and queen.

Hayston decided to take advantage of the land breeze, and so get away to South harbour at once, as we had business to do there. Chabral harbour was a difficult place to get out of, though easy enough to get into.

The trade winds blow steadily here for seven months out of the twelve. Now, though the largest ship afloat may run in easily through the deep and narrow passage, there is not room enough to beat out against the north-east wind. Neither can she tow out, as there is always a heavy swell rolling in through the passage, wind or no wind. Kedging out is also simply impossible, owing to the extraordinary depth of water.

In 1836, the *Falcon* of London, a whaleship, lay in Chabral harbour for 120 days. She had ventured in for wood and water. On making a fifth attempt to tow out with her five boats, she touched and went to pieces on the reef.

Hayston, however, had run in, knowing that at this season of the year—from January to March—the winds were variable, a land breeze generally springing up at dusk.

I stated that there was revelry on board the brig that night. The fact was that the Captain, in the presence of the king, queen, and myself, had made agreement with the refugee traders to take them to whatever island they preferred. The king was strongly averse to their retinue of excitable natives being domiciled among the peaceful Kusaie people. Inspired with courage by the presence of Hayston, he had told the traders that he wished them to vacate Lêlé. If they did arrange to leave in the *Leonora*, he told them that they could establish themselves at Utwé (South harbour), and there remain until they got away in a passing whaler or China-bound ship.

After conferring with Hayston, most of the traders decided to take his offer of conveying them and their following to Ujilong (Providence Island), which was his own property, and there enter into engagement with him to make oil for five years. Two others agreed to proceed to the sparsely populated but beautiful Eniwetok (or Brown's group), where were vast quantities of cocoa-nuts, and only thirty natives. These two men had a following of thirty Ocean islanders, and were in high delight at the prospect of having an island to themselves and securing a fortune after a few years of oil-making.

As the merry clink of the windlass pauls echoed amidst the verdurous glens and crags of the mountains that surround Lêlé, the traders, with their wives, families, and followers, pulled off in their whaleboats and came aboard.

What a picture did the brig make as she spread her snowy canvas to the land-breeze! Laden with the perfume of a thousand flowers, cooled by its passage through the primeval forest, it swept us along towards the passage, upon the right steering through which so much depended. The traders had half a dozen whaleboats; these, with two belonging to the *Leonora*, were towing astern, with a native in each.

The passage, as I have said before, was deep but narrow. As the traders gazed on either side and watched the immense green rollers dashing with resistless force past the brig's side, they looked apprehensively at the Captain and then at their boats astern.

Right in the centre an enormous billow came careering along at the speed of an express train. Though it had no "breaking curl" on its towering crest, I instinctively placed my hands in the starboard boat davits, expecting to see the vast volume of water sweep our decks. Some of the traders sprang into the main rigging just as the brig lifted to the sea, to plunge downward with a swift and graceful motion, never losing her way for a moment. No man of our crew took the least notice. They knew what the brig could do, they knew the Captain, and no more anticipated a disaster than a mutiny.

We made open water safely. Then the Captain descended from the fore-yard, whence he had been conning the ship. "Well, gentlemen," he said, "here we are, all on board the *Leonora*! I hope you think well of her."

The traders emphatically asserted that she was a wonder. Then, as we did not intend to enter Utwé harbour till the morning, we shortened sail. The brig was placed under her topsails only, and we glided slowly and smoothly down the coast. Still the reef surge was thundering on the starboard hand.

The light of the native villages—for the sudden night of the tropics was upon us—glimmered through the groves of cocoa-nuts and bread-fruit trees that fringed the snowy beaches. A shadowy, dreamy landscape, blurred and indistinct at times, while ever and anon the back-borne spume of the breakers fell in rain-mist over all, as they reared and raved, only to dash themselves in mad turmoil on the javelins of jagged coral.

It was a strange scene. Yet stranger still were the dramatis personæ—the wild band of traders that clustered around the giant form of the Captain, as he lay smoking his cigar on the skylight, in friendly converse with all.

Foremost in position and seniority comes old Harry Terry, a stalwart, grizzled veteran, brown-cheeked and bright-eyed still. Full of yarns of his cruise with Captain Waldegrave of H.M. *Seringapatan*, and Captain Thomas Thompson in the *Talbot* frigate, on the coast of South America. Clear and honest is his eye, yet he has a worn and saddened look, as from a sorrow, long past, half-forgotten, yet never to be wholly erased from memory's tablet. A deserter—of course. Yet had he a true Briton's love for the flag which he had once sailed and fought under. By his side stand four stalwart half-caste sons, hearkening with glistening eyes to the Captain's tales of lands they had never seen, scarcely heard of,—of polar bears, icebergs, dog sledges, Esquimaux, reindeer, far amid the solitudes of the frozen North.

Close by old Harry sits a tall, red-bearded man, with a look of latent humour in his countenance, which proclaims his nationality even if the richness of his brogue were not in evidence. This is Pleasant Island Bill, a merry good-for-nothing, with a warm heart and unlimited capacity for whisky. In his belt he carries—perhaps from force of habit—a heavy navy revolver, before which many a fierce Pleasant islander has gone down in the bloody émeutes so common in that wild spot. Behind Bill is his wife Tiaro—a fair-skinned native of Taputanea (Drummond's Island). She is certainly the "savage woman" of the poet's fancy—handsome withal, as, with her hand on her husband's shoulder, she gazes admiringly at the herculean figure of the far-famed Rover of the South Seas, the dreaded Captain of the *Leonora*. Near to or behind Tiaro are the other traders' wives, with their wild-eyed, graceful children.

Beside me, sitting upon a bundle of sleeping mats, is a bronzed and handsome young fellow, Charlie Wilder by name, a veritable Adonis of the South Seas. With clear-cut features and bright brown curling locks, contrasting well with a dark, drooping moustache, he lolls languidly on the mats, gazing dreamily at times at the animated forms and faces around him. He was the ideal sea rover—much untrammelled by the canons of more civilised life. To each of his four young wives he appeared equally devoted. Though a *blasé*, exquisite in manner, he was a man who simply laughed at wounds and death. A dangerous antagonist, too, as some of his fellow-traders had good reason to know.

There was yet another trader—a tall young American, who had run away at Pleasant Island from the whaleship *Seagull*—a difference of opinion with the captain having resulted in Seth's being put in irons.

Besides Dick Mills the boat-steerer, who had deserted also from a whaler, there was another well-known trader, a true type of the old-time escaped convict. Burnt browner than a coffee berry is old Bob Ridley, scarred, weather-beaten, and, in accordance with the fashion of runaway sailors in the early days, tattooed like a Marquesas islander. Very "dour" and dangerous was this veteran—thinking no more of settling a difference with his ever-ready revolver than of filling his ancient clay pipe. He had with him two sons and three daughters, all married save the youngest girl. Sons and daughters alike had intermarried with natives, and the old man himself—his first wife being dead—had possessed himself of a girl of tender years but unyielding character. A native of Rapa-nui or Easter Island, she possessed in a high degree the personal beauty for which her race is famed throughout Polynesia. The old trader, it seems, had lately visited Tahiti, and there had dropped across the beautiful Lālia, and rescued her from the streets of Papeite. When he returned to Pleasant Island she accompanied him. She was a clever damsel, and having once been an inmate of the military camp at Tahiti, gave herself great airs over her step-children, though she was the junior of the youngest girl. Amongst other accomplishments Lālia could swear fluently both in French and English, having besides a thorough command of whaleship oaths which, I may observe, are unique in their way, and never seen in print.

Singing and dancing were kept up until the galley fire was lit and coffee served out. Then as the tropic sea-mist was dispelled by the first sun rays, we saw, at no great distance, the verdurous hills that enclose with emerald walls the harbour of Utwé. Far back, yet seeming but a cable's length from the brig, rose the rugged coast, two thousand feet in air, of Mount Crozier.

The inner shore of the harbour, sheltered by the reef from the fury of the terrific rollers, is surrounded by a broad belt of darkest green mangroves and hibiscus, forming a dense barrier, monotonous in colouring, but blending harmoniously with sea and sky. A well-nigh impassable forest coloured the landscape from sea to mountain top. Only near the shore were groves of cocoa-palms waving their plumy banners to the soft trade breezes. Interspersed at intervals one descried plantations of bananas and sugar-cane, yams and taro. The humidity of the climate shows itself in the surpassing richness of the vegetation. Mountain torrents foam and "rivulets dance their wayward round" in many a sequestered glen. Cane thickets springing densely from the deep alluvial mould form a safe retreat for the wild boar, while the stately purple plumaged pigeons preen themselves in the green gloom of this paradisal wild.

The Captain walked the quarter-deck, giving orders to make sail on the brig, glancing in a half amused, yet contemptuous manner at the recumbent figures of the traders who, overcome by their potations, lay slumbering on the deck.

Utwé is but a small harbour, so that the Captain felt vexed when daylight broke and revealed four whalers lying at anchor in the little port, allowing us no room. But one of them had his canvas loosed, and we caught the strains of "Shenandoah" as the crew lifted the anchor. We backed our main-yard and lay to, while she sailed out. A fine sight it was, as the whaler stood out through the narrow passage! The huge rollers dashing swiftly past her weather-beaten sides, made her roll so heavily that the boats on the davits nearly touched the water with their keels. She came close under our stern. Her captain stood up in one of the boats and took off his hat.

"How air you, Capt'n?" he drawled; "that's a beautiful brig of yours. I've heard a deal of the *Leonora* and Captain Hayston. I'm real sorry I hav'n't time to board you and have a chat. There's another blubber-hunter coming out after me, so you'd better wait awhile."

Hayston answered him politely, and the *Marathon* soon ran round the lee side of the island. In a quarter of an hour she was followed by another ship, after which we filled again and ran in, anchoring between the mangroves and the *Europa* and *St. George,* New Bedford whaleships.

Our first care was to land the cattle, and here the traders and whalers were treated to a lively scene. The mate Jansen, of whom I have before spoken, had been knocked off duty by the Captain, who told him that he was no seaman, and a cowardly dog besides, as he was always ready to ill treat the native crew, but would not stand up to him.

An incident, in which I was an actor, goes to show the savage nature of the brute. One day, during our stay at Ponapé, I happened to require a pair of steelyards that lay in his cabin; on going for them he used insulting language, and dared me to enter. He was lying in his bunk, and his bloodshot eyes glared with rage as he took a pistol from under his pillow. Keeping one eye on the pistol I went in and took the steelyards. He leaped out, and a struggle began. We fell on the deck—his whole weight upon me—but I managed to get hold of the pistol, which I threw overboard. As he freed himself and rose, he gave me a savage kick on the knee which lamed me for a week. But I drew back and landed him a left-hander, which catching him fair in the face, sent him down senseless, while a stream of blood poured from his mouth and ears.

"Malie! malie!" shouted Black Johnny in Samoan (the equivalent to "*habet*"), and the crew took up the cry in tones of deep approval.

We never spoke again after this encounter.

However, just before we made ready to land the cattle, he came aft and begged the Captain to reinstate him.

"Mr. Jansen!" said Hayston, "I cannot permit you to resume duty as mate of this brig. I have given the position to Fiji Bill, as you are not fit for it. However, I will see how you behave for the future, and may give you another chance. Go on deck and assist to get these cattle into the water."

The traders and whalers were watching the operation with great interest. The longboat, in charge of Fiji Billy, was ready to tow the cattle on shore as soon as they were lowered into the water. The first beast was swung safely out of the main hold and over the side, when the tackle parted aloft and the animal plunged into the sea, just missing the boat. For a moment there was silence. We all ran to the side, where we saw the bullock reappear and strike bravely out for the mangroves, which he reached in safety.

The Captain walked slowly over to Jansen, who was engaged in bullying the boatswain.

"Who rigged that tackle?" he asked in his most unruffled tones; but I could see the colour mounting to his forehead, as the laughter of the whaling crews fell upon his ear.

"I did," growled Jansen (edging towards his cabin, in which he always kept loaded firearms), his sullen face showing fear and hatred combined.

"Keep to the deck, sir," broke forth the Captain, who had foreseen this movement; the harsh, severe tones I knew foretold disaster. "D—n you, sir, you are neither good enough for an officer nor man before the mast. There is not a kanaka on board this brig but could have rigged that tackle in a seaman-like manner. Boy George, or even one of the girls, could have made a better fist of it. You have disgraced the brig in the presence of other ships. Go to your bunk till after breakfast."

And now Jansen brought immediate punishment on himself. With one hand on the door of the deckhouse, he turned round and muttered, "Why didn't you let the women do it, then?"

The next moment both men were struggling fiercely on the deck,— Jansen making frantic efforts to fire a pistol he had concealed in the bosom of his shirt; but the hand which held it was gripped by the Captain, and the muzzle pointed upwards.

Jansen was an extremely powerful man, and, amid the babel of tongues that were let loose, I heard one trader say, "By ——! he's got the best of the Captain."

But I noticed that while Jansen was almost spent, and was breathing stertorously, the Captain had not yet put forth the tremendous strength which, on sea or shore, I never saw equalled. He was still holding Jansen's hand with a vice-like grasp, when the pistol fell to the deck. Suddenly freeing himself, he stepped back and dealt two blows with wonderful quickness on the mate's face, cutting his forehead and cheek to the bone. The man staggered wildly—his features streaming with blood—then fell senseless against one of the crew, who darted aside and let him drop on the deck. A murmur of applause, mingled with cries of pity from the women, arose from the spectators, while the whaler crews rent the air with cheers for "Bully Hayston."

The Captain drew forth his handkerchief, with which he removed a slight stain upon his face, then said in a mild and pleasant voice, as if nothing had occurred, "Steward! bring me a glass of water. Bill (to the Fijian) get these other beasts up and put them ashore. Antonio! get Jansen's traps together, and put them and him into the boat. The man that points a pistol at me on board of this brig only does it once. As I don't wish to hurt him again, I must get rid of him."

The cattle were soon landed and eating their fill on the rich tract of littoral between Utwé and Coquille.

A Modern Buccaneer

That day I bought various articles of trade—including ten tons of yams for Arrecifos. The Captain never interfered with my dealings with the natives; so when Likiak Sâ the missionary went to him, and in a whining tone complained of my paying them in trade, he got the following answer: "Don't want your people to be paid in trade, don't you? Precisely so! you white chokered schemer—you whited sepulchre! you want to see these hard-working slaves of natives paid in cash, so that you and your brethren may rob the poor devils of every dollar for church tithes. The supercargo has my fullest confidence, and will not rob any native of a cent. Go and talk to him."

The missionary came to the trade-room, where I was selling pigeon shot and powder to a man named Sree, and said that he wished the natives paid in cash. Every Strong's islander can speak English. So I turned to those present and asked if I had suggested their taking trade instead of dollars. On receiving this answer in the negative I told him to clear out. He disregarded me, upon which I assisted him to leave the cabin, while Lālia and Kitty covered him with flour from the pantry.

This provided me with a persistent and bitter enemy.

About six o'clock the Captain went below, but rather hastily returned, casting an anxious look to seaward. "The glass is falling fast," he said, "I can't make it out. I have never known it to blow hard here at this time of year. Still it is banking up to the westward."

He hailed the whaleships, and saw that they had also noticed the glass falling. In a few minutes the two captains boarded us to have a consultation. The heavy, lowering cloud to seaward had deepened in gloom, and the three captains gazed anxiously at it.

"Gentlemen!" said Hayston, "we are in a bad place if it comes on to blow. The land-breeze has died away, and that it is going to blow from the sou'-west I am convinced. We cannot tow out in the face of such a swell, even if we had daylight to try it. To beat out by night would be madness."

The faces of the Yankee skippers lengthened visibly as they begged Hayston to make a suggestion.

"Well," he said at length, "your ships may ride out a blow, for you've room to swing in, and if you send down your light spars and be quick about it, and your cables don't part, you'll see daylight. But with me it is different. I cannot give the brig a fathom more cable; there are coral boulders all around us, and the first one she touches will knock a hole in her bottom. But now every man must look to himself. I have two hundred people on board, and my decks are lumbered up with them. Adios! gentlemen, go on board and get your spars down for God's sake."

Then the Captain turned all his attention to getting the brig ready for the storm that was even then close upon us. In the shortest time our royal and topgallant yards were down, the decks cleared of lumber, the native passengers sent below, and five fathoms of cable hove in. Hayston knew the brig would swing round with her head to the passage as soon as the gale struck her, and unless he hove in cable, must strike on one of the boulders he had spoken of.

As yet there was not a breath of air, for after the last whisper of the land-breeze had died away, the atmosphere became surcharged with electricity, and the rollers commenced to sound a ceaseless thunder, as they dashed themselves upon the reef, such as I had never heard before. A pall of darkness settled over us, and though the whaleships were so near that the voices of their crews sounded strange and ghostlike in our ears, we could see nothing except the dull glow of the lamps alight in the cabins—showing through the ports.

Then we heard the voice of Captain Grant of the *St. George*, "Stand by, Captain Hayston, it's coming along as solid as a wall."

A fierce gust whistled through the cordage, and then a great white cloud of rain, salt spume, and spray enveloped the brig, as with a shrill, humming drone, like a thousand bagpipes in full blast, the full force of the gale struck us. The brig heeled over, then swung quickly round to her anchor, while the crew, every man at his station, sought through the inky blackness that followed the rain squall to see how the whaleships fared.

But now the darkness deepened, if such were possible. No star shone through the funereal gloom; while the enormous rollers, impelled by the increasing force of the wind, swept in quickest succession through the narrow passage. The three ships rolled heavily.

"Harry!" called out the Captain to the oldest trader, "take your boats and land as many of the people as you can. The sea is getting up fast—in half-an-hour it will be breaking aboard the brig."

The traders' boats were made fast to the ship's stern, except two on deck.

These were now hauled alongside, and old Harry, with his four stalwart sons—splendid fellows they were physically—manned one, and taking about fifty of their followers, who sprang over the side and were hauled into the boat, the sons gave a wild shout and disappeared into the darkness.

The other boat was equally lucky in not being stove in. Pleasant Island Bill was in charge, and in a lull of the wind I heard him call out to those on deck to throw the women overboard and he would pick them up.

Five or six of them leaped overboard and, swimming like otters, gained the boat; many others naturally held back. Standing on the deck clinging to the Captain's knees were the two children, Toby and Kitty. Seizing Kitty in his arms the Captain tossed her into the black waters close to the boat, where one of the crew caught her by the hair and pulled her in. Toby gave a yell of alarm and tried to dart below, but I caught him and slung him over after Kitty. Bill nearly missed catching him as he rose to the surface, but he was taken in. Then the boat headed for the shore, now only discernible by the white line of foam breaking; into the mangroves.

And now our troubles recommenced. The waters of the harbour, generally placid as a mill-pond, were now running mountains high, so quickly had the sea got up. The Captain, who was standing at the stern sounding, and apparently as cool as if he were trout fishing, beckoned me to him, and placing his mouth to my ear, shouted—

"Four fathoms under our stern—little enough if the sea gets worse. But if the wind hauls another point we'll touch that big coral mushroom on the port quarter, and then it's good-bye to the *Leonora!*"

The words had hardly left his lips when a strange and awful lull of the wind occurred, rendering more intense the enshrouding darkness, more dread and distinct the seething wash and roar of the seas that broke on the weather reef.

The Captain sprang into the main rigging and held up his hand to feel if the wind was coming from a new quarter. For some minutes the brig rolled so madly that it was all he could do to hold on.

Then his strong, fearless voice sounded out: "Men! who will man a boat to take a line to the *Europa*? If I can get a hawser to the whaler to keep the brig's stern from this boulder under our port quarter, it may save the ship. If not, we must strike. There's a lull now, and a boat could get away."

After a momentary hesitation, Antonio the Portuguese, Johnny Tilton, and two natives volunteered.

"Good lads!" cried the Captain; "stand by, men, to lower away the whaleboat." In a few minutes she was in the water, and a whale-line made fast to a stout hawser was coiled away in the bow, as with an encouraging cheer from those on deck, the men gave way, and passing under our stern made for the *Europa*.

After twenty minutes of anxiety, for we could see nothing, nor tell whether the boat had reached the *Europa* safely or been stove in alongside, we saw her dart past the stern again, and Antonio called out, "All right, Captain, heave away on the hawser, the end's fast to the *Europa*."

"Well done, lads!" cried the Captain; "but stay where you are, and I'll get some more women on shore."

The strange lull still continued, but a lurid glare showed me the glass still falling steadily; when I told the Captain this he sighed, for he knew that our best chance of safety was gone. But he was a man of action.

"Go below, Hilary!" he said quietly, "and get all the papers, letters, and articles of value together—I'll send them on shore with the women."

In the cabin were eight or ten women; they gazed at me with terror-stricken faces. "On deck, Mary!" I said. "On deck all of you! there's a boat alongside, and some of you can get ashore."

Five of them, with old Mary, at once left the cabin, and I heard their wild cries and screams of alarm as they were seized by the Captain and crew, and thrown overboard to be picked up by the boat.

Lālia and the others remained in the cabin, clinging to each other and sobbing with fear.

I picked up a heavy trade chest, and laying mats and rugs along the bottom and sides, stowed into it the chronometers, a couple of sextants, charts, and what gold and silver coin was in the Captain's secretary; also as many Winchester carbines and cartridges as it would hold.

"Here, girls! help me carry this on deck," I said in Samoan to Lālia, who understood the language. We dragged the heavy box on deck, and, by wonderful good luck, it was lowered into the boat, which was now under the ship's quarter, and in imminent danger of being stove in.

The Captain desired me to go ashore in the longboat and take charge of the boat. I was just about to jump when the brig gave a fearful plunge, and before she could recover, a heavy roller crashed over the waist and nearly smothered me. By clinging to the iron boat davits near me, I managed to save myself from being carried overboard with the debris of spars and timber that swept aft. When I regained my breath I could see nothing of the boat. She had, however, been swept ashore, and all in her landed safely except Bill, who was knocked overboard, but washed up into the mangroves.

I felt the Captain's hand on my shoulder, as he asked me if I thought the boat had gone under.

"I think not, or we should have heard some of them calling out; they can all swim."

"Well, perhaps so," he replied, "but I fear not. I don't care a cent about the loss of the dollars, but Bill is a good fellow."

Lālia had clung to the davits with me when the sea struck us, and was now almost exhausted. So with the Captain's help I carried her below into the now deserted cabin, for the other women were gone; had, I supposed, been washed overboard, for they were standing with us when we lowered the chest.

The Captain then hastened on deck, telling me that the wind was coming away from the south. He had scarcely left me when I heard the dismal drone of the gale again, and his voice shouting to the carpenter to stand by and cut away the masts, for the seas were now breaking clean over the bows, and sweeping along the decks with resistless force.

Being almost hove short, the ship could not rise quickly enough to the seas, and was besides rolling so much that she threatened to turn turtle every minute. It was impossible for any one to cross the deck, so madly was the brig rolling, and so fiercely were the seas sweeping her decks in quick succession; and so for a while all hands waited till a better chance offered to cut away.

In the mean time I had dragged out another trade chest, and first securing my own papers and placing them in the bottom, I filled it with such articles as I thought would prove valuable if we did not save the ship.

Lālia rendered me great assistance now. I filled a wineglass of brandy from the decanter, and made her drink it, for her teeth were chattering, and her lips blue with cold and terror combined.

Together we managed to get the chest half-way up the companion, when another plunge made me slip, and the heavy box jammed the girl's feet against the side of the companion lining. I called loudly for help, as I could not extricate her from under the box. Fortunately, four native seamen heard me, and lifted the chest off her legs.

Then I heard the Captain's voice calling out, "Well done, boys! Rotumah men, brave fellows, in a boat!"

Carrying the girl below again, I dropped her in the steward's cabin, told her to stay there till I came back, and ran on deck.

The Captain met me, and, pointing to a dark, indistinct mass, rising and falling near the ship's stern, said, "There's real grit for you!"

It was one of the trader's whaleboats, manned by four Rotumah men and a native of Danger Island. Two of these brave fellows had been washed ashore in the second sea that had struck us, and with three others, who had reached the mangroves in another boat, had put out again to return to the brig and save their shipmates.

The Captain now called out to those who were left on board, and told them that there was a chance of some of them getting ashore, by jumping over as the boat approached and getting into her. As for himself, if three or four good men would stand by him, he would attempt to cut away the masts, and perhaps save the ship as the hawser was made fast to the *Europa*.

It was a new one, and might not part; but if it did, nothing could help the brig from sticking on the detached coral boulders that lay so close under the stern.

Seizing her child in her arms, a powerfully-built Ocean Island woman sprang into the seething foam-caldron, and disregarding our cries to make for the boat, struck out for the nearest point of the mangroves. Next morning the child was found unharmed on a small beach, more than a mile away, and the body of the mother lying dead beside her, with a fearful gash on her temple and one foot missing,—the poor babe gazing at the cold face, and wondering why she did not wake when she called to her. Then others followed the women, some getting into the boat, and others letting the sea take them in the direction of the shore.

"Where is the second mate?" shouted the Captain to the coxswain of the rescuing boat.

"On shore with the traders, sir; all the boats but one are stove in on the beach, and he can't get out again."

"All right, lads, don't attempt to come out again; but wait a minute." Then turning to me, "You must go ashore now in this boat. She has not many in her; and if her head is kept right into the break between the mountains she'll run up into the mangroves."

But I said I would take my chance with the ship. I was a good swimmer, and in that time of danger, even despair, I could not leave the Captain.

He pressed my hand silently, then called out, "All right, men, give way, the supercargo stays with me and the ship"; one dash of the oars, a wailing cry, a shout which out-toned it, and the boat disappeared, as if swallowed up by the darkness or the deep.

We were not clustered together aft. Those of the crew that had stood by the ship were hanging on to the main rigging. The Captain, who had hitherto intended cutting away both masts at once, told me he fancied the ship was straining and plunging less, and that he would only cut away as a last resource.

Suddenly he bent his glance at the hawser that was made fast to the *Europa*, and then pointed over to the seething water under our stern. I saw we were almost over a huge coral boulder, which every now and then showed itself bare.

"By ——! those fellows on board the *Europa* are paying out the hawser. We were fifty feet from that rock when the hawser was made fast and had a strain on it, and now it's right under her stern. Can any of you see the whaler's cabin lights?"

The men looked through the blinding mists of spray that flew in our faces, and stung like whip-lashes when the brig was lifted high on a towering sea. The hawser tightened like an iron bar, but suddenly fell as if it had parted or been cast off.

"The cursed dogs!" said the Captain, opening and shutting his hands spasmodically, "they are paying out, and letting us go to the devil!"

And now a tremendous sea swept along and broke just as it reached abreast the mainmast. We felt the brig strike. Sea after sea tumbled in over the bulwarks, and a solid sheet of water broke over us in the main rigging, sweeping three or four men overboard.

When I cleared my throat of the water I had swallowed, I saw the Captain with a rifle in his hand, and then followed the flash as he fired in the direction of the *Europa*.

"Captain," I cried, "what good will that do? She may be ashore herself in as bad a fix as we are."

He pushed me aside as I placed my hand on his arm. "Stand clear, Hilary! I tell you these cowardly hounds are deliberately wrecking me. That ship is in a safe place, and could ride out a heavier gale than this."

"Captain," I began, when another sea lifted the brig's bow high in the air; then, with a dull crash, we struck stern on, and I saw the hawser had either parted or been cut away. The rudder had been torn from the stern-post, and ripped its way through the timbers with a fearful tearing sound. Again the Captain's face showed itself to me almost as white as the hell of boiling foam around us.

"My ship is dearer to me than my life!" he said, as he cast the rifle from him and stood gazing out into the howling storm, amid which all the voices of earth and air seemed to be contending.

Suddenly, with a pang of pity, I remembered that Lālia was in the steward's cabin. I dashed down below. Already the water was running into the hold, and as I gained the cabin the ship once more struck violently under my feet.

"Lālia! Lālia!" I called, "come with me. Can you walk?"

The girl was sitting up in the bunk, her hair unloosed, her eyes dilated with terror, as she gazed into the dimly-lighted cabin, and saw the water washing around it.

She could hardly stand with the pain in her bruised feet, but I lifted her out. Then she tore off her dress, stripped to the waist, and, hand in hand, we succeeded in gaining the companion-way just as a torrent of water filled the cabin and put out the lamps.

I felt the Captain's hand grasp me round the waist as we stumbled out on deck, and heard him say, "Hold on to me, Hilary! hold on like grim death, my girl!" as we were swept along by a sea against the bulwarks on the starboard side.

Some of the men had clung to a boat that we carried on top of the deck-house, which had been washed over the side. They had no oars, but the backwater from the reef dashed her up against the ship, and I have an indistinct remembrance of the Captain dragging us along with him, and attempting to lift the girl up, when a towering wave struck us right amidships and drove us all over together on top of the boat, which was already stove in.

I should have gone under then but for Lālia, for I had got a blow on the side from a piece of wreckage. Anyhow, what followed I cannot remember, for when I came to my senses it was daylight, and I was lying under some cocoa-nut trees with Lālia, and one of Harry Skilling's native retainers named Karta, bathing my back with fresh water.

My first inquiry was for the Captain, and I was relieved to hear from Lālia that he was visible at that moment, directing the crew to save wreckage from the brig. The two whaleships had ridden out the gale in safety, and the *Europa* was already under weigh. I thought it just as well it was so, for Hayston would, I am sure, have attempted to seize her.

Lālia told me that we clung to the boat till she struck a coral rock and went to pieces. Then every one was separated. She had been seized by Karta, and, still keeping hold of me, the three of us had come ashore together. She said also that my back was badly cut with the coral. The poor girl had a terrible gash on her arm, and this she had neglected to attend to me. I had a deep wound on my face, which caused me great pain, as a piece of tough coral had broken off in it.

Lālia was almost nude, and I had only the remnants of a pair of duck trousers. We did not feel cold, however, as the storm had ceased, and the sun was now shining brightly. The wind had gone down, and the harbour was nearly as smooth as a mountain lake. The only visible sign of the disaster of the night was the maintopmast of the *Leonora*, showing where she had gone down.

From the bank of mangroves on which we were located there was no access to the village of Utwé, where the rest of the ship's company were. Deep channels separated the two portions of the harbour. Karta was about to swim over to tell the Captain where I was, when Lālia caught him by the arm and pointed to the water. I have read a good many tall yarns about sharks, but never till now could I believe in their being as numerous as a shoal of minnows.

The channels were simply alive with the brutes dashing to and fro, lashing the water into foam, and contesting with each other for dark objects floating near the surface. I shuddered instinctively, but Lālia laughed, and explained that the dead bodies were those of pigs washed overboard from the brig.

Presently the tall figure of Karta attracted the notice of some of the people on the other side, and Lālia said the "ariki vaka" was coming over to us in one of the traders' whaleboats.

The Captain sprang out of the boat, and seeing me lying down with my head in the girl's lap thought I was dead.

"My dear boy," he said, taking both my hands and pressing them, "are you badly hurt?"

I showed him my back, and said I felt most pain in my side, and whereupon I suffered ten excruciating pains in one as he extracted the piece of flat coral from my face. He then called one of the boat's crew, and told him to take off his shirt, one sleeve of which he tore off and bound up Lālia's arm. He then gave her the mutilated garment to cover her bare body, saying in his old cheerful manner that her husband was all right, and was out searching the beaches for her. She made a gesture of indifference, and then fainted away. As soon as she revived she was lifted into the boat, and we pushed off for the village.

The Captain kept pressing my hand all the way over, and told me that since daylight he had been looking among the wreckage coming ashore and searching the beach for me, when some one saw our three figures in the cocoa-nut grove, and said two were white. Hayston knew this must be Lālia and myself, as she had a very fair skin. He was sincerely pleased at my escape, and no words need express my relief at his safety.

He took us forthwith to one of the villagers' houses, and told the people to attend to us, and see that we wanted for nothing. He further insisted that I should not attempt to render him any assistance until I was perfectly recovered. I could only nod acquiescence, as my side was paining me terribly.

A warm grasp of my hand and a kind look to Lālia and he was gone.

One of the Kusaie women in the house told us that a message had gone up to the king, and that a native doctor named Srulik would soon come down and cure my back with leaves in the island fashion.

She also informed Lālia that her husband had gone away in a canoe to look for her body, with two natives, but that he had come across a case of gin, and was now dead drunk on the opposite side of Utwé. It is hardly to be expected that a young girl could feel love for a man of her husband's years; but tears of humiliation coursed down her cheeks when the woman added that he had already asked an Ocean Island girl to be wife to him.

About four o'clock in the afternoon messengers arrived from Lêlé with a message of regret from the king to Captain Hayston, and an invitation for me to Chabral harbour, so that I could get better quickly; and he could send his own boat for me. But I did not want to be separated from the Captain, and said I would come and visit him when I got permission.

Queen Sê sent me a large basket of cooked pigeons and fruit. Taking out a few for myself and Lālia, I sent the rest to the Captain, who was glad of them for his weary and hungry men.

For the next few days I suffered fearfully with the pain in my side, and though the Captain visited me twice a day, and tried all he could to cheer me up, I fell into a hopeless state of despondency. All the time Lālia had remained in the house, her husband, not having finished the case of gin, never coming near her. Her stepsons and daughters disliked her, and therefore avoided the house where we were staying.

The Captain told me that her arm was cut to the bone, and that the trade chest that had fallen against her had injured one foot badly. Never as long as I live shall I forget the unwearied attention and kindness which the poor girl showed me during our stay in the village. Though lame, and with only the use of one arm, she never left my side, and strove by every means in her power to allay the agony I endured—answering to my petulance and irritability only with smiles and kind words.

The Captain told me that he had saved a good many articles from the wreck; that the big trade chest had come ashore, and that the money and firearms were in a safe place. A quantity of liquor had also been saved, and already some fierce fights had taken place, but the traders had in most instances behaved well, and assisted him to maintain order. He told me also that Lālia's husband had taken away a lot of liquor into the impassable forest that lines the north side of Utwé, and, with two of his sons and several women, was having a big carouse.

"The virtuous and Christian Strong's islanders had," he said, "stolen about a thousand dollars' worth of trade that had been washed ashore. But," he added quietly, "I'll talk to them like a father as soon as I get a house built, and knock the devil out of those Pleasant islanders besides. They seem disposed to cut all our throats."

A couple of days after this, Hayston came to me with a letter from Lālia's husband, which he handed to me. I don't know whether amusement or indignation predominated as I read it, written as it was on a piece of account paper.

Strong's Island, March 11th.

Supercargo Leonora Brig.

Dear Friend.—I heer my wife have took up with you, and say she do'ent want anny mo-ar truck with her lawful husban. Captin Hayston say No, but she must be cotton strong to you, not to come to me when I look for her neerly one week amung two thousan sharks, as I can prove, but I bare you no ill-wil, for I got anuther wife, but you must give me the three rings she ware, and I warn you I'm not responsble.—I remane, your true and sincere friend.

P.S.—Lal can read as well as me, and you can let her read this. She is a good girl, and I bear no ill-wil.

The Captain laughed when I read out this precious document, and told me not to take matters so seriously. He then sat down and chatted for half-an-hour, saying that as soon as he had finished saving the wreckage, he had called the traders together, and laid certain proposals before them to which they had agreed.

These were that the traders and their followers would consider themselves under his direction, in which case he would engage to provide food for them during their stay on the island. They were not to have any commercial dealings with the people of Strong's Island, and their natives were to assist the crew of the *Leonora* in erecting houses for their joint accommodation. After which he would endeavour to charter a vessel, probably a passing whaleship, to take the whole lot of us to Providence Island. Should no vessel call in six months' time, he would take a boat's crew and make for Millé Lagoon, six hundred miles distant. If the ketch I had brought down from Samoa was still afloat, he would bring her back, and take the people in detachments to Providence Island. He feared, however, that no more whalers would be calling in for ten months, as the *St. George* and *Europa* were the last of the fleet which was making, viâ Japan, for the Siberian coast, "right whaling."

He left us then, saying he had established a little republic on the narrow strip of land that lay on the sea-side of Utwé village.

Then I gave Lālia the letter I had received from her reprobate husband. She read it in silence and returned it to me, but I could see that the heartless old scoundrel's words had wounded her deeply. She took off some rings from her fingers, and sent them to the Captain to hand to the old man. "Do you think," she said, "that I can ever get back to Rapa-nui?" (Easter Island.)

Her father, she went on to say, was dead, and her mother had been among those unfortunate people who in 1866 were seized by three Peruvian slavers and taken to work the guano deposits on the Chincha Islands. She, when about fourteen, had married one of the captains of one of the ships owned by the great firm of Brander of Tahiti. The tales she told me of his brutality and ill-usage during his drunken fits of passion moved me to sincere pity. The unmitigated rascal deliberately sold his child wife to an American (or a man who called himself one), and by him she was taken to San Francisco and delivered into yet more hopeless slavery. Here she made the acquaintance of a Tahitian half-caste. She and this girl succeeded in escaping and paying their passages to Tahiti, where they landed penniless and starving.

From Tahiti she was taken by her present husband.

CHAPTER XI

A KING AND QUEEN

On the next day I walked to the new village in course of formation, when I received from whites and natives alike a most flattering reception. Outside of the sandy spit a solid sea-wall of coral had been built, the ground had been levelled, and an enormous dwelling-house erected. This was the work of the Ocean and Pleasant islanders. It was the Captain's house, and from a hole in the gable floated the starry banner of the great Republic. This flag had been the joint work of Nellie and Mila. It was composed of strips of white calico, navy blue and Turkey red. At the further end of the sea-wall stood the traders' houses; opposite the captains' were those of their people. Every one seemed busy, and the greatest animation pervaded the scene, while a number of Strong's islanders, squatted down in front of the big house, surveyed the operations with dismay. They dreaded, and with good reason, the fierce and intractable natives of Pleasant Island, who would have been only too pleased to have cut their throats and taken possession of their beautiful home altogether.

I was received by the Captain at the door of his house, and although the girls had frequently been to visit me, and bring fruit and fish from the Captain when I was sick, I was made as much of as if I had been dead and buried and come to life again. The Captain's merry blue eyes looked searchingly into mine, as I seated myself in an easy chair, "You see what it is to be *l'ami du maison.*"

I acknowledged the compliment, and then turned to shake hands with little Toby, who with a number of other children were being entertained by a sort of pig and yam tea-party by the Captain, each youngster having in his hand a junk of yam and piece of pork.

Those of the crew who were in the vicinity now came in, and I had quite a levee. Black Johnny nearly wrung my hand off. I was glad to see the Captain looking so bright, and evidently on such good terms with those around him. I could not but be struck with the way in which the traders, resolute and determined men themselves, deferred to his slightest wish.

For a few minutes he walked up and down the long matted floor, apparently lost in thought, while I sat and talked with the light-hearted, merry creatures around me. Suddenly stopping, he came up, and placed his hand on my shoulder.

"Hilary! I like this island so well, that as Henry the Fifth said in France, when the French queen asked him how he liked her country: I mean to keep it."

"Captain," I said, startled and alarmed, "are you serious?"

"Yes and no! If I cannot get a ship to take us to Providence Island within six months I will upset the missionaries' apple-cart and take possession of the island. If a ship does call here, and I can charter her, I am bound in honour to fulfil my promise to these traders."

"Captain," I said, "there are two hundred and fifty men on Strong's Island; surely you would not dispossess them? Besides, they will fight."

"So much the better," he said, with a smile of contempt, "once let a quarrel break out between them and these Ocean and Pleasant islanders, and every native of Kusaie will have his throat cut in twenty-four hours."

I turned the subject, for I saw by his stern expression that he meant what he said, and that any trifling incident would perhaps bring matters to an issue.

Presently he began again. "Yes, these Pleasant islanders, who two weeks ago were all attached to these traders, are now heart and soul devoted to me. They know I am a better man, according to their ideas, than all the traders put together, and if I stepped out of the house now and told them I would lead them, they would follow me and burn old Tokusar's town over his head, cut off a passing ship, or do any other devilry such as their bloody instincts revel in."

I tried to turn his thoughts into another channel, and succeeded so far that when I rose to return he was laughing and joking in his usual manner. He pointed out to me a separate part of the house, and told me that as soon as I liked to take possession he would be glad to see me in it.

I explained to him that for the present I had better remain in the native house, as the king daily sent me food, and considered me his guest. In this he concurred, as he said if the king took a liking to a white man he would live in clover. He advised me to go and see him as soon as I was strong, or else his dignity would be touched. Also that I would find it well to keep good friends with Queen Sê.

When I returned to the native house, however, I felt "sick unto death," and cast myself down on the mats in despair. The hurt I had received in the side seemed to have also affected my chest, as I could hardly breathe without suffering agonies. Happily I became unconscious; when I opened my eyes I found the Captain beside my mat, and during the whole night he remained with me and encouraged my sinking spirits. When daylight came he examined me carefully, after which he told me, that from the darkening colour of my skin, and the agony I felt from the slightest pressure, he thought I had received internal injury. He therefore insisted upon my coming over to his village, so that I might be under his immediate control. To this I consented at last, although young Harry (as we called Harry Waters) was eager that I should come and live with him on the north side of Utwé, where Hayston had formed a sub-station to make oil and given him charge.

I liked Harry very much; he was the only one of the traders whose age approached my own. His bearing and behaviour, too, contrasted favourably with those of his drunken and dissolute colleagues. However, I had to decline his kind offer, although, to my amusement, he emphatically asserted that I would be no trouble to him, as he had four wives, and Rosa, the youngest of them, was a clever nurse. I paid the Strong islanders who had attended on me, and then inquired of Lālia what she intended to do? She had, of course, no money to pay the people for keeping her, and the old custom of extending hospitality to strangers had naturally died out since the coming of the missionaries.

I had no other way of showing my gratitude than by offering her money. This she refused, but said she would be glad to get some clothes or material to make them. I gave a native money, and sent him up to Lêlé, where he bought several dresses from Kitty of Ebon, and as she was the same height and figure as Lālia, they fitted her capitally.

A couple of days after I had taken up my quarters with the Captain she came to see me, and say good-bye. She told me she was going to live at a village near Lêlé, and teach the Strong's Island women hat-making, at which she was clever. She would stay there till she got tired of it. I was sincerely sorry, and was not ashamed to show it, "being weak from my wound," and hardly able to refrain from tears. I felt quite pleased when the Captain came up and shook her little hand warmly, telling her that she really ought not to leave us. "Mind, Lālia, come to me if you are in any trouble, and I will see you righted," he said in parting.

"I know that, Captain! very well," she answered, looking up with a strange, sorrowful look in her large bright eyes, "but I must go now." Whereupon she walked slowly down the beach, and getting into a canoe with two Kusaie women, waved her hand and was soon out of sight.

I recovered slowly, but after a while was able to get about and to take an inventory of the property saved, while the Captain amused himself by overlooking the building of a large oil-store. He had demanded an immediate payment of two hundred and fifty thousand cocoa-nuts from the king, as part indemnity for the property stolen by the natives from the wreck. The king dared not refuse, and now a huge pile of cocoa-nuts was accumulating near the oil-shed, where the Pleasant islanders were daily scraping the nuts and making oil. A number of butts had come ashore, which were utilised for the oil, so that the village had already gained a settled look. About this time the Captain gave way to occasional bursts of passion, inflicting severe beatings upon two of the traders, who had got drunk and were careering about with rifles in their hands, threatening to shoot any one that interfered with them.

He also accused old Harry Terry of plotting with the king, and a violent scene ensued. Some of the natives still sided with their old master, and with knives and shark-tooth daggers surrounded him, uttering cries of defiance at the Captain.

I was in the big house when the row commenced, and saw the excited savages running up to where the Captain and old Harry stood. An encounter seemed imminent.

Boy George, with Nellie and the other women, now rushed in and demanded of me to give them the Winchester and Snider rifles, which stood ready loaded in a corner of the house. But, knowing that the Captain was ready to assert his authority without arms, I refused, and locking them up in a trade chest sat down upon it. I knew that the first shot would be followed by a scene of bloodshed and murder. George was persistent, saying the Captain would be killed, but changed his tone when he walked in unharmed, but with his fingers bleeding. Harry had given in when he saw the Captain dart in amongst the natives surrounding him, and knock two of the ringleaders down, but denied that he had been plotting to usurp Hayston's authority. A hollow reconciliation then took place, but there was bad blood between them from that time. He told me that I had done wisely in locking up the arms, and gave me the key to keep, as I had, he confessed, shown more prudence than himself. Then he sat down and began to sing like a schoolboy on a holiday.

One day we took the boat and went up a creek flowing into the harbour. We were the only men, as the crew consisted of Ocean Island women and some of the girls from the brig.

We were going to land them across the creek, where they intended to construct a fish weir, as the harbour was a bad place to fish in on account of the swarms of fierce and daring sharks.

Among the girls in the boat were two from Ocean Island, being of the party landed from the whaleships at Chabral harbour. One of these was the new wife of the old convict trader. She had come down on a visit, and kept us amused with her descriptions of the orgies and drunken freaks of the fierce old man, whose conduct had frightened—no easy matter—all who came into contact with him.

As we crossed over the in-shore reef and got into the channel of the creek, I saw a canoe with three figures in it ahead of us, and told the Captain that I thought I recognised Lālia. He said it was hardly possible, as she lived six miles away on the coast, and was not likely to come down here. At this mention of Lālia her successor looked frightened, and said she would like to go back, but was overruled by the others, who laughed at her fears. After rowing up the creek as far as the boat would go, the girls got out, and the Captain and I took our rifles and started up a spur in the mountain on the chance of getting a shot at the wild pigs.

We struck into the dense woodland, and in a few minutes the voices of the laughing girls sounded subdued and far away. The gloom of the primeval forest seemed to be deepened by the vast structure and domelike tops of the mighty trees, whose thick branches formed an almost perfect canopy, while underneath our footsteps fell soundless on the thick carpet of rotting leaves.

Here the Captain and I took different routes, agreeing to meet on the summit of the spur. As I walked along the silence that enshrouded all things seemed to weigh heavily; the darkening gloom of the forest began to fill me with childish fancies and misgivings. My nerves became strung to such a pitch that the harsh croak of some brooding frigate bird, or the sudden booming note of a wood pigeon, set my heart bumping against my ribs with that strange, undefined feeling which, if it be not premonition, is nearly akin to it.

I had ascended half-way to the spur when I heard a shot.

Its prolonged and tumultuous echoes startled the denizens of the forest, winged and quadrupedal, and as they died away a wild chorus of shrieks and growls seemed to electrify me into life. Waiting till silence resumed sway I called aloud to the Captain. Far down below I heard his answering call. Then he queried, "Have you shot anything?"

"No, I have not fired."

"Quick," he shouted, "come down—there's mischief among the women."

Rushing down the leaf-strewn spur I soon joined him. We ran together till we reached the boat. There a tragedy had been enacted. The girls were huddled up in the boat, which was drifting about from bank to bank. As we dashed through the scrub they pointed to a patch of green-sward amongst the cocoa-nut trees, saying, "She is killed."

There, lying on her face quite dead, was the Ocean Island girl with a bullet through her breast. The ball had passed completely through her body, and though her limbs were still quivering with muscular action, she must have died in a few seconds after she was struck.

The girls told us that while they were making the weir she had gone up to a pool of fresh water among the rocks to look for fresh-water shrimps. A few minutes after they heard a shot; she staggered forward and fell on her face dead.

The Captain and I looked at one another. Each read the thoughts that passed through the other's mind—Lālia had fired the shot! But, calling the women out of the boat, the Captain sternly forbade them to mention Lālia's name in connection with the matter, and said that they must all keep silence. A grave was hastily dug in the soft alluvial of the shadowy forest glade, where the body of the poor girl, wrapped in garments of her companions, was hastily buried.

I did not understand the meaning of the secrecy which was evidently considered necessary, until the Captain told me that as the girl was in his charge at the time of her death, he would be held responsible, and that the uncertain temper of her countrymen might at any time cause an outbreak.

We returned to the boat, and the women, as we neared the village, were instructed by the Captain to answer all inquiries for the dead girl by saying she had disappeared. Her countrymen took her departure very quietly, and came to the conclusion that the evil spirits of the mountain had carried her away, and their superstition forbade search.

I cannot, even after the time that has elapsed, recall without a pang of regret the total change in the Captain's demeanour and conduct at this time. Some demon appeared to have taken possession of him. His terrific bursts of violence drove every soul away at times, none daring to venture near him until he had cooled down except myself, to whom he never addressed a harsh or angry word. One day he declared that the men of the *Leonora* and some of the Pleasant islanders were concocting a meeting, and I was sickened and horrified at seeing three of each lashed to cocoa-nut trees, while the huge figure of Antonio, the black Portuguese, towered above the crowd as he flogged them. The Captain stood by with a pistol in each hand as, with a countenance blanched and disturbed with passion, he ordered Antonio to lay it on well.

I went into the house and, sitting down, tried to think out a course for myself. The Captain came in after a while and, drawing a seat to the window, gazed moodily out upon the sparkling, breeze-rippled sea. Then I knew that the dark hour had passed, and that he would listen to reason.

"Captain," I said, "I can stay here no longer with you. I am sick of seeing men flogged till their backs are like raw meat, even though they are mutinous. If I thought any words of mine would do good, I would earnestly beg of you to adopt milder measures. Every day that passes you run the gauntlet, so to speak, of these men's deadly hatred, I know; for how can I avoid hearing the mutterings and seeing the fierce glances of the people—that you are surrounded with foes, and that any moment may be your last."

He placed his hand on my shoulder in his old way. "True, my lad, true; but if they are dangerous to meddle with, so am I. The white men, young Harry excepted, would gladly see me lying out there on the sand with a bullet hole in my skull; but, by ——, I'll shoot every mother's son of them if I detect any treachery.... And so you wish to leave me?"

I considered a moment and then answered, "Sorry am I to say it, but I do."

"Come out to the beach, my lad, and talk to me there. This house is stifling; another month of this life would send me mad."

We walked along the weather side for about a mile, then seating ourselves on a huge flat rock, watched the rollers tumbling in over the reef and hissing along the sand at our feet. Hayston then spoke freely to me of his troubles, his hopes, and disappointments, begging me to remain with him—going, indeed, the length of a half promise to use gentler methods of correction in future.

I yielded for a time, but after another week the fights and floggings, followed by threats of vengeance, commenced anew. Two incidents also, following close upon one another, led me to sever my connection with the Captain finally, though in a friendly spirit.

The first was an attack single-handed upon the Kusaie village of Utwé, driving the men before him like a flock of sheep. Some who ventured to resist were felled by blows of his fist. Then he picked out half a dozen of the youngest women, and drove them to the men's quarters, telling them to keep them till the husbands and families ransomed them.

This was all because he had been told that Likiak Sâ had been to the village, and urged the natives to remove to Lêlê, where a man-of-war was expected to arrive from Honolulu, and that Hayston dared not follow them there.

The next matter that went wrong was that he desired me to bring the trade books, and go over the various traders' accounts with him.

One of these books was missing, although I remembered placing the whole bundle in the big chest with the charts and chronometers. He declared that the loss of this book, with some important accounts of his trading stations in the Line and Marshall Islands, rendered the others valueless.

I felt aggrieved at the imputation of carelessness, and having never since first I knew him felt any fear of expressing myself clearly, told him that he must have lost it, or it would have been with the others.

Starting from his seat with his face livid with rage, he passionately denied having lost it. Then he strode into his room, and with savage oaths drove out the women, cursing them as the cause of the brig's loss and all his misfortunes.

The next moment he appeared with his arms full of chronometers, and, standing in the doorway, tore the costly instruments from their cases and dashed them to pieces on the coral flagstones at his feet. Then, swearing he would fire the station and roast every one in it, with his hands beating and clutching at the air, his face working with passion, he walked, staggering like a drunken man, to the beach, and threw himself down on a boulder.

Three hours after, taking little Kitty and Toby with me, I found him still there, resting his head on his hand and gazing out upon the sea.

"Captain," I said, "I have come to say farewell."

He slowly raised his head, and with sorrow depicted on his countenance, gave me his hand.

I pressed it and turned away. I packed up my belongings, and then calling to Nellie, told her to give the Captain a note which I left on his table, and with a handshake to each of the wondering girls, made my way through the village, and thence to the bank of a lagoon that runs parallel to the southern coast of Strong's Island. I knew that I could walk to Coquille harbour in about a day, and thither I decided to go, as at the village of Moūt dwelt a man named Kusis, who had several times pressed me to visit him.

It was a bright moonlight night, so that I had no difficulty in making my way along the lonely coast. The lagoon, solemnly still and silver-gleaming, lay between me and the mainland. The narrow strip on the ocean side was not more than half a mile wide; on the lagoon border was a thicket well-nigh impassable.

The mood of melancholy that impressed me at parting with a man to whom, in spite of his faults, I was sincerely attached, weighed heavily. The deep silence of the night, unbroken save by the murmuring plumes of the cocoa-nut palms as they swayed to the breath of the trade-wind, and the ceaseless plaints of the unresting surge, completed the feeling of loneliness and desolation.

At length I reached the end of the narrow spit that ran parallel to the lofty mainland, and found that I had to cross over the reef that connected it to the main, this reef forming the southern end of the lagoon.

The country was entirely new to me, but once I gained the white beach that fringed the leeside of the island, I knew that I need only follow it along till I reached the village of Moūt, about four miles distant from the end of the lagoon. I hung my bundle across my Winchester and commenced the crossing. The tide was out and the reef bare, but here and there were deep pools through which I had to pick my steps carefully, being confused besides by the lines of dazzling moon-rays.

When nearly across, and walking up to my waist through a channel that led between the coral patches, I saw a strange, dark shape moving quickly towards me. "A shark!" I thought, but the next minute the black mass darted past me at an angle, when I saw it was an innocent turtle that was doubtless more frightened than I. After this adventure I gained the white beach, which lay shining like a silver girdle under the moon-rays, and flung myself down on the safe yielding sand. The spot was silent as the grave. The murmurous rhythm of the surf sounded miles distant, and but rose to the faintest lulling sound, as I made a pillow of my worldly goods and sank into dreamless sleep.

It was the earliest dawn when the chill breath of the land-breeze touched my cheek, and sent a shiver through my somewhat exhausted frame. I arose, and looking round found that I was not wholly alone: several huge turtles had been keeping me company during the night, having come ashore to lay their eggs. As soon as I stood up they scrambled and floundered away in dire fright. I felt badly in need of a smoke, but having no matches, decided to eat something instead. I had not far to seek for a breakfast. Picking up a couple of sprouting cocoa-nuts from the ground, I husked them by beating them against a tree-trunk, and made a much needed meal from the sweet kernels.

Although I was still far from well, and the pain in my side had returned with tenfold vigour, I felt a new-born elasticity of spirit. The glow of the tropic sun lighted up the slumberous main spread out in azure vastness before me.

Shouldering my bundle and rifle, my sole worldly possessions, except utterly valueless money and papers in the Captain's care, I descended to the beach and walked along in the hard sand. At about six o'clock I came abreast of two lovely verdure-clad islets, rising from the shallow waters which lay between the outer reefs and the mainland, and I knew I must be near Moūt.

Then I saw a canoe shoot out from the land about a quarter of a mile distant, with the native in it standing up poling it along. The next bend of the beach brought me in full view of the picturesque village. A loud cry of wonder greeted me. The next moment I was surrounded by smiling villagers. I felt a thrill of pride at the thought that of all those who had been cast away in the *Leonora*, none would have been welcomed so warmly as I was now by those simple, kind-hearted people.

"Kusis' friend, Kusis' friend has come!" the men called aloud. Crowding around, and taking my rifle and bundle from me, I was escorted to the farther end of the village, where out of a pretty little house embowered in a grove of palms, a man sprang out and fairly hugged me.

This was Kusis, in whose frank and open countenance nothing but joyous welcome and boundless hospitality could be read. Taking me by the hand, he led me inside. My cares were over for the present, evidently.

Words of mine can but faintly describe the generosity and kindness of these people to me during my lengthened sojourn among them. The memory of the peaceful days which I passed in that unknown, lovely village can never be effaced.

Kusis, it seems, had often been to see me when I lay sick at Utwé, and was unconscious of his presence. The Captain and Lālia had told me of how he would come softly into the house, bringing a present of fruit or fish for "the sick white boy," as he called me. He would sit by my side and gaze anxiously at me for hours at a time, always questioning the Captain concerning me. When I got better I had long chats with him, and to his inexpressible delight, gave him a shot gun which I had bought from the carpenter for a pound of tobacco. He had no shot, but he told me he could make some from strips of lead, and as there was plenty of that from the wreckage that came ashore, the Captain gave him as much as he could carry in the canoe, besides a large tin of powder and plenty of caps.

He was a tall, large-framed man for a Strong's islander—magnificently built, and with a heart in proportion. His wife Tulpé, and his only daughter, a little girl named Kinie, made up the family. He evidently wished to complete it by making me his son, for his sole aim in life seemed to be to keep me with him.

Unlike the people of Utwé, the villagers of Moūt were utterly unsophisticated, besides being free from the cant and hypocrisy that nearly always attaches to the native character when they profess

Christianity. No doubt this was the result of their village being so distant from Lêlé, where the natives were for ever chanting psalms and hymns, and keeping the letter of the law, while at the same time they departed as widely from the spirit as their heathen forefathers had ever done.

After a while I received a letter from Captain Hayston, and with it a large parcel. The letter ran as follows:—

MY DEAR BOY.—Have you entirely deserted me? I hope not. Come and see me again, even if you only stop a day: I miss you greatly, and the evenings are very dull without you to talk to. I gave that fellow Miles, the boatswain, a bad beating, and he has cleared out to the mountains with the Pleasant islanders. Had you been here you would have got him off. As it is, I have lost three men. Accept the things I send. (The hat was made for you by a friend.) They will do for presents for your Kusaie friends. Let me know when you can come up, and I will send the whaleboat.—Yours sincerely,

W. H. HAYSTON.

I sent back my thanks, saying that I would come and see him, but should come overland, as the messenger was returning in a canoe. Kusis put in two turtle as "present for Captin."

I opened the parcel, which I found contained all sorts of articles likely to be useful to me, with ten pounds of tobacco, and a bag of small scarlet and white beads, the delight of a Strong's Island girl's heart. Rolled up in a native sash was a beautifully-made Panama hat. This latter was a gift from Lālia, and at once excited the admiration of Kusis and Tulpé, when they examined its texture. The childish delight of Kinie, when I gave her the beads, gave me the greatest pleasure, and although her father and mother looked with glistening eyes at the other articles which I wished them to take, they firmly refused the offered gifts, Kusis only taking a few sticks of tobacco, and his wife a silk handkerchief with some needles and thread.

I was rapidly regaining my strength, now felt in much higher spirits as I accompanied Kusis on his shooting and fishing trips, returning home to the bright faces and welcoming smiles of his wife and daughter. After another week Kusis and I set out to visit the Captain, who, though I was thoroughly happy and contented with my new friends, was never absent from my thoughts. He received us with unaffected pleasure, and, calling his steward and making us sit down to lunch, he gave me an account of what had been doing since I had left.

The village had now a settled appearance, and the people were all busy making oil, another two hundred and fifty thousand cocoa-nuts having been paid by the king. The Captain asked me if there were not a vast quantity of cocoa-nuts at Coquille harbour, and on my assenting, said he would send a gang of Pleasant islanders under Fiji Bill and Antonio to live there, and collect the third part of the indemnity—another two hundred and fifty thousand cocoa-nuts.

This I begged him not to do, pointing out the injustice of such an action, inasmuch as the people of Coquille had no hand in stealing the property from the brig, and it would be cruel to make them pay for the misdoings of others. I told him also that at Coquille were situated the largest taro and yam plantations, with the best turtle fisheries, that I was sure the natives would destroy the plantations and abandon the villages if they had the savage Pleasant islanders quartered upon them. Besides, we might have to remain another eight or nine months on the island before the whaling fleet called here again, and that it was absolutely indispensable that he should be able to command a supply of food to subsist nearly a hundred and fifty people.

Kusis, who was seated on the mats near us, eagerly watched the Captain. At length a look of content overspread his face as the Captain said he would not touch the cocoa-nuts in Coquille harbour. To Kusis he said, "Tell your people to have no fear as long as the king continues to pay up, but once let me see any 'soldiering,' or desire to avoid paying the fine, I'll strip the island from Mount Crozier to the reef."

Then we strolled to and fro on the Plaza, as we called the local esplanade in front of the big house, and the Captain told me to come and look at his turtle pond, in which were a number of green turtle, and also the two hawkbills sent by Kusis.

I found that several of the traders had now openly broken with him, and leaving their native following, had retired to Lêlé, where they were under the protection of the king. The number of girls in the big house had now increased to nine or ten. At the time of my visit some were engaged in weaving an immense mat to cover the whole floor, others were drying and picking tobacco leaves for making cigars. Two of the new arrivals, I could see, were native girls. I asked the Captain what they were doing there. He answered somewhat testily, "Did I think they came to teach Sunday-school?"

I remained that night, and we spent a merry evening. In the morning, after a breakfast of turtle eggs and roast pig, Kusis and I prepared to return.

The Captain urged me to go by way of Chabral harbour, and pay my promised visit to the king.

"In that case I might let him know how his Majesty was taking matters." Kusis also urged me to see the king, who was anxious that I should spend a week with him.

We got a canoe to carry us across to the north arm of the harbour, where I remained an hour or two with young Harry, who had established quite a small village.

When we entered the fence surrounding his place, we found him lying in a hammock, slung between two pandanus-trees, smoking his morning pipe, and having his hair combed by two pretty little witches named Rosa and Taloe.

This was Harry's idea of island luxury. He always alleged that sleeping gave him a headache, and that having his hair brushed drove it away, particularly if the combing was performed by the soft hands of one of his four houris.

He sprang up and welcomed me heartily, urging me to stay all night. But I was anxious to get on. However, I said I should be glad to see him at Moūt, when he could bring his family with him, and give them a week's feast on pork and turtle.

Harry presently took me into a small room, saying, "Look here!" The place was closely packed with liquor in small kegs. These had been washed ashore, and he had found them, only a few days since, high up in the mangroves. The Captain told him to store it, as it was dangerous stuff to bring to Utwé. The Pleasant islanders are very fond of liquor, after imbibing which they always want to fight and kill some one, and generally do.

We had a glass of grog together, after which I said good-bye to the good-natured, handsome young trader and his wives, whom he used to call the "Three Graces, with another thrown in."

Kusis and I reached the south side of Chabral harbour about sunset. I was freshly enchanted with the loveliness of the scene, accustomed as I had become to this paradisal quarter of the globe. The trade-wind had died away, the transparent waters of the harbour reflected in their blue depths the tall shadows of the towering mountains that overhung the harbour on three sides.

A canoe put across from the king's wharf when I fired a shot to attract attention. So wonderfully clear was the atmosphere, so unbroken the silence of the lonely bay, that the quick "tweep, tweep" of the paddle, as it struck the water, reached our ears as distinctly as if the canoe was but a few yards distant, instead of nearly half a mile.

The old king received me graciously, but soon commenced a string of complaints, interlarded with Scripture quotations rounded off by quaint oaths. He feared the Captain greatly, and yet was anxious to keep up his authority. Then, with every grievance that was laid before me, he drank a stiff glass of grog to wash it down with, and insisted on my keeping him company.

Queen Sê now came in, saying in her prettiest English, "Oh! you naughty boy! Why you no come see king, see *me*? Long time promise, but never come out. How you bad pain side? How many Strong's Island girl Captain got now? I never see man like that. Debil, I believe. You got any wife yet?"

I told the queen I was still unmarried, and thought I should remain so.

"Oh! no, you say so now. By and by get like Captain. But don't you steal girl like him. You come to me! I pick you out nice girl. Cook, sew, make pyjamas; very pretty face too."

By this time old Tokusar was asleep, with his head on the table, his inevitable Bible open at the Psalms of David (printed in the Kusaie dialect) in the leaf of his armchair, and the half-emptied gin bottle encircled by his left arm.

Queen Sê was a tiny little creature—very good-looking, even at this time of her life—being about five-and-twenty, which is considered the *passée* period in Polynesia. She was extremely vain, but had a quick perception of humour. She and the Captain always got on famously together.

Drawing our chairs up to a side table, she brought me a number of bound volumes of *Leslie's Illustrated Paper*, sent to her by the queen of Hawaii.

While I looked at the pictures she plied me with questions, principally at random, about Captain Hayston, who, I was not long in discovering, had been a former admirer. Going into a side room, she unlocked a small box, and brought me out a photo of a gentleman wearing a post-captain's uniform in her Britannic Majesty's navy. "What do you think of him?" she asked. "Very, oh! very handsome man—that Captain Damer. Oh! that long time ago. I love him; he love me too"—and then, pointing to poor old Tokusar, "King know all about it. He don't like me to talk about Captain Damer. But, oh! such handsome man! He tell me I loveliest girl in all the world. What you think yourself? What Captain tell you; he think me pretty too?"

Her Majesty was an expert angler for flattery. I was not indisposed to humour a pretty woman, and a queen, and was evidently rising in her estimation. I resolved to turn my good fortune to account, by inducing her to effect a reconciliation between the king and the Captain, who wanted the king to visit him at Utwé, to see the wonderful change he had effected there. He felt certain that, when the king saw the magnitude of the station, knowing that it must, sooner or later, come into his possession when he, Hayston, left the island, he would forgive all that had passed.

Once the subject was broached I became an ardent advocate for the Captain, and told the queen how anxious he was to be on good terms with the king again. In fact, so eloquent did I become, partly through the potency of the schnapps of which I had partaken, that I represented the Captain as devoured with grief at losing the king's and her friendship.

The queen listened gravely, and then extending her shapely hand, caught me by the ear, and laughed, "Oh! you bad boy! Captain Hayston think Tokusar old fool; told *me* so plenty time. Well, never mind, I try make everything all right."

The queen, as beseemed her, had a number of young women with her, sitting round the sides of the great room. Some were making the girdles that the Kusaie natives of both sexes wear round the waist under their other garments. They are woven on an ingeniously constructed loom, the banana fibres which form the material being stained in various bright colours. These girls were sitting in the manner peculiar to the Strong's Island women, with their eyes cast down—it being considered a boldness to look at either the king or queen. When speaking to either their eyes were always bent on the ground.

The king, being carefully placed on a cane lounge, a meal was brought in. Both Kusis and I were presented with food enough to last for a month. As the queen bade me good-night she passed her arm round me, and tenderly inquired, "How my poor side feel?" adding that I was a very good boy, because I was kind to Strong's Island man. She also informed me that I could kiss her, which I did. Then putting the post-captain's photo in her bosom she went to bed, finally telling me that she "will make king friend once more with Captain."

For the next six months I lived with the kind-hearted Kusis, his wife, and little daughter. Except for an occasional visit to the Captain or the king, nothing disturbed the pleasing monotony of my existence.

Why Kusis should have taken such a violent and wholly unreasonable attachment to me is a mystery I never could unravel. Yet such is island life. And how strange it is, and hard of comprehension! Women take their fancies here, as in other worlds (surely this is a world in itself, distinct, mystic, unreal), but the extraordinary point in the social system is, that men will, as a matter of mere caprice, conceive the most ardent friendship for an utter stranger. In pursuance of which passion they will entertain him for any time which he likes to stay; will guide, help, and defend him, risking, and indeed sacrificing their lives for him in the most reckless and devoted manner. Such was the deep and sudden affection of Kusis for me. How he acquired it I don't in the least know. All my personal property seemed to be mixed up with his. As the weather was not favourable for attention to detail, I preferred to leave things as they were. My life at this time was chiefly uneventful. Yet it was not always so. I was fishing one day near the end of the lagoon which extends from Utwé to the lee side of the island. After I had anchored my canoe a very strange incident indeed occurred.

The sun had just set, and I had cast out my hooks, and was able to fill my pipe, when I saw two boatsful of Pleasant islanders land on the narrow fringe of the north side of the lagoon. There were about twenty men and seven or eight women. I saw that they had with them a small keg, doubtless one of the kegs of rum which had been washed ashore, and which they had discovered in the mangroves. A fire was lit. The women began to sing and the men to dance; and as the fiery spirit was passed round in cocoa-nut shells to the men—for the women touched none—a wild orgie began.

Suddenly bright flashes appeared from out the darkness in the surrounding grove, and the reverberating echoes of gun-shots pealed over the water, and ran far back, from mountain, crag, and cave.

Three of the dancers fell, either killed or wounded. Then the dark forms of their previously unseen enemies appeared through the firelight. The white shells worn in strings round their necks told me that they were Ocean islanders, between whom and the Pleasant islanders feuds were of common occurrence. Then began a bloody hand-to-hand fight, the twilight silence being broken by yells of rage and screams of mortal agony. When the Ocean islanders were beaten off seven or eight bodies lay motionless on the ground.

I quietly pulled up the anchor, and let the canoe drift towards the mainland. I did not care about visiting the scene of the fight as I had no arms with me, and learnt by experience the folly of meddling with the Pleasant islanders when they were sober. When they were drunk I knew that they would as soon cut my throat as not.

I mentioned this matter to the Captain on my next visit. He told me with a grim smile that he knew there had been a fight up the lagoon; so much the better, as he found the Pleasant islanders harder to manage every day, and the sooner their number was reduced the better.

One day, when Kusis and I were coming across the lagoon with some pigeons I had shot, we met the Pingelap girl, Peloa, paddling a canoe furiously, her plump face showing great excitement. "She had been sent for us," she said, "by the Captain. There was a sail in sight. I was to hasten back to Moūt, where I would find a boat outside the reef which he had sent down for me. I was to try and board the ship, in case he could not do so from Utwé, and tell the master that a shipwrecked crew were on the island."

Peloa hauled her canoe up on a little beach, and got in with us. We three then paddled along till we got abreast of the two islets near Moūt. We then saw a whaleboat coming round the point with a lug sail. She soon ran in for me, and I found she was manned by Pleasant islanders, who told me that the ship was coming round the point, about three miles off the land.

There was a strong breeze, and we slipped through the water at a great rate so as to meet the ship. As soon as we cleared the point I saw her coming down before the wind about two miles distant.

She was a large ship, and was running straight for us with her yards squared. At first I thought she had seen us, but she kept steadily on her course. Then I saw her take in her light sails and heave to. Standing up in the boat, I could distinguish a whaleboat under a fore and aft sail close to her. Behind this boat were two others, which, from their black paint and peculiarly-cut sails, I knew to be those the Captain had at Utwé.

The ship lay to till the first whaleboat boarded her, and then, to my great surprise, the yards were swung round, the light sails again set, and she stood on her course, but kept the wind more on her quarter so as to make the most of the breeze.

By this time I had got almost within hailing distance of the ship. She was deep in the water, and was, I supposed, some coal-laden ship bound from New South Wales to China, which had taken the outside or easier route to her destination. When the whaleboat lowered her sail and ran alongside, I saw that she was the king's new boat, and contained but two men. These, my crew said, looked like the two deserters from the *St. George*. As soon as they got on board the boat was hoisted in without delay, and, as I have said, the ship kept on her course.

It was of no use attempting to overtake her, as she was travelling now about twelve knots, so I signalled for the other two boats, and they ran down after us till we got under the lee of the land again in smooth water.

The men in these boats told me the following tale: — About daylight that morning the king's whaleboat, which was anchored in Utwé harbour, was found to be missing. The two deserters from the *St. George* were also gone. Captain Hayston instantly offered to send his boat in pursuit of the runaways, and curiously, just as they were being launched, there came a cry of "Sail ho." The Captain then saw the ship a long way off, and told the crews to try and board her, and get her to run in close to the land, and that he would then come off himself. In the mean time he manned one of the trader's whaleboats with a native crew, and sent her round to Coquille to pick me up, as he fancied the ship would be easier boarded from there than from Utwé. The three boats left together, two standing right out to sea, and the other running down the coast to pick me up.

When the two boats were within three miles of the ship, they noticed the fore and aft sail of the king's whaleboat showing up now and then as she rose and sunk again in the heavy swell, and noticed that she was also heading to meet the ship. The rest I had observed myself.

I suspected something from the manner of the coxswain in charge of the king's two boats, but did not question him, and telling him to give the Captain full particulars of our endeavour to board the ship, I got ashore in a smooth part of the reef, and walked back to Moūt, where I found the villagers in a great state of excitement, under the impression that I had gone away in the ship.

Hayston afterwards admitted that he had supplied the deserters with sextant, compass, and chart, had also given them provisions, and fifty dollars in money. They promised him to make straight for Ponapé, and wait there till some Californian ship called, which they would endeavour to charter, on the part of Hayston, to beat up to Strong's Island, and take us all away to Providence Island. Barney was a good navigator, and could he only have kept fairly sober would have long since had a ship of his own. He eagerly accepted the Captain's offer, and the next morning the crew of the king's whaleboat found she had disappeared; then followed the strange series of events by which Barney and his mate got on board the ship and evaded pursuit.

Barney was a highly intelligent individual, as the sequel will show, and was capable of making a rapid calculation of probabilities. He afterwards visited Samoa, and gave this account of his escape.

He said that when the Captain provided him with "a jewel of a whaleboat," he honestly intended to fulfil his promises. He lost some time in trying to persuade a native girl named Luta to share his fortunes, but she was afraid of a long voyage in a small boat. His pleadings, moreover, were cut short by the Captain, who told him to hurry up, and get out of the harbour before daylight.

As soon, then, as Barney sighted the ship a plan suggested itself to him. Once on deck he introduced himself to the Captain as "Captain Casey," and said, "For heaven's sake, sir, don't delay another moment. There are two boat-loads of bloody, cut-throat pirates coming after me, and they mane to take the ship! Have you never heard of 'Bully Hayston'?"

The skipper *had* heard of him,—things true, and untrue likewise. Then Barney told him a tale of how the *Leonora* had been wrecked on the island, and that ever since the fierce Captain and crew had planned to cut off the first ship that touched at the island—that he (Barney) and his mate had owned a small trading cutter, which Hayston had seized two days ago—but that he had managed to escape with one of his men, and thanked God that he was able to reach the ship in time, and save every one's throat from being cut.

The ship's captain took all this in; Barney's boat was hoisted in, and the ship kept away. The two boats, with their crews of excited natives yelling and shouting, gave colour to Barney's narrative, and when he pointed to my boat, and said, "Holy saints! there's another of the villains coming out under the lee side with a boat-load of pirates too," the captain's funk was complete. He landed Barney and his companion at Ponapé, and, purely out of compassion, bought the king's whaleboat and her contents for a hundred dollars, so that Mr. Barney landed there with a hundred and fifty dollars in his pocket, and got a free passage later on to Manila as a distressed American seaman.

The Captain took matters philosophically when the boats returned, saying that he never had expected to see Barney again. After which he resumed his oil-making and the government of his "kingdom by the sea" as usual.

As for me, my life was a quiet, deeply enjoyable one. I began at times to doubt whether I should ever wish to change it. But against this phase of lotus-eating contentment arose from time to time a haunting dread, lest by evil chance I should ever sink down into the position of those renegades from civilisation, whom I had known, in the strange world of "The Islands," and as often pitied or despised. In this Robinson Crusoe existence I even felt a mild interest in the three cattle that we had landed at Utwé.

They had found their way over to the lee side of the island, and made their way along the beach to Moūt.

One day little Kinie met them, and, with hair flying loose and eyes dilated in an agony of terror, fled wildly home. She explained to me incoherently "that she had met three huge pigs, with, long teeth growing out of their heads and eyes as big as cocoa-nuts."

Kusis and I, with some natives, went out and found them walking slowly along the beach. At the sound of my voice they stopped and let me come up to them, smelling me all over. I had only a mat round my waist, for my European clothes were only worn on great occasions; but they evidently knew me for a different being to those around them. We drove them to a rich piece of meadow land, where they remained during the rest of my stay on the island—fat, quiet, and contented.

Early one morning I made ready for a start back to Coquille harbour, and found Kusis awaiting me in the king's courtyard.

Shortly after the queen came out and told me that I must wait for breakfast, or the king would be offended. Old Tokusar then appeared, none the worse for the night's potations, and we sat down to a very good breakfast.

He told me that he had intended to go and see the Captain's village at Utwé, but that Likiak Sâ, had dissuaded him by telling him that Hayston would seize and imprison him.

I assured the king that this was a pure invention, upon which both he and the queen said they would take my word before that of Likiak Sâ, and from the kindness of the king and his subjects at Chabral harbour, I felt certain that my intercession with Hayston on behalf of the villages at Coquille had placed me high in their regard.

The queen pointed to a pile of beautiful mats, quantities of cooked fowls, pigeons, pork, fish, and fruit, which were being carried in and deposited in the courtyard, telling me that they were presents from the king and herself, and would be taken down to Moūt for me by native carriers.

As I was bidding my royal friends good-bye, promising to come and see them whenever I got tired of Moūt, Kitty of Ebon came in, and quite bore out the description Hayston had given me of her remarkable beauty. She seemed a very intelligent girl, and was much admired by the king, who kept nudging me, and saying in his wheezy, croaking voice, "Um, ah! What you tink girl like that?"

He then fell into moody silence, upon which Queen Sê gave him a scornful glance, exclaiming, "For shame! old man like you, sick all the time, look so much at young girl like Kitty Ebon! Captain Hayston teach you all that."

I learnt from Kitty that Lālia was then at her house on a visit, and, telling the king and queen of her kindness to me when I was ill at Utwé, said I should like to go and see her, as Kitty's house lay in the direction Kusis and I were taking. The queen generously gave me a small work-box, with the necessary fittings, which she said I could give to Lālia. It was quite a handsome affair, and had been given to the queen by a ship captain; but she had never used it. Shaking hands with Tokusar and Queen Sê, we set out on our journey, Kusis leading the way, Kitty of Ebon and I following, and the carriers in the rear.

Kitty was very lively, and startlingly simple in manner. She made me laugh at her description of the flirtations of Captain Hayston and the queen when he had visited Strong's Island three years before in company with Captain Ben Peese. For a missionary's housekeeper Kitty of Ebon was something unique, and her lively sallies kept me amused in her excellent English all the way. I was pleased to see Lālia, who was looking as beautiful as ever. Indeed, it was hard to say which was the handsomer, she or the hostess.

I gave her the work-box, which seemed to please her very much. Then Kitty proposed a game of cards, saying it was all right, as we need not play for money, and no one would tell Mr. Morland. But I had to decline, and, saying good-bye to them with some regrets, I rejoined Kusis, much wondering inwardly whether Lālia, with her sad, bright eyes, soft voice, and gentle manner, could really have been the perpetrator of the cruel deed in the mountain forest of Utwé.

CHAPTER XII

"MY LORDS OF THE ADMIRALTY"

In October I received another letter from the Captain, asking me to meet him in Chabral harbour. He had become so tired of waiting for a ship that he had decided to start in a boat for Millé. He had effected a reconciliation with the king, and was paying him a friendly visit. He meant to arrange with him regarding the people and the management of the station at Utwé during his absence.

I left Moūt at daylight, and, as I said good-bye to Tulpé and the little daughter, how little I thought that I should never cross their hospitable threshold again!

Kusis came with me, and we took the route by the weather side of the island, reaching Lêlé in the afternoon. On my way to the king's house we came across a number of women catching shrimps in the rivulet that runs into Chabral harbour, and among them were Kitty of Ebon and Lālia.

These two called to us to stop, as they had news for me. Coming out of the water, they threw off their wet clothes and put on dry ones. Then the four of us sat down on a low coral wall under the shade of some trees.

Kitty of Ebon began the conversation by saying that the Captain had arrived the night before, and had a long talk with the king, whom he told that he was going to try and reach Millé in the largest of the ship's boats, though he would have to contend against the north-east trades the whole way. He wished the king to become responsible for the management and safety of the station of Utwé.

This the king didn't see his way to do, as he could never control the Pleasant islanders. The remaining white men at Chabral harbour would regain their control over them as soon as Hayston had left; that it was not wise of the Captain to attempt to reach Millé.

He also showed great fear of being punished if the Captain came back and found his station pillaged.

Kitty of Ebon, who was present at the interview, further narrated that the king, finding that Hayston was bent on setting out for Millé, made another proposal to the Captain, who had accepted it on the condition that I would concur. This was that all the oil, boats, and stores, with the women, should be conveyed to Chabral harbour and put under the king's protection, who professed then to be anxious that I should come and live with him in case the traders made an attack on him, and tried to seize the property or carry off the women.

Both Kitty and Lālia urged me not to do this, for, they said, "as soon as the Captain goes away there will be fighting here; the king is weak, and the traders do not fear him. Besides, they are plotting with Likiak Sâ, the missionary, who has promised them to win the king over. They say that you and Black Johnny are the only two men that will stand by the Captain's property when guns and knives are out, as young Harry is to stay at Utwé till the Captain returns."

I inquired of the girls what the traders proposed doing with me?

"Shoot you, Black Johnny, and young Harry. Then, when the Captain is once away, they will be strong enough, and the king will not interfere with them."

Lālia then told me that one of the trader's wives had told her that they had arranged to have us three shot by some of their natives as soon as the Captain had left for Millé. The girls again urged me not to comply with the king's request, and to dissuade Hayston from his intended voyage. Indeed, they tried to prevent me from going to the king at all, Kitty urging me to come to her house, and write a letter to the Captain asking him to meet me there.

The thought of the Captain being a victim, as well as myself and young Harry, to such treachery decided me in an instant, and breaking away from the women, Kusis and I soon reached the king's house.

The traders who were living at Chabral kept carefully within doors. When I reached the courtyard of the king's house I found no one there but His Majesty and Likiak Sâ engaged in earnest conversation. The native missionary glanced uneasily at me, and I at once opened out on him by calling him a treacherous dog, striking him at the same time, and threatening him with the Captain's vengeance. He picked himself up and left.

"Where is the Captain?" I said to the king.

"In my oil-shed," he answered in a troubled voice.

But I said nothing to him, and, finding Hayston, shortly made him acquainted with what I had learnt from Kitty of Ebon. His face darkened as he strode off to the king.

At that moment the natives called out that there was a vessel in sight, upon which he turned back, and together we walked to the beach in time to see a fine fore and aft schooner sailing in, which Hayston declared was the *Matautu*, belonging to Captain Warner.

"He would never have ventured in if he knew I was here," quoth the Captain grimly; "and if I had a few of my boys he'd never go out again, unless the schooner had a new master."

I reasoned with him against the folly of such an action, when he said that he would use fair means at first, and would try and charter the *Matautu*. He then went to the king, and I could see meant mischief. I was glad to notice the traders getting into canoes and making for the schooner, where they no doubt thought they would be safe, as Hayston had only two native boys with him, and would hardly attempt to tackle the schooner single-handed.

Likiak Sâ was again with the king when we returned. However, he ran away at once, narrowly missing a chair which the Captain threw at him. Old Tokusar seemed scared, as he watched the Captain's darkening face. He inquired in a shaking voice, "Why you so much angry?"

"Because," answered the Captain, "the men who have been living on my food have been plotting against me, and that scheming missionary is at the bottom of it; but look you, King Tokusar, and mark my words well! If I suspect you, too, I will burn your house and town, and drown you like a rat in your own turtle pond!"

"Captain," I said, "what folly! You are here almost alone, and all but in the power of your enemies. Return to the boats and get back to Utwé."

He calmed down almost immediately, and said he would see Captain Warner. He asked me to come with him. I mentioned the fact of the traders being on board the ship, and urged him to be cautious.

We got in the boats, and pulled towards the schooner. Before we were half-way across the Captain laughed contemptuously, and pointed to the traders, who were already leaving the schooner's side in canoes, and making rapidly for the western side of the harbour.

Captain Warner seemed under great excitement when we stepped on deck, but the cordial manner of Hayston's greeting at once reassured him, so that we were received most politely and asked below.

Captain Warner seemed so intensely amiable that I could hardly help laughing, and as he kept his glass constantly filled, or rather emptied, his amiability increased proportionately.

In the course of conversation a discussion arose as to some business transactions with Hayston while we were at Ponapé, and the skipper laughingly remarked that he had over-reached him in the matter. The Captain, who was now perfectly calm, gave a pleasantly-worded denial, and said, "No, Captain Warner, I think my supercargo must have got to windward of *you* there."

A quarrel ensued forthwith. The burly skipper became offensive, and it ended in our agreeing to meet with pistols on the beach at daylight next morning.

However, at dawn the *Matautu* had towed out with the first breath of the land-breeze, and was already outside the passage standing to the westward. So the duel did not come off. I honestly think the skipper was not afraid, but I suspect he decided not to risk another encounter with Hayston, and so thought discretion was the better part of valour.

Next day we again heard the stirring cry of "Sail ho!" The new arrival was the *Morning Star* from Honolulu, from which about ten o'clock landed the Rev. Mr. Morland—a portly, white bearded old gentleman, who at once made his way to his residence, while the Captain and I returned to South harbour. Kusis went home, with a promise from me to follow him next day, the honest fellow begging me to delay as little as possible.

It was dark when we started, and a fierce black squall struck us just after we got out of the passage, nearly capsizing the boat. The Captain thought we had better return, but I was anxious to get back to Moūt, and said I was sure the squall would not last. So we reefed the sail and dashed out to sea close-hauled, for the squall came from the westward, and was dead against us. However, the wind continued to increase, and the little boat shipped two or three heavy seas. So we agreed to turn back.

We went about in a lull, and had made the entrance to the passage, as we thought, when the Captain called out, "Look out! here comes a sea!"

Looking back, I saw a huge black roller almost on top of us. The next minute I felt we had touched. I shouted, "By Jove! we're not in the passage at all—it's only a creek in the reef. Jump out, quick!"

We all sprang out of the boat on to the jagged coral, then the waves, poised high in air, dashed down upon us, and we were all washed clear over into a pool of smooth water. The boat was capsized, and with broken masts and oars gone, was swept in far ahead of us, till she disappeared in the darkness. We clung to the reef as best we could, and succeeded in reaching a coral "mushroom" that was just a wash. "We'll be all right here," said the Captain, in his cool, cheerful way; "are you boys all right?"—the two native boys were, like ourselves, cut about the arms and legs by the coral. But they thought nothing of that. What they dreaded were the *sharks*!

Fortunately the tide was falling, and the coral knoll was gradually showing more of its surface above the water. Otherwise none of us would have reached the shore; for in these deep water passages the sharks literally swarm.

A sea occasionally broke close to us, but not with sufficient force to wash any of us away. Suddenly the Captain said, "Boys, I see some people fishing ashore with torches," and he gave a resounding hail. An answer came back, and, what was more to the purpose, a canoe, in which we were rescued from our precarious position and taken ashore. The boat was searched for, and found drifting out to sea. But as long as I live I shall never forget the horrible feeling of standing on that coral knoll, in the wave-washed darkness, knowing that if we were once dislodged there was no chance of escaping the sharks. We were all good swimmers, but the Kusaie natives told us that the passage of Chabral harbour was swarming with the dreaded reef-shark, that seeks its prey, chiefly turtle, in the foam and swirl of the breakers on the reef. We slept that night in a native house, some distance from the village of Lêlé, and at daylight proceeded along the beach to the king's house. The old king did not appear; the queen was very hospitable to us, but seemed nervous and constrained in her manner to the Captain. Once when I was standing apart from him, she said in a low tone that I had better return to Moūt, where I would be safe, adding, "Don't stay along with Captain. Man-of-war come from Honolulu to take him away. By and by I tell him."

I afterwards regretted that I did not attach more importance to her warning, and tell the Captain; subsequent events showed that both the king and queen had been informed by Mr. Morland of the impending arrival of a man-of-war, which had been searching for Hayston for months previously. Later in the day, while the Captain was superintending repairs to the boat, Mr. Morland and the native colleague were announced. The white missionary requested to see the Captain. I may mention, that during our cruise to the north-west in the *Leonora* we had occasionally met with the missionary brig, *Morning Star*, and had been visited by Mr. Morland once or twice.

On this occasion he met us with the usual smile and outstretched hand.

"How do you do, Captain Hayston? I am glad—very glad to see you, and yet sorry; for you have my sincere sympathy for the loss of your beautiful vessel."

"Morland!" came the quick reply, "you know you are lying most infernally. You are no more pleased to see me than I am to see you. Our interests are too antagonistic for us to take kindly to each other. So let us at least be candid!"

"Oh! Captain Hayston!" rejoined Mr. Morland, "you terribly unkind man! Why must you hate the poor parson so? Oh! my friend, my countryman, let us shake hands as fellow-Christians should do when they meet in these lonely, beautiful spots of God's bright universe!"

Hayston smiled, but if he had but known that Mr. Morland was, even then, anxiously looking for the tall spars of one of Her Majesty's warships, and had actually been in communication with her captain a few days previously, he would possibly have half-strangled his pleasant-mannered visitor then and there.

After a short chat the missionary returned to the king's house with the Captain, while I busied myself with the repairs of the boat, when the startling cry of "Sail ho!" rang through the quiet village. I ran up to the king's house, and found the Captain in the courtyard playing a game of dominoes with Queen Sê.

The missionary and Likiak Sâ were just coming out from an interview with the king. The air of exultation on their faces as they saw the natives hurrying to and fro at the cry of "Sail ho!" struck me at once.

The Captain sprang up at once, and said, "Let us take the boat and go out to her, she may want a pilot"; and we walked through the house to the stone wharf that abutted on one side of the king's establishment. We jumped into the boat, and with a crew of four natives pulled quickly out of the passage. On gaining the open we could see no sail, and concluded that the ship must be coming round the north-eastern side of the island, where she had been sighted by the natives. We then set sail, and commenced beating to windward, and about half-an-hour afterwards, as the little boat rode on the swell, we got a sight of the lofty masts and square yards of a man-of-war under steam, as she rounded the high land on the north-east side of the island.

With a sudden exclamation the Captain stood up and gazed at the steamer. He then seated himself

and seemed lost in thought. The great vessel came steadily on, then altered her course by a couple of points, and steered in the direction of the passage. I could see that she was under a full head of steam, and was travelling at a great rate. A volume of thick smoke was issuing from the yellow funnel, and as there is always a heavy sea off

A Modern Buccaneer

the windward side of Strong's Island she rolled tremendously, the water pouring from her black painted sides in sheets.

The Captain watched her intently. "That's a man-of-war, Hilary! and a Britisher too," he said. "Though she may be an American—the *Portsmouth* or the *Jamestown*; I can't tell with that smoke blowing ahead of her. If she's an American cruiser, she'll take me prisoner right enough. It's no use attempting to escape now. It's too late; I must take my chance. In that case you must get away to Utwé as quick as possible, and do the best you can with the station and the people. You know where the money is stowed away, and what to do with it if we are fated not to meet again."

As he said these words the smoke cleared away from the cruiser, and we had a splendid view of her as she rose majestically to a heavy sea, and fell gracefully into the trough again. "A Britisher, by ——!" exclaimed the Captain, "and a beauty too; give way, my lads, she's stopped her engines. Let us get aboard, and I'll soon learn what's in store for me."

In order that it may be understood what reason the Captain had for these strong suspicions of arrest and imprisonment, I will here make quotation from the *Queensland Government Gazette*, an official journal of severely correct character, which, like "the *Apparatus*, cannot lie."

COLONIAL SECRETARY'S OFFICE,
BRISBANE, 20th August 1875.

His Excellency directs the subjoined circular despatch received from the Secretary of State for the Colonies, together with the enclosed correspondence with the Board of Admiralty, respecting the proceedings in the South Seas of W. H. Hayston, a United States' subject, and master of the American brig *Leonora*, to be published in the *Gazette* for general information.

A. MACALISTER.

The Admiralty to the Colonial Office.

ADMIRALTY, 12th January 1875.

Sir,—I am commanded by the my Lords Commissioners of the Admiralty to transmit herewith, for the information of the Earl of Carnarvon, a letter and its enclosures from Commodore Goodenough, Senior Naval Officer of the Australasian Station, reporting the proceedings of W. H. Hayston, a citizen of the United States, and master of the late American brig *Leonora*. It is requested that these papers be returned in order that they may be sent to the Foreign Office.—I am, etc.

(Signed) Robert Hall.

The Under Secretary of State,
Colonial Office.

Admiral Cochrane to the Admiralty.

Repulse at Callao, *28th February 1875*.

Sir,—I have the honour to forward for the information of their Lordships a copy of correspondence which I have received from Commodore Goodenough, commanding the Australian Station.

2. The correspondence has reference to the very irregular conduct of a master of a trading brig lately wrecked. The master is believed to be an American.

3. Commodore Goodenough requested that the documents containing evidence tending to substantiate the charges against the said master should be forwarded to the American admiral commanding the North Pacific Station. The islands where the occurrences referred to took place are not included in the Pacific Station.—I am, etc.

(Signed) A. A. Cochrane.

Rear Admiral and Commander-in-Chief.

H.M.S. *Repulse*,
Callao, *28th February 1875*.

Sir,—I have the honour to forward for your perusal copies of correspondence I have received from Commodore Goodenough in command of H.M. ships on the Australian Station, relative to the highly irregular proceedings of a master of a vessel trading among the South Sea Islands. He is believed to be an American citizen.

I should be much gratified if circumstances enable you to cause inquiry into the subject of the charges enumerated.—I have, etc.

(Signed) A. A. COCHRANE.

Rear Admiral and Commander-in-Chief.

Circular.

DOWNING STREET, *13th May 1875.*

SIR,—I have the honour to transmit to you copies of a correspondence with the Board of Admiralty respecting the proceedings in the South Seas of W. H. Hayston, a United States' subject, and master of the late American brig *Leonora*. In connection with the lawless conduct of Hayston, as reported in the papers now transmitted, I beg to refer you to my predecessor's Circular Despatch of 22nd December 1875, relating to the proceedings in the case of the *Atlantic*, and I desire to express my entire concurrence in the hope expressed by Lord Kimberley, that no opportunity may be lost of bringing the man to trial.—I have, etc.

CARNARVON.

To the Officer administering the
Government of Queensland.

Proceedings of H.M.S. *Rosario* in the South Sea Islands. Criminal acts of Mr. W. H. Hayston, master of the brig *Leonora*.

H.M.S. *Pearl, 16th November 1874.*

SIR,—I have the honour to enclose for the information of the Lords Commissioners of the Admiralty, a Report and various papers furnished to me by Commander Dupont of H.M.S. *Rosario*, concerning a Mr. William H. Hayston, master of the late American brig *Leonora*.

2. This Mr. Hayston has long been known among the Pacific Islands as a collector of produce, and has the reputation of defrauding natives and lifting produce collected by other traders. He has been spoken of in correspondence between this and the Chinese Station as

"the notorious Captain Hayston," but hitherto no evidence on which he could be convicted of any piratical act has been brought before me.

3. It seemed possible that Commander Dupont, while cruising in H.M.S. *Rosario* among the Gilbert and Ellice Islands, and watching the labour traffic, might be able to gather some evidence which would enable him to detain this person, who is doing much harm among the islands. A copy of my orders to Commander Dupont is enclosed.

4. Commander Dupont seems only to have obtained the evidence which he desired against Hayston after he had learned of his escape, and he is satisfied from inspection of Hayston's papers that he is an American citizen.

5. Commander Dupont brought away with him from Strong's Island the crew of Hayston's vessel, the *Leonora*, which was wrecked there in March last, and also one Hilary Telfer, who had proceeded from Samoa to Millé as supercargo of a vessel called the *E. A. Wilson*, and belonging to the sons and daughters of Mr. Wilson, H.M. Consul from Samoa.

6. This Mr. Telfer carried with him from Samoa orders from Mr. Wilson to put the *E. A. Wilson* and the cargo into Hayston's hands to be sold, and in course of business appears to have become so mixed up in Hayston's affairs, that the latter made him his agent and entrusted him with letters to all his subordinate agents, informing them that he had been seized by the *Rosario* for conveyance to Sydney.

7. I was in Samoa in H.M.S. *Pearl* in November 1873. The ketch *E. A. Wilson* was then there under repairs. Mr. S. D. Wilson told me nothing of his intentions regarding the vessel, but gave me to understand that Mr. Hayston was a great rascal, who had cleverly outwitted all inquiries. He offered to obtain evidence from a half-caste, and at my desire took the statements (which proved valueless) on oath. Yet on December 3, 1873, he enters into communication with this man, against whom he had pretended to give me information.

8. I consider the whole affair as most unsatisfactory, even regarding Mr. Wilson as a trader. In the position of Her Majesty's Acting

A Modern Buccaneer

Consul, I consider that he has been guilty of improper behaviour, rendering him unworthy to occupy such a position. The desirability of appointing a non-trading Consul in Samoa has already been pointed out by both myself and my predecessor on this Station.

9. The papers I enclose concerning Hayston will illustrate the life of a modern South-Sea filibuster.—I have the honour to be, your obedient servant,

JAMES G. GOODENOUGH,
Captain and Commodore, 2nd Class,
Commanding Australian Station.

To the Secretary.

Enclosure No. 2.

H.M.S. *Rosario*,
AT SEA, Lat. 2° 26' N., Long. 167° 19' E.,
10th October 1874.

SIR,—With reference to Mr. Hayston, master of the American brig *Leonora*, I beg to forward the following statement of facts relative to him that I have been able to collect among the different islands visited during my present cruise:—

1. There can be no doubt but that Mr. Hayston is a shrewd, unprincipled man, who has committed acts of violence towards the natives, and been guilty of unjustifiable acts towards other persons. Yet, so greatly has his name got to be feared, by both natives and white men on the islands, that, though it was evident that at nearly all the islands I visited he was well known, it was impossible to find out much about him.

2. With respect to Mr. Dunn's business, what evidence I could get was mainly in Hayston's favour, and tended to show that Dunn's agents had sold the trade to Hayston instead of his taking it. This is certainly the case as regards an Englishman named George Winchcombe, whom I found living on Nukufutau, one of the Ellice group. He himself stated to me that he left Sydney with Dunn, in the understanding that he was to be found at a station on one of the islands. He complained that Dunn treated him badly on board, and eventually sent him on shore on the island of Apaiari (Gilbert group)

to collect trade. He was dissatisfied with his life, much in dread of the natives, and on Hayston's coming there in the beginning of 1873, he begged him to take him off the island, and offered to sell him all the trade he had collected. Hayston accordingly took him. At another island, Tarawa, the only white resident had heard that some trade had been removed by Hayston, but was not on the island at the time. At other islands I heard things relative to Dunn's property, but could get nothing but hearsay evidence. I could not find a single individual, either white or native, who could furnish me with any positive evidence or proof against Hayston.

On entering Chabral harbour (Strong's Island) Mr. Hayston, as I have reported in my letter of proceedings, came out to meet the ship in a boat. He told that his vessel had been wrecked in South harbour of the island on the 15th of March this year, since which date he had been living on shore collecting oil.

Mr. Morland, an American missionary, who had just arrived from Ebon Island, and numerous white men—the late crew of the *Leonora*—were also there. A schooner under the German flag, Mr. Miller an Englishman master, lay in the harbour. I commenced making inquiries as quietly as possible about Hayston, but here, as at other places, I met with disinclination from all traders to tell me anything they might know; Mr. Miller, though hinting that Hayston had robbed him not long since, would at first say nothing, nor was it till after considerable persuasion and the delay of some days that I got the enclosed statement, with the various witnesses in the matter, from him.

But as he was sailing under German colours, I could not believe my duty was to do more than receive the statements and forward it through you to the German Consul in Sydney.

Hayston, apprised by some of the crew of the inquiries that had been made, left the island in a boat on the night of the 27th. His design was, I believe, either to make the island of Ascension or that of Pingelap. At their own request, and also considering it a good thing for the island to be rid of them, I took five of the crew of the *Leonora* on board for passage to Sydney, and also one other person who had been a passenger on board, and also, from what I could hear, a great friend of Hayston. This Hilary Telfer was the person who had been sent by Mr. Wilson, British Consul at Samoa, as supercargo of the ketch that I met at Millé, but leaving his charge there, had gone to sea with Hayston and been with him since January. I deemed it advisable that he should be removed, there being no chance of his getting back to Millé from Strong's Island, and also because the chief particularly desired his removal, as being likely to stir up trouble in the island. These six persons are now on board.

I visited Mr. Hayston's residence at South harbour; he had made a regular settlement of it, and had collected a large quantity of oil. No less than five young women were living in his house, who had all with one exception been living on board the *Leonora*. That vessel was sunk in fourteen fathoms, her topmast head a few feet above water.

The first mate I left on the island, recommending him to take charge of Hayston's property. The second mate, William Hicks, ran away into the bush and couldn't be found, otherwise I should have taken him to Sydney with the others. Thinking the case over quietly afterwards, I cannot see how I could have arrested Hayston. It is, therefore, with great regret that I am obliged to report my failure to collect sufficient evidence against him to warrant my doing so. The case of Mr. Dunn must have failed from want of such evidence. —I have, etc., etc.

A. E. DUPONT,
Commander.

To Commodore J. G. Goodenough,
H.M.S. *Pearl*.

Enclosure No. 13.

MESSRS. MILLER AND WARNE TO MR. HILARY TELFER, SUPERCARGO.

DEAR SIR,—You will proceed from hence to Millé, Mulgrave Island, for the purpose of selling the ketch *A.E.W.* You will find Captain Hayston there waiting for you, so you will please consult with him, as he is acquainted with the people who wish to purchase the ketch. Try to obtain oil or copra to the amount of £500 for her. Ship whatever produce you may get on board the *Leonora*, and get Captain Hayston to sign bills of lading. Do not sell the chronometer unless you get a good price for it. Sell the few things you take to the best advantage. None of the Samoans are to remain, but to come back to Apia. Have the ketch painted at Millé.—Wishing you a prosperous and speedy voyage, we are, etc.,

(Signed) MILLER AND WARNE.

Enclosure No. 15.

Know all men by these presents that I, William Henry Hayston, Master mariner, now residing on Strong's Island, in the North Pacific Ocean, have made, constituted, and appointed Hilary Telfer, of Sydney, New South Wales, at present residing on this island of Kusaie (or Strong's Island), to be my true and lawful agent for me, and, in my place and stead, to enter into and take possession of my station situated at Maloe, near the village of Utwé, South harbour, on the above-named island. Also all my oil, casks, tobacco, and other trade which may be on said station. Also boats, canoe, pigs, fowls, possessions—all and everything, whether of value or not, together with my furniture and private effects, and to take full charge of all my business on the above-named island during my trip to the eastward.

(Signed) W. H. HAYSTON,
In the presence of the undersigned witness,
this 19th August 1874.

(Signed) CHARLES ROBERTS.

Enclosure No. 16.

MEMORANDUM OF INSTRUCTIONS FOR MR. HILARY TELFER.

SIR,—As I am about to leave Strong's Island, and have given you power to act on my behalf, I wish you to close up all my affairs in the best manner you can. You will look after the property I leave behind, and dispose of it to the best advantage. Out of the remainder of the oil you can pay yourself for the chronometer, and Mr. Harry Skillings for the trade I had from him. Sell the balance, including the large cargo-boat, as soon as an opportunity offers. Anything left over you can give to the people that have been kind to you, and the natives. Out of the proceeds of the sale you can pay for the passage of my natives to Samoa, if they want to go there. If not, see them back on their own island, or on some of the Kingsmill group, that they may get with their own country people.

My native boy Toby I wish you to take to Samoa, and look after him as well as you can; also Kitty, as they have no father or mother. Both were given to me by the king of Hope Island. The stores I left behind are for you and the natives to live on till you can get away. Be careful of the little trade I leave you, as the Strong's islanders want payment for everything you get of them to eat. You will also bear in mind that the king owes me 12,100 cocoa-nuts, the balance of the 48,000 that he agreed to pay me for the property stolen by the Strong's islanders at the time of the loss of the brig.

I write an accompanying letter to each of my agents. You will have to settle with them by their own accounts, as my trade-book was lost, as you know. The balance, after paying for your own passage and expense, you can hand over to my agent at Samoa.—Wishing you a safe arrival there and every success, I remain, yours in good faith,

(Signed) W. H. HAYSTON.

Circular.

DOWNING STREET, *31st May 1875*.

SIR,—With reference to my circular despatch of 13th instant, I have the honour to transmit to you the accompanying copy of a note addressed by the Duc de Decazes to Her Majesty's Minister at Paris, in consequence of the communication on the subject of the lawless proceedings of W. H. Hayston in the South Seas, which the Earl of Derby caused to be made to the French Government, also those of Germany and the United States.—I am, etc.,

CARNARVON.

The Officer Administering
the Government of Queensland.

THE DUC DE DECAZES TO MR. ADAMS.

(Copy.)

PARIS, *le 10 mai 1875*.

M. LE MINISTRE,—J'ai porté à la connaissance de mon collègue les informations que vous m'avez fait l'honneur de me transmettre, relativement à un personnage dangereux, du nom de Hayston, qui se serait signalé par de nombreux actes de déprédation dans les Iles de l'Océanie. M. l'Amiral de Montaigne répondant à ma communication m'annonce qu'il signalera par le premier courrier cet individu au Commandant en Chef de notre division navale dans l'Océan Pacifique. Il adressera en outre à M. l'Amiral Rebout les instructions nécessaires pour que ce flibustier Psoit surveillé de près et mis, le cas échéant, hors d'état de poursuivre son industrie criminelle.—Agréez, etc.,

(Signed) DUC DE DECAZES.

M. Adams.

CHAPTER XIII

H.M.S. ROSARIO

As we pulled up alongside we saw her bulwarks forward crowded with the blue-jackets. The Captain's quick eye, which nothing escaped, detected among them the bronzed faces of Dan Gardiner and another trader whom he had left at Providence Island.

"She's come to take me, sure enough," he said to me. "The moment I looked at those two fellows they dropped back out of sight. Never mind, come aboard and I'll see it through."

As soon as we gained the deck he advanced towards a group of officers standing on the quarter-deck, and, raising his hat, said, "Good morning, gentlemen. I am Captain Hayston of the brig *Leonora*, cast away on this island in the earlier part of the year."

There was a moment's silence; then a tall man, the captain of the cruiser, stepped out from the others, surveyed Hayston from head to foot, and said, "Oh, ah, indeed! then you are the very man I am looking for. This is Her Majesty's ship *Rosario*, and you are a prisoner, Mr. Hayston!"

Hayston simply bowed and said nothing, retiring to the port side, where he was placed under the charge of the sergeant-major of marines, who, as also all others on board, looked with intense curiosity at the man of whose doings they had heard so much in their cruises in the Pacific Ocean.

The man-of-war captain then demanded my name, after which I was considerably staggered by the announcement that he had instructions to apprehend me on the charge of stealing the ketch *E. A. Wilson*, the property of Messrs. Miller and Warne of Samoa.

Hayston at once came forward, and, addressing the captain, said that I had simply brought that vessel to him at Millé, and could produce written instructions from the owners to hand the vessel over to him. To this no answer was returned, and silence was maintained, for the *Rosario* was now entering the passage, and so interested was I at the novel surroundings of a man-of-war under steam, and so lost in admiration of the perfect discipline on board, that for the time being I forgot that the Captain of the *Leonora* was a prisoner, and that I was also apprehended on a serious charge.

Slowly and gracefully the great ship steamed through the passage, and brought up within a cable's length of the king's wharf, where the anchor plunged below to its resting-place on the coral bottom. No sooner had the man-of-war come to anchor than Mr. Morland and the native missionary, who followed him like a shadow, came on board, and were received by Her Majesty's representative. A consultation took place, after which I was separated from my companion, and, without being able to exchange a word of farewell, was hurried down to the gun-room. As I placed my foot on the ladder leading to the "'tween decks" I turned. He waved his hand to me in farewell. *We never met again!*

While I was detained in the gun-room a midshipman told me that Captain Hayston had been permitted to go on shore, under the charge of an officer, to collect his personal effects and write letters, as he had been informed that I would not be permitted to have any further communication with him.

The midshipman said that Mr. Morland had seemed surprised at Captain Hayston's not being put in irons, and was at that moment collecting evidence in order to formulate a series of charges against him before the captain of the *Rosario*. My informant added, "If Captain Hayston is such a blood-thirsty ruffian as he is described to be he certainly shows no indication of it."

Several of the warrant officers now gathered around and pressed me with questions concerning Hayston. One of them jocularly inquired where the Captain's harem was located, adding that it was a pity to separate him from them, and that there was plenty of room on board the *Rosario* for ladies.

I was burning with anxiety to know on what particular charge Hayston had been arrested, and how the captain of the *Rosario* had heard of the loss of the *Leonora*. They told me then that the *Rosario* had been searching for Hayston for some time, under instructions from the Commodore of the Australian Station, to whom representations had been made concerning alleged depredations committed by him (Hayston) in the Line Islands. The *Rosario* had visited a number of islands, and endeavoured to obtain evidence against Hayston, but that it had resulted in a failure, nearly every one, when it came to the point, declining to make any statement against him. The captain of the man-of-war then decided to proceed to Arrecifos, or Providence Island, which he knew to be one of Hayston's depôts. On arrival he learned from the two white men there that so long an interval had passed since his last visit that they fancied that the *Leonora* had been lost.

These two men were taken on board, and the *Rosario* made for Strong's Island. When within 400 miles she met the little *Matautu*, who signalled a wish to speak. As soon as Captain Warner boarded the man-of-war he informed the commander of the loss of the *Leonora*, and of Hayston's presence on the island. He also handed in several written charges made by himself against Hayston, and, as well as I can remember from what I was told, was about to return to his schooner when the *Morning Star* hove in sight.

On board of the missionary brig was Mr. Morland, and a consultation then took place between the two captains and this gentleman, who was, of course, delighted to hear of the loss of the *Leonora*, and that Captain Hayston was to be taken prisoner.

The *Matautu* then bore away on her course, and the *Morning Star*, after landing Mr. Morland at the weather side of the island, went on her way, leaving him ashore, perfectly assured of his own safety and the immediate presence of the *Rosario* in Chabral harbour.

I could now understand the hints given me by the queen, as well as the expression of triumph on the faces of the missionaries as they returned from their interview with the king.

Presently an officer came down and asked me if I wished to obtain my effects from the shore. I at once sent a message to Kusis to bring me a small chest, in which were my worldly goods, as well as my power of attorney and letters of instructions from former employers in Samoa. I was going to make inquiries about Hayston, when the officer requested me kindly enough not to ask him questions, as he could give me no information. He told me, however, that the captain of the *Rosario* was at that moment engaged in hearing charges against Hayston made by the king, Mr. Morland, and two or three of the traders from Pleasant Island. Also that some of the crew of the *Leonora* had been induced to come forward and make statements. I also learned that Hayston had been taken to South harbour in charge of an officer, for what purpose I could never learn, unless it was to give him an opportunity of escaping, as he could easily have written his letters in the king's house.

Two of the boats' crews were piped away, and I was told by an old quarter-master, with a humorous grin, that some of the officers had gone away in the boats to South harbour to have a look at the "pirate's village, and bring away the unfortunate female captives." All this time I was kept in close confinement, and the time passed wearily away. I was growing tired of the ceaseless questions from every one that came near me about Hayston, the *Leonora*, and our voyage from the Carolines till the brig was cast away.

At night, however, the boats returned, and after the crews had been piped down to supper the good old sergeant-major of marines, suspecting the anxiety I was in as to Hayston's movements, startled me by telling me that he had escaped from custody when at South Island harbour.

He told me that as soon as the boat reached the village they found the place in a state of wildest confusion. A messenger had come down along the coast and told the Captain's people that a man-of-war was at Lêlé, and that Captain Hayston had been taken prisoner, put in irons, and was to be shot or hanged at once. A number of Strong's Island natives followed the man-of-war boats down from Chabral harbour, and these at once attempted to rush and ransack the station, which they were only prevented from doing by the presence of the blue-jackets.

Hayston was escorted to his station, where he was at once surrounded by the girls belonging to the house and many others, among them being the carpenter's, steward's, boatswain's, and Antonio's wives—all clinging to him and impeding his movements.

Calling them all together, with such others of the natives as had not fled from the village at the sight of the blue-jackets, he told them that they need not be under any alarm, that he was going away in the man-of-war, and might not return for a long time—perhaps many moons, but that the supercargo, Hilary Telfer, would be with them shortly, and they must be guided by him. Of course the Captain never for a minute imagined that I was then under the closest surveillance, and therefore would be utterly powerless to carry out his promises made to them.

He then quietly seated himself, and wrote a quantity of letters to his agents in the different islands in the Line and Marshall groups. These letters he directed and enclosed to me, together with a power of attorney which he had previously drawn up, and a letter of instructions—all of which he laid on the table.

He then told his captors that he was ready to return with them, when (according to the statement made by the marines on their return to Lêlé) he suddenly exerted his vast strength, and knocking several of them down, sprang into the sea and gained the mangroves on the opposite side of the harbour.

On my inquiring from the marine officer why he had not been pursued, that gentleman winked at me, and replied, "No orders, my boy, no orders; besides he swam like a beaver, and to search the mangroves for one man would take a month of Sundays." Thinking the matter over, I came to the conclusion that for some reason I could not fathom, the captain of the man-of-war was not particularly anxious to keep Hayston a prisoner, though I had heard him declare to Mr. Morland that the naval authorities would at last rid the Pacific of this man, who was a source of terror and dread from New Zealand to the China Seas.

When the boats returned from Utwé they brought up the man Jansen, whom Hayston had beaten and disgraced. He called himself, and was recognised by the captain of the *Rosario* as the chief officer of the *Leonora*, although he had long since lost his position on account of his rascally conduct. He seemed brimful of evidence as to Hayston's misdeeds, and I was afterwards informed that when brought into the ward-room of the man-of-war the officers expected to have some thrilling stories of rapine and bloodshed. However, they were disappointed, as his evidence was little more than confirmatory of that of Captain Warner of the *Matautu*, in reference to the taking of some gear from the brig *Kamehameha the Fourth*.

Mr. Morland and Likiak Sâ appeared to be the leading spirits in obtaining charges against the absent Hayston, for the commander of the man-of-war was strictly neutral, and certainly not furiously indignant at his escape. They succeeded in obtaining his approval of the appointment of Jansen to take charge of the people and the station, under the supervision of King Tokusar, at Utwé. It was at this juncture that the letters written by Hayston to his agents, as well as the power of attorney and letters of instruction to me, were produced by Mr. Morland. How they came to be in that gentleman's hands I do not know. A rough draft was made by him for the king's perusal, he said, and the originals were then brought to me by one of the lieutenants, who also handed me a bundle of papers which he said had been brought on board by a native.

These papers were my power of attorney, to hand over the ketch *E. A. Wilson* to Captain Hayston, and also a letter of instructions in reference to the crew—copies of which the reader has already seen. Feeling confident that I had but to show these documents to Commander Dupont to insure an interview and my instant release, I requested to be ushered into the autocrat's presence. The Reverend Mr. Morland was present, and greeted me with such a smile of active benevolence that I longed to kick him.

When I presented the letter to Captain Dupont I was considerably surprised when he denounced them as forgeries, calling me at the same time a d—d piratical scoundrel and accomplished young villain, adding that my cruel behaviour in aiding and abetting Hayston in his villainies made him regret that he could not run me up to the yardarm as a warning. He finished this tirade by tearing up my papers and throwing them at me. Calling the sergeant of marines, he ordered me put in irons, from which, however, I was released before the *Rosario* put to sea.

Early next morning, much to my relief, there appeared on board the black shining face of Johnny Tilton, the young negro, who among others of the crew had been brought away from Utwé, in one of the man-of-war boats. Johnny, with his shipmates, was taken below and examined by the captain and Mr. Morland. But as there was nothing against him personally or the Fijian half-caste Bill, they were permitted to return ashore. Before leaving, Johnny requested to be allowed to see me, which was granted.

The moment I saw his face I knew he had something of importance to tell me, for looking at the marine standing sentry over me, he said in Samoan, "Le—alu uā sola i te po" (the Captain escaped in the night).

"Yes!" I replied, "I know that already."

"Ah! but I mean that he has taken the small boat and gone away altogether. Listen, I'll tell you all about it. After the man-of-war boats had gone away from Utwé, and the Captain had escaped into the mangroves, a number of the Strong's islanders came down and said they were going to loot the place. Then the king sent down word that the captain of the man-of-war had declared that the station now belonged to him (the king), and that he could do what he liked with the place. The king forbade any of the people to go into the Captain's house till Jansen came down with Likiak Sâ, as these two had been appointed by the king and Mr. Morland to take charge. Well, there was a lot of us ran away into the mountains at the very first when we heard the Captain was taken prisoner. Bill Hicks and I were among them, also boy George and Sunday. Before we left I went to the Captain's house and told the girls that we were running away, and our wives were coming with us, and asked them what they intended to do. Old Mary said she would wait and see first if it were true about the Captain being taken prisoner.

"All the young women, too, though they were very frightened, said they would stay. I got Hope Island Nellie to give me three Winchester rifles and a bag of cartridges from the back of the big house. I cut a hole through the side of the Captain's sleeping-place, and Nellie passed the rifles out to me quietly. I told Nellie that we were going to hide in the mountains till we saw whether the man-of-war wanted to catch us as well as the Captain. If not we would return to Utwé.

"I took the rifles and wrapped them up in a long mat, and went down to the lagoon, where I found a canoe and took it. Bill and the others were waiting for me; they told me that the man-of-war boats were coming into the harbour, and that the Captain was in one of them; we watched them carefully and saw them go out of the harbour. Then Bill began to talk against the Captain, and said he would be glad if he were shot. He asked me if I was willing to make a dash into the village and help him to bring away Nellie and Sara, as if the Captain was taken away in the man-of-war he was going to have them for himself.

"I told him that until Captain Hayston was taken away or dead that I intended to stick to him. So we nearly had a fight over it. Then Bill said all of a sudden that he intended to have Sara and Nellie, right or wrong. And as he had nothing to fear from the man-of-war, he would try if he couldn't fool the captain, and pretend he could tell him all about Captain Hayston robbing Captain Daly's station on the Line Islands.

"I told him I was not going to turn dog on the Captain, and he might do his dirty work himself.

"So off he went, and we saw him cross over in a canoe to young Harry's place, and knew he was going along the beach to Chabral harbour. Then I talked to the others, and asked them what we ought to do, for I was afraid we would not see the Captain any more. Boy George laughed, and said he didn't care, but he meant to be beforehand with Bill and run off with Sara; that if I had any sense I would run off with Nellie, and let the other girls go adrift. He said we could easily live in the mountains till the man-of-war was gone, and then go back to Utwé. But I said I wouldn't do that, and that they would find that Sara would fight like a wild cat if boy George or any one else tried to take her away.

"Boy George then said if she wouldn't come he would put a bullet through her, and take Mila or Nellie instead. So then we had a row; he called me a black thief and said I could go to h—l. He and the others cleared out and left me alone.

"It was then very dark, and as everything seemed quiet, I walked across the coral and got into the house on the point where some Strong's Island people live, the one you were brought to when you were washed ashore. The man and his wife Nadup were frightened at first; but they were good to me, and gave me food, and then they told me Jansen was in charge of the station; that the Pleasant islanders were fled into the bush, and that the girls in the big house had run away when they saw him coming to them, drunk, with a loaded rifle in his hand.

"Only Nellie and little Kitty and Toby stayed behind. Nellie had a Winchester rifle and pointed it at Jansen, who was afraid to come into the house. Then she, Kitty, and the little boy collected as many of the Captain's things as they could carry, and taking a canoe, put out to sea, intending to paddle round to Moūt, where they thought they would find you, who would tell them all about the Captain, and whether he was killed or not.

"But, after they had gone four or five miles, the outrigger came off and the canoe capsized. They swam ashore and then walked back to Utwé, where they were told by some natives that you were also a prisoner on board the man-of-war. And the last that had been seen of Nellie, Kitty, and the boy, was that they started to walk to Chabral harbour to try and see the captain of the man-of-war, as they were afraid that Jansen would kill them.

"Well," continued Black Johnny, "when I heard that you were also a prisoner I thought I would run away into the bush again, as I knew Jansen would put a bullet into me whenever he saw me if I did not get first shot. Just as I was thinking very hard what I should do, I heard some one walking on the broken coral outside the house. I knew the footstep; it was the Captain! I crept outside, and saw him standing up leaning against a stone wall. He had two pistols in his sash and a Winchester rifle in his hand. He seemed to be considering. I whistled softly, and then spoke. He shook hands with me, and then raised his rifle and pointed it at the head of the Strong's islander, who, with his wife Nadup, had followed me. They ran outside and threw themselves on the ground, and grovelled in the way they do to old Tokusar, and swore they would not tell that the Captain had come back.

"We then had a hasty talk, and I told him about you being a prisoner. But he said you would soon be set free again and would return to Utwé, and I must stick to you and help to keep order; that after the man-of-war had gone he would come back again. When I told him that the station was broken up, and that Jansen was in charge of thirty Strong's islanders, and that the girls had run away, he said it was a bad case, and, picking up his rifle, he asked me where Jansen was sleeping. I saw what he meant to do, and begged him to let things be as they were, and not kill Jansen while the man-of-war was here.

"So he thought awhile, and then said if he could find a boat he would get away, as he didn't think the man-of-war would follow him. By and by he would come back again, when he hoped to find you and me here all safe.

"The Strong's Island women then told us that the dingey had been brought down from Chabral harbour by Jansen, and was then lying outside the coral at anchor. 'She'll do,' said the Captain; 'lend me a hand, and we'll bring her ashore.' But I made him lie quiet while I went for her; and I can tell you I was in a terrible funk all the time about sharks as soon as I began to swim out. Anyway I brought her in all right; and then the man and his wife brought a lot of cocoa-nuts and cooked food, and put it into the boat. I gave the Captain all the cartridges I had. He told me that he got the pistols from the place in the bush that you know of, and the rifle from young Harry, and that everything else there was all right."

By this I knew that Hayston had visited a place in the bush where he had secreted his bags of money, besides firearms and ammunition.

Going on with his talk the young negro said, "When everything was ready the Captain told me he meant to sail round the lee side of the island, and hide the boat in the mangroves till the man-of-war had gone, and then he would return and wipe out Jansen and the traders.

"He told me, though (for he felt sure of your being set free again), that if it so happened that he did not return in ten days you would know that he had cleared out towards the north-west, and would try to reach the Pelew Islands. He said if he reached there he would soon get a vessel, as there were always plenty of small Spanish schooners about those islands, and he could easily put his hand on one or two people in the Pelews who would help him to take one. I asked him what we should do if, when we came back to Utwé, you found that Jansen was too strong for us? He said we should make no attempt to take forcible possession, but go and live with your people at Moūt. That as soon as the girls knew where we were they would be certain to come to us with little Kitty and Toby. That we must wait till he returned, as he would never desert us.

"Then," said Johnny, whose glistening eyes showed how deeply attached he was to his Captain, "the poor fellow! he shook hands with me, and said I was made of the right stuff, and that the Almighty made a mistake when he gave me a black skin. Then, telling me to keep a stout heart, he got in and hoisted the sail. It was very dark, but there was a good land-breeze, and he sailed the dingey right along the edge of the reef till he came to the passage, and disappeared in the darkness. I ran across the strip of land on the sea-side of the lagoon and waited till I saw him pass.

"In about half-an-hour I saw the little boat sailing along close into the shore, just outside of the breakers, rising and falling like a sea-gull on the top of the heavy seas. I could see the Captain's figure in the stern, and every moment expected to see her lifted high up on a roller and dashed on the reef. But though I shouted to him to keep farther out, the white figure in the stern never moved, and my voice was lost in the roaring of the surf.

"Then, as I saw him still keeping steady to the southward, just clear of the last sweep of the seas before they curled and broke on the reef, I remembered that only a few cables' lengths from the breakers there was always a strong current setting to the north, and that with a light breeze the boat would never stem it. That was why he hugged the shore so closely. At last, as I kept running through the undergrowth following the boat, I came to that place where there is a thick cane scrub. When I got through it he was nearly out of sight, and I sat on a boulder and watched the sail gradually covered up by the night."

Such, in effect, was the young negro's story. I could not help being affected by his evident sorrow, and told him that I feared there was no chance of me at least ever seeing the Captain again. Then, when the time came to part, I shook his hand warmly, and advised him to sever his connection with the *Leonora's* crew; also to go and see the king, who would not, at any rate, object to his remaining on the island to follow out the Captain's wishes as far as lay in his power.

Soon after Black Johnny had bid me good-bye young Harry came to say farewell, and with him Kusis and his family, and Lālia.

Harry told me that he saw the Captain after his escape, and urged him not to think of returning to Utwé just then, as Jansen had a strong force of natives with him, and would certainly try to take or shoot him. But he was determined to find out how matters stood, and bidding Harry good-bye, set out across the mangrove swamp that lined the shore from Harry's station to the village at Utwé. He gave him the Winchester and cartridges, and the Captain assured him that he would not fire a shot except in self-defence.

I told Harry what I had learned from the young negro about the Captain's final movements, and that I was being taken away as a prisoner. He seemed very bitter against the other traders, whom he spoke of as trembling like whipped hounds before the Captain's frown when he was free, and who now, when he was a ruined and broken man, were loud in their threats and vapourings.

He also told me that he had received a letter from the king and Mr. Morland, commanding him to deliver up to Jansen all oil, casks, boats, and other property in his possession belonging to Captain Hayston, and threatening him with deportation from the island if he refused. To this he sent a written reply to the effect, that unless the king and Mr. Morland could back up their demand by a boat's crew from the man-of-war, he would shoot the first man who stepped inside his fence.

They then appealed to Commander Dupont, who told them that as young Harry was an American citizen, he could not force him to give up the property, but advised the king and Mr. Morland to take the law into their own hands.

Young Harry then armed his wives and native servants with rifles, and telling them to make short work of any one attempting to seize Captain Hayston's property, set out for Chabral harbour to interview the king. He told me that when he reached the king's house he found there the other traders, Mr. Morland, and the commander of the man-of-war. On the latter gentleman inquiring who he was, and what he wanted, Harry answered him very concisely by furnishing his name and nationality. He then stated that he had not come to see him (Commander Dupont), but the king, of whom he wished to ask by what right he dared to send him a letter threatening him with deportation from the island unless he consented to give up Captain

Hayston's property. He warned him to be careful how he interfered with an American citizen, as there was an American cruiser now in the Caroline Islands. He (the king) would find he had made a serious mistake if he committed any outrage upon a citizen of the United States.

"You should have seen the look in the British officer's face," said Harry, "when I stepped up to the old king, and nearly touching his face with my hand, said, 'and I warn you, king, that the captain of an American cruiser will listen to the tale and redress the wrongs of the honest American citizen. He would think little of knocking your town about your ears.'"

The old king never spoke, but glanced first towards the British officer and then to the missionary, but as neither of them offered suggestions, the poor old fellow could only mutter something to the effect that he was like a little fish in a pool, afraid of the sea because of the bigger fish, and afraid to stay lest the frigate birds should seize him. Young Harry quite enjoyed relating the scene to me, and said that as he was going away the king held out his hand and inquired in a shaky voice, "I say, Harry, what you tink, what you do? Suppose Captain Hayston come back, what become of King Tokusar? Oh! by God! now I be 'fraid every day; think I hear Captain Hayston speak me; make noise like bullock; I think better be poor native, no more king."

Harry refused to advise the king, and then taking a good look at the white men present, said, "Well, good-bye, King Tokusar! I am going back to my station — the station I am minding for Captain Hayston. I have six men and four women all armed, and the American flag on a pole in front of my door; and the first man that attempts to do me any mischief, white, black, or yellow, *I'll shoot him*. You can ask the white men from Pleasant Island if I am not a man of my word. They know me."

Harry then got into his boat and pulled on board the man-of-war, where the first lieutenant very kindly allowed him to see me. I felt sincere regret at parting with Harry, telling him to beware of the other traders. I repeated what had been told me by Kitty of Ebon and Lālia. He laughed, and said he was always prepared, and meant to do justice to the trust reposed in him by Captain Hayston. "I'm the wrong man," he said on leaving, "to abandon any station and property left in my charge." Then, with oft-repeated wishes that we might meet again, after hearing of the Captain's safety we parted.

Then came again good simple Kusis and his people with Lālia. She had in charge little Kitty and Toby. Poor Toby clung to my legs and sobbed as if his heart was breaking, when I told him that I did not know when the Captain would come back again. If no one else loved his master Toby did, and I tried in vain to assuage his grief. I was glad to hear from Lālia that she was going to young Harry's place with the two children. There I knew they would be well treated and cared for.

"Look!" said she, pointing to the little fellow, "the Captain had two good friends besides yourself, young Harry, and the nigger Johnny, but this little fellow has never ceased crying for 'Captin' since he left the village in South harbour. Never mind, little Toby, we will wait and the 'Captin' will be sure to come;" and then she stooped down, and tried by kissing and coaxing to prevent him from giving utterance to his doleful wails and sobs of grief.

Lālia told me, as with glistening eyes and trembling hands we said farewell, that her one hope now was to be able to get back to her distant home on Easter Island, that Captain Hayston would return with a ship; and, if he went towards Samoa or Tahiti, take her with him for that portion of the many thousand miles that lay between Strong's Island and her native land. That he would do this she felt confident. "For," she said, "he once told me that he would stand by me if I was in trouble—it was when we were all washed ashore together—you remember? *and he never breaks his word.*"

Whatever Lālia's past life had been, I could never help admiring her many noble traits of character. I owed her life-long gratitude for her heroic self-sacrifice on the fateful night of the wreck of the *Leonora*; by me, at least, she will never be forgotten. Poor Lālia! Brave, loving, lovely child of the charmed isles of the southern main! reckless alike in love and hate, who shall judge? who condemn thee? Not I!

Kusis, Tulpé, and Kinie clung to me as if they could not bear to say farewell. I see before me often the honest, kindly countenance of Kusis as, with his hand clasped in mine, he looked trustfully into my face and made me promise that some day I would return and live with him once more. And so freshly at that time came the remembrance of the happy days I had passed in his quiet home, dreaming the hours away within sight of the heaving bosom of the blue, boundless Pacific Ocean, so deliciously restful after the stormy life of the *Leonora* and her wild commander, that I believe I really intended to return to Strong's Island some day; but, as we used to say at Sydney college, "*Dîs aliter visum*."

Queen Sê sent me a letter as follows:—

DEAR FRIEND,—Kitty Ebon send Lālia to see you. We all very sorry, but must not say so, because Mr. Morland very strong man now. Where you think Captain Hayston go in little boat? I 'fraid he die in boat. I very sorry for Captain—very kind man—but bad man to natives sometimes.

QUEEN SÊ.

Enclosed were these pencilled lines from Kitty of Ebon:—

MY DEAR FRIEND,—All the people from Moūt been to Mr. Morland to ask why you are in prison, and he says you will be hung for stealing a ship. We all very sorry, all Moūt people love you very much—and me too. Good-bye, dear friend, come back to Kusis and Moūt people, for I don't think you be hanged in Fiji.—Your sincere friend,

CATHERINE EBON.

But when the light-hearted blue-jackets manned the capstan and merrily footed it round to lively music, and the great steamer's head was pointed to the passage, my thoughts were far away, where in fancy I discerned a tiny boat breasting the vast ocean swell, while sitting aft with his face turned to the westward, his strong brown hand on the tiller, was the once dreaded Captain of the *Leonora*; the lawless rover of the South Seas; the man whose name was known and feared from the South Pole to Japan, and yet through all, my true friend and most indulgent commander. With all his faults, our constant association had enabled me to appreciate his many noble qualities and fine natural impulses. And as the black hull of the *Rosario* rose and fell to the sea, her funnel the while pouring forth volumes of sable smoke, the island gradually sunk astern, but the memories connected with it and Captain Hayston will abide with me for ever.

Harry Skillings I never saw again, but heard that he went to Truk in the North-west Carolines. Black Johnny was murdered in New Britain. The other Harry with his native wife fell victims to the treacherous savages of the Solomon Islands. Jansen died a few years since on Providence Island. Some of the other traders and members of the crew I have heard of from time to time, scattered far and wide over the Isles of the Pacific. Lālia died in Honolulu about five years since, constant in her attempts to reach her distant home on Easter Island.

CHAPTER XIV

NORFOLK ISLAND—ARCADIA

And now, my innocence and lack of complicity in Hayston's irregularities having been established, a revulsion of feeling took place in the minds of the captain and officers of the *Rosario* with regard to me.

After the fullest explanations furnished by the traders and others, backed up by the manifest sympathy and good-will of the inhabitants of Strong Island, it became apparent that some sort of reparation was due to me. This took the form of a courteous invitation to accept a passage to Sydney in H.M.S. *Rosario*, and to join the officers' mess on the voyage. "I'm afraid that we acted hastily in your case, Mr. Telfer!" said Captain Dupont. "You have been thoroughly cleared of all accusations made against you. I am bound to say they were very few. And you seem chiefly to have acted as a peacemaker and a power for good. I have gathered that you are anxious to rejoin your friends in Sydney. I shall be glad to have your company on the return voyage. What do you say? I trust you will not refuse; I shall otherwise think you have not forgiven my apparent harshness."

Thus pressed to return to family and friends—from whom, at times, in spite of my inborn roving propensities, the separation had cost me dear—what could I do but thank the manly and courteous potentate, and comply with an invitation so rarely granted to a South Sea adventurer. I was the more loth to lose the opportunity as there had come upon me of late a violent fit of homesickness which I in vain strove to combat.

I had in truth now no particular reason for remaining at Kusaie, or indeed anywhere in the South Seas. Hayston was gone; his magnetic influence no longer controlled my will, as in our first acquaintance. The *Leonora*—our pride and boast, our peerless floating home—no longer "walked the waters like a thing of life," but lay dead, dismantled, dishonoured on the ruthless coral rocks which had crushed the life out of her on that fatal night.

I realised now with thankfulness that I had narrowly escaped being liable as an accessory for some of Hayston's ultra-legal proceedings—to call them by no harsher name.

How often, indeed, in the reckless daring of boyhood is the fatal line crossed which severs imprudence from crime! The inexorable fiat of human justice knows no shade of criminality. "Guilty or not guilty," goes forth the verdict. There is no appeal on earth. And the faulty, but not all evil-natured victim, is doomed to live out all the years of a life branded as a felon, or maddened by the fears which must ever torture the fugitive from justice!

If I stayed in the South Seas on my present footing, nothing remained but the trader's life, pure and simple. I had little doubt but that I could make a living, perhaps a competence in years to come. But that meant exile in every sense of the word. Complete severance from my kindred, whom my soul yearned to see again; from the friends of my boyhood; from the loved and lovely land of my birth; from the thousand and one luxuries, material and intellectual, which are comprehended in the word civilisation. I had slaked my thirst for adventure, danger, and mystery. I had carried my life in my hand, so to speak, and times without number had doubted whether I should retain that more or less valuable possession for the next ten minutes. I had felt the poisoned arrows at Santa Cruz hurtling around me, even hiss through my waving locks, when the death-scratch summoned a man on either hand. I had nearly been "blue sharks' meat" as Hayston phrased it, on coral strand amid "the cruel crawling foam." All chances and risks I had taken heedlessly in the past. But now I began to feel that I must pronounce the momentous decision which would make or mar my future career. The island life was very fair. For one moment I saw myself the owner of a trading station on Pingelap or Arurai. I am sitting in a large, cool house, on soft, parti-coloured mats, surrounded by laughing girls garlanded and flower-crowned. Around and above, save in the plantation which surrounds the house, is the soft green light of the paradisal woodland illumining its incredible wealth of leafage, fruit, and flowers. Before me lies the endless, azure sea-plain. And oh, my sea! my own, my beloved sea!—loved in childhood, youth, and age, if such be granted to me! In my ears are the magical murmurous surge-voices, to the lulling of which I have so often slept like a tired child. Fruit and flowers—love and war—manly effort—danger—high health—boundless liberty,—all things necessary to the happiness of primeval man, before he became sophisticated by the false wisdom of these later ages, should I not possess in profusion? Why, then, should I not remain in this land of changeless summer—this magic treasure-house of all delights of land and sea?

Long and anxiously did I ponder over my decision. Those only who have known the witchery of the "summer Isles of Eden," have felt the charm of the dream-life of the Southern Main—the sorcery of that lotus-eating existence, alternating with the fierce hazards and stormy delights which give a richness to life unknown to a guarded, narrowed civilisation—can gauge my irresolution.

I had well-nigh resolved to adhere to the trader's life—until I had made a fortune with which I could return in triumph—when I thought of my mother! The old house, with its broad, stone-paved verandah came back to me—the large, "careless-ordered" garden with its trailing, tropical shrubs and fruit-trees—the lordly araucarias, the boat-house, the stone-walled bath wherein I had learned to swim—all came back in that moment when memory recalled the scenes and surroundings of my early life. I could hear a voice ever low and sweet, as in the days of my childhood, which said, "Oh! my boy! my boy! come back—let me see my darling's face before I die."

I was conquered—the temptations of the strange life, with its sorceries and phantasms, which had so long enveloped me, were swept away like a ghost-procession at dawn. And in their place came the steadfast resolve to return to the home of my youth, thenceforward to pursue such modes of life as might be marked out for me. In a new land like my birth-place, with a continent for an arena, I had no fear but that a career would open itself for me. In no country under heaven are there so many chances of success, so many roads to fortune, as in the lone wastes upon which the Southern Cross looks down. On land or sea—the tracks are limitless—the avenues to fortune innumerable. Gold was to be had for the seeking; silver and gems lay as yet in their desert solitudes, only awaiting the adventurer who, strong in the daring of manhood, should compel the waste to disclose its secrets—only awaited the hour and the man.

For such enterprises was I peculiarly fitted. So much could then be said without boast or falsehood on my part. My frame, inured to withstand every change of temperature which sea or land could furnish, was of unusual strength. By hard experience I had learned to bear myself masterfully among men of widely various dispositions and characters. I took my stand henceforth as a citizen of the world—as a rover on sea and land—as more than a suppliant to fortune, a "Conquistador."

The homeward voyage being now fairly commenced, I began to speculate on the probabilities of my future career. During the years which I had passed among the islands I had acquired experience— more or less valuable—but very little cash. This was chiefly in consequence of our crowning disaster, the wreck of the *Leonora*. But for that untoward gale, my share of the proceeds of the venture would have exceeded the profits of all my other trading enterprises. As it was, I was left, if not altogether penniless, still in a position which would debar me from making more than a brief stay with my friends in Sydney, unless I consented to be beholden to them for support. That I held to be impossible. For a few weeks I felt that my finances would hold out. And after that, was there not a whole world of adventures—risks, hardships, dangers, if you will—all that makes life worth living—open before me; the curtain had fallen upon one act of the life drama of Hilary Telfer. What of that? Were there not four more, at least, to come?

Even the princess had not arrived. There had been a "first robber" on the boards, perhaps—even more of that persuasion. But the principal stage business was only commencing—the dénouement was obviously far off. Thereupon my hopes rose as if freshly illuminated. My sanguine nature—boundless in faith, fertile in expedient— reasserted itself. Temporarily depressed, more in sympathy with Hayston than with my own ill-luck, it seemed more vigorous and elastic in rebound than ever. The memory of my island life became faint and dreamily indistinct. The forms of Hayston, the king and queen, of Lālia, with sad, reproachful gaze—of Hope Island Nellie, lifting a rifle with the mien of an angered goddess—of Kitty of Ebon, incarnate daughter of the dusky Venus—of the bronzed and wrinkled trader, with blood and to spare on his sinewy hand—of young Harry and the negro Johnny. All these forms and faces, once so familiar, seemed to recede into the misty distance until they faded away from my mental vision.

With them passed into shadow-land the joyous life of my youth—of the untrammelled, care-free existence—such as no man may find again in this world of slow, tracking care and hasty disenchantment. "Was I wise?" I asked myself again and again, in quitting it for the hard and anxious pursuits of the Continent? Were there not a dozen places besides Strong's Island where I should be welcomed, fêted, caressed, almost worshipped as a restored divinity? Was it well to abandon the rank which I had acquired among these simple people? Was it— But no. For ever had I made the decision. Once resolved, I disliked changing my plans. Burdened with a regret which for days I could neither subdue nor remove, I adhered unflinchingly to my resolution, and addressed myself to the steady contemplation of the future.

Now had commenced for me a new life—a new world socially speaking. The quiet reserve and unemotional bearing of the British officer was substituted for the frank accost and reckless speech of the island trader or wandering mariner. I was prompt, however, to assimilate the modish bearing of my companions, and assisted by some natural alertness, or perhaps inherited tendencies, soon became undistinguishable from the honourables and lordlings of the gun-room. Upon my repose of manner, indeed, I was often complimented. "By Jove, old fellow," one of the offshoots of the British aristocracy would say, "one would think you had been at Rugby or Eton. And I suppose you have never seen England. Certainly you have the pull of us in make and shape. I can't think how they grow such fellows,—more English than the English,—with your blue eyes and fair hair, too, in these God-forsaken regions."

"Because," I said, "I am of as pure English blood as yourself; have been reared, and moulded, and surrounded by English people, and have all the traditions of the old country at my fingers' end. For the rest, I hold that this end of the world is more favourable to the growth of Anglo-Saxons, as you call yourselves, than the other."

"Well! it looks like it, I must say," said my new friend. "I only hope that when the time comes for fighting, by sea and land—and, mark my words, come it will—that you will be found as stanch as I think you are."

"Be sure we shall be," said I. "We have inherited the true English 'grit,' as Americans say. You all said *they* couldn't fight when their war began; when it finished, the world gave a different verdict. We are our fathers' sons, neither more nor less. The bull-dog and the game-cock still fight to the death in our country. Many a time have I seen it. And so will we when our time comes, and when we think it worth our while."

We carried an order from the New South Wales Government to call in at Norfolk Island—once the ocean prison of the more desperate felons of the old convict régime, who had been replaced by the descendants of the Pitcairn islanders. They, in their turn the descendants of mutinous sailors and Tahitian women—now the most moral, God-fearing, and ideally perfect race on the face of the earth.

What a miracle had been wrought! Who could have imagined that the last days of a rough old sailor, spent among the survivors of a group of savage women who had butchered their mates, could have so firmly fixed the morale of a whole community that virtue should have indelibly impressed itself upon a hundred families. Sydney lies about S.S.W. from Kusaie, but to avoid passing through the dangers of the New Hebrides, and the reef-studded vicinity of New Caledonia, a direct south course with a little easting was decided upon.

We made Norfolk Island, the distance being about two thousand miles, in ten days' easy steaming from Strong's Island. This lovely island was discovered by Cook in 1774.

A military man writing of it in 1798, draws a comparison between it and Sydney much to the disadvantage of the latter. "The air is soft (he says) and the soil inexpressibly productive. It is a perfect section of paradise. Our officers and their wives were sensibly affected at their departure, and what they regarded as banishment to Sydney."

Another officer writing of it in 1847, says: "It is by nature a paradise adorned with all the choicest gifts of nature—climate, scenery, and vegetable productions; by art and man's policy turned into an earthly hell, disfigured by crime, misery, and despair."

The island had been brought into a high state of cultivation by convict labour. Its roads, buildings, and gardens were in admirable order. But with the establishment of the new régime—a different race with different tasks—much was neglected, a part became decayed and ruinous. The island is now partitioned into blocks of fifty acres, of which each adult male is allowed one, drawn for and decided by lot.

Whale fishing is the favourite and most profitable occupation. From this and the sale of farm produce, which finds a market in Sydney, the inhabitants are furnished with all their needs require. Their wants are few, simple, and easily supplied.

The old convict town with its huge, dilapidated barracks, gaol-officers' quarters, and servants' houses, is situated on the south-east edge of the island, where the little Nepean islet gives sufficient shelter to form a precarious roadstead available in certain winds. The old town is occupied by the Pitcairn islanders—in number about three hundred.

Five miles across the island, on its north-eastern shore, and communicating with it by a fair road, lies the Melanesian Mission estate of a thousand acres. Sloping gently down to a low cliff and a rocky shore, the land is an undulating meadow, broken by ravines, and covered with a thick sward of conch grass or "doubh," said to have been imported from India, whence we drew our chief food supplies so many a year ago. Nothing more beautiful in a state of nature had ever been seen, I thought, when I first cast my admiring eyes on it. Here and there gigantic, graceful pines (*Araucaria excelsa*) stood in stately groves. Higher up on the flanks of Mount Pitt (a thousand feet above) grow the lemon and guava, cotton and wild tobacco. The island is nine hundred miles from Sydney and thirteen hundred and fifty from Cape Pillar, Tasmania. The Nepean and Phillip Islands lie to the south of the main island.

We were in such a hurry to see the famous island and still more famous islanders, that we omitted a precaution which had been earnestly impressed upon us the day before. This was not to attempt to land unless we had a Pitcairner to steer. When the long swell of the Pacific rolls in upon the shallow beaches of Sydney Bay there is no more dangerous place in the world—the roadstead of Madras hardly excepted—than the boat harbour at Norfolk Island.

Like most sailors, and man-of-war's men in particular, the crew was reckless and confident. For myself, I was a fair hand in a boat, and had mixed in so many cases of touch-and-go, where all hands would have fed the sharks in a few more minutes, that I had lost any sense of caution that I might have originally possessed. As we neared the shore, rising and falling upon the tremendous billows, which told of a scarce passed gale, I felt a sense of exhilaration to which I had been long a stranger. A party of the islanders, seeing a boat leave the ship, had come down to watch our landing, apparently with interest. As we came closer I noticed them talking rapidly to one another, and occasionally waving their arms to one side or the other as if to direct our steering. There were several women in the group, but as we neared the landing my attention was rivetted upon a girl who stood out some distance from the others at the end of a rocky point, which jutted beyond the narrow beach.

I had seen strikingly beautiful faces and faultless forms among the island girls, as all unconscious, they threw themselves into attitudes so graceful and unstudied that a sculptor would have coveted them for models. Among these children of nature, roaming at will through their paradisal isles, the perfection of the human form had doubtless been developed. But there was a subtle charm about this girl, as she stood with bare feet beside the plashing wave,—a statuesque presentment of nobility, courage, and refinement which I had never before recognised in living woman. Tall and slender of frame, she yet possessed the rounded outlines which, in all island women, promise a fuller development in the matured stage of womanhood. Her features were delicately regular; in her large dark eyes there was an expression of strong interest, deepening almost into fear, as she gazed at our incoming boat. She had bent slightly forward, and stood poised on her rock as if waiting for a signal to plunge into the boiling surf. Her complexion was so fair that, but for her attitude, which spoke her a daughter of the sea, one which no mortal born away from the music of the surges could have assumed, I might have taken her for an Englishwoman.

"In the name of all the divine maidens since Nausicaa" (I had not quite forgotten my *Odyssey*, rusty though was my Greek) "who can she be?" thought I.

At this point my reflections and conjectures came to an abrupt end, as, indeed, nearly did also "the fever called living" in my particular case. I felt the boat rise heavenwards on the back of a tremendous roller. The islanders shouted as though to warn us of danger, the steersman gave the tiller a wrong turn, or omitted to give it the right one, and the next moment the boat was buried beneath an avalanche of foam, with crew and passengers struggling for their lives. I could swim well, that is, of course, comparatively, for the difference between the best performance of a white man—well practised from youth though he be—and of an islander is as that of a dog and a fish. Still, having risen to the surface, I made no doubt but that I could easily gain a landing. In this I was deceived. As in other spots, the constant surf concealed a treacherous undertow against which the ordinary swimmer is powerless. Again and again did I gain foothold, to be swept back by the resistless power of the backward current. Each time I became weaker, and at length, after a long fruitless struggle, I closed my eyes and resigned myself to my fate. Borne backward and half fainting, I saw the whole party of natives in the water mingling with the crew, who, like myself, had been making desperate efforts to reach the landing.

My senses were leaving me; darkness was before my eyes, when dimly, as in a dream, I seemed to mark the girl upon the rock plunge with the gliding motion of a seal into the boiling foam. Her bosom shone as with outstretched arms she parted the foaming tide, her short under-dress, reaching only to the knees, offered no impediment to the freedom of her limbs. I felt soft arms around me. A cloud of dusky hair enveloped me. Strains of unearthly music floated in my ears. It was the dirge of the mermaidens, as they wail over the drowned sailor and bear him with song and lament to his burial cavern. All suddenly it ceased.

The mid-day sun had pierced the roof and side of the cottage wherein I was lying upon a couch, softly matted. When I awoke I looked around. Surely I had been drowned, and must be dead and gone! How, then, was I once more in a place where the sun shone, where there were mats and signs of ordinary life? I closed my eyes in half-denial of the evidences of my so-called senses. Then, as I raised myself with difficulty, the door opened and a man entered.

He was a tall, grandly developed Pitcairner, one of the men who had been on board the night before. His face was dark, with the tint of those races which, though far removed from the blackness of the Ethiop, are yet distinct from the pure white family of mankind. But his eyes, curiously, were of bright and distinct blue, in hereditary transmission, doubtless, from that ancestor who had formed one of the historic mutineers of the *Bounty*.

"You've had a close shave, Hilary. That's your name, I believe. A trifle more salt water and you'd have been with the poor chap that's drowned. We got all the crew out but him."

"I thought I *was* drowned," I replied, "but I begin to perceive that I'm alive. I see you're of the same opinion, so I suppose it's all right."

"It's not a thing to laugh at," the Pitcairner said gravely. "God saw fit to save you this time. To Him and Miranda you owe your thanks for being where you are now."

"There are people in Sydney," I said, "who will be foolish enough to be glad of it, and after I have a little time to think, I daresay I shall be pleased myself. But who is Miranda, and how did she save me?"

"Miranda Christian, my cousin, is the girl you saw standing on the rock. She had a strong fight of it to get you in, and but for one of us going on each side neither of you would have come out. We had been hard at it trying to save the crew, and nearly left it too late. She was just about done."

"I shall be uneasy till I thank her. What a brave girl! And what am I to call you?"

"Fletcher Quintal, and her cousin," the islander replied, drawing himself up and looking at me with a steady gaze. "You won't see her till the afternoon. She has gone home to rest after staying with you till you came to. My sister, Dorcas, will bring you food directly, and perhaps you'd better rest yourself too till sundown. Then some of us will pay you a visit. Good morning."

A pleasant-faced damsel, with the sparkling eyes and perfect teeth of the race, came in shortly afterwards, who smilingly informed me that her name was Dorcas Quintal, and that her cousin Miranda had told her she was not to talk much to me.

However, during the time occupied in making a creditable lunch — all things considered, — I succeeded in convincing her that I was strong enough for a decent dose of gossip, in the course of which I learned several interesting pieces of information about Miranda, who certainly had posed as my Guardian Angel in the late accident. She was, according to Dorcas, the leader in all sports and pastimes, and also the most learned and accomplished damsel on the island. "She sang and played in their church choir. She had read all the poets in the world," Dorcas believed. "She could recite pages and pages of poetry and history. Altogether she was a wonderful girl to be born and brought up in such a place as Norfolk Island, where we never see any one"—here Dorcas wreathed her lips into an expressive pout—"that is, except captains of ships and strangers like yourself."

"So she is quite perfect," I said, "alike on land and sea. I can vouch for the last. I suppose she can pull an oar and is quite at home in a boat?"

"Indeed she is," answered Dorcas, warming up. "She can sail a cutter with any man on the island, and steer a whaleboat besides. You should see her standing up with the big steer oar in those tiny hands of hers."

"So, then, she has no faults?" I queried, a little mischievously.

The girl smiled. "I suppose we have all some here as in other places. She is rather proud and quiet, the other girls say. I never saw it, and if there is anything else you must find it out for yourself. And now, as you have finished eating and drinking, I must go. Miranda will be here by and by."

"Only one word, Dorcas," said I, as she turned towards the doorway. "How many admirers has she—all the young men in the island, I suppose?"

"Only one," she replied, impressively, "my brother, Fletcher Quintal. He would die for her."

"And she?"

The girl paused before replying, and gazed earnestly at me.

"She says she will never marry." And with that she passed out and left me to my meditations.

I must have been fatigued, even bruised and battered by my conflict with sea and shore, as I felt a kind of lassitude creep over me, and presently fell into a dreamless sleep, which lasted till the sun was low and the dimness of the light told me that the day had passed.

I raised myself and saw Miranda sitting on a low stool near the window, or the aperture which served for one. As I turned, she smiled and came towards me, putting out her hand for me to take, and gazing into my face with a frank pleasure of the unspoiled woman of the woods and fields. "I have to thank you for my life," I said, as I pressed her hand warmly. "It is of no great value to any one, as things have been going lately, but being such as it is, you have my warmest gratitude. I should hardly have changed for the worse if I had been lying beside poor Bill Dacre."

"You must not talk in that mocking way," she said, with a pained expression like that of a hurt child. "God has given us all a life to use for some good purpose. Surely you have friends? perhaps a mother and sisters, who would weep when they heard you were lying under the waves?"

"You are right, Miranda, and I will not talk foolishly again; but I thank you with my whole heart for your noble courage in risking your life to save mine. I wonder now how we both got to land, in spite of that beastly undertow?"

"I never could have done it without help," she said. "I was nearly exhausted, yet I did not like to let you go, when Fletcher Quintal and Peter Mills, who had each brought out a man, swam in again, and we came in between them."

"You seem to be quite at home in the water," I said. "I thought I could swim, and at Strong's Island and other places could hold my own with the natives pretty well. But I found my mistake here."

"Of course we all swim well," she replied, smiling, "and know how to manage a boat. It would be curious if we did not; there is little else to do, in Norfolk Island, except when we are working in the fields. Our life is sometimes dull, I must allow."

"I hear that you can do all sorts of other things," I said. "That you are the chief musician and teacher, besides being commander of the fleet."

"Dorcas has been chattering, I am afraid," she answered, while a blush rose to her brow, tingeing the pallor of her ivory cheek with faint carmine. "I certainly have a variety of occupations, and very fortunate it is! Otherwise, I don't know what would happen to me, for I am scarcely as contented as my cousins and the other girls on the island."

"It is the old story," I said. "Now, why should you not be contented on this lovely island where you have all you could wish for in the world—perfect freedom, a matchless climate, exercise, adventure, the love of your kinsfolk, everything that satisfies the heart of woman?"

"Everything necessary to satisfy a woman's heart!" she said, rising and walking to where the casement admitted a view of the heaving deep with the *Rosario* lying on and off. "Can you look at the boundless ocean with its thousand paths to the cities of the earth and not wish to roam? To see the glories of the old world, all the varied richly-coloured life of ancient nations that I have read of and see in my dreams? Do you think men only are impatient of a hemmed-in life? It is not so. Women have their longings for a wider range, a larger sphere; and yet I am perhaps the only girl on the island that feels what I have described."

"You must have read much," I said, rather startled at this burst of feeling from the lips of a Norfolk Island damsel—a child of the most contented community in the world. "These strange yearnings must have been awakened in you through the word-painting of these wicked authors."

"And why not?" she answered, with heightened colour and flashing eye. "That my world is one of books I do not deny. I have daily tasks and occupations, but my evenings are my own, and in them I read and muse. Then this little island, with its patient, primitive people, seems to fade away. I spend hours in Italy, where I revel in Florence, the Pitti Palace, the Arno, and roam the streets of the Eternal City amid the monuments of the world's grandest era, their very decay 'an Empire's dust.' I fall asleep often when reclining on the banks of 'Tiber, Father Tiber, to whom the Romans pray.' But, oh! if I begin to wander away in the track of my visions I shall never stop. And you," she continued with an eager glance, "you, who have seen men and cities, are you contented to linger away your life under cocoa-palms and bread-fruit trees, taking in glorious ease among simple savages until you become one yourself in all but the colour? Is this what you were born and reared and educated for?"

As the girl thus spoke, with head upraised and exalted mien, her wondrous eyes flashing with almost unearthly light, her mobile lineaments changing with each varying mood, she looked in her strange and unfamiliar beauty like some virgin prophetess of the days of old, rousing her countrymen to deeds of patriotic valour or self-sacrificing heroism.

All enthusiasm is contagious, more especially when the enthusiast is fair to look upon, and belongs to that sex for, or on account of which, so much of the world's strife has resulted.

For the first time I began seriously to ask myself what motives had led me to waste so large a portion of my youth in heedless wandering among these fairy isles. What were my aims in life? What did I propose to myself? As I looked at the girl's face, aglow with the fire of a noble ambition, I felt humbled and ashamed.

"You have spoken truly, Miranda," I replied, after a long pause, during which my fair questioner looked with a far-away gaze across the ocean plain, now quenching its thousand shifting gleams in the quick-falling tropic night. "I have been idly careless and unheeding of the future, satisfied with the day's toil and the day's pleasure. But I am going back to my people in Australia; there I shall begin a new life. It is a land of duty, of labour, and its enduring reward. There I shall renew the tension of my moral fibre which has been too long relaxed. But you must not be too hard on me. I have had to face losses, dangers, and misfortunes. I have been wrecked; I lost everything I had in the world. I have been ill; have been wounded; and, but for some of those simple islanders you seem to despise, I should not have been a living man to-day."

"I do not despise them," she said; "of course every one knows that we are descended from those of Tahiti. I only say that they are not fit companions for white men—I mean of educated white men who in the end become as bad as they are—even worse—much worse. But tell me about your being ill. And who tended you? Was it a woman?"

"I will tell you all about it to-morrow if you will walk with me and show me some of the scenery of this beautiful island of yours. But it is a long story, and it is too late to begin to-night."

"I should like it above all things," she said frankly, "though you must have seen so many grand places in your roamings that our poor landscapes will hardly interest you."

"Much depends on the guide," I said, as I gazed admiringly at her eloquent countenance.

"I know that," she answered, meeting my too ardent gaze with perfect unconsciousness of any hidden meaning. "They tell me I am the best guide on the island, and indeed I should be, for my father and I were never tired of exploring and finding out traces of the old occupation by the Sydney Government, and many curious discoveries we made. So I will come here after breakfast to-morrow."

She was true to her appointment, and then commenced a series of delightful rambles which, perhaps, I more truly enjoyed than many later and more pretentious travels.

In despite of Miranda's depreciation of her lovely isle we found endless excuses for interest and admiration. It was truly a wonderful little "kingdom by the sea." Scraped along the side of a hill would be one of the beautiful roads constructed by the forced labour of the convicts which at one time almost filled the island. Rising from the valley slope were gigantic ferns, broad-leaved palms, lemons, oranges, guavas, all originally imported, but now flourishing in the wildest luxuriance in the rich soil and semi-tropical climate; while above all, stately and columnar, rose the great Araucaria peculiar to the island—the Norfolk Island pine of the colonists.

Hand in hand we roamed together through this Eden amid the main, as though our great progenitors had again been transplanted to this wondrous wild—a latter day Adam, by whose side smiled a sinless Eve—pure as her prototype, and yet informed of much of the lore which men had wrested from the rolling ages. Together we explored the gloomy corridors and echoing halls of the ruinous prison houses—once the dark abodes of sorrow, torment, and despair unutterable.

Miranda shuddered at the thought that these dismal cells and courtyards had echoed to the cries of criminals under the lash—to the clanking of chains—had even witnessed the death penalty inflicted on the murderer and the mutineer.

Mute and terrible witnesses were they to the guilt to which human nature may descend—to the abysmal depths of despair into which the felon and the outcast may be hurled, when, hopeless of help from God or man, he abandons himself to all the baser instincts.

We seldom lingered amid these sullen retreats, around which Miranda always declared she heard sighs and groanings, sobs, and even shrieks, as though the spirits of those who had suffered, and mourned, and died amidst the horrors unspeakable of prison life still lingered amid the ruins of their place of torment.

How strange, well-nigh impossible, it even seemed to me that the very earth, the dumb witness of crime immeasurable, was not polluted irredeemably by the deeds that she had perforce endured and condoned. And now—stranger than aught that dreaming poet or seer imagined—that this Inferno should have been transmuted into an Arcadia, purer and more stainless than the fabled land of old, and peopled by the most obediently moral and conscientious family of mankind that had ever gathered the fruits of the earth since the days of our first parents.

Day after day followed of this charmed life—magical, unreal, only in that it transcended all my other experiences in the degree that the glamour of fairyland and the companionship of the queen of Elfland may have exceeded the memorials of Ercildoune. If he was enchanted, I was spellbound even as true Thomas. Never had I met with a companion who combined all the charm of womanhood—the grace and joyousness of girlhood's most resistless period—with the range of thought and intellectual progress which this singular girl, amid her lonely isle and restricted companionship, had explored. And withal, she had remained in her almost infantine unconsciousness of evil—her virginal, instinctive repulsion of all things forbidden and debarred—like a being of another planet.

Naturally an end arrived to this blissful state of things. The man-of-war after a few days was compelled to continue her voyage and perform her allotted duties, which comprehended surveys of uncharted coast-lines and suspected rocks. I had to choose between going on to Sydney and remaining in this charmed isle. And here inclination and duty appeared to draw different ways with equal strength. I was naturally anxious to return to my birth-place, my family, and friends. My feelings of home-sickness had returned with redoubled strength after being long in abeyance. But all such doubts and distrusts were swept away like storm wrack before the swelling surges of Miranda's own isle. I was fain to yield to the resistless force of the passion which now dominated, nay, consumed me. True, I had not as yet definitely assured myself that this purest pearl of womanhood was within my grasp. I had made no proffer of my affections. I had not, in so many words, solicited the priceless gift of hers. But I was not so unskilled in affairs of the heart as to mistake many a sign and symbol from Love's own alphabet, denoting that the outworks of the citadel were yielding, and that the fortress would ere long open gate and drawbridge to the invader.

True to nature's own teaching, Miranda had not scrupled to confess and dilate upon the pleasure my companionship afforded her, to declare that never before in her life had she been half so happy, to wonder if my sisters would not die of joy when I returned, to chide me for my long absence from them and from such a home as I had often described to her. And all this with the steady eye and frank expression of girlish pleasure, which a less unsophisticated damsel would scarcely have acknowledged without conscious blushes and downcast eyes.

Miranda, on the other hand, stated her sensations calmly and fearlessly, her wondrous eyes meeting mine with all the trustful eagerness of a happy child, as if it was the most natural thing in the world. "You see, Hilary," she would say, laying her hand lightly on my arm, and looking up in an appealing manner, "I have never met any one before who seems to understand my feelings as you do apparently by instinct. You have travelled and been in other places besides the islands, and you have read books—nearly all those which I have. You know that story in the *Arabian Nights* about the prince that was changed into a bird? He knew that he was a prince, yet he was condemned to be dumb, and was unable to convey his feelings, because to all the world he was only a bird.

"I sometimes think we Pitcairn girls live the life of birds—like that one," and she pointed to a soaring white-winged sea-bird, which presently darted downwards, falling like a stone upon the blue ocean wave. "We swim and fish, we are almost more on the sea than the land, we sleep on the land like that white bird, walk a little, talk a little,—that is our whole life. I think the bird has the best of it, as she can fly and we cannot."

"But you all seem happy and contented," I said, "you and your cousins."

"*They* are, but I seem to have been born under a different star. I must have inherited some of the restless, adventurous spirit of my ancestor, Fletcher Christian.

"The feeling of unrest and the desire to see the world—the wonderful, ancient, beautiful world of which we, in this island prison, for lovely as it is, it is but a prison for free souls—becomes so intense at times that I almost dread lest I should end my life like his."

"And in what way was that?" I asked. "God forbid you should ever do a deed so terrible," I said.

"Do you not know? He used to go every day to the top of a high cliff on the south side of Pitcairn to gaze over the ocean—as I have done hundreds of times—thinking, perhaps, of the wonderlands beyond, where he had forfeited the right to live by his own act; and—and one day he threw himself over the cliff, and they found his body on the rocks below. Poor Fletcher! I can partly understand his feelings."

This was but one of our many conversations, always fascinating to me, as affording the rare privilege of exploring a mind naturally of high intelligence, developed by patient thought and a wide range of reading,—the island library, enriched by many generous gifts, being by no means a poor one,—guarded from deterioration by an exquisite natural refinement, yet withal clear and limpid as the transparent seas which encircled her home, where the more deeply the eye penetrated the more precious were the treasures disclosed.

So it came to pass that the *Rosario* sailed without me. The Captain and my jolly comrades of the gun-room chaffed me about what they called my imprudent attachment. "You'll have to turn Pitcairner," they said, "and settle down after old Nobbs has spliced you upon a fifty-acre patch, where you can grow sweet potatoes, yams, and maize to the end of your days. Surely a fellow like you, with a family to go back to, has something better in view than that!"

"I shall not stay on the island," I said, "I intend to live in Australia, perhaps near Sydney."

"Then your island princess will run away and leave you disconsolate. They can't live away from their people and where they were brought up. Some of them insisted on going back to Pitcairn, and are there now. They could not be persuaded from it. They had to let them go. They would have died else."

"I have resolved," I said. "I will take all risks. You shall all come and see us in Sydney. We will live at North Shore, and have a yacht built on the lines of the *Leonora*. Adios!"

So we parted. The *Rosario* got up steam, and once more I watched the black cloud of smoke pouring from her funnels and the waves breaking as she moved majestically across the bright-hued ocean.

Up to the last moment my simple and warm-hearted friends on the island had serious doubts as to whether I was not going off in the *Rosario*. They could hardly understand how I could prefer remaining as their guest and friend when the glory and dignity of a man-of-war—their highest expression of maritime splendour—were open to me.

They had, it is true, implored me to stay with them for a few months longer—the young men were equally pressing with the older members of the community. With artless candour the girls promised that if I would stay Miranda should be my constant companion, and, except on Sundays, when, as their chief musician and organist, she could not naturally be spared, I should have a monopoly of her society.

"You seem to like her so much," Dorcas Quintal repeatedly exclaimed. "And I am certain she likes you more than any one she has ever seen. The worst of it is that she will be so sorry when you have to go away. Clara Young nearly died when her friend went away. That was two years ago. But she got over it in time, and now she is happily married. But she *did* try to drown herself one day, only we were too quick for her."

"It is a bad thing to have strangers for friends," I said, "if it may end so tragically when they leave. I wonder you entertain such dangerous visitors."

"I suppose we can't help it," the girl replied, laughingly. "It is so pleasant to talk with men who know the great world we can only read about. We just take our chance. We have plenty to do, and that prevents us from fretting too much. I daresay you will hear a little crying to-night. We are all very sorry the big ship is gone."

"It's the old, old story, Dorcas! Girls are a good deal alike all the world over, I suppose, in many of their ways. But you Pitcairners are certainly different in some respects to any women I know anywhere."

"What do you mean?" asked the girl, eagerly. "I know we are simple, and have never been taught very much."

"It isn't that. I will tell you before I go, or rather, I will tell Miranda, and she shall tell you what I say."

So, with the full approbation of friends and relations of every degree of relationship, and, what was of more consequence, with the goodwill of the spiritual pastor and master of the island, whose authority was absolute and unquestioned, Miranda and I pursued our untroubled way. In this wondrous Arcadia there were no jealousies, no scandals, no asking of intentions, no fiery, disappointed aspirants, no infuriated brothers,—these obstacles to pure and true love were evidently the outcome of a higher or a lower stage of civilisation. No evil consequences had ever occurred from unrestricted freedom of intercourse between the young people since the formation of the community. No such result was regarded as possible. Immutably fixed in my own course, I knew that nothing—humanly speaking—could affect my unalterable resolve. I had discovered a pearl of womanhood, matchless in beauty of mind and body, combining the higher mental qualities, indeed, with such physical perfection as no girl reared under less fortunate conditions was likely to possess. With regard to the future, if she consented to link her fate with mine I was ready to take all the risks of fortune. The fickle goddess has always favoured the brave, and with Miranda at my side I felt that I could lead the forlorn hopes of desperate endeavour, or endure uncomplainingly the toil and self-denial of the humblest station. I had, it is true, led a careless, somewhat epicurean life in the past, surrendering myself perhaps too readily to the charm of island life. But this was of the past, and the half-instinctive folly period of youth. Henceforth I would essay the culture of the mental qualities with which I had been reasonably gifted, turning to account also that very sound and thorough early tuition through which I had fortunately passed. Thus equipped, and with a helpmate at once loving and practical—devoted to duty and the highest forms of unselfish charity—ambitious only for intellectual experience and development—I felt that hope became certainty and success a mere matter of detail. After the departure of the *Rosario* I became almost a son by adoption among the elders of the community. I learned to accommodate myself to their ways, after a fashion which was rendered more easy by my years of familiarity with island life. At the same time I was careful not to infringe in the slightest degree upon their peculiar customs, or to shock those religious prejudices which were so earnestly accepted in the community. It was taken for granted that I would settle among them in right of my bride. If I decided to marry Miranda, or any other island maiden, I should be put in possession of a landed estate of fifty acres, where I might dream away life in a round of labour that was half recreation, wandering amid the island groves, reclining under giant ferns or lofty pines, bathing in crystal founts or clear-hued seas at dawn or under the yellow moon. Passing contentedly from youth to middle age, from that half-way stage to a later span of life, which in this enchanted land implied little or no diminution of natural powers. Should it be so?

This question I had asked Miranda more than once. But she would not consent to take it seriously. One day, however, I compelled her to listen, though she had again declared that we were so happy as we were that no change could be for the better, possibly for the worse—even.

"Then, Miranda," I answered, "I must leave the island. Did we not hear from the last whaler that called in for fresh provisions that my old friend—the friend of the family, Captain Carryall, was to touch here in the *Florentia*?" He was the best known, the most popular of all the skippers next to Captain Hayston. Unlike him, however, his reputation was spotless, while for fair dealing and adherence to his promises his fame was proverbial. "Shall I go with him?" I said, "and must I go alone?"

"And would you leave me?" she asked, imploringly—her dark eyes turned towards my face in a passion of reproachful tenderness, of which she herself scarce understood the meaning, "Oh! I thought once that I could let you go, though it has been life and happiness untold having you to talk to and read with. I fancied I should only mourn for you for a while—like the other island girls who weep and lament, and then dry their tears and dance and sing as if nothing had happened. But, oh! It is not so with me. They always say the Fletcher-Christians are different. I shall die! I shall die! I know I shall."

And with that she cast herself on my neck, sobbing as though her heart would break. In the same breath declaring that she would never consent to spoil my life by marriage with a poor savage island girl, but a few degrees superior to the women of Pingelap and Ocean Island whom she had so often despised.

By degrees I persuaded her to listen to my pleadings, and then calmly set before her my plans for the future. We must be married here, and after remaining on the island, living the idyllic life we were revelling in now, we would sail for Sydney in the *Florentia*, or some other vessel, and there begin life in earnest. Some employment would be found, doubtless, which would pave the way, by which I might make a serious effort towards a career, perhaps a competency in the future, or even a fortune.

I had but little difficulty in carrying out my plan. The elders of the community, the relations and friends of Miranda, were overjoyed at the prospect of her marriage with a person of my position, who might also be enabled to do them many a good turn if I settled in Sydney, a port with which they had close business relations. I found, too, that I was not altogether an unknown personage. Some of the young men who had made voyages in whaleships had heard of my companionship with Captain Hayston. However, it would seem that all the natives whom they had met had given a good account of me as a fair dealer, and, moreover, generous in my treatment of them, — an apparently unimportant matter at the time, but serious enough now. Miranda told me afterwards, that had it been otherwise nothing would have induced her guardians to give their consent, or her to defy their decision.

As it was, however, all seemed *couleur de rose*. No great preparations were needed. The simple island fashion was not encumbered with any great multiplication of garments. On the happy day Miranda was escorted to the modest building which did duty for a church by a band of white-robed maidens, in whose dark hair was wreathed the crimson blossoms of the coral plant and the hibiscus, with little other adornment but nature's furnishing in the flower-time of life. My comrades were selected from the younger men of the island, among whom I had always taken care to stand well, joining in their sports, and entering as an equal competitor their athletic contests. I was therefore looked upon as a most desirable acquaintance, able to hold my own, moreover, in all manly accomplishments (except swimming), and much esteemed for a gift of relating adventures in strange lands, and describing the foreign manners and customs with which a roving life had made me familiar.

It might have been imagined that a girl so singularly gifted and attractive as Miranda would have had lovers in abundance, by whom a successful aspirant like myself would be regarded with jealousy. Unlikely as it may appear I observed no feeling of this kind. In that strange society, the passions which rage so fiercely in more civilised communities appeared to have lost their force, or to flow with the peaceful motion of the incoming tide rather than the resistless rush of a mountain torrent, which love, hate, jealousy, and envy in other lands so often resemble. The young men admired Miranda, indeed, worshipped her from afar. But they seemed rather elated by her good fortune, as it so appeared to them, than enviously disposed, and had no thought of other than the warmest friendship for their more fortunate companion. Even Fletcher Quintal, who might have been expected to view with dislike, if not a stronger sensation, my marriage with his favourite cousin, had apparently no feeling of this sort. He certainly expressed none, but congratulated me with all the warmth which a brother might be supposed to exhibit at the marriage of his best loved sister with his dearest friend. Truly it *was* the long lost rediscovered Arcadia. There were moments when I doubted whether it was wise to leave a land where care was unknown; where want, with its attendant evils, had never been heard of; where there were no rich men to envy; no bad ones to fear; no poor to despise; where no one died but of old age or mishap; whence all the ills that flesh is heir to had, like the snakes of Ireland, been banished by some good genius, and only the gifts of virtue, contentment, and regulated industry remained. But there was wild blood in my veins, long dormant as it had lain. The murmur of the ocean seemed to call me with a tone of magical power. I longed for the wave-music once more—for the voyage which was to speed me to my birthland. I hurried on the preparations for our wedding, and, lingering though were all the slow sweet hours, endless the days, almost tedious the soft starlight glow of the summer nights, the day of days at last dawned that was to herald the happiness of a lifetime.

Our small domain had been carefully measured and marked out for us. A cottage had been built, thatched with palm leaves, floored with the soft mats of the island, simply furnished, and, as it happened, near to a bubbling spring, and shaded by the wondrous wild orange, which here grows almost to the height and girth of a forest tree. It happened to be the flower-time of these charming fruit bearers, so that wreaths and garlands of the blossom sacred to Hymen were plentiful and profuse.

CHAPTER XV

EPITHALAMIUM

Our marriage day! Oh, day of days! Dawn of a new existence! All nature seemed to sympathise with us in our supernal joy. For us, for us alone in all the world the streamlets murmured, the breezes whispered together, the wavelets plashed musically, the blue sky glowed, the sun shone goldingly. The venerable pastor of the community—he who had watched over every man and woman present from infancy, who had christened, and married, and buried the whole population of the island as they require these offices—read the time-honoured service of the Church of England, which was followed with deepest reverential attention by all present. When he blessed our union in the solemn language of the ritual familiar to me in the days of my childhood, every head was bowed, each woman's eye was wet with heart-felt sympathy and warmest affection for their erst-while playmate.

The day was cloudless, a breeze at times sighed through the fragrant foliage of the grove wherein the little church had been built. The wavelets murmured on the beach, and the unresting surges seemed but to exchange loving memories of coral islands and crystal seas, of waving palms and the green gladness of tropic forests, of maidens, feather-crowned and flower-bejewelled, dancing on silver strands beneath the full-orbed midnight moon, or gliding, a laughing bevy of syrens, beneath the translucent wave. No sullen, dirge-like refrain on that paradisal day brought from the ocean voices the memory of drifting wrecks, of stormy seas, of drowned seamen—no hint of danger, of despair, of pestilence, and death; and yet all these phases of experience I had known and reckoned with even in my short life.

No; these and kindred ills were forgotten, banished from earth and sea. On this blissful morn the golden age of the earth seemed to have returned. Recalling the half-forgotten classics of my boyhood, I could fancy that I saw fauns peeping through the leaves of the orange grove, that the ages had reverted to the freshness of the elder world, when the flush of the fair Arcadian life informed all things with divinity.

And Miranda, my bride of brides! what words can describe her as she stood, with an expression half-timid, half-rapt, and inspired, before the humble altar that day? Her simple dress of virgin white which but slightly concealed while it outlined the curves of her statuesque form; her large dark eyes, which had often appeared to me to hold a shade of melancholy, were now irradiated by the lovelight which she, in the purity and innocence of her heart, made no attempt to conceal. Her soft, abundant tresses had been gathered up into becoming form and classic simplicity, and, save a wreath of scarlet berries and the traditional orange blossom, she wore no ornament. As all unconscious of her maiden loveliness she stood beside me, with her head raised and an expectant smile which disclosed her pearly teeth, she seemed to my enraptured gaze a daughter of the wave,—no mortal maiden, but a being compact of air and sea and sky, visible but beneath the moonbeams, and unrevealed to the dwellers of the garish day.

We had been but a month wedded; our simple home, our tiny domain, our forest rambles, our sea-baths at dawn and eve, as yet contented us—filled us with all fullest delight in which mortal beings can revel beneath this ethereal dome. And yet the spirit of unrest, the veritable serpent of the world's fairest Aidenns, gradually found means to discover himself.

Miranda and I had, indeed, begun to discuss our projected voyage to Sydney, and I had many times described to her an ideal home on one of the thousand and one bays which render the northern shore of the unrivalled Sydney harbour matchless in beauty and convenience for those who, like myself, have salt water in their blood. She agreed with me, that with a boat, a garden, a bath-house, and a cottage built of the beautiful white, pink-veined sandstone, which is so abundant beneath and around Sydney, existence might be endured away from her island home, with the aid of books and the inspiring idea of the coming fortune.

"And even if we do not make money," she said, "as people call it— what a strange idea it seems to me, who have hardly ever seen any— we shall be happy. I can't imagine people who are married and love each other ever being unhappy. Then your mother and sisters—I am so much afraid of them. They will regard me as a kind of savage, I am sure; and, indeed, compared with them, or real civilised people, I am afraid that I shall feel like one. And, oh! shall we ever be happier than we are now? Why should we change? Do you think we can come back now and then and visit my people? I should break my heart if I thought I should see them no more!"

I promised this and other things, doubtless, at the time. But before we had completed the conversation about our future life—which indeed supplied us with endless subjects of interest—the great island wonder-sign appeared. A shout—a rush of excited people past our hut told of a ship in sight. We were down at the beach nearly as soon as the others, and as a long, low barque came up before the wind, something told me that she was the *Florentia*.

A boat—a whaleboat, with a kanaka crew—put off soon after she was at anchor, and in the tall man at the steer-oar, whose commanding figure, even at that distance, I seemed to know, there was no difficulty in identifying our old friend Captain Carryall.

Directly he jumped ashore, a dozen of the islanders dashed into the surf and ran the boat up on the beach. Our recognition was mutual.

"Well, young fellow!" he said, "I've been hunting you up half over the South Seas. Wherever have you stowed yourself all this time? Why, what a man you've grown—a couple of inches taller than me, and I'm no pony. Brown as a berry, too! You'll have to come home with me this trip. Your old man's beginning to get anxious about you—and you know he's not much in that line—and your mother and sisters."

"Captain Carryall," I said, "there's no necessity for more reasons. I'm going to Sydney with you if you'll give me a passage."

"Half a dozen if you want it," quoth the jolly sailor. "And now I must have a word with my friends. Anybody been married since I was here last; no Quintals—no Millses! Mary, how's this? Dorcas—Grace—Mercy Young, I'm ashamed of you. And Miranda! Nobody run away with you yet? I see I must take you to Sydney and show you at a Government House ball. Then they'd see what a Pitcairn girl was like."

"You may do that yet," I said, "for, seriously, Miranda is now Mrs. Hilary Telfer. We have been married more than a month."

The captain could not refrain from giving a prolonged whistle at this announcement, which certainly appeared to take him by surprise. However, he rallied with ease and celerity, and addressing Miranda, whose hand he took as he spoke, said, "My dear! let me congratulate the son of my old friend, Captain Telfer, upon his marriage with the best, cleverest, and prettiest girl I have fallen across in all my wanderings. I don't suppose you have any great amount of capital to begin life with; but if two young people like you don't manage to find some path to fortune in a country like Australia, I'm a Dutchman. He needs to be a good fellow, and a man all round, to be worthy of Miranda Christian; but he can't help, as the son of his father and his mother, being all that, and more. So now, my dear! you must let me kiss you, as your husband's old friend, and wish you all happiness."

Miranda blushed as the warm-hearted fellow folded her in his arms, but submitted with becoming grace; and leaving her among her young friends, he and I strolled away towards our hut to talk over affairs more at leisure.

"Well, youngster!" said he, laying his hand on my shoulder, "I suppose you've had enough island life for a while, and won't be sorry to see Sydney Heads again. Nor I either. I've been out fifteen months this time, and that's rather long to be away from one's home and picaninnies. They'll be glad to see your face again at Rose Bay, I'll be bound. But they certainly will be taken aback when you turn up as a married man. Nineteen times out of twenty it's a mistake to tie one's self up for life at your age. But all depends upon getting the right woman, and Miranda is the one woman in a thousand that a man might be proud to marry, whether he was rich or poor, and to work and wear out his life for all his days. I've known her since she was a baby, and, taking her all round, I don't know her equal anywhere. It seems queer to say so, considering her birth and bringing up. But these Pitcairners are well known to be the best and finest women, in all womanly ways, that the world can show. And your wife is, and has always been, the flower of the flock."

I grasped the captain's hand. I knew that I had secured a powerful ally; and though I felt so secure in the wisdom of my choice that no disapprobation of family and friends would have had power to affect me, yet, in such matters, it is well to have a friend at court, and the captain's reputation for sense and sagacity stood so high, that I felt not only my relatives, but my acquaintances and friends, would be strongly swayed by his judgment.

"Now that we've got so far," he said, "you had better make your arrangements to sail with me on Sunday morning; this is Thursday, but my passengers want to see the island and the people of whom they have heard so much."

"Passengers!" I said. "How many? and where from?"

"Well, I picked them up at Honolulu. Half a dozen, and very nice people, too. They came in an English yacht that went to San Francisco for them, and they wanted to see Australia, and so came with me. They're rather big people at home, I believe, though they're very quiet, and give themselves no airs."

"Any ladies?"

"There are two married couples, and a young lady, with her brother."

"That's very serious, captain," said I. "I don't quite know how Miranda will get on with travelling Englishwomen—they're rather difficult sometimes."

"Miranda will get on with any one," answered the captain, with a decided air. "She will sit on my right hand, as a bride, and no one in my ship will show her less than proper respect. Anyhow, these people are not that sort. You'll see she's all ready to start on Sunday morning. 'The better the day, the better the deed.'"

So the captain went to pay a visit to the people of the settlement, among whom his free, pleasant manner and generous bearing had made him most popular. The girls crowded around him, laughing and plying him with questions about the commissions he had promised to execute for them, and the presents he had brought. These attentions he never omitted. Full of curiosity they were, too, about the English ladies on board. "How they were dressed?" "How long they would stay in Sydney?" "What they would think of the poor Pitcairn girls?" and so on.

With the elders he told of the whaleships he had spoken, and of their cargoes of oil—of the Quintals, or Youngs, Mills, or M'Coys who were harpooners and boat-steerers on board some of the Sydney whalers, and of the chances of their "lay" or share of profit being a good one. Besides all this, the captain consented to act as their ambassador to the Governor-General in Sydney, and lay before that potentate certain defects of their island administration—small, perhaps, in themselves, but highly important to the members of an isolated community. In addition to all this, he (as I heard afterwards) specially attended to my marriage with Miranda, of which he highly approved; telling the old pastor and the elders of the community that he had known my father for ever so many years; that he was highly respected now, when retired, but had been well known in the South Seas and New Zealand many years ago as the captain of the *Orpheus*, one of the most successful whalers that ever sailed through Sydney Heads.

"Captain Telfer of the *Orpheus*!" said one of the oldest men of the group, "I remember him well. I was cast away on Easter Island the time the *Harriet* was wrecked in a hurricane. He gave me a free passage to Tahiti, a suit of clothes, and ten dollars when I left the ship. He wanted me to finish the voyage with him and go to Sydney. I was sorry afterwards I didn't. He was a fine man, and a better seaman never trod plank. No wonder Hilary is such a fine chap. I can see the likeness now. I don't hold with our young women going off this island in a general way, but Miranda is a lucky girl to have Captain Telfer's son for a husband." All this the captain told me afterwards with slight embellishments and variations of his own.

My reputation had fairly gone before, but this light thrown on my parentage placed me in a most exalted position—next to their spiritual pastor and master, before whom they bowed in genuine respect and reverence. Perhaps there is no man in the whole world more honoured and admired in the South Seas than the captain of a ship. And now that the name of my father's barque, once pretty well known south of the line, had been recalled from the past, every doubt as to the future of Miranda and myself was set at rest.

We were invested, so to speak, with the blessing of the whole community, and began our modest preparations with added cheerfulness and resolve.

In the afternoon we saw a boat put off from the *Florentia* and the visitors land. They were five in number. We could see them walk over to the village, where they were met by some of the principal people and a few of the women and girls. We had been making ready for our voyage, and having finished our simple meal, sat in the shade of our orange tree, near the door, and awaited the strangers whom I judged rightly that curiosity and the captain would bring to our dwelling.

In less than an hour's time we saw them strolling along the path which led to our nest. As they approached we arose and went to meet them, when the captain with all due form introduced us, "The Honourable Mr. and Mrs. Craven, Colonel Percival, Mr. Vavasour, and his sister, Miss Vavasour." Mrs. Percival had remained on board, as her little boy of four or five years old was not well. Miranda, rather to my surprise, was perfectly unembarrassed, and talked away to the stranger ladies as if she had been accustomed to the society business all her life.

I could see that they were pleased and surprised at her appearance, as also gratified with the manner in which she invited them to inspect our simple dwelling.

"Oh! what a charming nest of a place—quite a bower of bliss!" cried Miss Vavasour. "I declare I will come here when I am married and spend my honeymoon. What shade and fragrance combined! What a lovely crystal lakelet to bathe in! and I suppose, Mrs. Telfer, you go out fishing in that dear canoe? What an ideal life!"

"I quite agree with you and feel quite envious," said Mrs. Craven. "Charlie and I have been married too long to have our honeymoon over again; but it would have been idyllic, wouldn't it, Charlie?"

"Splendid place to smoke in," assented her husband. "No hounds meet nearer than Sydney, though, I presume. Drawback rather, isn't it?"

"You men are always thinking of horses, and hounds or guns," pouted Miss Vavasour. "What can one want with them here? What can life offer more than this endless summer, this fairy bower, this crystal wave, this air which is a living perfume? It is an earthly paradise."

"And the beloved object," added Mrs. Craven, with quiet humour. "You have left him out. It would be an incomplete paradise without Adam."

"Oh! here he comes!" exclaimed Miranda (as she told me afterwards), who had not been attending to the enthusiastic speech, but was watching bird-like for my approach.

"Who? Adam?" said Miss Vavasour, laughingly.

"Oh, no!" answered she, smiling at the apparent absurdity. "You must excuse me a little, but I was looking out for Hilary."

"Now, then, ladies!" said the cheerful voice of Captain Carryall, "we must get back to our boat. It's dangerous to stop ashore all night, isn't it, Miranda? We must leave you to finish your packing. It's a long voyage to Sydney, eh? It may be years before you see the island again."

We all went down together to the boat, where the visitors were seen off by all the young people of the island, the girls wondering with respectful admiration at the English ladies' dresses, hats, boots, and shoes—in fact, at everything they did and said as well. It was a revelation to them, not that they had any envious feeling about those cherished possessions. They had been too well trained for that, and were secure in the guidance of their deeply-rooted religious faith and lofty moral code. On the other hand, their visitors admired sincerely the noble forms and free, graceful bearing of the island maidens, as well as the splendid athletic development of the men.

"Here, you Thursday Quintal, come and show these ladies how you can handle a steer-oar," called out the captain. "He was the boat-steerer on board the *Florentia* one voyage, and steered in the pulling race for whaleboats at the regatta on anniversary day, which we won the year before last in Sydney harbour. We'll bring you ashore in the morning."

"Ay, ay, captain," said the young fellow, showing his splendid teeth in a pleasant smile. "It will feel quite natural to take an oar in a boat of yours again."

The wind had freshened during the afternoon, and the rollers on the beach lifted the whaleboat as she came up to the landing rather higher than the ladies fancied. However, they were carefully seated, and at the captain's word, "Give way, my lads," the crew picked her up in great style, while Quintal, standing with easy grace at the stern, the sixteen foot oar in his strong grasp, directed her course with instinctive skill so as to avoid the growing force of the wave. As he stood there—tall, muscular, glorious in the grace and dignity of early manhood—he seemed the embodiment of a sculptor's dream.

"What a magnificent figure!" said Mrs. Craven to her young friend. "How rare it is to see such a form in Mayfair!"

"I surmise, as our American girl said at Honolulu," replied Miss Vavasour, "that you might look a long time before you saw such a man among our 'Johnnies'; and what eyes and teeth he has! Really I feel inclined to rebel. Here's this Mr. Telfer, too, and what a grand-looking fellow he is, and an English gentleman besides in all his ways. He can make his way to this out of the way speck in the ocean, and secure a Miranda for a life companion—glorious girl she is too—while we poor English spins have to wait till a passable *pretendu* comes along,—old, bald, stupid, or diminutive, as the case may be,—and are bound to take him under penalty of dying old maids. I call it rank injustice, and I'd head a revolution tomorrow; and oh!—"

The interjection which closed the speech of this ardent woman's righter was caused by the onward course of a breaking wave, which was not avoided so deftly as usual, and splashed the speaker and Mrs. Craven.

"Hulloa! Quintal, what are you about?" said the captain, "is this your steering that I've been blowing about to these ladies and gentlemen? Miss Vavasour! I'm afraid it's your fault, you know the rule aboard ship? Passengers are requested not to speak to the man at the wheel."

"But there's no regulation, captain, that the man at the steer-oar is not to look at the passengers," said Mrs. Craven. "However, here we are nearly on board, so there's no harm done, and we're only a trifle damped."

Clear-hued—calm—waveless—dawned our farewell day. I was glad of it. Rain and storm-clouds lower the spirits more distinctly when one is about to make a departure than at any other time, besides the inconvenience of wet or bedraggled garments. It was the Sabbath day, and the pastor arranged a special service in commemoration of Miranda's marriage and departure from the island. All the ship's company that could be spared came, of course; the visitors made a point of attending. The little church was crowded. Except the youngest children and their guardians, every soul on the island was there.

After the Church of England service, which the islanders had at their fingers' ends, and in which they all most reverently joined, hymns were sung, in which the rich voices of the young girls were heard to great advantage. There was a strange and subtle harmony pervading the part-singing, which seemed natural to the race, more particularly in those parts in which the whole of the congregation joined. As Miranda played on the harmonium, it may have occurred to her friends and playmates for the last time, many of them could not restrain their tears. The aged pastor after the Liturgy preached a feeling and sympathetic address, which certainly went to the hearts of all present. He made particular allusion to our union and departure.

"One of the children of the island," he said, "who had endeared herself to all by her unselfish kindness of heart, who had been marked out by uncommon gifts, both mental and physical, was to leave them that day. She might be absent for years, perhaps they might not see her face again,—that face upon which no one had seen a frown, nor hear that voice which had never uttered an unkind word," here the greater part of the congregation, male and female, fell a-weeping and lamenting loudly. "But they must take comfort; our beloved one was not departing alone, she had been joined in holy matrimony with a youth of whom any damsel might feel proud; he was the husband of her choice, the son of a master mariner well known and highly respected in former years throughout the wide

Pacific. He himself had often heard of him in old days, and the son of such a father was worthy to be loved and trusted. The child of our hearts would go forth, even as Rebecca left her home and her people with Isaac, and God's blessing would surely rest upon all her descendants as upon the children of the promise.

"He would ask all now assembled to join in prayers for the welfare of Hilary Telfer and Miranda, his wife."

As the venerable man pronounced the words of the benediction, echoed audibly by the whole of the congregation, the sobs of the women were audible, while tears and stifled sighs were the rule, and not the exception. As the congregation rose from their knees, he walked down to the *Florentia's* boats, it having been so arranged by the captain, who had invited all who could by any means attend, to lunch on board his vessel. Farewells were said on the beach to all who were perforce detained by age, infirmity, or other causes, and at length we were safely seated in the captain's boat, and putting off, were followed by a perfect fleet of every size and carrying capacity.

Miranda hid her face and wept silently. I did not attempt to persuade her to moderate her grief, as the outlet of over-strung feelings, of genuine and passionate regret, it was a natural and healthful safety-valve for an overburdened heart.

"I don't think I was ever more impressed with our Church service," said Mrs. Craven. "That dear, venerable old man, and his truly wonderful congregation! How earnestly they listened, and how reverently they behaved!"

"Think of our rustics in a village church!" said Miss Vavasour, "the conceited choir, the sleeping labourers, the giggling school children, where do you ever see anything like what we have witnessed to-day? However did they manage to grow up so blameless, and to keep so good and pure minded? Can you tell me, Mr. Telfer?"

"My knowledge of my wife's people is chiefly from hearsay," I said; "I can remember the old tale of the Mutiny of the *Bounty* when I was a school-boy in Sydney. Captain Bligh, of the ill-fated ship, was afterwards the Governor of New South Wales. Whether his conduct provoked the mutiny, of which Miranda's great grandfather was the leader, or whether the crew were overcome by the temptations of a life in that second garden of Eden, Tahiti, has been disputed, and perhaps can never be definitely known. This much is certain, that the sole surviving mutineer, John Adams, deeply repentant, changed his rule of life. Morning and evening prayer was established, and a system of instruction for the children and young people regularly carried out. Such was the apparently accidental commencement of the religious teaching of the little community at the beginning of the century. Some of the results you have witnessed to-day."

"It certainly is the most wonderful historiette in the whole world," said Miss Vavasour, who had listened with deep interest. "I never saw so many nice people in one place before—all good—all kind—all contented, and all happy. It makes one believe in the millennium; I must try what I can do with our village when I get back to Dorsetshire."

"You'll have your work cut out for you, Miss Vavasour," said Colonel Percival. "Fancy the old poachers and the hardened tramps, the beer-drinking yokels and the rough field-hands. Work of years, and doubtful then."

"Oh! dear, why do we call ourselves civilised, I wonder?" sighed the enthusiastic damsel, just awakened to a sense of the duties of property in correlation with the "rights." "I really believe Englishmen—the lower classes, of course—are the most ill-mannered, uncivilised people in the world. Look at those dear islanders, how polite and unselfish they are in their behaviour to each other, and to us! It makes me feel ashamed of my country. Why, even at a presentation to Her Majesty people push, and crush, and look as black as thunder if you tread on their absurd trains."

"You ought to come out and join the Melanesian Mission, my dear," said Mrs. Craven. "There is no knowing, with your energy and convictions, what good you might do."

"I wish I could," said the girl eagerly. "But I'm not good enough, I wish I was. If I felt I could keep up my present feelings I'd go to-morrow. But I'm selfish and worldly-minded, like my neighbours in Christendom. It would be no use. I should only spoil my own life, and not mend theirs."

"Such has been the confession of many an earnest reformer, who had started in life with high hopes and a scorn of consequences," said Mr. Vavasour quietly; "it is by far the most common result of heroic self-sacrifice. If we did not occasionally see the accomplished fact, as in this case, we might well despair."

"And this was an accident of accidents," said Miss Vavasour sorrowfully. "No missionary society sent away the pioneer preachers to the heathen with prayers, and flags, and collections. No, here is the grandest feat ever accomplished in the world's history. The most religious, contented, consistent community in the whole world evolved from a crew of runaway sailors and a few poor savage women! Really there must be some good in human nature after all, reviled and insulted as it is by all the extra good people."

The *Florentia* had not had so large a party on board since the last successful affair in Sydney harbour. That one included dancing, which did not enter into this entertainment. Nothing, however, could have gone off better. The curiosity of the young women about the ladies' belongings was amply gratified, and the luncheon voted the very best one at which they had ever been entertained.

A mirthful and joyous gathering it was. The visitors were charmed with, the naturally refined and courteous manners of the guests. And, finally, as the day wore on, and the breeze from the land promised a good offing, Miranda came up from her cabin, to which she had elected to retire, and bade farewell to friends and kinsfolk, who departed in their boats, much less saddened of mien than they had been in the morning.

Once more at sea. The *Florentia*, though a whaler, and not ornamented up to yachting form, was yet extremely neat and spotlessly clean, as far as could be managed by a smart and energetic captain. She was a fast sailer, and as the wind off the land freshened at sundown, she spread most of her canvas and sped before the breeze after a fashion which would have made her a not unworthy comrade of the *Leonora*.

Miranda had retired to her cabin. Her heart was too full for jesting converse, and after she had watched the last speck of her loved island disappear below the horizon, she was fain to go below to hide her tears, and relieve her feelings by unrestrained indulgence in grief.

For my part, after a cheerful dinner in the cuddy, I remained long on deck, pacing up and down, and revolving in my mind plans for our future. As I felt the accustomed sway of the vessel, listened to the creaking of the rigging, which was music in my ears, and watched the waves fall back from her sides in hissing foam-flakes, as the aroused vessel, feeling the force of the rising gale, drove through the darkening wave-masses, and seemed to defy the menace of the deep, the memories of my early island life came back to me. The luxurious, halcyon days, the starlit, silent nights, when ofttimes I had wandered to the shore, and seating myself on a coral rock, gazed over the boundless watery waste, wondering ever about my career, my destined fate.

Then returned the strange and wayward memories of Hayston and his lawless associates—the reckless traders, the fierce half-castes, the savage islanders! Again I heard the soft voices of Lālia, Nellie, Kitty of Ebon, and smiled as I recalled their pleading, infantine ways, their flashing eyes, so eloquent in love or hate. All were gone; all had become phantoms of the past. With that stage and season of my life they had passed away—irrevocably, eternally—and now I possessed an incentive to labour, ambition, and self-denial such as I had never before known. With such a companion as Miranda, where was the man who would not have displayed the higher qualities of his nature, who would not have risen to the supremest effort of labour, valour, or self-abnegation? Before Heaven I vowed that night, that neither toil nor trouble, difficulty nor danger, should deter me from the pursuit of fortune and distinction. So passed our first day at sea.

With the one that followed the gale abated, and as the *Florentia* swept southward under easy sail, comfort was restored. The passengers settled themselves down to the enjoyment of that absolute rest and passive luxuriousness which characterise board-ship life in fine weather. Miss Vavasour and Miranda were soon deep in earnest conversation, both for the time disregarding the books with which they had furnished themselves. Mrs. Craven had devoted herself to an endless task of knitting, which apparently supplied a substitute for thought, reading, recreation, and conversation.

I was talking to the captain when a lady came up the companion, followed by the colonel, who half lifted, half led a fine little boy of four or five years of age.

"Oh," said the captain, with a sudden movement towards the new arrivals, "I see Mrs. Percival has come on deck. Come over and be introduced." We walked over, and I received a formal bow from a handsome, pale woman, who had evidently been sojourning in the East. There is a certain similarity in all "Indian women," as they are generally called, which extends even to manner and expression. Long residence in a hot climate robs them of their roses, while the habit of command, resulting from association with an inferior race, gives them a tinge of hauteur—not to say unconscious insolence of manner—which is scarcely agreeable to those who, from circumstances, they may deem to be socially inferior.

So it was that Miranda, in spite of Miss Vavasour's nods and signals, received but the faintest recognition, and retreated to her chair somewhat chilled by her reception. She, however, took no apparent notice of the slight, and was soon absorbed in conversation with Miss Vavasour, her brother, and Mrs. Craven, who had moved up her chair to join the party. The colonel deserted his former friends to devote himself to his family duties, while the captain and I walked forward and commenced a discussion which had, at any rate, a strong personal interest for me.

"Now look here, Hilary," said he, as he lighted a fresh cigar. He had been smoking on the quarter-deck under protest, as it were, and thus commenced: "Listen to me, my boy! I've been thinking seriously about you and Miranda. Your start in life when you get to Sydney is important. I think I can give you a bit of advice worth following. You understand all the dialects between here and the Line Islands, don't you?"

"More than eight," I answered; "I can talk with nearly every islander from here to the Gilberts. I have learned so much, at any rate, in my wanderings."

A Modern Buccaneer

"And a very good thing, too, for it's not a thing that can be picked up in a year, no matter how a man may work, and he's useless or nearly so without it; you can keep accounts, write well, and all that?"

I replied that I had a number of peculiar accounts to keep as supercargo to the *Leonora*, as well as all Hayston's business letters to write; that my office books were always considered neat, complete, and well kept. Then he suddenly said, "You are the very man we want!"

"Who are we, and what is the man wanted for?" I asked.

"For the South Sea Island trade, and no other," said Captain Carryall, putting his hand on my shoulder. "Old Paul Frankston (you've heard of him) and I have laid it out to establish a regular mercantile house in Sydney for the development of the island trade. The old man will back us, and the name of Paul Frankston is good from New Zealand to the North Pole and back again. I will do the whaling, cruising, and cargo business—cocoa-nut oil, copra, and curios—while you will live in one of those nice white houses at North Shore, somewhere about Neutral Bay, where you can see the ships come through the Heads; Miranda can have a skiff, and you a ten-tonner, so as not to forget your boating and your sea-legs. What do you think of that, eh?"

"It is a splendid idea!" I cried, "and poor Miranda will be within sound of the sea. If she were not, she would pine away like her own araucarias which will not live outside of the wave music. But how about the cash part of it? I haven't much. Most of my savings went down in the *Leonora*."

"Oh, we'll manage that somehow! Old Paul will work that part of the arrangement. I daresay your father will advance what will make your share equal, or nearly so, to ours."

"It sounds well," I said. "With partners like Mr. Frankston and yourself a man ought to be able to do something. I know almost every island where trade can be got, and the price to a cowrie that should be paid. There ought to be a fortune in it in five years. What a pity Hayston couldn't have had such a chance."

"He'd have had the cash, and the other partners the experience, in less than that time," said the captain, smiling sardonically. "He was a first-rate organiser if he had not been such a d—d scoundrel. He had some fine qualities, I allow; as a seaman he had no equal. In the good old fighting days he would have been a splendid robber baron. But in these modern times, where there is a trifle of law and order in most countries, even in the South Seas he was out of place."

"He was far from a model mariner," I said, "but it hurts me to hear him condemned. He had splendid points in his character, and no one but myself will ever know how much good there was mixed up with his recklessness and despair. I left him, but I couldn't help being fond of him to the last."

"It was a good thing for you that you did—a very good thing. You will live to be thankful for it. He was a dangerous beggar, and neither man nor woman could escape his fascination. However, that's all past and gone now. You're married and settled, remember, and you're to be Hilary Telfer, Esq., J.P., and all the rest of it directly, and the only sea-going business you can have for the future is to be Commodore of the Neutral Bay Yacht Club, or some such title and distinction. And now I've done for the present. You go and see what Miranda thinks of it. I won't agree to anything unless she consents."

Miranda was charmed with the idea of a mercantile marine enterprise, so much in accordance with her previous habits and experiences. The added inducement of living on the sea-shore, with a boat, a jetty, and a bathing-house, decided her. She implicitly believed in Captain Carryall's power and ability to make our fortune; was also certain that, with Mr. Frankston's commercial aid, we should soon be as rich as the Guldensterns, the Rothschilds of the Pacific. She surrendered herself thereupon to a dream of bliss, alloyed only at intervals by a tinge of apprehension that the great undiscovered country of Sydney society might prove hostile or indifferent.

So much she communicated to Miss Vavasour as she and Mrs. Craven were reclining side by side on their deck chairs, while the *Florentia* was gliding along on another day all sunshine, azure, and favouring breeze.

"Don't you be afraid, my dear," said the kind-hearted Mrs. Craven, "you and your husband are quite able to hold your own in Sydney society or any other; indeed, I shall be inclined to bet that you'd be the rage rather than otherwise. I wish I had you in Northamptonshire, I'd undertake to 'knock out' (as Charlie says) the local belles in a fortnight."

Miranda laughed the childishly happy laugh of unspoiled girlhood. "Dear Mrs. Craven, how good of you to say so; but, of course, I know I'm a sort of savage, who will improve in a year or two if every one is as kind as you and Miss Vavasour here; but suppose they should be like her," and she motioned towards Mrs. Percival.

This lady had never relaxed the coldness and hauteur towards Miranda and myself. She had been unable to modify her "Indian manner," as Captain Carryall and Mr. Vavasour called it, and about which they made daily jokes.

As she passed the little group, she bowed slightly and without relaxation of feature, going forward to the waist of the ship, where she sat down and was soon absorbed in a book. The three friends smiled at each other, and continued their conversation.

"I should like to dress you for a garden-party, Miranda," said Miss Vavasour; "let me see now, a real summer day, such as we sometimes get in dear old England—not like this one perhaps, but very nice. A lovely old manor house like Gravenhurst or Hunsdon—such a lawn, such old trees, such a river, a marquee under an elm a hundred years old, and the county magnates marching in from their carriages."

"Oh, how delicious!" cried Miranda. "I have read such descriptions in books, but you—oh, how happy you must be to have lived it all!"

"It's very nice, but as to the happiness, that doesn't always follow," confessed the English girl with a half sigh. "I almost think you have the greater share of that. Anyhow, just as the company are assembled, I am seen walking down from the house. We are of the house party, you know, Miranda and I. She is dressed in a soft, white, embroidered muslin, very simply made, with a little, a very little Valenciennes lace. Its long straight folds hang gracefully around her matchless figure, and are confined at the waist by a broad, white moiré sash; white gloves, a white moiré parasol, a large Gainsborough hat with fleecy white feathers, and Miranda's costume is complete—the very embodiment of fresh, fair girlhood, unspotted from the world of fashion and folly."

CHAPTER XVI

A SWIM FOR LIFE

The words died on her lips as a shriek, wild, agonising, despairing, rang through the air, and startled not only the little group of pleased listeners, but all who happened to be on deck at the time. We started up and gazed towards the spot whence the cry had come. The colonel, who had been reading on the opposite side of the deck, calmly smoking the while, dropped his book and only saved his meerschaum by a cricketer's smart catch. The captain came bounding up from below, followed by the steward and his boy; the foc'sle hands, with the black cook, hurled themselves aft. All guessed the cause as they saw Mrs. Percival wringing her hands frantically and gazing at an object in the sea.

Her boy had fallen overboard! Yes! the little fellow, active and courageous beyond his years, had tried to crawl up to the shrouds while his mother's eyes were engaged in the perusal of the leading novel of the day. Weary of inaction, the poor little chap had done a little climbing on his own account, and an unexpected roll of the ship had sent him overboard. Light as the wind was, he was already a long way astern.

Long before all these observations were made, however, and while the astonished spectators were questioning their senses as to the meaning of the confusion, Miranda had sprung upon the rail, and in the next moment, with hands clasped above her head, was parting the smooth waters. Rising to the surface, she swam with rapid and powerful strokes towards the receding form of the still floating child. With less rapidity of motion, I cast myself into the heaving waste of water, not that I doubted Miranda's ability to overtake and bear up the child, but from simple inability to remain behind while all that was worth living for on earth was adrift upon the wave.

I followed in her wake, and though I failed to keep near her, for the Pitcairn islanders are among the fastest swimmers in the world, I yet felt that I might be of some use or aid. Long before I could overtake her she had caught up the little fellow, and lifting him high above the water, was swimming easily towards me.

"Oh! you foolish boy!" she cried, "why did you come after me? do you want to be drowned again?" Here she smiled and showed her lovely teeth as if it was rather a good joke. It may have been, but at that time and place I was not in the humour to perceive it.

"I came for the same reason that you did, I suppose—because I could not stay behind. If anything had happened to you what should I have done? Here comes the boat, though, and we can talk it over on board."

Some little time had been expended in lowering the boat. The ship had been brought to, but even then—and with so light a wind—it was astonishing what a distance we had fallen behind. It was a curious sensation, such specks as we were upon the immense water-plain which stretched around to the horizon. However, the *Florentia* was strongly in evidence, and nearer and nearer came the whaleboat, with the captain at the steer-oar, and the men pulling as if they were laying on a crack harpooner to an eighty barrel whale.

We were now swimming side by side, Miranda talking to the little fellow, who had never lost consciousness, and did not seem particularly afraid of his position.

"How tremendously hard they are pulling!" I said; "they are making the boat spin again. One would think they were pulling for a wager."

"So they are," answered she, "for three lives, and perhaps another. See there! God in His mercy protect us."

I followed the direction of her turned head, and my heart stood still as my eye caught the fatal sign of the monster's presence at no great distance from us. It was *the back fin of a shark*!

"Do your best, my beloved," she continued; "we must keep together, and if he overtakes us before the boat reaches, splash hard and shout as loud as you can. I have seen a shark frightened before now; but please God it may not come to that."

The boat came nearer—still nearer—but, as it seemed to us, all too slowly. The men were pulling for their lives, I could notice, and the captain frantically urging them on. They had seen the dreaded signal before us, and had commenced to race from that moment. But for some delay in the tackle for lowering, they would have been up to us before now.

As it was we did our best. I would have taken the child, but Miranda would not allow me. "His weight is nothing in the water," she said, "and I could swim faster than you, even with him." This she showed me she could do by shooting ahead with the greatest ease, and then allowing me to overtake her. I had to let her have her own way. We were lessening the distance between us and the boat, but the sea demon had a mind to overtake us, and our hearts almost failed as we noticed the sharp black fin gaining rapidly upon us. Still there was one chance, that he would not pursue us to the very side of the boat. It was a terrible moment. With every muscle strained to the uttermost, with lung, and sinew, and every organ taxed to utmost tension, I most certainly beat any previous record in swimming that I had ever attained. Miranda, with apparently but little effort, kept slightly ahead. The last few yards—shorter than the actual distance—appeared to divide us from the huge form of the monster now distinctly visible beneath the water, when with one frantic yell and a dash at the oars, which took every remaining pound of strength out of the willing crew, the boat shot up within equal distance. At a signal from the captain every oar was raised and brought down again with a terrific splash into the water, and a simultaneous yell. The effort was successful. The huge creature, strangely timid in some respects, stopped, and with one powerful side motion of fins and tail glided out of the line of pursuit. At the same moment the boat swept up, and eager arms lifted Miranda and her burden into it. My hand was on the gunwale until I saw her safe, whence with a slight amount of assistance I gained the mid-thwart.

"Saved, thank God!" cried the captain, with fervent expression, "but a mighty close thing; the next time you take a bath of this kind, my dear Miranda, with sharks around, you must let me know beforehand, eh?"

"Some one would have had to go, captain," she answered; "we couldn't see the dear little fellow drowned before our eyes. It was only a trifle after all—a swim in smooth water on a fine day: I didn't reckon on a shark being so close, I must say."

"I saw the naughty shark," said the little fellow, now quite recovered and in his usual spirits. "How close he came! do you think he would have eaten us all, captain?"

"Yes, my boy—without salt; you would never have seen your papa and mamma again if it had not been for this lady here."

"But you took us in the boat, captain," argued the little fellow; "he can't catch us in here, can he?"

"But the lady caught you in her arms long before the boat came up, my dear, or else you would have been drowned over and over again; that confounded tackle caught, or else we should have been up long before. It's a good thing they were not lowering for a whale, or my first mate's language would have been something to remember till the voyage after next. However, here we are all safe, Charlie, and there's your mother looking out for you."

A painfully eager face was that which gazed from the vessel as we rowed alongside. Every trace of the languor partly born of the tropic sun and partly of aristocratic *morgue* was gone from the countenance of Mrs. Percival, as her boy, laughing and prattling, was carried up the rope ladder and lifted on deck. His mother clasped him now passionately in her arms, sobbing, blessing, kissing him, and crying aloud that God had restored her child from the dead. "Oh, my boy! my boy!" she repeated again and again; "your mother would have died too, if you had been drowned, she would never have lived without you."

By this time Miranda had reached the deck, where she was received with a hearty British cheer from the ship's company, while the passengers crowded around her as if she had acquired a new character in their eyes. But Mrs. Percival surpassed them all; kneeling before Miranda she bowed herself to the deck, as if in adoration, and kissed her wet feet again and again.

"You have saved my child from a terrible death at the risk of your own and your husband's lives," she said. "May God forget me if I forget your noble act this day! I have been proud and unkind in my manner to you, my dear. I humble myself at your feet, and implore your pardon. But henceforth, Miranda Telfer, you and I are sisters. If

I do not do something in requital it will go hard with me and Charlie."

"Now, my dear Sybil," interposed the husband, "do you observe that Mrs. Telfer has not had time to change her dress—very wet it seems to be—and I suppose Master Charlie will be none the worse for being put to bed and well scolded, the young rascal. Come, my dear."

Colonel Percival, doubtless, felt a world of joy and relief when the light of his eyes and the joy of his heart stood safe and sound on the deck of the *Florentia* again, but it is not the wont of the British aristocrat to give vent to his emotions, even the holiest, in public. The veil of indifference is thrown over them, and men may but guess at the volcanic forces at work below that studiously calm exterior.

So, laying his hand gently but firmly on his wife's arm, he led her to her cabin, with her boy still clasped in her arms as if she yet feared to lose him, and they disappeared from our eyes. As for Miranda and myself, such immersions had been daily matters of course, and were regarded as altogether too trifling occurrences to require more than the necessary changes of clothing.

We both appeared in our places at the next meal, when Miranda was besieged with questions as to her sensations, mingled with praises of her courage and endurance in that hour of deadly peril.

"And *her* child, too," said Mrs. Craven; "what a lesson of humility it ought to teach her! Had you, my dear girl, been swayed by any of the meaner motives which actuate men and women her foolish pride might have cost her child's life."

"Oh, surely no one *could* have had such thoughts when that dear little boy fell overboard! I couldn't help Mrs. Percival not liking me. I really did not think much about it; but when I saw the poor little face in the sea, more startled, indeed, than frightened, I felt as if I must go in after him. It was quite a matter of course."

After this incident it may be believed that we were indeed a happy family on board the *Florentia*. Every one vied with every one else in exhibiting respect and admiration towards Miranda. Mrs. Percival would not hear of a refusal that we should come and stay with her, when we had done all that was proper and dutiful in the family home. Miss Vavasour and Mrs. Craven depended on me to show them all the beauties of Sydney harbour; while Captain Carryall pledged himself to place Mr. Frankston's yacht at the service of his passengers generally, and to render them competent to champion the much-vaunted glories of the unrivalled harbour to all friends, foes, and doubters on the other side of the world.

Colonel Percival privately interrogated the captain as to the nature of the commercial undertaking in which he was about to arrange a partnership for me, and begged as a favour, being a man of ample means, that he might be permitted to advance the amount of my share. The captain solemnly promised him that if there was any difficulty in the proposed arrangement on account of my deficiency of cash he should be requested to supply it. "He seemed to feel easy in his mind after I told him this, my boy," said the commander, with that mixture of simplicity and astuteness which distinguished him, "but fancy old Paul and your father admitting outside capital in one of their trade ventures!"

"This time to-morrow we shall be going through Sydney Heads," said the first mate to me as we walked the deck about an hour after sunrise one morning, "that is, if the wind holds."

"Pray Heaven it may," said I, "then we shall have a view of the harbour and city worth seeing. It makes all the difference. We might have a cloudy day, or be tacking about till nightfall, and the whole effect would be lost." I was most anxious not only that Miranda's first sight of my native land and her future home should impress her favourably, but I was naturally concerned that our friends should not suppose that the descriptions of the Queen City of the South, with which the captain and I had regaled them, were overdrawn. We sat late at supper that night talking over the wonderful events and experiences that were to occur on the morrow. Plans were discussed, probable residence and inland travel calculated, the Fish River caves and the Blue Mountains were, of course, to be visited—all kinds of expeditions and slightly incongruous journeys to be carried out.

Colonel and Mrs. Percival had been asked to stay at Government House during their visit, which was comparatively short; while Mr. and Mrs. Craven and Miss Vavasour were to go primarily to Petty's Hotel, which had been highly recommended; and the gentlemen had intimation that they would receive notices of their being admitted as honorary members of the Australian and Union Clubs. With such cheerful expectations and forecasts we parted for the night.

The winds were kind. "The breeze stuck to us," as the mate expressed it, and about an hour after the time he had mentioned we were within a mile of the towering sandstone portals of that erstwhile strange, silent harbour into which the gallant seaman Cook, old England's typical mariner, had sailed a hundred years ago.

I had been on deck since dawn. Now that we were so near the home of my childhood, the thoughts of old days, and the parents, brothers, sisters, from whom I had been so long separated, rushed into my mind, until I felt almost suffocated with contending emotions. How would they receive us? Would they be prepared to see me a married man? Would their welcome to Miranda be warm or formal? I began to foresee difficulties—even dangers of family disruption—consequences which before had never entered into the calculation.

However, for the present these serious reflections were put to flight by expressions of delight from the whole body of passengers, headed by Miranda, who then came on deck. By this time the good ship *Florentia* had closely approached the comparatively narrow entrance, the frowning buttresses of sandstone, against which the waves, now dashed with hoarse and angry murmur, rose almost above us, while a long line of surges, lit up by the red dawn fires, menaced us on either hand.

"Oh, what a lovely entrance!" said Miss Vavasour, after gazing long and earnestly at the scene. "It seems like the gate of an enchanted lake. What magnificent rock-masses, and what light and colour the sun brings out! It is something like a sun—warm, glowing, irradiating everything even at this early hour—and what a sky! The dream tone of a painter! I congratulate you, you dear darling Miranda, and you, Mr. Telfer, on having such a day for home-coming. It is a good omen—I am sure it must be. Nothing but good could happen on such a glorious day."

"The day is perfection, but more than one good ship coming through this entrance at night has mistaken the indentation on the other side of the South Head for the true passage, and gone to pieces on the rocks below that promontory. But, at any rate, *we* are now safely inside; and where is there a harbour in the world to match it?"

As we passed Middle harbour and drew slowly up the great waterway, which affords perhaps more deep anchorage than any other in the world, the ladies were loud in their expressions of admiration. "Look at those sweet white houses on the shores of the pretty little bays!" said Mrs. Craven; "and what lovely gardens and terraces stretching down to the beaches!"

"And there is a Norfolk Island pine, one—two—ever so many," cried Miranda. "I did not think *they* grew here, I am sure now that I shall be happy."

"Yes, of course!" said Miss Vavasour, "what is to hinder you? And you are to live in one of those pretty cream-coloured cottages—what lovely stone it must be!—with a garden just like that one on the point, and a boat-house and a jetty. One of those little steamers that I see fussing about will land Mr. Telfer, when he returns from the city, or you can get into that little boat that lies moored below, and row across the bay for him."

Miranda's eyes filled as she glanced at the pretty villas and more pretentious mansions, past which we glided, some half-covered with climbers, or buried amid tropical shrubs of wild luxuriance. Her heart was too deeply stirred for jesting at that moment. She could only press her friend's hand and smile, as if pleading for a less humorous view of so important a subject.

The harbour itself was full of interest to the strangers. Vessels of all sizes and shapes—coasters, colliers, passenger-boats, yachts, and steam launches, passed and re-passed in endless succession. Two men-of-war lay peacefully at anchor in Farm Cove, a Messagerie steamer in the stream, while a huge P. & O. mail-boat outward bound moved majestically towards the Heads through which we had so recently entered.

We had just cleared Point Piper, where I remember spending the joyous holidays of long ago with my schoolmates, the sons of the fine old English gentleman who then dwelt there, when a sailing boat sped swiftly towards us, in which stood a stout, middle-aged man waving his hat frantically.

"I believe that is Paul Frankston himself come to overhaul us," said the captain, raising his glass. "He's sailor enough to recognise the rig of the *Florentia*, and if we had been a little nearer his bay, he'd have wanted us to stop the ship and lunch with him in a body. As it is I feel sure he'll capture some of the party."

"What splendid hospitality!" said Mrs. Percival. "Is that sort of thing usual here? you must be something like us Indians in your ways."

"There is a good deal of likeness, I think," said the captain. "I suppose the heat accounts for it. It's too hot to refuse, most of the year. But here comes Paul!"

The sailing boat by this time had run alongside and doused her sail, while one of the crew held on to a rope thrown to him, as the owner presented himself on deck with more agility than might have been expected from a man of his age.

"Well, Charley, my boy, so you're in at last—thought you were lost, or had run away and sold the ship, ha, ha! What sort of a voyage have you had? Passengers, too—pray introduce me. Is there anything I can do for them in Sydney? Must be something. Perhaps I shall hear by and by. Who's this youngster?

"No! surely not the son of my old friend, Captain Telfer? Now I remember the boy that ran away to the islands, or would have done so, if they hadn't let him go. Quite right, I ran away myself and a fine time I had there. I must tell you what happened to me there once, eh! Charley?"

Here the old gentleman began to laugh so heartily that he was forced to suspend his narration, while the captain regarded him with an expression which conveyed a slight look of warning. "But I am forgetting. By the way, Charley, have you any curios in your cabin?" The captain nodded, and the two old friends disappeared down the companion. Only, however, to reappear in a very few minutes, which we employed in favourable criticism.

"What a fine hearty old gentleman!" said Mrs. Craven, "any one can see that he is an Englishman by his figure and the way he talks; though I suppose colonists are not so very different."

"Mr. Frankston has been a good deal about the world," I said. "But he was born in Sydney, and has spent the greater part of his life near this very spot. He was at sea in his earlier years, but has been on shore since he married. He is now a wealthy man, and one of the leading Sydney merchants."

"One would think he was a sea captain now," said Miss Vavasour. "He looks quite as much like one as a merchant; but I suppose every one can sail a boat here."

"You are quite right, Miss Vavasour. Every one who is born in Sydney learns to swim and sail a boat as soon as possible after he can walk. There is no place in the world where there are so many yachtsmen. On holidays you may see doctors, lawyers, clergymen, even judges, sailing their boats—doing a good deal of their own work in the 'able seaman' line; and, to tell truth, looking occasionally much more like pirates than sober professional men."

About this time Mr. Frankston reappeared, carrying in his hand a couple of grass-er-garments, which he appeared to look upon as very precious. "These are for my little girl," he said, "she has just come down from the bush with her husband to spend the hot months with her old father. It will give her the greatest pleasure to see these ladies and their husbands at Marahmee, next Saturday, when we can have a little picnic in the harbour and a sail in my yacht, the *Sea-gull*. The captain will tell you that I am to be trusted with a lively boat still."

"I never wish to go to sea with a better sailor," said the captain, "and if our friends have no other engagements, I can promise them a delightful day and a view of some of the finest scenery south of the line."

Barring unforeseen or indispensable engagements every one promised to go. Mr. Frankston averred that they had done him a great—an important service. He was getting quite hipped—he was indeed—when his daughter luckily recognised the *Florentia* coming up the harbour. She is a sailor's daughter, you know—has an eye for a ship—and started him off to meet his old friend Captain Carryall, and secure him for dinner. Now he felt quite another man, and would say good-bye. Before leaving he must have a word with his young friend.

"My dear boy," said he, laying his hand on my shoulder, "I have known your father ever so many years. We were younger men then, and saw something of each other in more than one bit of fun; and at least one or two very queer bits of fighting in the Bay of Islands; so that we know each other pretty well. I've heard what Carryall has to say about you and your charming wife. I think we shall be able to 'fix up,' as our American friends say, our little mercantile arrangement very neatly. But that's not what I wanted to talk to you about. You've been away a good while, so many years, we'll say."

"I have indeed," I replied.

"Well—you've grown from a boy into a man, and a devilish fine one too." Here the dear old chap patted me on the back and looked up at my face, a great deal higher up than his. "Well! naturally, you've changed. So have your people, your young brothers and sisters have turned into men and women while you've been away. And then again, another change—a great one too—you're married."

"Yes! thank God I am."

"I am sure you have good reason, my boy. But my idea is this, people—the best of people—don't like surprises,—even one's own friends. Now, what I want you to do is to bring your wife and come and stay at Marahmee for a week, while they're getting your rooms ready for you at North Shore. There's nobody there now but Antonia and her husband. It wants another pair of young people to enliven the place a bit. And Charley Carryall will go over and tell them all about you and your pretty Miranda, while you and I settle our partnership affairs."

I could see how it was; our good old friend, with a kindness and delicacy of feeling which I have rarely seen equalled, had all along made up his mind that Miranda and I should begin our Sydney experiences with a visit to his hospitable mansion. After a talk with the captain, for which purpose he had feigned an interest in South Sea "curios," they had come to the conclusion that it would be more prudent that the family should have a few days to accustom themselves to the idea of my marriage. In the mean time his daughter, Mrs. Neuchamp, would be able to give Miranda the benefit of her experience as a Sydney matron of some years' standing, and to ensure that she made her introduction under favourable circumstances.

Miranda, naturally nervous at the idea of then and there making her appearance among a group of relatives wholly unknown to her, was much relieved at the delay thus granted, and cheerfully acceded to the proposed arrangement.

"That being all settled, I'll get home and have everything ready for you when you arrive. The captain will take care of you. He knows the road out, eh, Charley? night or day; so good-bye till dinner time. Seven o'clock sharp."

Still talking, Mr. Frankston descended to his boat, and making a long board, proceeded to beat down the harbour on his homeward voyage, waving his handkerchief at intervals until he rounded a point and was lost to our gaze.

It was not very long after this interview that we found ourselves in our berth at the Circular Quay, where, unlike Melbourne and some other ports, nothing more was needed for disembarkation but to step on shore into the city. Our good comrades of so many days were carried off in cabs to their destinations, with the exception of the Percivals, who, having been invited to Government House, found an aide-de-camp and the viceregal carriage awaiting them on the wharf. At such a time there is always a certain amount of fuss and anxiety with reference to luggage, rendering farewells occasionally less sentimental than might have been expected from the character of marine friendships. But it was not so in our experience. Miss Vavasour and Mrs. Craven exchanged touching farewells with Miranda, mingled with solemn promises to meet at given dates—to write—to do all sorts of things necessary for their keeping up the flame of friendship. Then at the last moment Colonel and Mrs. Percival came up. "My dearest Miranda," said this lady, "don't forget that you are my sister, not in word only. Put me to the proof whenever you need a sister's aid, and it shall be always at your service. Kiss Auntie Miranda, Charlie darling, and tell her you will always love her."

"She picked me up out of the sea, when the naughty shark was going to eat us all. She's a good auntie, isn't she, mother?" said the little chap responding readily. "Good-bye, Auntie Miranda."

"I am not a man of many words, Mr. Telfer!" said the colonel; "but if I can be of service to you, now or at any future time I shall be offended if you do not let me know;" and then the stern soldier shook my hand in a way which gave double meaning to the pledge.

It was yet early in the day, and the captain had duties to attend to which would keep him employed until the evening. "I've ordered a carriage at six," he said, "when we'll start for Marahmee, which is about half-an-hour's drive. Until that time you can go ashore if you like; the Botanical Gardens are just round that point, or walk down George Street, or in any other way amuse yourselves. Meanwhile, consider yourselves at home also."

"I think we'll stay at home then, captain, for the present," said Miranda, "and watch the people on shore. You have no idea how they interest me. Everything is so new. Remember that I have never seen a carriage in my life before, or a cab, or a soldier; there goes one now—isn't he beautiful to behold? I shall sit here and make Hilary tell me the names of all the specimens as they come into view."

"That will do capitally," said the captain. "I might have known that you could amuse yourself without help from any one."

The time passed quickly enough, with the aid of lunch. The decks were cleared by six o'clock, by which time we were ready for the hired barouche when it drove up.

Miranda and I had employed our time so well that she had learnt the names of various types of character, and many products of civilisation, of which she had been before necessarily ignorant, except from books. "It is a perfect object lesson," she said. "How delightful it is to be able to see the things and people that I have only read about! I feel like those people in the *Arabian Nights* who had been all their lives in a glass tower on a desert island. Not that our dear Norfolk Island was a desert—very far from it. And now I am going to the first grand house I ever saw, and to live in it—more wonderful still. I feel like a princess in a fairy tale," she went on, as she smilingly skipped into the carriage. "Everything seems so unreal. Do you think this will turn into a pumpkin, drawn by mice, like poor Cinderella's? Hers was a chariot, though. What is a chariot?"

"I remember riding in one when I was a small boy," I answered; "and, by the same token, I had caught a number of locusts, and put them into my hat. I was invited to uncover, as the day was warm. When I did so, the locusts flew all about the closed-up carriage and into everybody's face. But chariots are old-fashioned now."

Onward we passed along the South Head road, while below us lay the harbour with its multitudinous bays, inlets, promontories, and green knolls, in so many instances crowned with white-walled gardens, surrounding villas and mansions, all built of pale-hued, delicately-toned sandstone.

"Oh! what a lovely, delicious bay!" cried Miranda; "and these are the Heads, where we came in. Good-bye, old ocean, playfellow of my childhood; farewell, wind of the sea, for a while. But I shall live near you still, and hear you in my dreams. I should die—I should feel suffocated—if nothing but woods and forests were to be seen."

"If you don't die until you can't see the ocean, or feel the winds about here, you will live a long time, my dear," said the captain. "I don't know a more sea-going population anywhere than this Sydney one. Half the people you meet here have been a voyage, and the boys take to a boat as the bush lads do to a horse. But here we are at the Marahmee gates, and there's my pet Antonia on the verandah ready to receive us."

As we drove up the avenue, which was not very long, a very pretty, graceful young woman came swiftly to meet us. I knew this must be Mrs. Neuchamp, formerly Antonia Frankston, the old man's only child. She was not grown up when I left Sydney, and I heard that she had lately married a young Englishman, who had come out with letters of introduction to Mr. Frankston. We had seen each other last, as boy and girl, long years ago.

"Well, Captain Charley," she said, making as though she would have embraced the skipper, "what do you mean by being so long away? We began to think that you were lost—that the *Florentia* had run on a reef—all sorts of things—been cut off by the islanders, perhaps. But now you *are* back with all sorts of island stories to tell dad, and a few curios for me. And you are Mrs. Telfer! Papa has told me all about you—his latest admiration, evidently. But you mustn't get melancholy when he deserts you; he is a passionate adorer while it lasts, but is always carried away by the next fresh face, generally a complete contrast to the last. I am sure we shall be great friends. I used to dance with your husband when we were children. Do you remember that party at Mrs. Morton's? You have grown considerably since then, and so handsome, too, I suppose I may say—now we are all married—no wonder Miranda fell in love with you. You're to call me Antonia, my dear; and now come upstairs, and I'll show you your rooms which I have been getting ready all the morning. Papa and Ernest will be here in a few minutes."

"Mrs. Neuchamp evidently takes after her father," I said, "who can say more kind things in fewer minutes than any one I ever knew—and do them, too, which is more to the purpose. I am so glad that Miranda has had the chance of making her acquaintance before she sees many other people."

"She is a dear, good, unselfish girl," said the captain, "and was always the same from a child, when she used to sit on my knee in this very verandah, and get me to tell her the names of the ships. I never saw a child so thoughtful for other people, always wondering what she could do for them; she is just the same to this day. She will be an invaluable friend for our Miranda, I foresee. She can give her all sorts of hints about housekeeping, and I've no doubt one or two about dress and the minor society matters. Not that Miranda wants much teaching in that or any other way. Nature made her a lady, and gave her the look of a sea princess, and nothing could alter her."

"Did you ever hear of a handsome young woman being spoiled by flattery, captain?" I said. "I don't want to anticipate such a disaster, but it strikes me that if you are all going to be so very complimentary, I shall have to go on the other tack to keep the compass level."

"There are dispositions that flattery falls harmless from," said the captain solemnly; "there are women that cannot be spoiled,—not so many, perhaps, but you have got one of them, Antonia is another. They will make a good pair, and I'll back them to do their duty and keep a straight course, fair weather or foul, against any two, married or single, that I ever saw, and I've seen a good many women in my time. But now we had better be ready for dinner, for old Paul and Mr. Neuchamp will be here directly."

They were not long in making their appearance, and a very merry dinner it was. Mr. Frankston wanted to hear all about the islands, and Mrs. Neuchamp was much interested in Captain Hayston, and thought he resembled one of the buccaneers of the Spanish Main, for whom she had a sentimental admiration in her girlhood.

"What a pity that all the romantic and picturesque people should be so wicked!" she asked. "How is it, and what law of nature can it be that arranges that so many good and worthy people are so deadly uninteresting?"

"Antonia is not quite in earnest, my dear Mrs. Telfer!" said Mr. Neuchamp, remarking Miranda's wondering look; "she knows well that it is more difficult to live up to a high ideal than to fall below it. There is a false glamour about men like Hayston, I admit, by which people who are swayed by feeling rather than reason are often attracted."

"I am afraid that Captain Hayston was a wicked man," said Miranda, "though I can't get Hilary to tell me much about him. However, there were very different accounts, some describing him as being generous and heroic, and others as cruel and unprincipled."

"Whatever he was, there was no doubt about his being a sailor every inch of him," said Captain Charley. "I saw him handle his ship in a gale of wind through a dangerous channel, and I never forgot it."

"I suppose he had his faults like the rest of us," said Mr. Frankston, who did not seem inclined to pursue the subject. "Never mind, when Frankston, Telfer, and Co. get the control of the South Sea Island trade, there won't be any room for dashing filibusters, will there, Charley?"

"I hope not; his day is over," said the captain. "I am sorry for him, too, for he was one of the grandest men and finest seamen God Almighty ever permitted to sail upon His ocean. Under a different star he might have been an ornament to the service and an honour to his country."

After dinner we all sat out on the broad verandah, where we lighted our cigars, and enjoyed the view over the sleeping waters of the bay. It was a glorious night, undimmed by mist or cloud. The harbour lights flamed brightly, anear and afar, while steamers passing to the different points of the endless harbourage lighted up the glittering plain with their variegated lamps, as if an operatic effect were intended.

"What a wondrous sight!" said Miranda. "It certainly is a scene of enchantment, though it loses some of its beauty in my eyes from being so restless and exciting. There is no solitude; all is motion and effort, as is the city by day. Our sea-view is as still and silent as if our island had just been discovered. It lends an air of solemnity to the night which this brilliant, many-coloured vision seems to want."

"Antonia and I enjoy this sort of thing thoroughly," said Mr. Neuchamp; "our country is hot and dry as the summer comes on, and the glare is something to remember. But I must say I prefer the winter of the interior. The nights are heavenly, the mid-day warm without being oppressive, and the mornings are delightfully cool and bracing."

"As weather it is as nearly perfect as it can be," assented Mrs. Neuchamp, backing up her husband. "Then the rides and drives on the firm sandy turf and the delightful natural roads! It's nice to think you can drive thirty or forty miles in any direction without going off your own run. Miranda must come and stay with me for a month or two when you get settled, Mr. Telfer. We must see if she can't be persuaded to leave the seaside for a while."

"We'll make up a party," said Mr. Frankston; "it's a long time since I have seen any station life. I had half a mind to try squatting once myself. But I'm like Miranda—I don't sleep well unless I can hear the surge in the night; but for a month or two, in May or June, it would be great fun, and do us all good, I expect."

"Yes, my dear dad," said his daughter, patting his shoulder, "think of the riding and driving. You're not too old to ride, you know. I'll lend you Osmond—he's my horse now, and he's a pearl of hackneys. I'll ride out with you, and Ernest can take Miranda and Courtenay in the four-in-hand drag."

"Well, that's a bargain, my dear!" said her father. "When the summer is over and the autumn has nearly come to an end, and the nights and mornings are growing fresh and crisp, that's the time to see the interior at its best. I haven't forgotten the feel of a bush-morning at sunrise; there's something very exhilarating about it."

"Is there not?" replied Mrs. Neuchamp, "'as you see the vision splendid, of the sunlit plains extended,' an ocean of verdure. You trace the river by the heavy timber on its banks, and the slowly-rising mists along its course. Then the sun, a crimson and gold shield against the cloudless azure, the cattle low in the great river meadows, you hear the crack of a stockwhip as the horses come galloping in like a regiment of cavalry, and the day has begun. It seems like a new world awakening to life."

"I know a young woman," said her husband, "whose 'inward eye' by no means made 'the bliss of solitude' when she first went into the bush."

"That was because I was newly married—torn away from my childhood's home, and all that," laughed his wife. "Besides, you used to stay away unconscionably long sometimes; now everything looks different. You will have to pass through that stage, my dear Miranda. So prepare yourself."

"I am sure Hilary will never stay away from our home unless he is obliged; and then I must sew and sing till he comes back, like my countrywomen at Norfolk Island and Pitcairn when their men are at sea."

"A very good custom, too," said Paul. "That reminds me that we must have some music to-night. Antonia will lead the way, and our cigars will taste all the better in the verandah."

Mrs. Neuchamp had a fine voice and a fine ear. She had been well taught, and played her own accompaniments, while she sang several favourite songs of her father's, and a duet with her husband.

"Now, it's your turn, Miranda," said Mr. Frankston. "I've heard all about you from the captain."

"I shall be very glad to sing," she answered, seating herself at the piano, "if you care for my simple songs. I have always been fond of music, but our poor little harmonium was, for a long time, my only instrument. What shall I sing?"

"Sing the 'Lament of Susannah M'Coy for her drowned lover,'" said the captain, "that was a song brought from Pitcairn, wasn't it? I always liked it the best of all the island sing songs."

"It is simple," replied Miranda, "but it is true; I believe the poor girl used to sit by the sea-shore singing it at night, and died of grief a year afterwards."

She struck a few chords on the grand Erard piano, and commenced a wailing, dirge-like melody, "a long, low island song," inexpressibly mournful. The movement was chiefly low-toned, and in the minor key, but at times it rose to a higher pitch, into which was thrown the agonised sorrow of irrevocable love, the endless regret, the void immeasurable and eternal, the hopeless despair of a desolated existence.

The words were simple, and more in recitative than rhythm. There was a certain monotony and repetition, but as an expression of passionate and hopeless sorrow it was strangely complete.

The tale was old as life and death, as love and joy, hope and despair. The maiden watching and waiting, during the voyage of the whaleship, the year long through. The sudden delight of the vessel being sighted; the boats going off; the intensity of the anxiety; the returning crew; the eager scanning of the passengers; the refusal to believe in mischance; the guarded half-told tale, then the unmistakable word of doom! *He had been drowned at sea*; the fearless, fortunate harpooner had, in the sudden flurry of the death-stricken whale, been thrown overboard and stunned. When the half-capsized boat was righted, Johnnie Mills was missing! They rowed round and round, all vainly, then sadly returned to the vessel. This was the tale they had to tell, the tale Susannah M'Coy had to hear. Her overwrought feelings found relief in the "Maiden's Lament," and after her death her girl companions in singing it preserved the memory of the maiden and her lover, of his doom and her unhappy fate.

There was nothing unusually melodious in the song itself, but as the low, rich notes of Miranda's voice struck on the ear of the listeners, those who had not heard before seemed spell-bound. Not a motion was made, not a sound escaped them, as they listened with an intentness which said far more than the ready and general praise at its close. Knowing, as I did, the extraordinary quality of her voice, I had expected that some such effect would be produced, but I hardly reckoned on such complete and universal admiration.

When the cry of the heartbroken girl rose and echoed through the large room, the effect was electrical; the higher notes were sweet and clear, without a suspicion of hardness, and yet had wondrous undertones of tears, such as I never heard in another woman's voice. Long before the wailing notes had faded into nothingness Mrs. Neuchamp's eyes were wet. While old Paul, Mr. Neuchamp, and the captain, seemed in no great hurry to express their approval.

"That's the most wonderful song I ever heard," said the old man. "I've heard the girls in Nukuheva sing one something like it, and there are notes in Miranda's voice that take me back to my youth, the island days, and the good old times when Paul Frankston was young and foolish. God's blessing on them! Miranda! my dear, take an old man's thanks. I foresee that I shall have two daughters: one at Marahmee in the summer, and the other in the winter, when Antonia is in the bush."

After this no one would hear of her leaving off. She sang other songs which were not all sorrowful. Some had a livelier tone, and the transient gleam which lit up the dark eyes told that mirth had its due place in her rich and many-sided nature.

"Would you like to hear one of our hymns now?" she asked, with the simplicity of a child. "We used to sing them in parts, and many a night when the moon was at the full did we sit on the beach and sing for hours. I can hear the surge now, and it puts me in mind of our dear old home."

"Oh, by all means," said Antonia, and without further prelude, she began a well-known hymn, the deep tones of her voice rising and falling as if in a cathedral, while the organ-like chords which she evoked from the Erard favoured the faultless rendering. We involuntarily joined in, and I saw Antonia looking admiringly at the singer, as with head upraised, and all the fervour of a mediæval penitent, she poured forth a volume of melodious adoration.

All were silent for some seconds after the last cadence had died away. At length the pause was broken by Antonia.

"After that lovely hymn, my dear Miranda, let me first thank you warmly for the pleasure you have given us all, and then suggest that we retire. The gentlemen may stay and smoke a while longer, but this has been an exciting day for us, and you require rest. Besides, you have to make acquaintance with your new relations."

"A sensible suggestion, my darling," said Mr. Frankston. "So we'll say good night to Mrs. Telfer and yourself. We must have one more cigar in the verandah while we think over that great song of hers."

It was arranged between Mr. Frankston and the captain that I should take my bride to my old home on the morning after next, and present her to my family. It might have been thought that, after so long an absence from my parents, it would have been more in keeping with filial duty to have rushed off at once and, in a manner, cast myself at their feet like the prodigal. But that unlucky, yet eventually fortunate younger son, did not bring a wife with him, in which case the paternal welcome might have been less distinct. I had put myself in the hands of my more experienced friends, who, as men of the world, knew the value of first impressions.

"You and Miranda will be all the better for a day's rest, and a little cheering up at Marahmee," had said the captain. "Antonia, too, will see that your sea princess is properly turned out, and fit to bear inspection by the ladies of the family. *They* won't have much to criticise, I'll be bound. I'm an early man, so I'll go and breakfast with your father, and give him a general idea of your doings and prospects. You had better turn up about mid-day. It will be high tide then, and Miranda will see Isola Bella at its best. Come on board the *Florentia* first, and I'll send you over in proper style."

Acting upon this prudent advice, Miranda and I alighted from the Marahmee carriage at the Circular Quay, and once more set foot on board the *Florentia*, where we found the captain ready to receive us. He made us come down into the cuddy and partake of fruit and wine (that is, Miranda took the first and I the latter), while he gave us a sketch of his interview with my father.

CHAPTER XVII

"OUR JACK'S COME HOME TO-DAY"

"The old skipper was walking in the garden, glass in hand. I knew I should find him up, though it was soon after sunrise. No fear of *his* being in bed and the sun up. 'Hallo! Carryall,' he said, 'I was just thinking about you; thought I could make out the *Florentia* yesterday. What sort of a voyage have you had, and what luck among the right whales?'

"'Pretty fair. Rather longer out than I expected, but didn't do badly after all; had some trading among the islands; cocoa-nut oil has gone up, and the copra I got will pay handsomely.'

"'That's good news,' he said; 'and look here, Carryall, my boy, I've been thinking lately that a very paying business might be put together by going in regularly for island trading. They're ready and willing to take our goods, and their raw material—oil, copra, fruit, ever so many things that they are only too glad to sell—would pay a handsome percentage on the outlay. What is wanted is a partner here with capital, a few ships to go regularly round the islands, and a manager who knows the language and understands the natives. If I were a little younger, by Jove! I'd go into it myself. You'll stay and breakfast with us of course. We're not late people. By the by you haven't heard of my boy in your travels, have you?'

"'Well I *have* heard of him, and—'

"'Heard of him!' he said, not giving me time to get further; 'where? what was he doing?'

"'Well, he was supercargo on board the *Leonora*—Hayston's brig. They had been at Ocean Island just before me.'

"'Hayston, Bully Hayston?' the old man said, looking stern. 'I'm sorry he was mixed up with that fellow. A fine seaman, but a d—d scoundrel, from all I've heard of him; what were they doing there? However, I know young fellows must buy their experience. Perhaps he's left him by this time.'

"'The *Leonora* was wrecked in Chabral harbour,' I said, 'and her bones lie on the coral reef there. She'll never float again.'

"'Ha! and did Hilary get off safe? I suppose it was a heavy gale. Heard anything of him since?'

"'He stayed at Moūt for some time,' I said, 'and then was lucky enough to get a passage to Sydney in the *Rosario*, but he left her at Norfolk Island.'

"'Left her—left her—why the devil didn't he come on in her, and see his old father, and mother, and sisters? Hang the fellow, has he no natural feeling? Here have we been wearing our hearts out with anxiety all these years, and his poor mother having a presentiment (as she calls it) that he's drowned or sold into slavery, or something, and d—mn me, sir! the young rascal goes and stays to have a picnic at Norfolk Island! The next thing we'll hear, I suppose, is that he's married one of these Pitcairn Island girls. Not but what he might do worse, for I never saw such a lot of fine-looking lasses in my life, as I did the last time I was there; and as good as they are handsome, by George! But to stay there, so near home too! If I didn't know that he was a good boy, and as honest as the day, from his cradle upwards, I'd say he was an unnatural young— But I won't miscall the lad. To stay there—'

"'But he didn't stay there, captain.'

"'What!' he roared, 'didn't stay there—went back to the islands, I suppose, to have a little more beach-combing and loafing? Why couldn't he have come home when he was so near? He *might* have thought of his poor mother, if he didn't give *me* credit for caring to see his face again.'

"And here the old skipper frowned, and put on a terribly stern expression. 'Why, he might have come home and married a wife, and settled down and been the comfort of our old age.'

"'So he has!' I said; 'that is, he is married, and he has come to Sydney.'

"'Married? Come to Sydney? How can that be? Why isn't he here? Carryall, my boy, you wouldn't play a joke on an old man? No, sir! you wouldn't *dare* to do it. How *could* he come to Sydney and be married?'

"'He came with me in the *Florentia*,' I said, 'and brought his wife with him.' And here, Miranda, my dear, I told him what a very unpleasant young woman you were, and took about a quarter of an hour to do it; at the end of which narration the breakfast bell rang.

"'Come into the house, Carryall,' he said, 'and tell it all to his mother. I'll break it to her by saying that you bring news of Hilary, and that he's quite well, and so on, and likely to come home soon.'

"So we went in. I shall never forget the look that came into your mother's eyes when the skipper said, 'Here's Captain Carryall straight from the islands; he's brought you girls some shells and curios as usual, and better than that, news of Hilary.'

"'News of my boy, my darling Hilary! Good news, I hope. Oh, Captain Carryall! say it's good. Oh! *where* is he, and what was he doing?'

"'It is good news, my dear lady,' said I, 'or I should not have come over to tell you. I saw him quite lately as near Sydney as Norfolk Island.'

"'Of course he was coming here—coming here; he would not have the heart to stay away from his poor father and mother any longer, when he was so near as that. And was he quite well? Oh! my boy— my precious Hilary! What would I not give if he were to come here and settle down for good?'

"'He is thinking of doing so,' I said. 'His fixed intention was to marry and live in Sydney for the rest of his days.'

"'Thank God! thank God in His mercy!' she said, clasping her hands. 'And do you think he will be here soon—how many weeks?'

"'It will not be a matter of weeks, but days; I know that he took his passage in a certain ship, and that you may expect him every hour.'

"Then she looked keenly at me. Your mother is a clever woman. She began to think I had been leading her on.

"'You are not treating me as a child, Charles Carryall, are you? My son is here, and you have been afraid to tell me so. Is it not so?'

"'Only a harmless deception, my dear Mrs. Telfer. Your son and his wife came here in my vessel. They stayed at Paul Frankston's last night, and will be here at mid-day.'

"The dear lady looked as if she could not realise it for a moment, then sat back in her chair, and raised her eyes as if in prayer.

"One of the girls moved as if to support her, but she waved her off. 'No, my dear, you need not be afraid. I shall not faint; I have borne many things, and can bear this. I am returning thanks to our Almighty Father, who has restored my son to me. "My son, who was lost, and is found." My son, who was dead to me, and is now restored to life. Oh, God! most heartily and humbly do I thank Thee—most merciful—most loving!'

"After this we were a very happy party. The girls, of course, wanted to know all about Miranda here"—here my darling smiled, and took his hand; "I dashed off a sketch, and some day you can ask Mariana and Elinor—both great friends of mine they are—if it is a good likeness."

"I am afraid it was too good," sighed Miranda, "and they will be dreadfully disappointed."

The end of it was that we left the *Florentia* at eight bells, in great state and majesty, in a whaleboat—upon which Miranda insisted, despising the captain's gig as a trumpery skiff—and a picked crew, with the skipper himself as the steer-oar.

"That's really something like," she said, as she stepped lightly on to the thwart. "If there was a little swell on, I should feel quite myself again, and think of the dear days when I was a happy little island girl, bare-footed and bare-headed, and thought going off to a strange vessel through the great, solemn, sweeping rollers the wildest enjoyment. But I am a happy girl now," she added, with a look in her deep eyes which expressed a world of love and rich content; "only the thought of learning to be a lady sometimes troubles me."

"You will never need to do *that*," I said.

"There is the house?" I cried; "there's Isola Bella!" as we rounded a point, and a picturesque stone house came full into view. It had been built in the early days of the colony by an Imperial officer, long resident in Italy, and showed the period in its massive stone walls, Florentine façade, and wide, paved verandah. The site was elevated above the lake-like waters of the bay, towards which a winding walk led, terminating in a massive stone pier, into which iron rings and stanchions had been let. The beach was white and smooth, though the tide ran high, and the wavelets rippled close to the pale sandstone rocks, which lent a tone of delicacy and purity to the foreshore.

The weather-stained walls of the house were half covered with climbers, a wilderness of tropical shrubs, and richly-blooming flower-thickets. There were glades interspersed, carpeted with the thick-swarded couch or "dhoub" grass, originally imported from India, and which, nourished by the coast showers, and delighting in a humid atmosphere, preserves its general freshness of colour the long Australian summer through.

I had been so preoccupied with speculations as to Miranda's reception by my family, that my own emotions, on returning to my childhood's home, lay in abeyance. Now, however, at the near view of the house—the pier, the walled-in sea-bath—the scenes and adventures of my earliest youth came back with overwhelming force and clearness. There was the boat-house, into which I had paddled so many a time after nightfall, returning from fishing or sailing excursions. There was the flagstaff on which was displayed the Union Jack and other flags on great occasions. The old flag floated in the breeze to-day. I knew for what reason and celebration. I could see my mother, as of old, walking down to the pier to welcome and embrace, or to remonstrate and fondly chide when I had remained absent in stormy weather. How many fears and anxieties had I not caused to agitate that loving heart! And my stern and mostly silent parent—did I not once surprise him in scarce dignified sorrow at my night-long absence and probable untimely decease. Yet all his words were, "God forgive you, my boy, for the misery you have caused us this night."

And now the years had passed—had flown rather, crowded as they were with incident—that had changed the heedless boy into the man,—matured, perhaps, by too early worldly knowledge, and the grim comradeship of danger and death. I had returned safely, bringing my sheaves with me in the guise of one dearer to me than life. I had, during the intervals of reflection I had lately enjoyed, repented fully of the unconsciously selfish sins of my youth, and was fixed in firm resolve to atone, so far as in me lay, by care and consideration in the future.

As we dashed alongside of the pier, the years rolled back, and as of old I saw my mother pacing the well-known path to the boat. She was followed by my father at a short distance. I fancied that the dear form told of the lapse of time, in less firm step and the bent figure which age compels. My father was erect as ever, and his eye swept the far horizon of outer seas as of old; but surely his hair and beard were whiter.

Miranda's step was first upon the pier—she needed no help in leaving or entering a boat. Side by side we walked to meet my mother, who, with a sob of joy, folded me in her arms. "My boy! my boy!" was all she could articulate for some moments; then, gently disengaging herself, "and this is my new daughter?" she said. "May God bless and keep you both, my children, and preserve for us the great happiness which His providence has ordained this day."

"Well, neighbour!" in the well-remembered greeting which he affected, rang out here my father's clear tones, "and so you have finished your cruise for a while! What a man you have grown!" he exclaimed, as he looked upwards half-admiringly at my head and shoulders, markedly above his own. "Filled out, bronzed, you look a sailor, man, all over."

"And so you wouldn't give the Sydney girls a chance, and have brought a wife back with you for fear there mightn't be a 'currency lass' to spare. I must say I admire your taste, my boy. No one can fault that. Welcome, my dear Miranda, to your own and your husband's home. Give your old father a kiss and the ceremony is complete." Here the governor gravely embraced his new daughter, and then, holding her at arm's length, regarded her admiringly, till she playfully ran back to the girls. "Charley here guarantees she is as good as she is handsome. He said better, indeed; but that's impossible. No woman with her looks could be better inside than out. So, Hilary, my boy, I congratulate you on your choice. You've fallen on your feet in love and friendship both, according to what Carryall tells me of Paul Frankston's partnership arrangement. And now we'll come up to the house and drink the bride's health. I feel as if I needed a refresher after all this excitement. I little thought when I saw Charley come over so early what was in store for us, eh, mother?"

Before we reached the house the two girls, Mariana and Elinor, had taken possession of Miranda and carried her upstairs to the rooms which were to be allotted to us while we dwelt at Isola Bella. "Now that the other boys are up the country," said Mariana, who was the elder, "we have more houseroom than we need. So, directly we heard that you were in Sydney, Elinor and I set to work and arranged these two rooms, so that you and Miranda should be quite independent. There's such a pretty view of the harbour. You can use this one as a sitting-room, and there's a smaller dressing-room which he can make a den of. Men always like a place to be untidy in."

"Oh, how nice it will be," said Elinor, the younger one, whom I remember a curly-headed romp of ten when I left home, "to have a mate for rowing and boat-sailing. Mariana here doesn't care for boats, and dislikes rough weather. I suppose no weather would frighten you. Oh, what lovely trips we shall have, and mother can't be nervous when you are with me."

"I suppose you think Miranda is a sort of mermaid," said I, now arrived and joining in the conversation, "and impossible to be drowned. But what would become of me if anything happened to her? Do you think I can trust her with you? What a grand room! I remember it well in old days when it used to be the guest chamber. I was only allowed into it now and then, and always under inspection. I feel the promotion."

"Now, we'll run away and leave you," said Mariana. "Lunch is nearly ready; you will hear the bell."

We sat down on a couch and gazed into each other's eyes with clasped hands. The harbour, with its variously composed fleet, lay wide and diversified before us. Every conceivable vessel—barge, steamer, collier, skiff, yacht, and row-boat—made progress adown and across its waters. How fair a scene it was on this, one of the loveliest days which sun and sky and wavelets deep ever combined to fashion! After all my adventures by seas and lands—after all the sharp contrasts of my chequered life—now lotus-eating amid the groves or by the founts of an earthly paradise—now ignorant, from one day to another, of the hour when the death-knell would sound—now free and joyous, handsomely dressed, in foreign seaports with ruffling swagger and chinking dollars—anon ragged, shoeless, shipwrecked, and forlorn—nay, starving, but for the charity of the soft-hearted heathens whom we in our pride are prone to despise.

And now I was at home again. Home! sweet home! in fullest sense of the word—welcomed, beloved, fêted! What had I done to deserve this love and trust now so profusely showered upon me? My better angel, too, my darling Miranda, by my side, sharing in all this wealth of affection. How could I have foretold that such good fortune would be mine, all unworthy that I felt myself, when, bruised and bleeding, I was hurled ashore in the midnight storm from the wrecked *Leonora?*—when I felt in thought the deadly shudder which ever follows the scratch of the poisoned arrow—when I sank to eternal rest (as I then supposed) beneath the surf-tormented shore of the island? How had I jostled death, disease, danger in every form and shape,—and now, almost without thought or volition of my own, I was placed in possession of all those things for which through a long life so many men toil and struggle vainly and unsuccessfully.

"Thank God! thank God!" I exclaimed aloud involuntarily, for truly our hearts were filled in that hour of realised peace and happiness with grateful wonder.

"Let us give Him thanks," whispered Miranda, "who only has done this wondrous thing for us."

Captain Carryall, my father, and Mr. Frankston were men of action—all through their lives the deed had followed quick on the resolve. Thus, within a week after our arrival, premises were purchased on the shore of the bay; stores and warehouses were planned, while upon an office in the chief business centre of Sydney, at no great distance from Macquarie Square, a legend of the period presented the firm of "Carryall, Telfer, and Company, South Sea merchants and purchasers of island produce." This was the commencement, as it turned out, of a prosperous mercantile enterprise, ramifying in divers directions. It was arranged not only to purchase or to ship on commission the raw material so easily procurable, but to advance on whaling and trading ventures; the projectors, better equipped with experience than capital, being always willing to pay high interest, for which indeed the margin of profit amply provided. Here I was in my element, whether directing labourers, interviewing seamen, shouting in the vernacular to the native crews, or calculating the value of cargoes. My father came over every other day to watch me at my work, and of my style of management he was pleased to express approval. "You have not altogether wasted your time, my boy," he said one day. "The great thing in all these matters is energy. With that and reasonable experience a man is sure to be successful in a new country—indeed in any country. Pluck and perseverance mean everything in life. Never despair. You know our family motto—*Fortuna favet fortibus*. And you would smile if I told you how often in the history of my life a bold bid for fame or fortune has been my only resource."

Whether I had exhibited the proverbial fortitude, or whether, indeed, the capricious goddess was mollified in my case, cannot with certainty be decided. The fact, however, was there, that our luck, from whatever cause, was in the ascendant, inasmuch as business of a profitable nature began to pour in upon us. The average gains beyond expenses were so apparent that it was evident that before long we should be in a position to set up housekeeping on our own account.

In the mean time nothing could be more harmonious and satisfactory than our composite home life at Isola Bella, difficult as it is sometimes to arrange the housing of two families, however closely related, under one roof. The natural amiability of Miranda's nature fortunately prevented the slightest friction. Constitutionally anxious to please, it was the chief article of her simple faith to seek the happiness of others rather than her own. Prompt in compliance, eager to learn all minor matters with which she had been necessarily unacquainted, ready to join in the harmless mirth of the hour, or to tell of the wonders of her island home, she was, as all agreed, a constant source of interest and entertainment.

More than all, her pervading, fervent, religious faith endeared her to the pious heart of my dearest mother, in whose visits to the poor and in charitable ministrations she was by choice her constant companion; while her unfeigned pity for the half-fed, half-clothed children of the neglected classes with which every city abounds excited my mother's wonder and admiration.

"Your wife is a pearl of womanhood, my dear Hilary," she would say to me. "You are a good boy; I hope you are worthy of her. I can hardly think that any man could be. When you see the women so many men are fated to pass their lives with, you have indeed reason to be thankful."

"So I am, my dear old mother," I would say. "Every day I feel minded to sing a song of joy and gratitude. I feel as life was a new discovery and creation. I am in a Paradise where no serpent that ever crawled has power to harm my Eve. I feel sometimes as if there was an unreal perfection about it all, too bright to last."

So indeed it appeared to me at that time. Fully employed as I was by day and in the exercise of all the faculties that my island life had served to train, it was impossible to overtask the health of mind and body in which I revelled. I was sensible, too, that the joint enterprise upon which I had embarked was growing and improving daily, while much of its success was attributed by Mr. Frankston and Captain Carryall to my management. At night, when I returned there was one who never failed to catch sight of my skiff when half across the bay. Then our family evenings, cheered with song and harmless mirth, were truly restful after the labours of the day.

Our neighbours, too, with all the old friends of the family, seemed desirous to welcome the son of the house who had been so long absent, and had wandered so far. Whether from curiosity, or a higher feeling, they were equally anxious to call upon "the son's wife." The positions, and dispositions, manners, and habitudes of the different types were well explained to Miranda by my socially-experienced sisters, so that she was saved from any misapprehension which might so easily have arisen.

Our friends the Neuchamps, too, were often with us, and made the greater part of our quiet recreations. On alternate Sundays nothing would content Mr. Frankston short of our all dining with him, to be sent back in his sailing boat if the weather was favourable, or to remain for the night in the ample guest-chambers of Marahmee if otherwise.

Our Saturday afternoons, indeed, were almost entirely devoted to picnics and cruises in his yacht, at which time he insisted upon Miranda steering, or, as he said, taking command, at which times he was always loud in admiration of her nautical skill—declaring, indeed, that she was fit to take charge of any vessel in Her Majesty's navy.

We had also seen a good deal of our fellow passengers, Mr. and Miss Vavasour, who, after a first introduction, were always included in Mr. Frankston's Saturday picnic invitations. That lively damsel professed a great admiration for Mr. Frankston, who responded so promptly that Antonia reproached him for turning faithless to Miranda.

"It's his nature, he can't help it," she said.

"But Miss Vavasour will have some day to suffer whatever pangs are supposed to fall to the lot of the deserted fair; then she will repent of her fascinations."

"Not at all—sufficient for the day, you know. I begin to think that one's admirers ought to be past their first youth. They're more thoroughly appreciative. 'On his frank features middle age Had scarcely set its signet sage,' and so on. I'm sure that quite describes Mr. Frankston. How should you like me for a mamma-in-law, Mrs. Neuchamp? Marahmee is such a dear house, and these yachting parties are all that are wanted to make life perfect."

"I give my consent," said Antonia, "but beware of delay. 'Men were deceivers ever,' and if you wait more than a fortnight your charms will be on the wane, so I warn you."

"I like decision," responded Miss Vavasour, "but perhaps 'two weeks,' as our American friend used to say, is *rather hurried* legislation. The trousseau business and the milliner's objections would be fatal. Even Miranda must have stood out for a longer respite. How long did you take, Miranda, dear? You're the pattern woman, you know, the first girl I ever saw that men and women equally delighted to honour."

Miranda blushed charmingly, then looking up with her clear, frank eyes, that always appeared to me to be fountains of truth, as she replied—

"Hilary and I were married just a month after he asked me to be his wife, you know very well."

So, jesting lightly, and with a breeze that sufficed just to fill the great sails of the yacht, we glided along until we had explored the recesses of Middle harbour,—a spacious inlet winding amid the thick growing semi-tropical forest which clothed the slopes of the bays and promontories to the water's edge.

Here and there were small clearings in which might be discovered a tent or cabin, just sufficient for the needs of a couple of bachelors or a hermit, who here desired to live during his holiday amid this "boundless contiguity of shade"—"The world forgetting, and the world forgot."

"Oh, how lovely!" said Mrs. Percival, as we swept round a point and came suddenly upon a fairy-like nook, a tiny bay with milk-white strand and fantastic sandstone rocks. There was a fenced enclosure around a cabin. There was a boat, with rude stone pier and boat-house. The owner, in cool garb and broad-leafed sombrero, was seated on a rock reading, and occasionally dabbling his bare feet in the rippling tide. As the yacht glided past in the deep water which came so close to his possessions, he raised his hat to the ladies, and resumed his studies.

"What a picture of peace and restful enjoyment!" said Mrs. Craven. "How I envy men who can seclude themselves like this within an hour's sail from a city! Now, people are so fond of generalising about colonists, and how wrong they are! They always describe them as wildly energetic and restless people, perpetually rushing about in search of gain or gold."

"That's Thorndale," said one of the younger guests. "He works hard enough at his business when he is about it, but his notion of enjoyment is to come here on a Saturday with only a boat-keeper, to fish, and read, and smoke till Monday morning, when he goes back to his law and his office."

"Sensible fellow!" said the colonel. "There's nothing like tent life to recruit a man's health after a spell of official work. We used to manage that in India, when we couldn't go all the way to the hills, by forming small encampments of a dozen or twenty fellows, having a mess-house in common, and living in tents or huts separately when we were not hunting or shooting. Splendid life while it lasted! Sent us back twice the men we were, when we left the lines!"

We anchored for lunch in one of the fairy nooks of which that enchanted region is so lavish. There was tea for the ladies and something presumably stronger for the seniors. We had mirth and pleasantries, spoken and acted—all went merrily in that charmed sunshine and beneath the shadowy sea-woods. We had songs—"A mellow voice Fitz Eustace had"—that is, one of the young fellows, native and to the manner born, lifted up his tuneful pipe and made us all laugh, the air he sang being certainly not "wild and sad,"—the reverse, indeed.

"Now, is not this an ideal picnic,—a day rescued from that terrible fiend Ennui, that haunts us all?" cried Miss Vavasour. "I might truthfully, perhaps, except myself, who am frivolous, and therefore easily amused—but of course it sounds well to complain and be mysterious. But, really, this is life indeed! The climate makes up for any little deficiency. I shall positively go home and arrange my affairs, make sure of my allowance being paid quarterly, then take a cottage near Miranda, on that sweet North Shore,—isn't that what you call it?—and live happy ever afterwards like a 'maid of Llangollen.'"

"Nothing can be nicer," said Mrs. Neuchamp. "We'll all three live here in the summer, within reach of the sea-breeze. In June you must come up and stay with me at Rainbar; then you will know what the glory of winter in our Riverina is like."

The breeze freshened as we glided swiftly on our homeward course. We had expended most of the daylight before we left our fairy bower. Sunset banners flared o'er the western horizon. "White and golden-crimson, blue," fading imperceptibly into the paler tones, and swift-appearing shades which veil the couch of the day god. The stars tremulously gleamed at first timidly, then brightly scintillating in pure and clustered radiance. Our merry converse had gradually lessened, then ceased and died away. All seemed impressed by the solemnity of the hour—the hush of sea and land—the shimmering phosphorescent sparkle of the silver-seeming plain over which we swept all swift and silently. Then the lights of the city, brilliant, profuse, widely scattered as in a lower firmament!

Miss Vavasour sat with Miranda's hand in hers. "How lovely to live in an hour like this, and yet it is like this with such surroundings that I should like to die."

"Hush!" said Miranda, "we must all die when God wills it. It is not good to talk so, my dear."

During the next week our good friends and fellow-passengers of the *Florentia* were to leave us on their return voyage. We arranged to meet as often as we could manage the leisure, and, as it happened, there was to be a ball at Government House—one of the great functions of the season, which, it was decided, would be an appropriate conclusion to our comradeship. Mr. and Mrs. Neuchamp were going back to their station, Captain Carryall was under sailing orders, and our friends the Colonel and Mrs. Percival were leaving for India and "going foreign" generally.

Miranda was not eager to attend the extremely grand, and, as far as she was concerned, strange entertainment. But the whole party were most anxious for her to make her appearance in public—at least on that occasion. Partly from natural curiosity, partly on account of my wishes, and my sisters' and Mrs. Neuchamp's strong persuasion, she consented—pleading, however, to be relieved from all anxiety on the score of her dress.

"Oh! we'll take that responsibility," said Elinor. "Antonia Neuchamp is generally admitted to dress in perfect taste. We'll compose a becoming ball-dress amongst us or die—something simple and yet not wholly out of the fashion, and becoming to Miranda's style of beauty."

"I'm afraid you'll make me vain," she answered, smiling. "What will you do if I spend all Hilary's money on dress? However, it must be a lovely sight. I have read of balls and grand entertainments, of course, and when I was a girl longed to be able to take part in them. Now that I am married," and here she gazed at me with those tender, truthful eyes, "I seem not to care for mere pleasure. It leads to nothing, you know."

"You are going to be a pattern wife, Miranda, I see," said Mariana, my elder sister. "You must not spoil Hilary, you know. He will think he is the only man in the world."

"And is he not for me?" she asked, eagerly. Then blushing at the quick betrayal of her inmost heart, she added, "Should it not be so? Are civilised people in a great city anxious to attract admiration even after they are married?"

"There are people who do this and more in all societies, my dear," said my mother, with a seriousness which rebuked our inclination to smile at Miranda's ignorance of the world. "But do you, my dear child, cling fast to the faith in which you have been reared. You will neither be of them nor among them that follow the multitude to do evil."

"I don't think there is as much evil in Miranda as would fill a teaspoon," said Elinor. "This isle of hers must have been a veritable Eden, or she must have come down from the moon, dear creature. You must be very good to deserve her, I can tell you, Master Hilary."

The day arrived, the night of which was to realise all manner of rose-coloured visions, in which the youth and maidens of Sydney had for weeks indulged. It was to be the ball of the season. The grand entertainment at which a royal personage, who had arrived in a man-of-war but recently, had consented to be present! The officers of the squadron were, of course, invited. They were gratified that the ball was fixed for a week previous to their sailing on an extended cruise among the islands. As it happened, too, the great pastoral section—the proprietors of the vast estates of the interior—were still at their clubs and hotels, not yet departed for their annual sojourn amid the limitless wastes of "The Bush." The *jeunesse dorée* of the city, the *flaneurs*, and civil servants who, like the poor, are "always with us," were specially available. Lastly, the Governor's wife had openly stated that she wished to show her friends, the Percivals, what we could do in Sydney. And she was not a woman to fail in any of her undertakings.

It was arranged that we should comply with Paul Frankston's imperious mandate, and meet at Marahmee early in the day for the greater convenience of driving thence to Government House, instead of taking steamboat from the North Shore. All our plans prospered exceedingly. The day was calm and fair; the night illumined by the soft radiance of the moon. We dined in great peace and contentment, the ladies having devoted—as it appeared to me—the greater portion of the afternoon to the befitting adornments of their persons. We were all in good spirits. I had reason indeed to be so, for that day I had concluded a highly profitable trade arrangement, which augured well for my future mercantile career.

"What a glorious night!" said Paul Frankston. "Don't be afraid of that Moselle, Ernest, it's some of my own importing—a rare wine, as most judges think. Do you remember the ball we went to, Antonia, given by that fellow Schäfer? Such a swell he looked, and how well he did the thing! He has different quarters now, if all's true that we hear."

"The poor Count!" answered Mrs. Neuchamp, "I can't help feeling sorry for him though he was an imposter. Is it really true that they put him in prison in Batavia? What a fate after such a brilliant career!"

"Carryall was there last year and saw him. Got an order, you know, from the Dutch authorities. Said he was fairly cheerful; expected to be out in three years."

"He was very near not being imprisoned in Batavia or anywhere else," interposed Mr. Neuchamp, with some show of asperity. "If Jack Windsor had come up a little earlier in the fray we'd have broken the scoundrel's neck, or otherwise saved the hangman a task."

"Now, Ernest, you mustn't bear malice," said his wife, reprovingly; "after all it was Harriet Folleton and not me whom he wished to carry off. It was an afterthought try ing to make me accompany her. But 'all's well that ends well.' He has paid for his misdeeds in full."

"Not half as much as he deserves," growled Neuchamp, who evidently declined to perceive the humorous side of the affair—the attempted abduction of an imprudent beauty and heiress, besides the ultra-felonious taking away of Miss Frankston, as she was then— as a pendant to a career of general swindling and imposture practised upon the good people of Sydney. Mr. Frankston's eyes began to glitter, too, at the reminiscence. So the conversation was changed.

"I really believe that women never wholly repudiate admiration," continued Mr. Neuchamp, reflectively, "however unprincipled and abandoned the 'first robber' may be. It's a curious psychical problem."

"You know that is untrue, Ernest," quoth Mrs. Neuchamp, with calm decision. "Don't let me hear you say such things." An hour later our carriages had taken up position in the apparently endless line of vehicles which stretched along Macquarie Street and the lamplit avenues which led to it. After nearly an hour's waiting, as it seemed to me, we drove through the lofty freestone gateway which led to the viceregal mansion, and descended within the portico, amid a guard of honour and attendant aides-de-camp. Passing through a vestibule, and being duly divested of wraps in the cloak-rooms, we were finally ushered into the Viceroy's presence, and duly announced.

Paul Frankston took the lead, with Miranda on his arm. I followed with Mrs. Neuchamp, whose husband escorted my sisters. As we were announced by name, I noticed that Colonel and Mrs. Percival, with a few other people of distinction, were standing on the dais, close to the Governor and Lady Rochester, the latter talking to a young man in naval uniform, whom I conjectured to be the Prince.

As we approached I saw Mrs. Percival speak to Lady Rochester, who at once came forward and greeted us warmly. "Mr. Frankston," she said, "I know the Governor wishes to talk to you about the fortifications; will you and your party come up here and stay with us. And so this is Mrs. Telfer, the heroine of my friend, Mrs. Percival's romance! I am delighted to see her and congratulate you, Mr. Telfer, on bringing us such a sea princess for your bride. She has all the air of it, I declare."

Miranda secured a seat near Mrs. Percival, who watched with pleasure her evident admiration, mingled with a certain awe, of the brilliant, unaccustomed scene before her. Much to her relief Miss Vavasour came up with the Cravens, and commenced a critical review of Miranda's and other dresses, which soon obliterated all trace of timidity and strangeness.

"Well, my princess," began Miss Vavasour, "and how does this gay and festive scene strike you? Isn't it a fairy tale—a dream of the *Arabian Nights*? Don't you expect to see the fairy godmother come when the clock strikes twelve, and your carriage turn into a pumpkin and white mice?"

"It is a scene of enchantment," said Miranda. "I hardly expected anything so dazzlingly beautiful. How the naval uniforms seem to light up the throng, and the soldiers too. I don't wonder at all the pretty things we read about them in books."

"Yes, they do strike the unaccustomed eye," said Miss Vavasour. "I wish I saw them for the first time. I'm afraid I'm growing old. Oh! my coming-out ball! I didn't sleep for a week before in anticipation of delicious joy, or a week after in retrospection. Ah! me, my youth is slipping away unsatisfied, I much fear. And now, unless my eyes deceive me, we are going to have the first quadrille. Miranda, we must show these good people that we dance in our island. How about partners and a *vis-a-vis*?"

We were not left long in doubt. One of the aides-de-camp, a gorgeous apparition in gold and scarlet, came up bowing, and intimated his Royal Highness' wish to dance with Mrs. Telfer. This, of course, was equivalent to a command. I looked for some indecision or hesitation on the part of Miranda. But it appeared to her evidently just as much a part of the proceedings as if (as had happened before) she had been asked to dance with the captain of a man-of-war at one of their island fêtes, where waltz, quadrille, and polka had long been familiar. I had provided myself with an enviable partner in the shape of Mrs. Neuchamp; and her husband having promptly arranged matters with Miss Vavasour, we betook ourselves to the next set, where we had a full view of the viceregal party. My sisters had apparently no difficulty in deciding between several aspirants for their respective hands, as they and their partners helped to make up the set.

When the melodious crash broke forth, in commencement from Herr Königsmark's musicians, recruited from an Austrian military band which had visited Australia, a murmur of admiration made itself audible, as the Prince and his partner stepped forth in the opening measure of the dance. I turned my head and was lost in astonishment as I noticed the unconscious grace with which Miranda moved—calm as when rivalling the fairies in rhythmic measure on a milk white beach beside the moonlit wave. How many a time had I watched her!

"Who in the world is that lovely creature dancing with the Prince?" I heard a middle-aged dame behind me ask. "She has a foreign appearance, and I think she is the most exquisitely beautiful woman I ever saw in my life. What a figure, too! How she smiles, what teeth, what eyes! Is there any news of a migration of angels? Such strange things happen nowadays on account of electricity and all that. Who and what is she, Mary Kingston, again I ask you?"

"My dear Arabella!" answered the other dame, evidently one of the aristocracy of the land, "you are so enthusiastic! She came with the Frankston party. That's her husband quite close to us, dancing with Mrs. Neuchamp. He's the son of Captain Telfer of North Shore, and has been away among the islands and nobody knows where for ever so long. He married her at Norfolk Island. I believe she is one of those wonderful Pitcairn people that we hear such good accounts of."

"H'm; he's a young man of distinctly good taste, I must say. I wish my Cavendish had gone to the islands too, if that is the sort of girl they grow there. Mrs. Percival seems to be a great chum of hers. How did that come about?"

"I believe they came back in the *Florentia* together. Captain Carryall touched at Norfolk Island on the way from Honolulu, and it seems that Mrs. Percival's little boy fell overboard on the voyage, and the girl was into the sea after him like a shot, and swam with him in her arms till the boats came. There was something about a shark too. Mrs. Percival tells everybody she saved his life. No wonder she raves about her."

"What a pearl of a girl! No wonder, indeed! And to think of her having a world of courage and fire in her with all that delicacy and beauty. I can't take my eyes off her. The Prince admires her, apparently, too; and she smiles like a pleased child, with as little thought of vanity or harm, I dare swear, as a baby. She ought to be a princess, no doubt of it. So I see it's the last figure. I must go and look up my old friend, Paul Frankston, and make him tell me all about her."

After the dance and the usual promenade, Mrs. Neuchamp and I recovered our respective spouses, and took the opportunity to make a detour of the ball-room, and even to go through the next apartment, where refreshments were procurable, into the ample gardens. The night was superbly beautiful. The full moon lit up the grove of tropical foliage and richly-flowering plants, the glades carpeted with velvet lawn, the wide sea-plain traversed by shimmering pathways of silver. Below, in the sleeping bay, lay several men-of-war, half in shadow, half illuminated with coloured lamps hanging from their rigging. Gay and mirthful, grave or earnest, the frequent partners passed to and fro like shadows of revellers beneath the moon, or turned to the lower paths to gaze at the motionless vessels, the silver sea, the whispering wave. It was an ecstatic experience, a fairy pageant, a supernal revelation of an enchanted landscape.

Miranda pressed my arm. "Oh, Hilary! how lovely all this is! But you must not laugh at me. Now that I have seen it, I do not think I shall be anxious to follow it up. There is something almost intoxicating about it all. I can imagine it unfitting people for their everyday life."

We had hardly returned to the ball-room when the glorious strains of the "Tausend und einer nacht" waltz pealed forth from the band, and hurrying and anxious swains in search of their partners, not always easy to discover in such a crush, were seen in every direction. Instant request was preferred to Miranda by a naval officer high in command, but to my surprise, as we had not spoken on the subject, she graciously, but firmly, declined the honour. He protested, but she quietly repeated her negative: "I only dance round dances with my husband, Captain Harley! and, indeed, these not very often."

He was inclined to be persistent, though most courteous. "I am sure you used to dance them once. Indeed, I heard such an account of your waltzing, Mrs. Telfer."

"That was before I was married, Captain Harley!" she replied, with such evident belief that this explanation fully answered every objection that neither the captain nor I could help smiling.

"Look at your friend, Mrs. Neuchamp!" he said, as that dainty matron came gliding past with a military partner, looking like the very impersonation of the waltz, "and Mrs. Craven, and Mrs. Percival."

"I am so sorry that I can't comply," she answered. "They are quite right to dance waltzes if they please. I do not care for them now, and am only going to have one with Hilary to-night. He is fond of it, I know. I will dance the Lancers with you, if you like."

"Anything with *you*," murmured the captain gallantly, as he carefully wrote her name on his card, and departed to secure a partner for the yet unfinished portion of the dance.

"I see by this lovely programme," she said, "that there is another waltz, a polka, and then the Lancers, which I used to know very well; and after that I will dance the next waltz with you, Hilary, just to feel what this wonderful floor is like. You are not angry with me for refusing Captain Harley? I really feel as if I *could* not do it."

"You can follow your own way, my dear!" I said, "in this and all minor matters. It concerns you chiefly; and, considering how many husbands think their wives are rather too fond of dancing, I shall certainly not quarrel with mine for not caring for it enough."

I was not altogether without interest as to this set of Lancers which she had promised to the gallant captain of the *Arethusa*, knowing as I did that the fashion had changed considerably since the Lancers was a decorous, somewhat dull dance, differing from the quadrille only in a more complicated series of evolutions, and, like that very proper performance, affording much opportunity for conversation. Not intending to take part in it myself, and being, indeed, more than sufficiently entertained as a spectator of the novel spectacle, I stationed myself near the "tops," one couple of which Miranda's partner elected to be. I saw by the composition of the set, and the looks of some of the youths and maidens who eagerly took their places with their pre-arranged *vis-a-vis*, that the pace would be rapid and the newest variations introduced.

I provided, therefore, for a *contretemps*. My younger sister having professed herself tired with the previous waltz, had declined the invitation of a partner not wholly acceptable as it appeared to me. I therefore persuaded her to walk up with me to a seat near Miranda, so that we, as I explained, might see how she got on.

What I anticipated exactly came to pass. The first few non-committal quadrille steps were got through without unusual display, but when Miranda saw the damsel next to her leaning back as far as she could manage, while her partner swung her round several times, as if he either wished to lift her entirely off her feet, or drag her arms out of the sockets, a look of amazement overspread her features. She stopped with a startled air, commingled with distaste, and saying to her surprised partner, "I cannot dance like this—I did not know—why did no one tell me?"—walked like a queen to the nearest seat. Now my foresight came in. Knowing that a girl of nineteen would be willing to dance with a naval officer of the rank and fashion of Captain Harley, if she was ready to drop with fatigue, I said promptly, "Allow me to introduce you to my sister Captain Harley, who will, I am sure, be happy to take my wife's place;" a look of joyful acquiescence lit up her countenance, and before any serious hitch took place in the figure the vacancy was filled.

I fancied that my sister Elinor, who was at the age when girls are not disinclined for a little daring frolic out of pure gladsomeness, performed her part in the figures with somewhat less unreserve after noticing the look of quiet surprise with which Miranda observed some of the more vivacious couples.

We contented ourselves, when the next series of waltzes commenced, with a single dance, which we enjoyed as thoroughly as the perfection of floor, music, and surroundings warranted.

"Oh, what a floor!" said Miranda; "if I were as fond of dancing as I used to be, I could dance all night; and such music! Quite heavenly, if it is not wicked to say so. And there is the sea, too, with the moonlight on it as in old days! We have been taken to an enchanted castle!

"But there is something different. I can hardly describe my feelings. Why, I cannot explain, but going back to dancing now for the mere pleasure of it, when I have entered upon the serious duties of life, appears like returning to one's childish passion for dolls and playthings."

"And yet, how many married people of both sexes are dancing now, not with each other either."

"I see them, and I wonder. I am not surprised at married men dancing—if they like it. If they come at all, they may as well do so as sit down and get weary. But I think the married women should leave the round dances to the girls."

"Would not balls be rather slow if the married women only danced squares?"

"I don't see why. Yet many of the girls have no partners—wall-flowers, I think you call them. And that is hardly fair, surely."

As this dance only came before supper, which was now near at hand, we danced it out. I hardly noticed until the music closed how many of the other couples had stopped, or that quite a crowd had collected around us. This was a tribute, I found, to Miranda's performance, which had an ease and grace of movement such as I never saw any living woman possess. She hardly seemed to use the ordinary means of progression. Hers was a half-aerial motion, in time to every note and movement of the music, while the rhythmic sway and yielding grace of her figure presented the idea of a mermaiden floating through the translucent waves rather than that of a mortal woman.

As she swayed dreamily to the wondrous music of "Tausend und einer nacht," her head thrown slightly back, her parted lips, her wondrous eyes, her faultless form so impressed the by-standers with the ideal of supreme beauty, that they scarce repressed an audible murmur as the music ceased and the dance came to an end.

When supper was announced there was the usual crush, but before the doors were opened a few of the more favoured guests, including the Frankstons and ourselves, were conducted by one of the aides-de-camp to a place near the viceregal party. Miranda was taken possession of by another of our naval friends, who seemed to think that they had special claims upon her, as having knowledge of her island home. I was requested to take in our good friend and fellow-voyager Mrs. Percival, who was more warm and effusive in praise of Miranda than I ever thought possible before her child's danger broke through the crust of her ordinary manner. Now nothing could have been more sisterly and unreserved than her tone and expression.

"It has been quite a luxury to all of us to look on at that wonderful darling of a wife of yours dancing! The whole room, including Lady Rochester, was in ecstasies, I assure you. You came in for your share of compliments also, which I mustn't make you vain by repeating. How exquisitely, how charmingly she does dance! I have seen some of the best *danseuses* in Europe and India—on and off the stage—and not one worthy to be named with her. She is a dream of grace—the very poetry of motion. I said so before to-night, and now every one agrees with me. It is rather a disappointment in some quarters that she declines to dance except with you. It would seem odd for some people, but being the woman she is I understand it."

"She is free to follow her own course socially," I said. "She will soon decide upon her line of action, and will not be turned from it by outside influence. Fortunately she and my mother are much in harmony as to leading principles, which relieves my mind considerably."

"You are fortunate in that, then, as in several other respects; may I add that I think you worthy of your good fortune. I trust that my boy's simple prayers for your welfare—and he prays for you both every night—may be answered."

A Modern Buccaneer

Just before the conclusion of the supper I saw that Miranda had been presented to his Excellency the Governor, who was standing near the Prince. Both of these personages were most complimentary and flattering in their attention to her, and when we left, as we had arranged, immediately after that most important function supper, leaving the girls to go home with Mr. and Mrs. Neuchamp, we were gratified to think that we could not have been more graciously received—treated even with distinction—and that nothing had occurred to detract in the slightest degree from the unwonted pleasure and modest triumph of the night.

After this, our first experience of "society," in the higher sense of the word, unexpectedly agreeable, as it had been, Miranda's fixed resolve, in which I fully concurred, was to detach ourselves from it and its code of obligations, except at rare intervals—to live our own lives, and to trouble ourselves as little as might be with the tastes and fancies of others.

I was likely to have my time fully occupied in the development of my business. Miranda had, partly from observation, partly from information supplied by my mother and sisters, discovered that there was even in prosperous, easy going, naturally favoured Sydney a section of ill-fed, ill-clothed, ill-taught poor. "While I meet them daily, such as I never saw on our island, I cannot occupy myself with the vanities of life." My mother was delighted to find a daughter willing to co-operate with her in the benevolent plans of relief which she was always organising for the poor and the afflicted. Between them a notable increase of efficiency took place in the management of children's hospitals, soup-kitchens, and other institutions, commonly regarded with indifference, if not dislike, by the well-to-do members of society. Outside of these duties, our chief pleasure at the end of the week, when only we could afford the time, was a cruise in our sailing boat the *Harpooner*, which soon came to be known as one of the fastest in the harbour, as well as one that was rarely absent from the Saturday's regatta, when a stiff breeze was sending the spray aloft.

Our life henceforth was that of the happy nations "that have no history." My business prospered, and as it largely increased and developed from its original proportions, Captain Carryall began to tire of his voyages and settled down on shore.

Within a year of the founding of our commercial enterprise one of the ideal houses we had so often pictured came into our possession. In an afternoon stroll, Miranda and I had ventured into a deserted garden, lured by the masses of crimson blooms on a great double hibiscus. The heavy entrance-gate was awry—the stone pillars decaying—the avenue weed-grown and neglected—the shrubberies trodden down and disfigured by browsing cattle. Exploring further behind a screen of thick-growing pines, we found the house,—a noble, wide-balconied freestone building, which I well remembered in my boyhood. Then it was inhabited, carefully tended, and ringing with the voices of happy boys and girls in holiday-time. What blight had fallen on the place, or on the pleasant family that once dwelt there? On the north-eastern side the land sloped down to a little bay, sheltered from the prevailing wind, and provided with pier and boat-house—all marine conveniences, in short. "Oh! if we had a house like this," said Miranda, clapping her hands, "how happy we should be! Not that I am otherwise now; but I should enjoy having this for our own. We could soon renovate the poor garden." I assented, but said nothing at the time—resolved to take counsel of our good friend and trusted adviser then and now—who else but Paul Frankston?

From him I learned the history of the house and its old-time inmates. Some were dead and some were gone. The story was long. The gist of it was, however, that it was now in the hands of certain trustees for the benefit of the heirs-at-law. "I think I can find out about it," he concluded. "And now come down and look at my little boat. I've had some painting and gilding done lately; I want you all—father, mother, sisters, wife, and everybody—to come for a sail next Saturday. I'm going to have a race with Richard Jones to the Heads and back, and I want your wife to steer. Then we'll win, I'm sure, and we'll call in at Edenhall—that's the name of the old place you saw—been its name for fifty years or more—and we'll have another look at it."

I said "Yes, by all means."

The next Saturday proved to be a day specially provided by the gods for boat-sailing. The wind was in the right quarter, the weather fine. The *Sea-gull* swept across the harbour like a veritable sea-bird, spreading her broad wings. The whole party had punctually assembled at our jetty after an early lunch. The breeze freshened as the day wore on; we had our friendly race against an old comrade of Mr. Frankston's—like him, not all ignorant of the ways of those who go down to the deep in ships—which we won handsomely, thanks to Miranda's steering, as Paul loudly averred. And that young woman herself, as the *Sea-gull* went flying past her sister yacht in the concluding tack, lying down "gunnel under," with every inch of canvas on that she dared carry, was as eager and excited as if she had been paddling for her life in one of the canoe races of her childhood.

We got back to Neutral Bay in time for afternoon tea, a little later than the established hour. But instead of having it on board, Paul proposed to have it at Edenhall, where he said he had permission to go whenever he pleased. He had arranged with the caretaker too.

We landed at the long unused pier. "How many times have I been here before, in poor old Dartmoor's time," said Mr. Frankston, "and how many a jolly night have I spent within those old walls! Well, well! time goes on, and our friends, where are they? Life's a sad business at best. However, we can't make it better by crying over our losses. Ladies and gentlemen, follow me!"

With a sudden change of tone and manner, Paul stepped briskly along the upward winding path, long unused, which led to the house. The hall door stood open, and passing along a noble hall and turning to the right, we entered a dining-room of fine proportions. In this was an improvised table on trestles whereon was spread a tempting collation. Two men servants, whom I recognised as the Marahmee butler and footman, stood ready to serve the company. A needful amount of sweeping and repair had been effected. The windows had been cleaned, and a fine view of the bay thereby afforded. Altogether the effect was as striking as it was unexpected; a general exclamation broke from the company.

"Ladies and gentlemen," said Paul, "I have prepared a surprise for you, I know; but oblige me by making your selves at home for the present, and dining with me in this informal fashion—I will explain by and by."

The day was nearly spent. It would probably be near the time of twilight, which in summer in Australia is nearer nine o'clock than eight, before we reached our homes. So the majority of the guests hailed the idea as one of Paul's eccentric notions with which he was wont to amuse his intimates. The Marahmee champagne was proverbial, and after a reasonable number of corks had been drawn a progressive degree of cheerfulness was reached. Paul rose to his feet, and requested the usual solemnities to be observed, as he was about to propose a toast. "Those of my friends who have been here before, in its happier times, will remember the former owner of this once pleasant home. Little is left now save the evidences of decay and desertion—the memories of a long past happy day. But there is no reason why it should not be again inhabited, again be filled with pleasant and pleasure-giving inhabitants. It is solid and substantial; if somewhat old-fashioned, all the better I say. There was no jerry building in the old days. The garden is here—to be easily renewed in beauty—the jetty, and the boat-house. The sea is here, much as I remember when as a boy I used to get 'congewoi' for bait off those very rocks."

"Hear, hear!" from the guests, and Mr. Richard Jones.

"And now I come to a piece of news which I am sure you will hear with pleasure. The house and grounds have been purchased by a young friend of mine, whose health, with that of his charming wife, I now ask you to drink with all the honours. The health of Mr. and Mrs. Telfer, their long life and prosperity! and may we all have many as pleasant a sail round the harbour as we have had to-day, and come here to enjoy ourselves at the end of it."

The applause which followed was tumultuous. Paul has sprung a surprise upon his guests with a vengeance. I was as much astonished as anybody; for though I knew that he had promised to make inquiries about the price put upon the property, I had no idea that he would go further in the matter, still less that he would purchase it on my account, as it was evident that he had done.

I said a few words, chiefly to the effect that it seemed to me quite unnecessary to go through the form of exerting myself for my advancement in life, as my friends, Mr. Frankston and Captain Carryall, were bent on making my fortune for me. I trusted to prove not wholly unworthy of such unselfish friendship, and thanking them all in the name of my wife and myself, trusted that a meeting like this would often conclude a happy day such as we had just completed. As for Miranda, she went up to the old man, and placing her hand in his, looked up into his face with an expression of heartfelt gratitude, which hardly needed the addition of her words: "You have made us both perfectly happy—what can I say? My heart will not let me speak. We have nothing to wish for now in this world."

The old man looked at her with an expression of mingled admiration and paternal affection. "I have two daughters now," he said, "and two sons; I was always wishing to have another pair, to gossip with when Antonia and Ernest were away. Now I have found them I am sure. The only thing we want now is another boat."

Miranda's eyes glistened at the allusion, and she looked as if she was only prevented, by a half-instinctive doubt as to the fitness of the occasion, from embracing Paul before the assembled company.

Years have passed since that day. Children's voices have long since echoed in the wide verandahs and amid the shrubberies of Edenhall. The house, thoroughly renovated, is one of the most comfortable, if not the most aristocratic, of the many embowered mansions which look over the Haven Beauteous.

My boys have been "water babies" from earliest childhood, and we can turn out a crew not easy to beat, particularly when their mother can be persuaded to steer. My girls have inherited a large proportion of their mother's fearless spirit, though people say not one has equalled her in beauty. Their partners in the dance, however, appear to consider them sufficiently good-looking, if one may judge by the competition which their appearance at balls usually produces.

Our business, always aided by the cool heads and steady courage of the senior partners, has increased, with the growth of the city of

Sydney and the development of the island trade, beyond all hope and expectation. I am a rich man now, and, indeed, somewhat in danger of the occasional mood of discontent with the uneventful, unvarying tide of success upon which life's barque appears ever to float. But one look at Miranda's face, serenely happy in her children, in her daily life of charity and almsgiving, in the devoted love and trust of my parents, is all-sufficient to banish all vagrant ideas.

Sometimes, in the train of unbidden fancies which throng the portals of the mind, the scenes and sounds of a far clime claim right of audience. Again I see the paradisal woodland, the mysterious mountain forest, the ceaseless moan of the billow upon the reef sounds in my ear; while forms, now fair, now fierce, flit, shadow-like, across the scene. I hear again the soft voices of the island girls as in frolic race they troop to beach or stream. I see the sad, bright eyes of Lālia, or mark the fierce regard of Hope Island Nellie as she stands with bared bosom full in the track of the deadly arrow flight. I hear the lion roar of Hayston as he quells a mutiny, or towers, alone and unarmed, above a crowd of hostile islanders. I shudder in thought at the dangers which I have escaped. Once more sounds from afar the weird voice of the tempest in the midnight wreck of the *Leonora*. Lastly, the harbour lights disappear as I sit in my cane lounge in the verandah of Edenhall, and in place of the wooded heights and distant city I see the breakers upon the reef of Ocean Island, and discern a solitary figure in the stern of a small boat sailing out into the illimitable gloom; I fall a musing upon the mysterious problems of Fate—of man's life and the strange procession of circumstance—until the hour strikes and I retire. Yet my thoughts are still dominated by the majestic figure of the Captain, grand in his natural good qualities, grand in his fearless courage, his generosity, his friendship—grand even in his vices. He was not without resemblance to a yet more famous corsair, immortalised by the poet—

Who died and left a name to other times,
Link'd with one virtue and a thousand crimes.

THE END

A Modern Buccaneer

Copyright © 2023 Esprios Digital Publishing. All Rights Reserved.